Cover design by Pixel Squirrel Studio

HOLIDAY HAVOC

A PARKER PHOTOGRAPHY COZY MYSTERY

SUZANNE BOLDEN

LAUGHING DEER PRESS

CONTENTS

CHAPTER ONE

"Hard to believe this is our last night here, isn't it, Libby?"

I wrapped a throw blanket around my shoulders and slipped into my moccasins before facing the cold December air. My dog Libby stepped out through the French doors with me on to my small, second-floor balcony.

Between the evergreens and through the bare maples of the village green below, I looked out across the empty marina to an ice-covered Lake Harmony. Any visible cabin lights on the far-off shoreline were extinguished hours ago, leaving behind a cold, lonely darkness. Below me, the special string lights for our Winter Wonderland celebration were still lit, giving the entire downtown a magical fairyland look.

The skating rink had closed, but a small group of teens lingered by the hot chocolate stand. Probably friends of the Harris brothers waiting for them to clean and close up the place. Tony must have been about fourteen now and Thad was close to seventeen.

Memories of me with my friends Val and Wanda at that age brought a smile to my face. We sure had some fun times together. Christmas break had meant so much then. The winter sports, like skating and sledding, kicked into high gear. Harmony even had a small ski hill nearby, but most of us didn't have the gear for it.

Eventually, they added a ski rental shop because the runs were now long enough to draw from the Milwaukee and Chicago area, especially on weekends and during these school breaks.

Store displays were left on overnight, and the twinkling holiday lights kept the celebratory mood of the holidays alive all night, even as the streets emptied. Libby heard the crunch of snow underfoot. She stuck her nose through the railing posts to see who was walking by. Probably late-night patrons leaving Shorty's, the small neighborhood tavern a couple of doors down the street.

My small bistro table and chair set had been brought inside weeks ago. The garland and large red ribbons I'd strung on my balcony's edge would stay for now. I took one deeper inhale of the crisp, cold air before bending to pet Libby.

"It's been just you and me, and I'm going to miss our little lookout up here."

Libby leaned against my leg, snuggling closer. "What is that? You feeling it too? Things will be different. Now you'll have a forest to run in and squirrels to chase. But I totally get that it's a sad-glad time."

I walked back in and closed the French doors, shutting out the winter night. What had been my cozy living area was now filled with packed boxes of my belongings. Tomorrow, the moving crew would appear, and this place would be swept clean of my possessions. Also tomorrow morning, I would pack my bags for the three nights I'd be staying with Aunt Ruth in her little cottage.

Strangely enough, I was anticipating sleeping on her not-so-comfortable couch again, just like I had done many times before when I visited Harmony after leaving. How many hours had I spent with Ruth in this apartment when she lived here? It had to be hundreds of hours! Like when I worked with dad and Ruth in the photography studio below, I would join her up here for lemonade after we closed. And then the times hanging out up here with Wanda and Val, who loved talking over our teen lives with Ruth. She was an important mother figure in my life, even as my own mother spent her time at her dress shop across Main Street.

Again today, my fiancé Scott suggested I move in with him instead of staying with Aunt Ruth until we were married. He didn't have to remind me that our wedding day was Sunday, and we were both adults in our sixties. His claims that it wouldn't matter to anyone if we lived together before we were legally wed were true, but I'd made up my mind early on.

Even though he was right in his reasoning, and believe me, it was tempting, I wanted to wait. This was my first and only marriage, and traditions from my past were weighing heavily in the decisions I was making. I looked forward to spending those final days as a single woman with girlfriends and family. However, I drew the line at throwing a bachelorette party!

My life had been spent building my skills as a photographer, then traveling the world using those skills to support myself. I did well in my career, and it provided me with financial independence. Now, returning to my hometown of Harmony, I used my financing and business savviness to reinvigorate Parker Photography while bringing it into the twenty-first century.

My phone rang, jolting me as it echoed in the empty space around me. It was Scott. The little anticipation flutter in my heart was still there. I prayed it never went away.

"I'm mighty lonely up here in this big house," his sexy, low, Sam Elliot voice said.

I let the shivers travel through me before saying, "Libby and I are even lonelier in this empty apartment." I wasn't very good at a sexy come-hither voice.

"My house is too big for one person. Come here tonight."

"Oh baby, you poor thing. I'm sorry you're all alone. But Sophia and Jack will be with you tonight."

A low chuckle came through the phone. "Way to burst my bubble. Change of plans. They're taking a flight tomorrow instead. But back to a minute ago. Want me to come up to your place and keep you company?"

"Thanks, but no thanks. I've got Libby here with me, and we were just going back to the bedroom. Finished up the packing I had to do, and now it's time to put my feet up."

"I could give you a foot massage."

With a laugh, I said, "Tempting, but I'll take a rain check. You all set up with a cleaned-out garage for my furniture and boxes coming your way tomorrow?"

"Yep, I am. And I'm looking forward to getting your things mingled in with mine after we get back from our honeymoon."

"So am I, Scott. But I will admit to some bittersweet thoughts here. I loved this little apartment."

"Understood, Jackie, but it will still be a part of your life. When we get back from Florida, the breathtaking transformation of your historical building will be well underway. Accolades will come pouring in from across the globe, or at least from across the Driftless."

"Well then, let the renovation begin!" I said. "Goodnight hon. See you tomorrow."

CHAPTER TWO

*L*ibby and I had a restless night, and I was up before dawn packing my bags to take to Aunt Ruth's. I filled a small tote with Libby's favorite toys, her water and food dishes, and her leash. We didn't go on long walks in the winter, but she still needed her outside potty time. I loaded the things into my car before opening the studio for the day.

Todd and Mandy showed up early as well. They'd been busy filling Christmas gift orders. Our social media, email, and snail mail announcements of the studio and gallery being temporarily closed had gone out weeks ago. Customers were directed to our online store for updated progress on the extensive remodeling project that would take over both stories of the building that had housed my family's photography business for decades.

Todd would be handling the updating on the website as well as our Facebook page. He suggested we share more history of the business, including its place in the community. I welcomed his savviness with modern marketing.

He wanted to include a photograph of my family in front of our large home on Oak Street. My mother, father, and I had lived there, while Aunt Ruth had preferred to live in the apartment above the studio.

Age caught up with Aunt Ruth, and in her eighties she eagerly agreed to my plan to retire, move to Harmony, and take over our family business. She bought one of the cute cottages in our local retirement village, Shady Pines, and settled in to enjoy time away from the demands of running a business.

By taking over the second-story apartment, more gallery space would be created, which meant we could display more guest photographers' works alongside my own. Mandy's framing business had grown exponentially. It was an appreciated part of what we offered to customers. She looked forward to the additional room to work and store her materials.

Scott's construction company would be doing the work. His son Matt, Mandy's husband, was going to be taking over Drake Construction soon. Keeping this in the family made for a great working arrangement. We'd spent many hours together tossing around ideas for the project and had completed plans this fall. Ordered materials were waiting for us to close our retail operations before they were delivered. Scott wanted the remodeling completed in time for the summer tourist season.

"How's your move going?" Mandy asked as I walked into her framing room in the back.

"Good. The movers will be coming for my personal items and furniture in about an hour. When will you be taking your framing equipment out of here?"

"After the holidays. Matt said it won't be in their way right now. All my holiday gift framings were sent out last week, so there's no big last-minute rush. I allowed for the pause so I can enjoy Christmas and get settled into my new temporary digs."

Todd appeared in the doorway. "Ah, there you are, Jackie. Got some burly-looking guys out front looking for you. Want me to send them around back?"

Wow, this was really moving fast!

"Yeah, thanks. I'll show them the alley entrance. Hope the moving van fits back there."

Thankfully, the weather was holding steady. No snow was in today's forecast, and the alley had been plowed the night before. I spent the next half-hour directing the movers as to what they would be packing and moving. I gave them Scott's address and explained that someone would meet them when they arrived there.

Knowing they were ready to get to work emptying my apartment, I went back downstairs. The studio was open for the day, and already we had customers. We were running specials on everything, trying to get the inventory down so when Todd was ready to move operations to Scott's basement, it wouldn't be such a big chore.

Mandy was talking with a clean-shaven, square-shouldered man, and Kim Walters, our realtor extraordinaire. Kim excused herself to come up to me while Mandy took the client to the display of our current guest photographer. The young up-and-coming gal out of Mackinac Island was in no rush to pick up her remaining pieces as the island shut down for the winter. I made a mental note to ask Todd if he was planning to hold onto them for online sales.

"Jackie!" Kim's hug was a little over the top, but that was Kim. "We're going to miss you. When will you open up again? It will be super exciting to see the new space."

She leaned in conspiratorially. "That tall hunk of a man is looking at the vacant mill space. I'm finally thinking this will work out. Remember how we all looked at it that night when we thought Tara Steele would be buying it?"

"I do. What a tangled mess that whole time was. My high school buddy Keith murdered…"

"And the widow moving in on Scott. Not very nice," Kim said, wagging her finger in the air. "But nothing nefarious going on with my new client. He's staying in town for a few days. I'm showing him around and, of course, had to bring him to the studio of our local celebrity, world-famous photographer Jacqueline Parker. He loved your shots of the Cliffs of Moher and the Anar Islands."

"It's the Aran Islands," I corrected her, but I didn't think she even heard me.

"He seemed especially impressed with the local wildflower photography exhibit. The framing on those is totally amazing!"

"I agree. Mandy did a beautiful job. And good luck with the sale of that property. What sort of business is he looking to put in there?"

Kim's eyes narrowed in concentration. "I'm not sure exactly. He said he has several ideas, though. He's totally serious. And he has money. Just look at that watch he's wearing. Top of the line. I can tell those things you know. He wants to look at housing here too. Can you believe it? I'll just bet he's ready to send employees."

Kim was naturally an exuberant person, which lent itself well to her profession. She knew everything about Harmony and led the charge to keep improving our village.

Tourism was becoming ever more important here. It stabilized the village that, even with its natural beauty and the deep roots of the residents, had been quietly slipping into decline. Young people moved away for better-paying jobs. Shops like my mother's Vogue on Main had long ago gone out of business or moved to bigger markets. Now online selling was a boon for my photography business, but I understood that it was a two-edged sword, hurting other small businesses.

"What on earth is that ruckus upstairs?" Kim asked. She didn't wait for my answer as her client approached us. "Gerard Singleton, meet Jackie Parker. She's the photographer I was telling you about."

With a sincere smile, he said, "You have a lovely place. Your work is top-notch."

"Why thank you. I understand you're thinking of opening something in our little village. As a small business owner here, I know you'll find it to be a welcoming place."

He nodded. "I'm most definitely on the hunt. Though the holidays can be a difficult period for real estate, Kim here is giving me all the time I need to snoop around Harmony."

"Hope you find what you're looking for," I said. "Now if you'll excuse me, the movers are upstairs. I need to check out their progress."

Kim quickly steered Gerard toward another display, giving me a thumbs-up.

I hope she gets a sale out of this, I thought as I climbed the stairs.

CHAPTER THREE

"Welcome to my humble abode!" Aunt Ruth stood in the open doorway as I pulled my bags from my SUV.

Libby leaped out and dashed toward her, as she reached into her pocket for the treat Libby knew would be waiting.

"I've made fresh coffee if you'd like some, and I made some space in the corner for your bags and laid out fresh towels for you in the bathroom."

Libby sat and accepted Ruth's good-girl praise before snatching the treat from her hand and jumping up onto the couch I'd be sleeping on tonight.

"Way to make yourself at home, Libby," I said.

The cottage's interior could be dark, since it sat tucked under the tall white pines that dominated the grounds. Ruth always made sure to light lamps, particularly during the long winters of Wisconsin, which created a warm, welcoming, cozy atmosphere.

Small cabins on the grounds, which had once been used as a Lutheran summer camp for children, had been converted to cottages for Harmony's aging population. The original camp's main lodge had been made over into a community center. Its sturdy log walls and large stone fireplace were kept as is, but other interior spaces were freshened up. The wood floors were redone, and the kitchen and bathrooms were updated.

What was especially treasured by anyone who'd stayed there over the years was the community's setting on the Wisconsin River. Well-maintained walking paths meandered throughout the expansive grounds. What had once been narrow gravel paths were updated to paved roads, as most of the residents here still drove.

"Thanks," I said, bending to give Aunt Ruth a quick kiss. "Coffee sounds perfect."

"Can I go with you to your final fitting today?" Ruth asked as she stepped into the kitchen area and pulled two cups down from the cupboard. "Maybe your dress will be done, and I could help you bring it and the coat back."

"Sure. That would be great. One more thing checked off. Thank you again for doing this for me, it really meant a lot. Marrying this late in life, I skipped over some of the traditional things. But you're the closest thing to a mother I've had all these years since Mom passed, so buying my wedding attire was such a sweet gesture. And to make your couch available for me one last time was ideal!"

Aunt Ruth waved off my words. "It's a small thing, but I know what you're trying to say. Now, before we go getting all mushy and stuff, let's have our coffee and get you two settled in."

* * *

The roadways were clear, and our walk to Sonja Bernardi's cottage at the rear of the grounds only took about five minutes.

Sonja welcomed us with a big smile. "Your dress is waiting on my bed. You can step in and slip it on. I'm looking forward to seeing you in it on Sunday, and I want it to fit you perfectly."

The white plantation shutters covering her bedroom windows were tilted to allow the afternoon sun in. A queen-size bed with an elegant, periwinkle blue damask bedspread dominated the small room. Her nightstand held a reading lamp, tissue holder, reading glasses, and a novel lying askew on a leather journal. A colorful area rug covered almost the entire room.

I slipped into my wedding dress. It felt perfect just as it was.

In the full-length mirror hanging on the back of the bedroom door, I took a moment to soak up the beauty of Sonja's creation. The porcelain silk crepe fabric floated across my body as I turned to admire her work. Six small pearl buttons lined up along the seams rising from the bottom of the long sleeves, lending an elegant touch.

I stood on the balls of my feet as if I was in the heels I would be wearing. The mid-calf length she'd hemmed hit just right. I turned my hips side-to-side to flare the skirt. The movement was dreamy. The seams of the gores that created the skirt's fullness rose smoothly to shape the fit of the bodice.

"Jackie, dear, come out and show us," Aunt Ruth called.

"I'll help with zipping you up," Sonja offered.

A long, drawn out *ohhh* came from Ruth. "Jackie, it's so very lovely."

Sonja ran the long zipper to its end at the edge of the bateau neckline. I felt her closing the row of delicate pearl buttons in their loops before circling around me, carefully taking in the fit of the garment. Then, with a bit of tugging and adjusting, she said, "I don't like the way the back of this neckline fits. Are you standing up straight?"

Readjusting my posture didn't seem to satisfy her. "I can correct that. It's not a big fix, but I will need to steam the seams and things anyway, so I'd prefer to do the neckline adjustment and then get this to you in the morning. Now let's see how the coat looks with it."

The crimson velvet evening coat turned out just as I had pictured it. My inspiration came from a coat in the Harmony family's historical garment collection.

"Exquisite! You are certainly going to be an elegant bride, Jackie. I'm so delighted you commissioned me to create this dress and coat for you. It felt so good to get back to designing and feeling the garments come to life under the presser foot of my sewing machine." She reached to take the coat off me. "Now let me mark that neckline adjustment."

"And I'm over the top pleased with how it worked out," I said. "I couldn't have imagined a more serendipitous meeting at that fall potluck dinner. How's our winter treating you? After living in Los Angeles, this must be quite an adjustment."

Sonja nodded slowly as she slipped a stick pin out of her mouth to pin the gap on my neckline and stepped back to see the effect. "I've lived through these kinds of winters in my childhood, so it's not completely new. Can you turn to the side for me?"

"My half-sister and her daughter are coming from Los Angeles for the wedding. She's in the film and television business. Maybe you two knew each other."

Sonja quickly replied, "I doubt it." She finished her adjustment marking and told me I could take the dress off. "I've not done costuming for productions in many years."

"She played Pauline Dubois in the soap opera *Times of Our Life*," Ruth said. "And her daughter Alli is a director."

That stopped Sonja in her tracks. "Beverly Turner?"

"That's her. Then you do know her?"

"I sure do. I worked in the wardrobe department of that soap. They had a generous budget. Soap operas were king back then. In fact, I've been reminiscing about working there. The producer gave me carte blanche to design what I wanted. 'Just keep it classy and high end. The audience doesn't want to see themselves,' he'd say. 'They want to escape to a world of love, intrigue, and glamour.' Always glamour. So, you say she'll be in town. Could I meet up with her?"

"I'll do you one better. She wrote a memoir, *Becoming Beverly*. Why don't you surprise her by showing up at our bookstore on Saturday? She's doing a book signing then."

Sonja shrugged. "I don't know if she'd remember me. It was so long ago and so much time has passed."

"Nonsense, Sonja," Ruth said. "This is another serendipitous moment. You must do it. Besides, it seems that other than this dress for Jackie, you've been holed up here at your cottage since you arrived. You should get out more to experience the village. Have you even been downtown to see our Winter Wonderland?"

"No, I haven't. You're right. Maybe I'll get some Christmas spirit going."

"Great. We'll be there on Friday night. Say, did you ever join the quilting group?" I asked.

"That's not really my thing, but I stopped in at the quilting circle once. Didn't get a good feeling about it. I felt like an interloper—an intruder. They're local ladies and have known each other for so long. Maybe I'll try it again after the holidays and after the work I've been having done here in my cottage is completed. I found an excellent older man who lives here in the Pines. He's been working with me on the things I want updated. So, I've been keeping busy with that and with your wedding garments. You can take the coat with you today and I'll finish up the dress."

"I'm so happy with it," I said. "It's perfect for the

sleigh ride I'll be taking to the Harmony House. I hope you'll make it to the reception. You seemed unsure when we spoke last. You could ride in with someone from Aunt Ruth's gang."

"Gang? What a way to describe your friends," Sonja said, grinning at Ruth. "I'll think about it. But now off with you. I have a friend coming to visit tonight. She's staying in a little retro motel outside of town. I wish I had space for her here, but until Don's work is completed, I'm just not prepared for an overnight guest."

"Should I wait until Saturday to pick up the dress?" I asked. I really wanted to get it sooner, but tried to respect Sonja's time with her friend as well.

"Oh no, tomorrow is fine. I plan on spending the next hour or so doing the adjustment and then the final light steaming. Plan on coming by tomorrow morning at, say, 11:00?"

"See you then."

CHAPTER FOUR

Once we left the fitting, Ruth agreed to come to the Harmony mansion with me to finalize my wedding plans. We stopped to grab Libby and headed through town and up the hills to the mansion.

Our village founders, the Harmony family, had built a beautiful stone mansion atop one of the hills just outside of town. When Eleanor Harmony, the matriarch of the family, decided to move to a smaller home, she donated the mansion and surrounding grounds to the Harmony Historical Society. The setting was now home to a museum, nature center, and event grounds.

Staff there always seemed very professional, and today was no different. They walked me through my checklist, answered all my questions, and settled my mind that things were in order. The fact that Harmony

House staff, the florist, the caterer, and the musicians had all worked together at other events made things easier all around.

Next stop for us was the studio. Mandy and Todd had things under control here.

"With only two more days of Parker Photography being open this year, you can let go of concerning yourself with the business," Mandy said. "You need to just enjoy these last few days before the wedding."

"What are you up to tonight?" Todd asked.

"I have her all to myself," Ruth answered for me. "We're going to relax and hunker down in case the weatherman is right for once and that winter snowstorm hits. I have a pot roast in the crock pot."

Todd rubbed his tummy and licked his lips. "Yum. If you need help eating it, I'm available."

The movers were almost done, which meant I could go to Scott's and let them in. I dropped him a text letting him know I had the movers' arrival at his place handled. He sent a teasing text back, saying I might as well just stay if I was driving all the way out there.

My response that *I have gas for the return trip to Shady Pines* prompted a laughing emoji to pop up on my screen.

"Want to check upstairs and see if they got everything?" Ruth asked.

"I suppose I should," I said, dreading to see the place emptied out.

Mandy read my cue and said she'd run up there and confirm that they'd not missed anything. "I'll catch them if I see a problem, but I'm sure it's fine. If we find anything during the remodeling, we'll bring it over to Scott's… I mean to your home."

Todd had some questions that I went through before Mandy came bounding back into the gallery. She tossed a yellow tennis ball toward Libby. "Here girl. Found this in the corner. But that's it, Jackie. Now get going and let them into your new place."

Ruth was right about our relaxing evening being what I needed. Today was not only a physically busy one, but emotionally too. And now I needed to leave this apartment behind, meet the movers at my new home, and begin the next phase of my life. I was getting married!

* * *

The pot roast dinner was the perfect cold weather comfort food. Later in the evening, Ruth made popcorn for our movie night. The two of us each snuggled into a corner of the couch and Libby laid down between us as *When Harry Met Sally* began. The quiet and darkness of a Shady Pines' winter night was something new to me after living on Main Street, where dim streetlights were on all night and people moved about at all hours.

Scott's house sat on a bluff outside of town. His property afforded him the peace and quiet he loved. Trees buffered any noise from the rural road and, though there was a walking trail between his house and the river, the land's downward slope and distance from the back deck afforded privacy there as well. His view down to the river was breathtaking. I know that the difference in lighting, noise, and proximity to others would take some getting used to.

A car's headlights passed by on the small road and pulled into the parking space at Ruth's nearest neighbor.

"Annie is expecting her son for the weekend. He always makes the trip here to spend a few days before Christmas, and then takes her to his place in the Upper Peninsula. She made the cutest baby quilt for her new great grandbaby. It has pink and purple unicorns."

"How nice. Ruth, do you think the quilting women were knowingly rude to Sonja like she said?" I asked.

"Could have been. We're not all nice little old ladies, you know. Annie, sweet as she is, can be off-putting, if you know what I mean. She's one of those take-charge types. And Jean is quite gossipy. Martha is… oh, anyway, don't listen to me. If Sonja experienced a chill or felt she had overstepped, I could picture it. I'll mention it to Eunice. She knows them better than I. And I'll make a point to get Sonja to the wedding. I meant it when I said she's been very reclusive. Though she does have Don Stone helping her with repairs and replacing things at her place. He's a nice guy. And easy on the eyes, too."

Another car pulled past our cottage.

"Regular highway tonight," Ruth said. "Maybe that's Sonja's friend arriving."

"How did you handle the transition to Shady Pines after leaving the apartment?"

Ruth gave me a knowing grin. "Worried you'll go stir crazy without some activity right outside your door?"

"Sort of. Except for my life as a child here in Harmony, and now moving back, I've always lived in big cities. I've never lived out in the country. Are you ever scared of all that darkness outside? I mean, like someone could be looking in and you'd never see them with your lights on."

"Nah, not me. I'm okay with it. Maybe you and Scott watch too many scary movies. We're off the beaten path here. No one comes here mistakenly. We all watch out for each other, but also give each other privacy."

"Good to hear that it's safe here. Repurposing the old summer camp to make it a retirement community was one of the best moves ever made. That way, the old-growth trees weren't taken down, and the land wasn't covered by a subdivision hiding the riverfront."

"We've noticed that people walking along the trail by the riverfront have been wandering into the edge of our forest and leaving behind trash. And once Harry, who has anointed himself some sort of watchman, discovered a couple of teens making kissy-kissy. He had fun scaring them half-to-death by creeping around, making noises, and throwing a stone at a bush on the other side of them. But my point is that type of thing is the most edgy thing that's happened here since I moved in. Now you, my dear, have seen a lot more murder and mayhem here than I ever had in my entire eighty-three years."

"No kidding. I'm sure hoping that moving out to Scott's will keep me away from involvement in future cases that happen. I won't be around the studio as much either. So yes, I do suppose my life will move at a different pace."

My evening ended with taking Libby out for her last potty break of the day. I couldn't resist extending my walk with large soft flakes falling around me. Instinctively, I tipped my head back, letting the flakes melt on my tongue. Libby chose to jump and bite at them. Good, she'd tire herself out for the night's sleep.

I turned back before I reached Sonja's house, but

noticed a car parked there. It must have been nice to have her friend visiting. Maybe Sonja would invite her along to our Winter Wonderland. I must remember to welcome her friend to my wedding reception on Sunday as well.

CHAPTER FIVE

*L*ibby woke me for her morning walk before I was ready to get up, but she wouldn't take no for an answer. I flicked on the coffee maker, then dressed and brushed my teeth in the kitchen while the coffee brewed. Pouring a cup, I felt ready to face the cold.

A couple inches of fresh snow fell during the night. There was very little drifting, as the trees prevented the winds from moving things about. The sound of snow crunching sharply under my feet cut through the quiet. In the predawn dimness I noticed lights on in a few of the cottages. Ruth was right, it felt safe here.

After Libby did her business and my coffee cup was empty, we returned to the cottage. The smell of applewood smoked bacon hit me before I even opened the door.

"There you two are. Did you have a nice walk? Breakfast is almost ready." Ruth moved efficiently in her little kitchen area. "What kind of running around do you have to do today?"

"I'm going to catch up with Beverly. She and Alli got in late last night and texted me that they were going right to Kay's B&B. This morning, she's meeting up with Ginger at the Book Nook. We're catching coffee at Murphy's after that. Since I'll be picking up my dress from Sonja later, I thought I'd go in early and check on things at the studio."

"Yesterday, you asked about my life after moving here. One thing I found hard was letting go of the day-to-day stuff."

"Really? I thought you wanted to retire," I said.

"I did. And believe you me, I got over thinking about all the little details in running a business. Just sayin' it was a change and took time. But it turned out to be a very good change," Ruth said with a smile. "Breakfast is served."

.   .   .

Walking into the studio, I saw my niece, Alli. "Well, this is a nice surprise!"

Alli ran toward me with her arms spread wide. "Aunt Jackie! I'm so happy to see you again."

Her hug felt wonderful. "Is your mom here too?"

"No, she's at the bookstore. I just wanted to stop in and say hi to Todd." She ducked her head. "And Mandy too, of course."

Todd stood behind her with a broad grin. "She surprised me."

"Well, that's sweet," I said, wondering if theirs was still just a 'close friendship,' as they liked to say, or if it was moving into new territory. "Looks like things are under control here, so I'll head over to the bookstore. Want to come with me?"

Alli declined, saying she'd like to stay and catch up with Todd. "If I won't be in the way."

"I'm sure you'll be fine. I'll see you later. Some of us are meeting up tonight to enjoy our Winter Wonderland festivities. Hope you'll join us."

Todd spoke up, "I was just about to ask her. In fact, I'm going to try to get her up on ice skates. Bet you never did that in California."

The corner of Alli's mouth twisted up in a little smirk. "Ah, I wouldn't bet on it." She stepped clear of us and did a fast spin on one foot. "Might see if I can still do an axel spin tonight. Or maybe a sit spin. Gosh, there's so much I haven't practiced since my days as a competitive figure skater."

"Wow! I had no idea. So, you'll be skating circles around me," Todd said, hanging his head.

"Probably not. My career lasted for a year and a half, until I aged out at nine," Alli said, giving Todd a hip bump. "But I think I can beat you in a race on the ice."

"Challenge accepted," Todd said.

"Okay, you two, no racing. The rink will be full of little kiddos and middle-aged couples. But Alli, I'll look forward to watching you skate with whatever skills you have left."

* * *

The snowfall last night had freshened up the Main Street area. Hannah Sutton was knocking accumulated snow off the awning over the doorway of Sutton's Antiques and straightening the green boughs edging her windows.

Val was whisking snow from the bench in front of her Cut-N-Curl Beauty Salon. "Morning Jackie. Time is ticking down. Ready for the big day?"

"Yes, I am," I said. "See you tomorrow for my manicure and pedicure."

Steam rolled out of Dolly's diner door as a customer opened it to leave. She was busy as usual. Rain or shine, people loved the down to earth, old-fashioned atmosphere of the diner. And Dolly's smart, sassy remarks added just the right touch of spice.

Across the village square sat Murphy's Coffee Shop and Bakery, my next destination. Grace and Dermot Murphy owned the entire building including the Book Nook. They'd cleverly created an interior doorway so that the two spaces were joined. It was perfect for a day like today.

As I walked the street toward the coffee shop, I saw Beverly sitting at one of Murphy's window tables. It wasn't long ago that I'd learned I had a half-sister and a niece. After the initial shock at learning the story of her birth, I grew grateful to have her in my life. My mother's indiscretion did not break up my family, and life went on here in Harmony while Caroline, Beverly's birth name, was being raised in a good home in Florida.

Looking into the bookstore, I saw Ginger lighting the fire in her fireplace. The treasure of the wood-burning fireplace had been found hidden behind a false wall.

"It's wonderful seeing you again, Beverly," I said, after grabbing a cup of coffee.

She stood, and we exchanged warm hugs.

"It's wonderful being back, though this weather, brrr." She wrapped her arms around her Irish cable-knit sweater. The cream-colored sweater, most likely hand-knit in Ireland, was a pleasing contrast to her deep hunter-green wool slacks. She pulled a chair out for me. "Now let's catch up. All plans in place for the wedding?"

"Knock on wood, they are. Checked on the venue, caterer and flowers yesterday. Did I tell you I rented a horse and carriage to bring me to the Harmony House?"

"I love that idea. Very photogenic too."

"Maybe Alli and Todd would like a private ride like that too. I could ask the driver to give them a quick romantic go around," I said with a grin before blowing on my coffee to cool it.

"What is up with those two?" Beverly asked.

"I get the feeling that their special friendship is growing in a new direction. Say, I ran into someone you may know. At the final fitting of my dress yesterday, the woman who designed and created it told me she used to work in the costume department for *Times of Our Life*."

Beverly's eyebrows arched questioningly as she took a sip of her coffee. "Really? How unusual that she would end up here. What's her name?"

"Sonja Bernardi."

"I know her! She didn't just work there, she ran the department. Her designs won an Emmy for Outstanding Costumes for a Series. I loved her work. Then she just sort of disappeared from the LA scene. I kept some of the garments she created. Very well done, and they fit like a glove. Will she be at your wedding? I'd love to see her. Or maybe you could let her know I'm in town and perhaps she could come to the book signing tomorrow. Or the village green tonight. I'm looking forward to checking out the winter festival."

"I've already mentioned it to her."

Beverly let out a low chuckle. "You know, Jackie, two of the garments that I kept from the soap's wardrobe department were wedding dresses. Remember how I was married four different times in that show?"

"Then I know where Sonja got her experience doing wedding garments from. Love these small world moments. And I have another one for you. I was recently bemoaning the fact that I wished we had a party planner, someone like your Katie, here to help with what I thought would be a simple wedding. Turns out that the owners of this coffee shop are Katie Murphy's aunt and uncle!"

"Whoa, that is surprising news. I love Katie. She's created such special parties for me. I was sad when I received an email from her saying she had to get away from LA for a while."

"Is she okay?"

Beverly reached for her cellphone, peering at the screen as she slid her fingers up it. After finding what she was looking for, she handed me her phone. "This is what she sent."

It was an email explaining that Katie was putting her business on a temporary hold due to personal matters, but that she looked forward to returning in the near future.

"So that's all I know about Katie leaving."

Grace was clearing a table nearby and stopped to tell Beverly how nice it was to see her back in town.

"Grace, remember when I talked to you about your niece, Katie? Do you know anything about her quitting her party planning business in LA?" I asked.

"I do. I don't want to share too much personal information, but I will tell you that I'm grateful she turned to her family to heal. As to what caused her to leave LA, we are thinking it's boyfriend issues. She was with my brother-in-law Paddy on the Florida Panhandle for a couple weeks, and now she's on her way here. She'll be spending Christmas with us and her cousin Patrick. I don't like her driving by herself all over the country, especially in winter, but she says if she can drive in LA at rush hour she can make it to Harmony from Florida."

"Beverly, you might remember Grace's son, Patrick. Around here, most of us call him Murph." I turned back to Grace. "When do you expect her?"

"She should be here later today if the weather holds. We're excited for her to see our small-town holiday celebration. We hope she isn't too tired from the drive, because we want to get out among all the festivities tonight. Are you coming to our Winter Wonderland, Beverly?"

"I most certainly am. And now I'll look forward to seeing two familiar faces there, Sonja and Katie," Beverly said.

"I have to head back to Shady Pines now to pick up my dress. I'll be sure to let Sonja know you want to say hello."

CHAPTER SIX

At Shady Pines I noticed Dorothy sweeping the light fluffy flakes off her porch. Eunice, who lived next door, was at her window and waved as I drove past.

I almost missed the turn that would take me to the back of the grounds where Sonja's cottage sat. It surprised me to see two vehicles parked there. One was a typical midsize sedan and probably a rental belonging to Sonja's friend. The old but well cared for pickup must mean that the man doing her small remodeling projects was here as well.

A petite, dark-haired woman stood talking with Aunt Ruth. The women both spun to look in my direction when they heard my car approach.

That's when I noticed Don come walking around

from the back of the cottage. He was looking down, watching that he kept within a trail of footprints left in the deep snow, but his head jerked up when Ruth called out my name.

"Jackie, thank goodness you're here. Have you heard from Sonja?"

"Not this morning. Is something wrong?"

The petite woman spoke. "I'm Sonja's friend, Lynette Vaughn. We were supposed to meet up last night, but I got in late and called her. She seemed like she'd rather just wait until today. We agreed to go out for lunch."

"And this is my niece, Jackie. She had an appointment to pick up her wedding dress at eleven, and I came to join her," Ruth said. "Don, were you able to see anything through the back windows?"

Don took time to stomp the snow from his boots before speaking. "Can't make out too much. She has the blinds closed on the back windows too. But I could see through a crack at the bottom edge. Things look sort of messed up. I'm part of that with the work I'm doing," he said in a slow considered way, "but this seems unusual. I think we should try to get in. Maybe I should have checked the back door."

Lynette began pacing. "We must find her. Does she go out for walks in the morning? Maybe she slipped on the snow and is lying injured somewhere."

"Don, go back and try that door please," Ruth said before explaining that she doubted Sonja would be out walking, but added, "I'm going to call friends and see if they saw her this morning. Lynette, you spoke to her last night, correct?"

"I did."

"But on the phone? Um, then the car I noticed here last night wasn't yours?" With a confused expression I looked at the car she drove. "It looked just like that one."

Lynette stopped her agitated pacing. "Oh yeah, sorry. It was a long day. I spoke incorrectly. I did come by, but since it was late, she said she would rather just meet for lunch today. This is not like her."

"When you saw her, she seemed fine?"

She gave a sharp annoyed nod. "Of course, she did."

I stepped to the front door and cupped my hands against the thin curtained covered window in it. I thought I might be able to see inside, especially because there were lights on. Instinctively I tried the front door-knob. It was locked.

Don had circled to the back, and in just moments the lock on the front door clicked. The door opened to reveal his pallid countenance and drooping figure.

CHAPTER SEVEN

"She's outside her bedroom door." Don's shallow breathing made his shock obvious to all of us. His hands fumbled as they opened his phone. "I'm calling 911."

We pushed past him.

Sonja's blood-soaked body lay in the narrow hall just outside her bedroom door. Lynette wailed and dropped to her knees, crying Sonja's name. She reached for the long, knife-edged shears lying against her shoulder and threw them aside, before pressing two fingers against her friend's neck.

"No pulse. She's cold. Oh dear God, she's dead!" Lynette screamed.

We heard Don speaking to the 911 operator from the other room. Apparently, he heard Lynette, because he walked to where Ruth and I stood, looked in our eyes, and in a surprisingly calm tone told the operator there was no pulse.

The silky, padded hangar holding my wedding dress hung on the bedroom door. Questions went through my mind in the next seconds. Who would have done this? Had Sonja fainted and fallen on her dressmaker shears? And then in a repugnant and selfish moment the thought that there might be blood spatter on my wedding dress darted through my mind.

Then the next second the pragmatic in me kicked in. This was a possible crime scene. I'd been at enough of these over the last two years to understand the importance of preserving evidence and as sirens sounded, I spoke. "Everyone, let's wait outside for the ambulance and the Chief of Police to get here. Please back out. We don't want to taint any evidence."

Without hesitation Don and Ruth left, but Lynette still knelt next to her friend.

I took her by the shoulders. "Lynette."

She turned to look up at me. "I can't just leave her lying here alone."

"There's nothing you can do for her now. Please, the paramedics will be here and the police too."

With a low soft sob, Lynette reached for my hand to help herself up.

"I'm so sorry, Lynette. Sonja was a good woman."

Lynette squeezed my hand. "Thank you. Yes, she was. I'm just in shock. I think it best I go back to the motel now."

Then without another word, she walked outside. Tearfully nodding at Ruth and Don, she headed to her car with a dull, zombie-like expression. I thought she'd want to stay, but then realized she had lost her reason for being here. Her friend was gone. She started her car, shifted it into gear, and began to back up, but by this time the ambulance had arrived, and he tooted his horn. She didn't respond quickly enough, because the ambulance jerked as Lynette's rear bumper hit it.

Her head swiveled sharply, and I noticed her movements growing more frantic as she pulled forward trying to find a way to leave. The driver repositioned his ambulance, giving her more room to slip out and drive past him.

Jeff's cruiser was already parked tight against a snowbank. "Who was that?" he asked as he approached the three of us standing on the porch.

"That was Sonja's friend," Ruth said. "Poor dear, she's in shock."

"Well, she'd better calm down before she gets out on the roads. There's some icing, and it's getting slippery. But now tell me what happened here," Jeff said, his eyes scanning the scene ahead of him through the open door.

I explained why Lynette, Ruth, and I were here.

"And you are?"

Don choked on a sob, then composed himself. "Don Stone."

"Mr. Stone, why were you here?" Jeff asked.

"I was working on her cottage. Replacing bathroom fixtures. Making repairs. Stuff like that."

"You live here in Shady Pines?"

"Yes sir, I do." Don's voice broke again. "Sorry."

Ruth reached to take Don's hand. "Don found the body, Jeff."

Jeff tilted his head, keeping his eyes on Don. "I see. So those are your footprints heading toward the rear of the cottage?"

Don nodded.

"And you went in through the back door, which was unlocked?"

Don nodded again, his hands nervously twisting and pinching his red and black plaid wool cap.

Jeff, noting his distress, said, "If you'd like to go now, please leave your phone number with my deputy. I'll need to talk to you again later."

A curious neighbor walked over from next door and two other women approached us from the road, one of them leading a timid black dog. Ruth took them aside to explain what had happened.

Jeff noticed them as well. "Jackie, maybe you can take Ruth home, and tell the neighbors it would be best if they go home and get out of the cold too."

"Sure," I said.

"Jackie, I'm sorry you were here to see this."

"Me too, Jeff. Too many times we've been together like this. Am I a jinx?"

CHAPTER EIGHT

uth ushered the women away from the scene. I heard her explain the sad reason the police were here. As the two women walked away, I heard snippets of their remarks. *She was different... outsider... brought trouble...*

The next-door neighbor told Ruth she'd not seen or heard anything out of the ordinary before crossing back over a snowbank to her own yard. This surprising and unsettling news would travel fast across this quiet community.

Don had driven away, but my car was blocked in by the ambulance. I walked Aunt Ruth home, deciding to stay with her until Rocco arrived. I was glad she called him not only to comfort her, but so he might provide insight that would help the police. After all, he'd been involved in investigating crimes most of his life, and he knew Sonja.

Ruth took off her winter gear and plopped down at her kitchen table, propping her elbows on one of the quilted placemats. "I can't believe someone was murdered in Shady Pines. It's not sinking in. I hope they find this murderer, lock him up, and throw away the key."

"At least now I know the car there last night was Lynette's."

"Don't be too sure, Jackie. You said it was hard to see. Maybe the one you saw belonged to someone else. Do you remember the time?"

"Not really. It was after the movie. Guess I wasn't paying attention. Jeff will be working up a timeline and he'll get Lynette's information on the time she was there."

"I couldn't believe she backed into that ambulance. What a poor driver."

"She was pretty shaken up, Ruth. And the ambulance was at an odd angle. Didn't look too damaged."

"Boy oh boy did she want out of there though. She was probably the last person to see her alive."

"Good point. When Rocco gets here, I'm walking back for my car. Jeff will probably still be there, and I'll talk to him about Lynette."

And I wanted to get my dress. Maybe Sonja hadn't done the alteration. It was such a small detail. It would be fine without it.

Oh my gosh! What a horrible, self-centered person I am. How can I be thinking about this? A woman was killed.

But still, I would be getting married. What if…

"Oh dear. What if your wedding dress has blood splatters on it? What will you do?"

Ruth spoke the words I couldn't, but her expression mirrored mine. "I'm ashamed to say that crossed my mind too. Even now it feels like the dress will have witnessed a murder. Do you think it's a bad omen?"

"Nonsense. It's a dress. A garment. It's just a thing. It cannot see what happened nor absorb any bad vibes from it." Ruth scolded, but I saw the doubt in her eyes.

I've always been the sort who has a Plan B. But I don't have a Plan B for the fact that my wedding dress was at the scene of a murder and could have the victim's blood on it. Dye the garment? If I could get the blood out, or covered up somehow, would I even want to wear it?

Ruth was relieved when Rocco arrived. We quickly caught him up on what we knew about Sonja's murder, offering condolences on the death of his friend.

"I never imagined something like this would happen

here," Rocco said. "I'm shocked. Where would a suspect even come from? Who knew she was here?"

"She had a friend in town, and they were supposed to go to lunch," I said. "Her friend's name was Lynette Vaughn. Do you recognize that name?"

"Has a familiar ring to it, Jacqueline. Perhaps a relative?" We watched Rocco's face pinch in concentration. "I'm seeming to recall that it might be her sister-in-law. But don't quote me on that. And I certainly don't think she would have murdered her."

"I just mentioned her as someone who knew Sonja was here. But that bodes your question about who knew she was here. Was she in hiding?"

"Let me address that by saying she's been lying low for many years. I guess I can say more now that she's gone, but at one time she was offered witness protection by law enforcement."

"Whoa," Ruth exclaimed. "What happened?"

"I'd be happy to provide a condensed version of what I know, but please keep it to yourself as I have not verified the veracity of these things that came to me secondhand. Sonja confided in my wife, and later, she shared those conversations with me. Other pieces of what I am about to tell you came from my connections in two very different, but affiliated, worlds. Law enforcement and those operating in the criminal realm."

Rocco paused, adjusting his position on the side chair and steepling his fingers. "We were living in Los Angeles at the time that my wife met Sonja. She was referred to her by other performers."

"Your wife was a jazz singer, right?" I asked.

"Yes, she was. Sonja's performance creations were stunning. My wife and Sonja became fast friends and kept in touch after we moved to Chicago. Sonja's husband was an interesting person and a nice enough fellow. We rarely did social things together as couples, but every time we did, it was clear that Sonja was deeply in love with him. My wife remembered Sonja mentioning that her husband was in the jewelry business, but that was the only inkling I had of what he did for a living.

"We were living in Chicago when news of his death in an automobile accident reached us. Sonja was in shock, disbelief. But I also sensed an evasiveness and fear in her words. My wife grew deeply concerned for her friend. I decided to make discrete inquiries of my California contacts. I learned the husband had a periphery involvement with the mob, or as they were called, the LA Mafia. Upon learning that the FBI was involved with the case, I shared what I'd uncovered with my wife."

"Was it a mob hit and not an accident?" Ruth spoke

breathlessly, leaning in close to hear Rocco's answer. "Do you think she knew what her husband was caught up in?"

"Or who he was involved with?" I asked.

Rocco paused, taking a deep breath. "I simply don't know, Jacqueline. But the FBI certainly thought she did and spent hours questioning her. Based on what my wife learned, it was the FBI keeping surveillance on her that led to them finding out that she herself was being surveilled by others."

"By the bad guys?" Ruth asked.

Rocco nodded. "We began to feel her distance herself from us, the calls were less frequent. Eventually they stopped."

"Do you think she testified against the LA Mafia?" I said.

"We've all read stories or seen movies about those sorts of things, but this didn't play out in a movie style way. I learned that the LA detectives, together with the FBI, had a difficult time proving the automobile accident was intentional, much less who did it. But either way, both the FBI and the mob thought Sonja had something they wanted. Or knew information that was valuable to them."

"So, the FBI wanted to give her protection?"

"Hard to say, Jacqueline. Did they want to keep her

in their radar, under their watch? We lost touch, and I didn't hear from her until a few months ago. The only other contact had been the beautiful orchid arrangement delivered to my wife's funeral. The card was signed with the initials SB. It had to have come from her."

"Did you know of any other family members?" Ruth asked.

"I did not. They didn't have children. Perhaps she began reaching out to others, such as myself, because the case was so old, or she was no longer worried about it making any sort of trouble for her. Maybe I should go to Jeff with this information. I'd be happy to check with those old contacts regarding the current situation."

"Probably would be a good idea. What a sad story. And now she died here, alone and far away from friends and family, except for Lynette. And it appears she was the last one to see Sonja alive."

Ruth added, "except for her killer."

CHAPTER NINE

The police presence at Sonja's cottage had grown. I was met with an apology from Jeff when I asked him to get my wedding dress out as he said it had to stay hung where it was, but he thought I could retrieve it tomorrow.

"This may sound crass Jeff, but can I please just look at it and see if, oh this sounds so awful..."

Jeff tilted his head ever so slightly. "My life is full of unpleasant things like this crime scene. Ask away, Jackie, so I can get back to work."

"I want to see if there are blood splatters on my wedding dress." There, I'd said it. I felt awful. Like my dress was more important than a woman dying. And I knew life goes on and all that, but still.

Jeff squeezed my hand "I understand. Where is your dress in the cottage?"

"The one hanging on the bedroom door."

"Right above the body?"

I nodded and grimaced. "Yes."

"Okay, come on Jackie, I'll take you in to look."

Other officers moved about the small space, taking crime scene photos and fingerprints. The body was covered. I was thankful for that. It would have been hard to see it again.

My question was answered. I would not be wearing the dress Sonja had designed for me.

Jeff asked me if I was up to making a quick survey of the interior. "You've been here numerous times. Is there anything you notice missing? Unlikely as it might seem, it could have still been a robbery gone awry."

"And the thief, instead of running when Sonja woke up, grabbed the shears and stabbed her? I don't believe that."

"Like I said, we're trying to rule things out, Jackie."

My quick look around didn't pick up on anything missing. The plantation blinds were closed, but police scene lights had been set up to illuminate the dim interior. The living room seemed to be in order. The kitchen table had been taken over by her sewing equipment and looked messier than I remembered, but maybe she was saving the final cleanup for when my dress was done. The ironing board with a pressing ham lying on it was standing against the wall. But the iron lay on its side on the floor. The bedroom was about the same as I'd seen earlier in the day.

I gulped the cold, fresh air as soon as we stepped back outside. "Jeff, do you have a moment? I think you should hear about what Rocco just shared with Ruth and me."

"About this murder?" Jeff asked.

"Possibly," I said. "He and his wife were friends with Sonja when they lived in Los Angeles. This could be a lead on who would want to murder her."

"Rocco's an experienced investigator. If he thought it was important enough to mention, I want to hear about it. But not now, and not second-hand from you, Jackie. I know this is personal for you, but you have a joyful occasion coming on Sunday and I'm going to keep you as far away from the havoc of this murder investigation as possible. I'll contact Rocco myself, but I do appreciate you letting me know about their relationship."

"You're right that it is personal. But I get what you mean. It's just that you're asking a hard thing from me."

Jeff groaned. "Jackie Parker, stop. Go home. No, wait, you can't go home. You're staying with Ruth. Go back to Ruth's, and I'll let you know when you can get the dress."

"I can't wear that dress. Not with her blood on it."

"Can't you wash it out?"

"Seriously, Jeff? No. Even if I could, it wouldn't feel right. Will we see you and Kay tonight at the festival?"

Jeff smiled. "I sure hope so. Kay is looking forward to it."

CHAPTER TEN

*P*iped Christmas music playing at the ice rink floated across the village green. Smells of sugar roasted pecans from one of the vendors mingled with those of wood burning in large metal barrels, Wisconsin's version of heat lamps.

Harmony's traditional nativity scene sat on a riser near the village hall. This year it was softly lit by a low-wattage floodlight that was hanging from a tree limb above it. All the characters, from Mary, Joseph, and baby Jesus, to the ornately garbed three wise men, had been touched up with a fresh coat of paint by an artist from Greensville. Because of budgetary issues, the stable animals' coats were due to be tidied up next year.

Putting on an event like the Winter Wonderland involved a great deal of hard work, but local businesses were happy to chip in to make it happen. This year, an innovation was being introduced. At the far side of the ice rink sat plastic see-through igloos. Renters of the domes could experience the outdoor surroundings while seated at tables in cozy, heated interiors.

With a squint of my eyes toward the domes, it appeared that a group from Shady Pines had reserved one for tonight. Good idea! It meant they could have a coffee or hot toddy without wearing their mittens and without staying in the chilly night air for an extended period.

After leaving the crime scene earlier in the afternoon, I'd gone to Scott's with the news both about Sonja and my wedding dress.

"What am I going to do? It's ruined, and the wedding is in two days."

"Aren't you going to at least try to get the spots out?" Scott had asked.

"I don't think so. I'll be thinking about that blood even if it can't be seen with the naked eye."

He was trying his best to help me figure out what to do, but nothing was bringing me out of my funk until he said, "Naked! That gives me an idea, Jackie, how about you wear only that crimson velvet coat?"

"And nothing underneath?"

"You could button it up and only I would know what

lay beneath. Everyone else would just think what a stunning bride. Course, you might get kind of hot while you're dancing."

I burst out laughing at his suggestion. So very Scott! He looked slightly offended.

"I know you're halfway serious, but I don't think I could pull that off." I gave him a quick kiss. "I love you for trying."

The decision to not wear the dress had been made. I'd go to Madison tomorrow and see if there was a simple cream sheath or maybe a Christmas holiday dress in one of the shops. After all, it was a festive season, and that meant dressing up. But being so close to Christmas meant that things would be picked over. I would just have to make do with what I could find.

Sophia, Scott's sister, and her husband Jack arrived from Florida in time to join us at the Winter Wonderland. Sophia listened to my sad tale of the dress and said she'd be honored to go dress shopping with me. She suggested that maybe there would be some sample dresses at the bridal shops that would fit me. "Might be glitterier than you pictured, but hey, it's your time to glitter and glow. It's your big day."

"That's a great suggestion. But I draw the line at strapless or mermaid style dresses."

We strolled past the Christmas tree lot where there

were ample evergreen trees available for those still look-ing. Young children running around with sugar cane energy were helping their parents pick one out. We ran into Matt and Mandy with their little boy Ty bundled in his stroller.

"We're having a hard time choosing a tree this year," Mandy said. "Ty is getting into things, and we are taking advice from anyone and everyone as to how to keep him away from the tree lights and ornaments. We're consid-ering decorating only the top half of the tree to elimi-nate temptation."

Scott reached in to take Ty's little fingers in his working man's hand. I quietly pulled out my cell phone to take a photo of the two. Scott was relishing his grandpa role.

He said, "We all survived. If I remember right, Matt managed to tip our tree over one year."

"Mom told me that, but I didn't know if I should believe her," Matt said.

"I think we have photos to prove it. But, the point being things will happen."

"Maybe keep the more breakable ornaments off for the next couple of years," I suggested. "I'll ask Ruth if she has any advice about it."

We all got a loaded hot chocolate in a souvenir mug. Scott and I chose a mug with the year printed on it, seeing as this would be our first official Christmas together. The rim was edged with chocolate and sprinkles, much like a margarita is rimmed with salt, and the whipped cream was topped with peppermint slivers.

Several booths held Christmas crafts and other items to purchase. Sophia chose a hand-painted ornament with the words *Our First Christmas* painted on it and gifted it to us.

Kim strolled arm in arm with her husband Stu. Her red and green plaid, mid-calf length coat stood out in the crowd. Patti and Charlie Hunt had just arrived to meet up with Matt and Mandy. Patti was soaking up her grandma role and had taken over pushing Ty in his stroller. Ginger and Murph skated on the rink with an attractive young woman with auburn curls peeking out of her white stocking cap.

I pointed her out to Scott. "That's Katie. She's the party planner I told you about. Isn't she just the cutest? Beverly should be nearby."

I scanned the crowd and saw her bundled up in a long, shawl-collared coat talking with Grace and Dermot. She looked happy and relaxed. This wouldn't be a good time to let her know about Sonja's death, but I didn't want her to hear it from a stranger. I'd wait until I had a private moment with her.

"Thinking about accepting that skating challenge?" I asked Todd as he walked by with Alli.

"We're on. Heading that way now."

Someone jostled me from behind. I turned to see if I'd stepped in someone's path, but it was Wanda and Val, my two high school friends, kidding around and giving me a hard time by beginning to chant, "Scott and Jackie sitting in a tree, K-I-S-S-I-N-G."

"Real mature," I said.

Val gave Scott a big loud smooch on his cheek, prompting him to say, "Where's the old man? He might be a little jealous."

"In hiding. This is not his thing. 'Too cold to be walking around outside,' he said. But if anyone suggests ice fishing, he's all in. Go figure. So, I convinced Wanda here to come with me."

"Hey, want to go over and say hi to Beverly and Alli? You can meet Dermot's niece, Katie. She's in town for Christmas with her aunt and uncle," I said.

As we made our way to the ice rink, I asked Wanda, "How is Lynette doing?"

"Who's Lynette?" Wanda asked.

"Oh sorry, guess you wouldn't know her. She's a friend of Sonja's who's staying at your motel. You heard about the murder this morning, right?"

"I did. So sorry to hear something like that

happening at Shady Pines of all places. Hope they get the lowlife that would do something like that to an elderly woman."

"Turns out Lynette was the last person to see Sonja alive. They'd made plans to have lunch together today, but when she showed up at the cottage Sonja didn't answer the door and that led to us finding her murdered."

"Oh boy, that had to be rough for her. I can't say I've seen her, but I'm not behind the front desk as much anymore. Nadine might have checked her in."

"Do you have any leads on who could have done this?" Val asked.

"Not that I know of," I said. "I think this will be a tough one for Jeff to solve."

Scott's big smile popped out, and he put his hands together in prayer style. "I like the sound of you saying Jeff needs to solve it. That means you will be sticking to the sidelines on this one, right? Please!"

CHAPTER ELEVEN

"Well..."

"Jackie! It's our wedding weekend. Please, no sleuthing!" Scott pleaded.

"I was just teasing. My weekend plan is to get married. That's it. No detective work involved, except investigating the dress shops in Madison tomorrow."

"What?" Val practically shouted. "You're supposed to relax. I have someone coming in to Cut-n-Curl to give you a manicure and pedicure."

"Well, there's been a little complication. My wedding dress is no longer wearable. I'm afraid I'll have to find a different one. Sophia and I are going to have to spend tomorrow dress shopping."

We'd caught up with Beverly, and she took hold of

my arm. "What? Your wedding dress? The one Sonja was making? What happened?"

Oh no, my flippant exchange with Val meant I'd messed up. No private moment now. How awful that Beverly was hearing about the murder this way.

"I'm so sorry you had to hear this here," I said. "But Sonja is gone."

"What do you mean, *gone?*"

"She died last night."

In an incredulous tone Beverly said, "No! That can't be." Then, slowly, her mouth dropped open as a sad acceptance softened her eyes. "First the joy of hearing our paths came together again after all these years, and now... gone. The world can work in cruel ways. She came here to grow old in a quiet, simple, soul-filling place. And then to have this happen. Was it her heart? Or a car accident?"

"No. It was a murder." I felt bad having to tell her this in front of everyone.

Beverly's mouth dropped open. "What? How can that be? Who would even know her here, much less want to kill her?"

"That's just what we were talking about," Wanda said. "It's so strange. But Jackie just told me about a friend of Sonja's who came to visit and is staying at my motel.

Maybe she'll have a clue as to who might have done this."

"And that brings us back to the fact that Jackie can't wear her wedding dress now," Val added. "Can you imagine? I heard about bridal salons going bankrupt and brides-to-be not being able to get their dresses out, but nothing like this."

"Why does this mean you can't wear your dress?" Beverly asked.

"It was still with her because she was doing some final adjustments. And now... well, let me just say it's not wearable."

"Can't you find someone to do the final adjustments?" Grace asked. "I do a little sewing. Maybe I could help."

"It's not that." I didn't want to explain this in front of everyone, but all eyes were on me.

I was rescued by Todd crashing into the sidewall of the rink in front of us. He clung tight to the wood until his skates stopped slipping and sliding under him.

"Whoa there, cowboy," Scott said. "You almost went over the barrier and took all of us down with that move."

Alli did an ice spraying hockey stop right next to him, followed by a tight twirl.

"Hi guys! This Midwest boy learned not to diss this

California girl's skating ability. Ready for another go round, Todd? I'll hold your hand this time."

Todd winked at us. "That's what I was aiming for." And off they went.

Ginger and Murph had exited the rink, along with Katie Murphy. The three of them stopped for hot chocolates from Val's grandsons' stand right next to the skate rental booth. With red noses and glowing cheeks, they did the skate waddle walk toward us.

"Alli sure knows how to skate," Katie said to Beverly. "I can't believe I ran into you guys here in Harmony."

"And I'm so happy about it too," Beverly said. "It's been good to lay eyeballs on you after that cryptic email you sent out. Katie, do you remember my sister Jackie from the party you put on for me?"

Katie extended her hand. "Yes, I do. Nice to see you again. And this must be Scott Drake, am I right? Beverly told me about you earlier when we spoke. I think she was getting weary of my bending her ear a bit too much about my own sad state of affairs."

"Nonsense. From what you've been through, you deserve a break," Beverly said.

"The visit to Uncle Paddy in Florida was a great start. And now to spend time with Uncle Dermot and Aunt Grace is just what I need. Big bonus in seeing cousin Murph again too. It's been way too long."

"Staying here for a while?" Val asked.

"Probably for New Year's Eve. Does it get pretty wild and crazy here?"

Wanda burst out laughing. "Let me tell you, Harmony has been known to throw a wild New Year's Eve celebration. Times Square has nothing on our village square. Only beer caps popping instead of champagne corks."

"Ah, we'll show you a fine time lassie," Dermot said. "Is Paddy ready to throw a New Year's Eve bash at his new place?"

"Not even close. Lots of work to do there yet," Katie said. "I'm going to drive back down that way when I leave here."

"My sister Sophia is around somewhere. We left her waiting in line for hot pretzel bites with mustard. But she lives just a couple of hours from Paddy's town," Scott said. "We're leaving soon to head down for our honeymoon."

Katie smiled and clapped her hands. "Yay! It'll be so fun for you guys."

Sophia and Jack showed up with hot pretzel bites to pass around. Everyone dove into the hot and salty morsels. Katie and Sophia were introduced and found out they were each in the event planning business, though on different scales. I joined with them in making plans to get together while we were visiting Florida. We all found out that Sophia and Jack's boat was kept in a marina near Paddy's town of Seaside Cove. Katie promptly tried to convince her to harbor it in the Seaside marina.

Jack nodded and put his arm around his wife's shoulders. "I've heard good things about that harbor area. It's well protected from the waves of the gulf, and a substantially sized river feeds into it. Good salt and freshwater fishing. Let's look into it. Seaside would be closer for us to get to. The drive would be easier because we wouldn't get all caught up in weekend traffic on the interstate."

"I'm good with checking it out," Sophia said. "Let's exchange phone numbers, Katie."

"Absolutely. I'd love to show you around if I'm still there."

"You're going back to Florida after the holidays?" I asked. "Then how long until you return to LA?"

"Not sure. LA holds little interest for me now. I'll probably be with Uncle Paddy a few more weeks, but I don't want to wear out my welcome. It's a good feeling being with family again," Katie said, before grabbing a pretzel bite. "I'm reconnecting with my Irish roots."

"Maybe when you're in Florida you could use your

expertise to help your uncle plan a grand opening," Sophia suggested.

"Hmm. That's a thought." Katie's eyes lit up. "A good thought, actually. I might be of help with that, though I don't know local vendors. But then he's setting up a bar and restaurant, so food and drinks would be taken care of."

"Maybe Dermot and I could sneak away and come down for it," Grace said. "Not that we don't love this part of our winter here, but a couple of weeks in Florida, now that I could live with."

We all shuffled closer to one of the fire barrels to stay warm as the temps dropped around us. Soon Kay Whitlow, along with Patti and Charlie Hunt, joined us.

"Where's Jeff?" Scott asked.

"He had to take a call. With the holidays and vacations, the department is short-staffed."

"Nothing serious I hope," Scott said.

"He didn't say," Kay answered. "I feel bad for him. He works such long and odd hours. But I guess that's what he signed up for."

The door of the plastic igloo holding the Shady Pines gang opened. Ruth and Rocco stepped out and looked around. When they saw me, they hurried over. They didn't hide the anxious expression on their faces.

As they made their way through the crowd, the

voices of those around me began tunneling and the people gathered nearby began to blur.

Something was horribly wrong.

Ruth jerked her head to one side indicating I should step away from our group.

Rocco quickly explained that Jeff had called him. "There's been a break-in at Sonja's cottage. Jeff thought this and the murder might be tied together. He asked me to meet him there. Ruth is coming with me. Maybe you could join us. You are someone who's gotten to know Sonja, and you might be able to shed some light on what Jeff is going to be looking at."

"Of course. Let me tell Scott I'm leaving. I can't believe this. What could there possibly be in her cottage to steal?"

Ruth seemed especially shaken. "And the place was ransacked. What's going on?"

CHAPTER TWELVE

Scott insisted on driving with us. Things were starting to wind down for the evening, so luckily we managed to slip away with little explanation. I noticed Murph giving Ginger a quick hug before he also left. He headed directly toward his police cruiser parked at the station.

As we headed to Shady Pines, Rocco explained that a neighbor had made the 911 call because she noticed movement in Sonja's cottage.

"'Like someone had a flashlight,' was the way she'd described it to the 911 operator. And seeing that a murder had been committed there, it didn't seem right for anyone to be at the house. The caller had not observed a vehicle or a person coming or leaving the residence."

"Why did Jeff call you?" I asked.

"I spoke with him this afternoon as you suggested, Jacqueline. I felt compelled to share what information I had about Sonja's past life, both her husband's suspect business dealings and the questionable accident causing his death. When she was murdered, I began to think that she'd been found living here by someone that law enforcement had wanted to protect her from. That her past had found her. I must assume that the conversation we had was why he reached out to me just now."

The entrance to Shady Pines was lit with decorative lampposts, but once we got further in, there was only soft down-lighting along the path. The bluish glow from television screens showed in some of the cottages we passed, and several residents had their porch lights on. But if we didn't know our way around here, a person could easily get lost, because every cottage was angled differently and had different setbacks from the narrow roads.

"What is going on in our little community?" Ruth murmured. "Now I imagine a murderer or a robber watching us from behind every tree. The darkness seems blacker. More sinister."

Rocco put his arm around Ruth. "This is an isolated incident, my dear, unique to Sonja. And I'm beginning to feel guilty. I encouraged her to move to Harmony, telling her what a safe and quiet place it was."

Scott pulled up to the cottage, where police cruisers were parked. Jeff stood talking with two people in the beams from his headlights.

Before getting out, Scott turned to Rocco and in a stern voice said, "Seriously, man, this is not your fault. This is and always will be a safe place for retirees. Sonja Bernardi's past found her. Now to figure out why so we can all get back to normal." Scott banged his fist against the steering wheel. "Jeff has to solve this. And the vile, ugly people who were after her for whatever happened in her past will be locked behind bars. I don't like this cloud hanging over us."

He turned to look me in the eye while gently tilting my chin up. "And I will not let it spoil my wedding to this lovely lady."

"Well said, Scott. Now let's get going on clearing this all up," Rocco replied.

Don Stone, the man who'd been working in the cottage, was one of the people talking to Jeff. Ruth identified the other person as Martha, the neighbor who'd been there that morning. She pointed to her home just beyond the snowbank.

Jeff made introductions all around and began to catch the four of us up on what happened here.

"Martha was the one who called 911. She was working late into the evening on her quilting project when flashes of light at this place caught her eye. She put her overcoat on and walked out to get a closer look."

"Put on my boots too, don't forget," Martha added. "I decided to take the shortcut to see better, but that involved crossing over a snowbank. Didn't know if I'd break through, and I didn't want to get my slippers wet."

"Right. Anyway, when she stepped out, her little dog Max ran out ahead of her and stood barking in this direction."

"That's when I saw the lights go out. Place was dark. Then he comes out the back from the kitchen door, real shadowy and moving quickly. I was never so scared in my life. I snatched Max up and ran into my house to call the police."

"You did the right thing," Jeff said. "Your quick actions might mean the robber's tracks will still be there. And Don here is apparently a restless sleeper and takes late-night walks. He was nearby when I pulled in and came over when he saw where I'd stopped."

Don, with his hands tucked in his Carhartt jacket, stood quietly to one side. Jeff turned to look up behind me. "Looks like word is spreading."

Harry approached. "We just got back home from the

Christmas festivities, and I noticed activity here. What's going on?"

"Robbery," Martha proclaimed. "And I reported it."

"Well, I'll be darned, that Sonja was a mysterious creature. Kind of exotic. Got things all stirred up here."

"Why do you say that?" Jeff asked.

"Murdering and thieving are outright rarities here." Harry pointed toward the house. "And now in only twenty-four hours look what's happened. I'd say she brought it on us."

Ruth scolded, "Why say such unpleasant things about an innocent woman?"

Betty seemed to appear out of nowhere, with Dorothy at her side. "She's right, Harry! Sonja just wanted to live here quietly for the rest of her life. She certainly didn't ask for this."

"And, mister big mouth, mister neighborhood watch leader, what about the guy you saw watching this place from the road? The stalker you called him, if I remember right?" Dorothy said. "Or did you use even more colorful language? Like he was casing the joint?"

"Are you saying I misread him? That he could be the murderer?"

"Why not? Or do you have a better idea, Jeff?" Dorothy asked.

Jeff didn't respond to Dorothy, but instead spoke to

Harry. "What is she talking about? How come you never told me about him?"

Harry faltered under Jeff's critical stare. "Uh... he stopped showing up."

"What happened, Harry? What was the guy's story?" Jeff asked.

"He told me he was looking at properties in the area and that he'd stopped to make phone calls before he got to the busier part of town."

"Then why tell your friends he was casing the joint?" Eunice scolded.

Harry's face reddened, and it wasn't from the cold. "I might have exaggerated a little."

"Did you see him after that?" Jeff asked.

"I saw him here again, but he just waved like we were old buddies. He didn't look guilty of anything," Harry said.

From Martha's yard, a group of three ladies approached in varying layers and colors of winter gear.

"I called my friends for support," Martha explained.

"Again, the place of that fancy lady in trouble," one of the women, who was dressed in a puffy coat, proclaimed.

I recognized her as the one with the black dog from this morning. I couldn't help but think about what a strange remark that was. Is that how Sonja was seen by her neighbors?

"It is, Jean. She's the one that they found dead this morning. Now someone's broken into her place, and I reported it. Max scared the robber off." Martha struggled to hold her little wiggly Max.

"You told us that in your message. Put Max down before he falls out of your arms," Jean snipped.

"Maybe the murderer broke in because he was afraid he'd left evidence behind," one of the other women said.

"Didn't we see that on that Hallmark Mystery story just a couple of weeks ago? The police missed the evidence at first, then the bad guy went back and removed it," Martha replied.

"Ladies, please, we need to stay focused on what we have in front of us," Jeff said. "We'll be questioning the residents of Shady Pines. Someone might have seen the thief's vehicle."

"Why is Don here?" Jean asked. "You call him too, Martha?"

"I didn't. Chief said he was just walking around and saw the lights."

I thought I heard a snicker come from one of the ladies. "I see him walking around this way a lot. Isn't it out of your way, Don? A dead end?"

"He saw the police cars and came to help," Martha

insisted. "For goodness' sake, let him be. He probably knew her better than any of us."

"I probably did." Don finally spoke up, his jaw visibly clenched. "She hired me to help her, and I took the job. Mrs. Bernardi was a very nice woman. And you all were not very nice to her in return."

As he began to walk away, Jeff stopped him. "Don, I'd like you to go inside with me and see if any of your tools are missing. Maybe it's just a theft of construction tools, the sort of things that can be easily fenced."

Don hesitated, then mumbled that he'd stay if it was necessary. He obviously was uncomfortable being back at the cottage after finding Sonja that morning.

Jeff sighed and shook his head. "Now everyone, unless you have anything to share involving this robbery, please go home."

Jeff directed Murph to begin canvassing the area, only talking to residents whose lights were on. Scott offered to go and do the same on the far side of the community. Jeff asked Rocco and me to join him and Don inside.

CHAPTER THIRTEEN

Ruth agreed to have Scott drop her off at her place before he began canvassing the far side of Shady Pines. I could tell the shocking events of the day had taken a toll on her. These past twenty-four hours had done that to all of us.

Before entering the house, Rocco, Don, and I were given paper booties and thin plastic gloves.

"What a sad state of affairs." Jeff's dry, exhausted tone surprised me. He usually was so professional. "Wonder if they found what they were looking for?"

"Any idea what that might be?" I asked.

"At this point no, but that's why I wanted the three of you to come in here. You're the ones who seemed to have been with her the most since she moved to Harmony."

My eyes scanned the living area and through the kitchen to the back door's broken glass. That must have been how the robber gained entry. Easy enough to break the glass and then reach in to unlock the door. Now what was he here for?

The place was a mess, but with an overpowering flowery odor. It looked like the set of a television crime show. Sofa cushions flipped. Drawers dumped out. Lamps knocked over. My dress still hung on the bedroom door above the blood stains on the floor.

"The murder hasn't been publicized except for a mention in our *Harmony Happenings* online edition. This seems an unlikely place for a common robbery," Jeff said before warning us to be careful where we stepped, even with our fancy slippers on. "The place has been searched for prints and blood spatter, but now a new crime scene has been created."

"What's a common robbery?" Don asked.

"Bad way to put it," Jeff said, with an uncomfortable chuckle. "A random robbery would be the better term. But this appears to have been targeted. My sense is the person knew her and broke into the cottage looking for something specific. But what? We took her personal identifying papers and any obvious things of value like jewelry into custody, so if that is what they were after, they didn't find it."

"Is it possible that since she was what Martha called exotic, someone came here thinking she harbored unusual pieces of art or unique memorabilia from her years in Hollywood?" Rocco asked.

"I heard that expression too. Where did anyone get that idea?" I asked Don.

Don stuttered and stammered. "Well, it's like… oh, I don't know. But she was… she was different. People could tell, you know? Not in a… bad way. Different in a good way. But sometimes that's… Oh, forget it. I don't know how to explain it."

"You must have learned a great deal about her, what with all the time you spent here working on her house," I said.

"She was a pretty woman and from out of town, so maybe that's what they were trying to say," Rocco said.

"I guess," Don murmured. "But I could tell something was haunting her. She didn't join in with things around here. That time she met up with you at our monthly potluck was the only time she participated in anything."

"I see. You're saying she was reclusive?" I asked.

"Right," Don said.

I noticed Jeff moving about while keeping a close ear on our conversation.

Rocco nodded. "I understand."

But I could see his wheels turning. Was he thinking what I was? Don Stone was here when the body was found, and he showed up tonight saying he'd been out for a walk. Had he wanted more from Sonja than being hired to do construction work? Maybe she'd rejected him.

Jeff stepped in. "Don, you were going to check if any of your tools are missing."

Rocco added. "Good idea. That is a common thing that thieves will steal. I've even heard they sell things online now, letting Facebook or Amazon fence the stolen goods for them."

"Sure. I'll check around," Don mumbled.

"Thanks, man," Jeff said. "Let's hope it is something that obvious."

"Thinking what I am?" I asked Jeff after Don was out of earshot.

"It's a possibility. I'll get him in for questioning. Maybe the neighbor or her quilting friends saw things like that happening. Jackie, any observations you have? You were in here quite a lot while she was working on your wedding stuff."

"Yes, I was."

Rocco noticed my glance at the dress.

"I am sorry you must deal with that unwearable

gown, Jacqueline. I heard you're heading to Madison tomorrow to get another dress. You will look lovely in whatever you wear," Rocco said.

"Thanks. It'll be what it is."

Jeff rubbed his chin and looked up at Rocco. "After what you told me earlier today, I'm thinking that the man Harry saw might be a possible connection to all of this."

"Agreed. I had the same thought," Rocco said. "Could have been looking for her or looking to protect her. Either way, he might be involved. I will check with my sources if there is any word on the street. But if you get a description of the car or the man, please forward it to me."

"Sure, will do. Appreciate the help, Rocco," Jeff said.

I'd stepped away to look around. I realized I hadn't been very observant while I was here over the past weeks. My focus had been elsewhere. I looked around the walls in the living room. Any artwork I'd noticed seemed to be in place. The Lalique Bacchantes crystal vase I'd admired had been knocked to the floor but appeared unbroken. Sonja had remarked that she looked forward to spring, when she could pick wildflowers to put in it. Her Miele coffeemaker still sat in its place on her kitchen counter.

I'd used her bathroom and didn't see anything out of

place except her perfumes, which had been swept off the shelf. That explained the pleasant, flowery scents in here. The bedroom was a mess. Things knocked off the nightstand, dresser drawers open, and items strewn about.

What were they looking for?

CHAPTER FOURTEEN

The next morning, Libby's nose rubbing against my shoulder meant she was ready for her walk. The icy air cut cold against my skin, but Libby loved it. She ran her nose up in the loose, light fluff of snow that had fallen during the night. Thankfully, Aunt Ruth had her coffee pot on a timer, so I slipped out the door with a fresh cup of coffee and Libby off leash.

The local guy hired to plow the roads hadn't been here yet, but this was not worthy of plowing. It would probably melt this morning. Libby and I broke new footpaths on the roadways. The silence enveloped me as I headed out toward the community center to catch a glimpse of the frozen river.

Along the way, the crime scene photographer in me

took photographs of the only two sets of tire tracks I saw. From the look of it, they were made at some point early this morning, so probably nothing to do with the thief, but hey, digital film was cheap and convenient. I looped around to walk in toward Sonja's cottage, stopping there to absorb all that had happened yesterday.

Libby sat at my feet. She sensed my contemplative mood. How sad. Who would want to take this woman's life? Here, where she thought she could live out her remaining years in peace.

I remembered her creative delight at working on my crimson velvet evening coat. The full-length style was elegant. The sophisticated Harmony woman who'd worn the original coat would never have imagined it would inspire a garment created in this Lutheran camp cabin. Now what was to have been my wedding dress hung behind those walls, droplets of blood soaked into the silk crepe fabric.

"Come on girl, let's get home. I need another coffee."

I turned to leave, deciding this was the last time I would think of that dress. Today I would find a new one. I had to find a new one, was more the way it was.

No purpose in regrets, I'm getting married. Life is good.

We'd gone just a short distance when Libby disappeared into the forest. I saw her head pop up between trees as she bounced through the snow.

"Libby, come girl! Libby. Come."

Snow clinging to her fur, Libby bounded back out to the road, taking a low snowbank with ease. She had something in her mouth.

"Drop it," I commanded.

Libby was especially playful this morning, and it took over a minute to get her to drop the object. I quickly snatched it up. It was a leather glove. Not a dress glove, more of a worker's glove. Practical. Well worn. I turned to look back at Sonja's cottage then down at the glove. I knew I had to give it to Jeff. It was a distance away from the scene, but it might be a clue.

Aunt Ruth was wide awake when we got back. She had started breakfast, and the smell of cinnamon rolls tickled my nose. Libby's, too, because she sat begging at Ruth's feet.

"Okay if I give her a piece?" Ruth asked, putting the rolls aside to cool.

"Sure, why not? Just one piece though, or you'll spoil her more than she already is."

After we finished breakfast and Ruth began clearing dishes, she said, "Last night, when I had a hard time sleeping, I was thinking on what Dorothy said about the man who seemed to be hanging around here."

"The stalker?"

"That's a term Eunice coined. She likes to stir things up, as you know. But yes, him. He told Harry not to worry, that he was looking at properties in the area. Maybe Kim should be asked if she was approached by him. That could confirm his story. Surely Kim would be the realtor he'd go to if it was commercial property he was looking for."

"Excellent idea, Ruth! I'll leave that information at the station for Jeff. I need to drop something off there this morning."

Ruth spun around from her spot at the kitchen sink. "Jacqueline Parker, you are not getting more involved with this murder, are you? You have your plate full already, and today you want to find a wedding dress for goodness' sake."

"Not to worry Auntie, I'm good. It's just a glove Libby found. It wasn't far from Sonja's, and I wanted Jeff to have it."

"Can I see it?"

"Sorry, but I put it in my car so I won't forget it. It's just a leather work glove."

Ruth turned back to finish with the dishes in the sink, but I could hear her tsk-tsk over the sound of running water. "What about that friend of hers? Since there weren't signs of a forced entry this morning, it had to be someone she knew."

I got a chuckle over Aunt Ruth scolding me about getting involved, when she'd put a lot of thought into the murder herself.

"Or maybe she didn't lock her doors at night like most everyone here?" I said.

"Did Jeff figure out how the burglar got in last night?"

"The back door window was broken. He probably did that to reach in and unlock the door. They took photos of the new footprints in the snow last night."

"Where did the tracks lead?"

"They followed them for a short distance, but then lost them on the asphalt roadbed which had been plowed. He figured a getaway car was parked some-where else. Murph and Scott both set off to talk to residents. Murph will be out again today. Something might turn up. I took photos of tire tracks on my walk, but it looked like they were made in the new snowfall that came early this morning."

Ruth ordered Libby to sit and then tossed her another bite of the roll. "Now off with you, Jackie. Let me cuddle up with Libby and enjoy my quiet morning."

CHAPTER FIFTEEN

As I approached Murphy's Coffee Shop and Bakery, the marvelous smell of the wood-burning fireplace in the Book Nook greeted me. Ginger's bookstore was a warm, welcoming place for our Wisconsin winter days. Through the bookstore's front windows, I saw Ginger chatting with Beverly. Even though I no longer had the luxury of time to spend relaxing today as I'd planned, I decided to pop in and say hello.

I stomped the snow off my boots before I pushed the door open. The cold air caught their attention. After giving Beverly a quick hug, I apologized for dashing off so quickly last night.

"I understand," Beverly said. "What did you discover at Sonja's place? Ginger told me it appeared to have been robbed. It's so hard to imagine that this has all happened since I arrived."

"Not sure if the person got what they were looking for. The police had removed all the smaller things of value after her murder. I didn't notice anything missing as far as artwork on her walls or obvious stuff like that, but then I'd only been there a few times, and was focused on my wedding dress and coat."

"Murph told me he's going back today to see if any of the residents witnessed something unusual," Ginger said. "Still planning on going wedding dress shopping?"

"Yep. There's nothing in my wardrobe that will fit the bill."

"That's such a bummer. I wouldn't be handling it as well as you are," Ginger said as she excused herself, returning to setting up her book signing table.

"Thanks again for doing this author appearance here, Beverly," I said.

"My pleasure. Being in Harmony for Christmas is perfect. It's like a fairytale. The last time I was in snow for the holidays I was skiing in Aspen."

"You ski?"

"Well, not skiing, but keeping up my image. I make a cute snow bunny!" Her self-deprecating laugh filled the air as she puffed her hair and stretched her neck. "My public expects so much of me."

Through the opening arch to the coffee shop, I heard another burst of laughter. It sounded familiar. I stepped aside and bent my head to look through the doorway between the two businesses. And I smiled. That was Val's laugh. She was talking with Sophia.

Ginger came and tapped Beverly on the shoulder. "I hate to break up a sisters' conversation, but it's time to sit down and greet your readers."

"Okay, thanks. Bummer about your dress, Jackie, but good luck with the shopping today!" Beverly said.

That was my cue to head over and grab a coffee and donut to go.

"Surprise!" Wanda jumped out toward me from behind the doorway corner. "Gotcha, didn't I?"

"The fact that I jumped and squealed would be a good indicator you did," I said, punching her in the shoulder. "What's going on? Val, aren't you opening the shop by now for your Saturday regulars?"

"I did a little shuffling and rearranging so I could close the place for the day."

"Why? Just because I had to cancel my mani-pedi?" I looked at the three of them with their Cheshire cat grins.

"No, because Wanda and I are going dress shopping with you! We're your oldest friends and want to help

Sophia. We want to make this a fun girls' day for you, Jackie."

I was on the edge of bursting into tears. I'd been holding in my disappointment about the dress, but now to have these two here… it was overwhelming. "You are the best! This is wonderful. But who set this up?"

Sophia gave me a conspiratorial smile as Wanda and Val pointed at her. "I knew what happened with your dress was horrible. And I just thought the more the merrier by having these two along for our trip to Madison."

As we were getting our road trip cookies and coffees, Lynette Vaughn walked into Murphy's, followed by Kim Walters.

Kim came hurrying over to me. "Are you okay, Jackie? I just heard about your wedding dress mess. Whatever are you going to do? I have a couple of evening gowns. They might not be long enough for you. You're so tall. But maybe they could be cut off and hemmed. Mid-calf is all the rage now. I'd allow that on the red one. Bad vibes from that dress, though.

"And in the very place you'll be getting married. Are you going to walk down the grand staircase that I managed to tumble down? What a night that was. Remember Luella Hagge ended up being shoved down those stairs? But she had a red dress like…"

"Kim, slow down. Yes, I remember that night. And yes, I'm okay. But my dress isn't okay, so I'm going on a very last-minute dress hunting trip." I didn't bother explaining the bad vibes that Kim was carrying on about, because Val and Wanda knew the story. But I noticed Sophia's confused expression and told her that I'd explain later.

"If you didn't find anything in LA, how on earth will you find something around here?" Kim asked with an incredulous expression.

"My acceptance bar has been lowered substantially! Say, while you're here, I wanted to ask how it's going with Gerard Singleton? Did he settle on a property he'd like to buy?"

"Not yet. But he's running me ragged looking. Though if he does buy something, I'll be happy for the village. And for my pocketbook."

Val asked if he was in the market for a beauty shop.

Kim grabbed her by the shoulders. "No! You cannot stop doing hair. Never ever. I will not allow it."

"I'm getting too old for it. My feet and back grumble at the end of every day, and my mind can't multi-task like it used to. I'm starting to make scheduling mistakes and double ordering."

"Nonsense," Kim exclaimed. "Come with me to my yoga class. You'll be feeling better soon. And the paperwork, sheesh, that's just organization. I have a terrific planner program in my laptop. You can handle that easily enough when your feet and back don't hurt. There's a new dietary supplement I've been using. I'll order you a sample."

Val rolled her eyes. "Thanks Kim, but I just want to be free of all the work. Spontaneous is what I want to be again."

I interrupted by saying, "So Kim, is Gerard still in town?"

"He is as far as I know. He seemed very determined to find something. Why do you ask?"

"There was a man that caught the attention of some of the Shady Pines gang. He stopped near the entrance road several times and said he was here looking at properties. I was just wondering if that could have been Gerard."

"Ohh… is this connected to your murder investigation?" Kim's eyes brightened as she licked her lips. "Do you need my help?"

CHAPTER SIXTEEN

*I*nfamous words from Kim Walters. But then I had to appreciate how she had helped with other investigations. I was pondering how much to tell her here in front of everyone.

Wanda must have wanted to help me out by slipping away from further conversation with Kim. "We're ready to hit the road."

"Sure, give me just a minute, I'll meet you all outside. I have to talk to Lynette. I won't be long."

I'd watched Lynette head to the bookstore and when I went back there, Kim followed me. "What should I question Gerard about, Jackie? I don't want to make him think we suspect him."

"Kim, stop. Please. It's just that Jeff was trying to figure out who that stranger was. He's not necessarily involved with the murder. But if he knew it was your client, it would clear the air."

"I see." Kim's squinted eyes and sage nod of her head meant she hadn't let go of the fact that her client might be a suspect. She leaned close. "You can't say things here where they can be overheard. Good thinking. I don't want to scare him off with too many questions. I'll phrase it casually. Did Harry get a good description of the stalker?"

"Stalker? How did you know it was Harry who talked to him?" I found myself in awe of what Kim knew about the goings on in our little Harmony.

"Heck, Jackie. Everyone knows Harry is a one-man neighborhood watch committee. And at the hardware store on Thursday, I overheard Eunice telling Clarence that they had a stalker at Shady Pines. I'm no dummy. I put two and two together."

"Look Kim, it's not that big of a deal, but if you have a photograph of him from a business card, or his website, that would be helpful."

"I should ask him directly if he talked with Harry."

"No, just give Jeff contact information for him."

"That convinces me you suspect him! Don't worry. I'll try to get a photo and see if I can remember what car he was driving. Hmm… I think it was a rental. Maybe charcoal gray. No, a deep navy blue."

"Kim, if you'll excuse me, there is someone I need to talk to, and the girls are waiting for me outside. If you could just let Jeff know what you found that would be helpful."

"Sure. I got this one covered, Jackie. Ohh… look at those cool boots! Those are not Wisconsin winter proof at all," Kim said. "Have fun and find a dress. I'll report to Jeff."

Whew! What a whirlwind. The boots Kim admired belonged to Lynette. She was telling Beverly that Sonja mentioned working on her soap opera. Beverly smiled and sympathetically patted Lynette's hand, but her attention had to return to a customer waiting in front of her table with a book for her to sign. I took the opportunity to talk to Lynette. She needed to be told that her friend's home had been burglarized last night.

"I overheard you telling Beverly that Sonja mentioned her by name. That was very nice of you. Beverly is my half-sister."

"Oh really? What a small world. When I noticed the sign for Beverly's book signing, I popped in to get a copy. She was so gracious in extending her sympathy to me."

"Ah Lynette, something happened last night, and I wanted to be the one to tell you about it. I'm sorry this is so rushed, but I have some friends waiting outside for me," I said. "Sonja's cottage was broken into last night. It was ransacked as though the thief was looking for something specific."

Lynette's hand flew to cover her mouth as she slowly moved her head from side to side. She seemed to tip toward me as she reached for a bookcase to steady herself. "This can't be."

I touched her shoulder lightly. "Would you like to sit down?"

"No, I'll be alright. It's just that this is such a shock."

"Of course. You just lost a dear friend."

Under her breath, but loud enough for me to hear, Lynette mumbled. "I hope they didn't steal it." She softly gasped. "I'm sorry you heard that. There's another reason I'm here. Sonja was to give me a ring."

"Why would she have your ring?"

She ignored my question. "I can't believe this has happened. The poor thing. And after all she went through. Who do I contact about getting my family's ring?"

"I thought you were a friend. How are you related to her?"

"I understand your confusion. We were friends as well as being sister-in-laws. We were a close Italian family. The ring was to stay in the Bernardi family."

"Why don't you go to the police station and talk to

Chief Jeff. They removed valuables from the home Friday morning. He might have it."

"Thank you, I will. And I have proof that it was to be returned to our family. I have emails between us explaining the entire thing. I'm sure he'll hand it over." Lynette straightened up and pulled her gloves from her coat pocket. "Is the police station nearby? I'd like to get this straightened out."

"I'm leaving now too. I'll point it out to you when we get outside."

But as I passed the author table, Beverly crooked her finger at me and whispered, "I know an actor when I see one."

CHAPTER SEVENTEEN

*I*t had been fun flying to LA to spend time there with Beverly and Alli, but the shopping excursions had proved fruitless. Ah, but the mysterious twist to have a well-respected dressmaker and designer land in Harmony and create a custom gown and coat for my wedding… couldn't beat that. I had been riding high for the past couple of months, but that all came to a screeching halt yesterday.

Now, a shopping trip with these friends was just what I needed. As we drove toward Madison, I explained what my wedding dress looked like, as no one else had seen it.

"Sonja and I collaborated on the design over a couple days, including an evening with more than one glass of wine, celebrating the final sketches. I chose the fabric from a sample selection she'd obtained and agreed with her suggestion of using silk crepe. The fabric had just the amount of body I liked. It held its shape beautifully and the soft fabric had a glow. I didn't want a glossy shine. Next, the color. I chose one named porcelain. It had a flared, almost full circle skirt with gored panel seams rising to the bodice."

"Wow! That sounds stunning," Val said.

"It was. But here I am blathering about something I don't have. I promised myself I wouldn't even think about it again."

"And you sure won't find one anywhere close to it on a Saturday in Madison. But I went online and found some likely shops for us to check out," Sophia said. "I'm not familiar with the town, so if one of you would watch the map that would be great."

Wanda agreed to take charge of navigation and Sophia gave her addresses of the first six dress shops as we drove through the hills of the Driftless region.

Sophia wanted to hear more about the coat I would be wearing. I explained that Sonja had done an amazing job on the velvet evening coat too.

"It was over the top for my normal way of dressing here in Harmony. What an impression it would have made at one of the charity balls in a wintery Chicago. To stroll around wrapped in the luxurious full-length coat with white fur trim would have drawn every eye in the room. Not that it was my style to do so, but this is going to be a once in a lifetime event, and I wanted to dress up."

"As a snow princess! I can't wait to see you and Scott riding up to the Harmony mansion in that sleigh," Val said. "It's your big day and we couldn't be happier for you, Jackie."

"And for your brother, Sophia. He's a lucky man," Wanda added. "He's not getting cold feet, is he?"

"He is not! I can say that definitively. I didn't know if he'd ever marry again after what happened with Patti, but you were the one to do it," Sophia said as she pulled her car into the first shop's parking lot.

This one was a bridal salon, and since it was the Saturday before Christmas it was quiet. The woman who approached us seemed puzzled as to where the bride was.

"Ah, is the bride on her way?"

When I announced that I was the one getting married, and the wedding was tomorrow, she stepped back in surprise.

"You're not the mother and aunts of the bride, then? Well now, we are going to have a difficult time getting something for you today."

"Oh, it will be close to impossible, I'm sure. I can't be picky. Don't you have anything I can buy off the rack?"

Wanda said, "Classy, not flashy. No sequins or cutouts."

"No mermaid style." Sophia looked at me. "And no… what was that other one you didn't want?"

"No strapless gown. Nothing too young and glitzy," I said.

The poor stylist began walking the rows of gowns. Pulling out and putting back a dozen gowns before she found three that I tried on. They just weren't right. And when I walked out to show Val, Wanda, and Sophia, they gave them all a thumbs down.

Next stop was Macy's in the Hilldale Shopping Center. The picked over selection of holiday dresses was another bust. A highly regarded dress shop had one likely dress, and we asked the clerk to hold it for us, which she was happy to do when she heard our story. It was at the fourth stop, another bridal salon, that I found what I thought might be my best bet.

The stylist, after hearing what had brought baby boomers to the salon, suggested we look at mother-of-the-bride dresses.

She saw our hesitation. "They aren't all in mint green with a lace overlay."

"Well, that's good to hear," Val said.

"And though there is not time to allow for any alterations, I can sell them off the sample racks. You look to be about a ten? Most of these run small, so I'll bring out both size ten and twelve."

After she'd settled us in one of the bridal rooms with glasses of champagne, she disappeared, reappearing about ten minutes later with a rolling rack of dresses in shades of pastels and creams. I felt hopeful.

"I feel like we're in an episode of *Say Yes to the Dress,*" Wanda said.

The stylist laughed. "And we are going to find one you'll be glad to say yes to."

"We have to. Time has run out," I said.

Some were dismissed out of hand by unanimous agreement. We managed to narrow it down to five dresses for me to try on. One was too small, two were too big, and two were just right. Goldilocks jokes aside, the stylist suggested I take those two home with me, and she'd allow me to return the one I didn't wear after the holidays.

As I turned to admire the dress in the elegant three-way mirror, I said, "I hadn't expected to like this one, but it is probably my favorite. I love the color, but the style seems too sedate."

"Nonsense, Jackie. You're thinking it's a mother-of-the-bride dress. But no one at the reception will even know that," Sophia said. "And I swear I won't tell Scott until Monday morning."

Val burst out laughing. "I'd like to see his face when you tell him."

"So how are you feeling? Did we do good?" Wanda asked.

I smiled at my friends. "You all did good. Thank you for being with me. I'm very happy with what we found."

"And it will produce the desired result," Val said.

"Which is to make me look like a mature bride?" I asked.

"Hey, buck up, Jackie. Look back on the other dresses we saw today. The sequined white sheath? The red, glitter-laden ball gown? The pastel pink garden party look? None of those would have done what this one will do. Show off your ageless beauty. Cheers!"

And we all raised our refilled champagne glasses as the stylist came back with two garment bags.

"Congratulations!" she said. "I've got a feeling this will be one fun wedding, despite the circumstances that brought you here today."

CHAPTER EIGHTEEN

Sophia dropped me back off at Murphy's to pick up my car. As I carefully laid the two garment bags on the back seat of my SUV, I saw the glove Libby discovered that morning. Oh gosh, I forgot to give that to Jeff this morning. I made the decision to run the glove over to the police station before heading to Ruth's.

I could have just left it at the front desk, but when I saw that Jeff was in his office, I poked my head in the doorway. "Didn't think I'd see you working late on a Saturday."

"Me either. But tomorrow I'm taking off. I have a big and very important event to attend." He winked and gestured at the papers and photographs spread across his desktop. "So, I'm doing some work on the case load here. What can I help you with?"

"I'm dropping off a work glove that Libby found in the snow near Sonja's cottage this morning. Didn't know if it could be important."

"Thank you. Never know. Come on in and tell me exactly where you found it. And if you have a minute, I'd like to run through how things are looking on the two Bernardi cases."

I walked in and dropped down on a chair near his desk.

"Good! I'll take that as a yes," he said.

"It was just south of her place. I was walking along the road and Libby dashed over the snowbank and into the woods. When I called her back, she returned with this in her mouth." I laid the glove down on Jeff's desk. "I didn't bother with an evidence bag, sorry."

"Excuse me." Jeff walked out and returned with a plastic glove on one hand and an evidence bag in the other. He lifted the glove and turned it over to examine it before placing it in the evidence bag. "This looks like it's been in the elements for a while. Might have been lost earlier and covered by snow for weeks. But kudos to Libby for finding it. Some of these stains might be blood. I'll have someone here run a phenolphthalein test for a start. Staffing is low all over with the holiday season. We're not sure when results of our fingerprint and DNA samples will be returned."

"Oh, and Jeff, I took photos of fresh tire tracks I found on the roads when I went walking this morning. Should I send them to you or just hang on to them for now?"

"Go ahead and email them with the image metadata. You've been busy. Anything else?"

"Earlier today I spoke with Kim and Lynette. They both were going to talk with you. Did they reach you?"

"Yes, they both did." Jeff let out a puff of air before leaning back in his chair. "The conversations with them are what I wanted to run by you. Let's start with Kim. She had Mr. Gerard Singleton's business card and brought it to me. It was very sleek and modern. Expensive looking. There was no business name or website, only a phone number. She had left a message for him earlier, and while she was here in my office, he returned her call. I listened in on it. He told her that he'd decided to drop the idea of doing anything here in Harmony."

"Oh boy, I bet she was disappointed by that," I said. "Did he say anything more?"

"Not really. He sounded very professional. I slipped her a note to request his address. Kim is quick on her feet, I'll give her that. Without missing a beat, she explained that she wanted to send him her information with a small thank you gift for considering Harmony, and to keep us in mind with any future business plans."

"Clever!"

"He declined, saying he already had her card and would recommend her to any of his business associates, should they ask. She was rambling on. You know Kim. But he was firm and said he had to hang up now."

"You have no way of knowing if he was the man that Eunice called the stalker? At least you have a phone number."

"Well, about that." Jeff cleared his throat. "It's been shut off, disconnected, unavailable as of, oh, about an hour ago. That raised a huge red flag for me, so I contacted Kim to see if she had any photographs of Mr. Singleton or the vehicle he was driving. She said she'd check, especially mentioning that we could check security cameras at some of the places she took him."

"Was she able to give you a good physical description of the man?"

"He is tall, middle-aged, well-spoken, and polite. 'Brown hair with a good haircut,' is how she put it. He often wore sunglasses. Was neatly dressed in pricey clothing, and he wore a high-end watch. You can tell why she was excited. In her eyes, the guy had money to spend on properties."

"I met him, and those things fit. She couldn't remember much about his car," I said.

"Told me the same thing. She mentioned he always showed up at her office next to the Harmony Happenings and parked in back. No security camera there."

"Maybe Stu noticed what his car was?"

"No luck there either."

"Hmm, that doesn't give you much to go on to compare him to the man Harry encountered, does it? Did she know where he was staying?"

"She didn't, though she thought it was at one of the chain hotels out by the expressway. We might have luck checking up there, but that doesn't leave Rocco much to go on. He was trying to get word from the street about Sonja Bernardi or anything new involving her husband's death."

"Maybe you should go back and talk to Harry. Try to draw out more about his encounters with the Shady Pines stalker, for lack of a better word."

"I'll do that. Now on to Sonja's friend Lynette," Jeff said. "But you go first and tell me about running into her at the Book Nook and then we can compare notes to see if she was consistent in what she told me."

I went over the morning in my mind, explaining as best I could about Lynette almost collapsing when I told her about Sonja's house being broken into.

"Then she explained that she was supposed to pick up a family ring from her. Did she tell you she was Sonja Bernardi's sister-in-law?" I asked.

Jeff nodded. "She said the ring was an heirloom that her brother wanted her to keep in their family. And she asked me to check the items we removed from the house. I could have pulled up the inventory of the things taken from the cottage, but I wanted to hear more from her first."

"She said she had proof that Sonja had the ring and was going to give it to her. Something about an email. Did she show you anything like that?"

"She did. The email she showed me on her phone was addressed to Sonja Bernardi. It explained that Lynette's brother always wanted a particular ring to remain in the family. She even described it and what it would mean to fulfill his wish. It was dated over a year ago though, so I'm not sure if she couldn't find Sonja, and only had contact through email?"

When I asked what the response had been, Jeff told me Lynette said he should just read on, but there was no responding email, only the one sent to Sonja. "Lynette seemed surprised and stumbled over her words trying to explain that she usually did her email on her laptop and couldn't figure out where the reply would have gone to on this stupid phone email app. Then she again asked if I could check if we'd recovered a ring like that from the cottage." Jeff rubbed his forehead. "Do you think it all was an act?"

I shrugged. "I don't know, but after Lynette's dramatic reaction to the news that the cottage had been robbed, my sister Beverly told me that she knew an actor when she saw one."

CHAPTER NINETEEN

"I'd say your sister has a point. At first, I felt sorry for Lynette. I could empathize with her exasperation trying to find the email responses in her phone. But then things started to turn. Her understandable frustration turned to anger, not at phone applications, or technology, but toward me, as though I was standing in the way of getting what she wanted.

"Do you think it might have been her who tore the house up Friday night looking for this ring?" Jeff asked.

"Remember, she was at the cottage briefly Thursday night, but Sonja suggested they meet for lunch on Friday because it was so late. She initially misled us to believe she wasn't there on Thursday at all, but she tripped herself up."

"That's a possibility. But why go through ransacking

a house if what she wanted was a family heirloom and she could claim it legally?"

"Could her so-called proof email have been faked?" I asked.

"That thought crossed my mind, but she claims she'll return with the rest of the email chain. We'll see."

"Do you have a ring like she described among Sonja's things?" I asked.

"Yes I do, and it's staying with me for now, locked up at the station. Even if she brings further emails, I need more than that. As you said, they can be faked."

"Has another thought regarding her guilt crossed your mind?"

"It has, and it is not a pleasant thought by any measure, but with the timing of things so far, she seems like a likely suspect for both crimes."

"I've considered that. Have you gotten her prints?"

Jeff pointed to the glass on the top of his desk. "I did this morning. From right about where you're sitting. Clean and clear ones."

"I've been thinking about the morning the body was discovered. Lynette dropped to her knees and touched the murder weapon. Was that planned? Or were her actions that of a shocked sister-in-law?"

"Could have been either," Jeff said.

"Remember her backing into the ambulance in her

hurry to leave? Was that because she'd done what she needed to do to cover her tracks by leaving her prints? It would give her plausible deniability."

"And if she did the break-in, she wised up and was smart enough to wear gloves," Jeff mused. "You're thinking they got into an argument on Thursday night when she arrived, probably over the ring. By the way, what's with that ring? What's the big deal about getting it now?"

Shrugging my shoulders, I said, "What some people consider just an object, others place emotional value on. Sometimes things, small things, become bigger, carry more significance, and deeper meaning to a person or a family than an outsider can fathom."

"Could the murder have been an impulsive action in the heat of the moment?" Jeff asked. "No answer necessary, I'm just talking out loud here."

"Jeff, as an aside, I noticed, or rather I should say Kim noticed, Lynette's stylish boots. If she was the one who broke into Sonja's house looking for the ring, you might compare the footprints found at the scene to her style of boots."

"I'll do that, but remember only a light snow fell since Don walked around the house on Friday morning. We didn't get very good ones, but I will check into that. I'll have to count on you or Kim to help me with the prints from fancy boots," Jeff said. "Without knowing what the burglar stole, or what he was looking for, it's hard to focus on suspects. But for suspects in the murder, I'll keep Lynette, Don Stone, and our mystery guy Gerard. As for the robbery, it still could be a random crook, Gerard Singleton, or Lynette."

I nodded in agreement with his opinions on suspects. His focus would be on them, but not at the exclusion of other possibilities.

"Mr. Stone gave me his fingerprints willingly when I told him I needed them for elimination purposes. He understood that, but then became nervous. He reminded me his prints would be all over the cottage, as he'd been doing work there."

"The glove Libby found could be his."

"Sure, or from landscapers, or lots of other workers. Now if it has the blood of our murder victim on it, I elevate finding the owner to top of my priorities. But what I don't get with Mr. Stone is what was his motive?"

"Unrequited love?"

"At their age? Seriously, Jackie? Just because you found that young love feeling again doesn't mean the population of Shady Pines is doing the same," Jeff said.

"Hey, you and Kay are like that. You both felt those butterflies in your stomach and light-headed, giddy feelings again, didn't you?" I leaned in to look more closely at his face. "Is that a blush I see on the Harmony Police Chief?"

Jeff straightened his back and squared his shoulders. "Please, Ms. Parker, this is a professional conversation. Don't let it veer off into personal matters."

I winked at Jeff. "Yes, sir!"

CHAPTER TWENTY

That quick *drop off the glove* business went on longer than I'd expected. As I drove out to Shady Pines, my mind went over what I thought Jeff needed. It was just a brain exercise, I told myself. My curiosity needed a workout. Ha... I wasn't kidding myself. It was hard to step back from the intrigue, the mystery, and the peculiar interest I had in solving puzzles.

Jeff needed Kim's help with information on Gerard for a couple of reasons. He could be involved with Sonja, maybe someone from her husband's shady past. And if Jeff learned more about Gerard, he might have some clue that would show him to be the mysterious lurking figure at Shady Pines, the stalker.

Then there were unanswered questions about just

who Lynette was and what she was here for. She was no longer just a friend visiting as Sonja said, but a sister-in-law coming after a family ring. Was it an innocent, cordial relationship? Or confrontational and hostile? Could Lynette prove she communicated with Sonja regarding a family ring via an email chain?

Jeff was still waiting on fingerprint results. With the holidays, getting results back would take a while. Would my photos of tire tracks be of any value?

Now, though, I needed a mind-shift to focus on getting ready for tonight's pre-wedding dinner at the Wildwood, which I was looking forward to! It was time to relax with Scott and our families after the fun, but hectic day in Madison.

Aunt Ruth pulled the door open before I'd even exited my SUV. "Hurry, Jackie, come see what is waiting for you. It's a package that came by special delivery. Overnight from Los Angeles. Very personalized service. Not UPS or FedEx. Some exclusive courier service."

"Alright, hold your horses. I have to bring in the dresses we found in Madison."

Ruth took the garment bags from me and laid them down on her bed. "Why two?"

"The stylist suggested I bring two with me. They both fit well, and the girls liked them. Now I'll make a final decision in the morning. I think I know which one I want, but at least I have an option."

"Okay, who all went with you?"

"Sophia surprised me by having Wanda and Val come along. She thought they seemed like the friends who I would have asked to be bridesmaids if I'd stayed in town and gotten married back in my twenties."

"That was so sweet of her! But back to the package, I've been staring at it for a couple of hours. What can it be?" Ruth handed me an envelope that the courier had given her. "He said you should open this first."

The card read,

To my sister Jackie. When I heard what happened to your Bernardi designed wedding dress I went into action to offer you an option. Inside this package are two previous wedding dresses she created. No pressure, but it would be amazing if you fall in love with one of them and decide to wear it to your wedding tomorrow. Surprise me, xoxoxo Beverly aka Pauline Dubois.

A warmth rose in me as I reread the note. Could these be the gowns Beverly had worn on *Times of Our Life*? She'd said she kept clothes from those productions.

I handed the note to Ruth and carried the oversized package to the kitchen table. With shaking hands, I pulled the gold seal off the outer wrapping. The pristine, glossy white wrapping paper fell away from an embossed gift box.

"Jackie," Ruth spoke in a low tone after reading the message. "What does this mean? Sonja designed other wedding dresses? How did Beverly know that?" Ruth joined me at the table.

I paused in my unwrapping, but my hands kept stroking the elegant box. "Aunt Ruth, I think my sister just gave me an unbelievable gift. She told me that Sonja Bernardi designed wedding dresses for the cast of *Times of Our Life*. Beverly's character was married four times on that show, and she kept many of the costumes she wore."

In an emotion-filled voice, Ruth replied, "I didn't know that. And what a gesture."

"I didn't either until yesterday."

"You two are about the same size."

I smiled at Ruth. "We are."

"Open the box, Jackie."

With a small choke in my throat, I said, "Good idea. But I want to, for just a second more, enjoy this wonderful feeling of anticipation."

"Enough already. Open away," Ruth exclaimed. "I've been experiencing excited anticipation enough for both of us. And we have a celebration dinner to go to!"

I took a deep breath and grinned at her. "You're right."

CHAPTER TWENTY-ONE

Aunt Ruth, Rocco, and I were the last to arrive for our dinner at the Wildwood Supper Club. Everyone else was already seated in an alcove that provided us some privacy from the main dining area. As soon as I saw Beverly, I ran and gave her a long hug before turning toward everyone else.

"I have received a most welcome gift from my sister." I bit my lip to avoid tearing up. "Beverly has somehow managed to get not one, but two Sonja Bernardi wedding dresses shipped here to Harmony. And I am overwhelmed and full of gratitude to her for this priceless gift."

Everyone started talking at once as Beverly stood and took my hand. "Let me explain. Sonja Bernardi, may she rest in peace, was the head of the wardrobe department on the *Times of Our Life* soap opera. Which, as you may remember, I acted in for many, many years. And, as soap opera stars are prone to do, I married numerous times."

Low chuckles rose from the smiling family members surrounding me. Goosebumps went up my arms. From tragedy just a day ago to this overwhelming moment of joy.

"The wedding dresses created for those television events ended up in my personal closet. How'd that happen?" Beverly did an exaggerated shrug. "When I heard that Jackie had to find a new wedding dress with a day's notice, I leaned on my assistant back in LA to get them here pronto. I chose the two most likely to fit Jackie's style."

"And she did it! I just opened the overnight package arriving at Ruth's cottage to find the two dresses. They are simply perfect. I'll have a hard time deciding which one to wear. Today I had a hectic but super fun time with you, Sophia," I said, nodding in her direction. "And many thanks for inviting Val and Wanda along. We managed to find something for me to wear on my wedding day. As an aside, it was from the mother-of-the-bride section of the salon."

Sophia started laughing. "I made a pinkie swear that none of us would mention that."

"And I love you three for turning the day from stressful to enjoyable by being with me and keeping my spirits up. I know you'll understand if I return both dresses we bought back toMadison."

"I'll offer to take care of that," Mandy said. "You have enough to do before you leave on your honeymoon."

"Aww, thank you! That's so sweet."

"Have you tried the new ones on?" Alli asked.

"I did, and both fit. I love the classic lines. No poofs or tulle or…"

"Mermaid tails," Sophia said. "Jackie had her limits."

Beverly clapped her hands. "I'm so glad to hear you like them. They are elegant designs."

"And age appropriate," I added. "Now let's order dinner. I'm starving."

I took the seat next to Scott in the center span of the table. He stood and kissed me before pulling out my chair. Instantly, the air filled with the ting-ting of silverware tapping lightly against glasses. We both grinned and kissed again.

"Want us to move out of your place a night early?" Sophia asked. "Hubby has booked a place at Kay's Bed and Breakfast for Sunday night, but I could see if she has an opening tonight."

"No!" I said, pulling away from Scott and laughing. "Did he put you up to this? I'll spend our wedding night there and wake up as Mrs. Scott Drake on Monday."

"Did the movers get all your things moved in okay?" Mandy asked.

"Yep, they did."

"All you have left is a suitcase at my place." Ruth teased.

Scott rested his hand on my shoulder. "You all might as well give up. She's sticking to her word about not moving in with me until she's Mrs. Drake. Not that there haven't been a few nights where we, well… I'll just leave that to your imagination. But seriously, I am a very lucky man to have found the love of my life, so one more day isn't going to matter when I know we have the rest of our lives to spend together.

"Now please everyone, raise the glass of champagne that has been poured for you. I'd like to toast you all, our family members. Thank you for your support and encouragement in our journey to this point. And may the blessings of family love continue as Jackie and I begin our new life as husband and wife."

"Here, here!" Everyone shouted and took a sip of champagne.

"Now let's eat!" Scott signaled to the waitress that she could begin serving.

As the salads were brought out, I took a moment to

take this all in. The Flower Girl, who was setting up flowers at the Harmony House for the wedding tomorrow, had done an enchanting floral and candle arrangement that spanned the table here for us tonight. It was low, so no views of my guests were obstructed. The combination of flickering candles and dimmed lighting created a charming effect.

To my left, I noticed Ruth holding hands with Rocco under the corner of the table as he talked with Beverly. Across from me, Mandy and Alli were chatting while Matt asked Jack about fishing in Florida. Sophia sat next to Scott, and I heard her explaining how far her home in Tallahassee was from Seaside Cove, where Jack and she kept their boat.

Conversation continued as empty salad plates were taken away and our dinners arrived. We'd chosen a traditional Saturday night dinner of mouth-watering prime rib, baked potatoes, and asparagus, but added Maine lobster tails to the meal as a special treat.

CHAPTER TWENTY-TWO

"We are looking forward to stepping back from the day-to-day duties of our businesses," I told Beverly. "We want to change our lifestyle to allow for more relaxation and travel. Scott's son Matt will take on added responsibility with Drake Construction, and his wife Mandy has become my partner at Parker Photography."

Beverly congratulated Matt and Mandy and then asked me, "Where do you hope to travel to?"

"Well for one thing, we want to do active travel, like to golf and hiking destinations. Scott's never been to Ireland, so I'd really enjoy going there again. Grace and Dermot have family on the west coast of Ireland with guest houses, so we'd have a personal welcome."

"That's Katie's aunt and uncle at the coffee shop here?" Beverly asked.

"Right. And then remember she has Dermot's brother Paddy and his wife Maeve in Seaside Cove. They are the ones trying to open an Irish pub. He was our Chief of Police before Jeff took over."

Alli joined our conversation, saying, "I hope Katie decides to come back to LA."

Beverly nodded. "I know what you mean. She's so talented and had her business going gangbusters. But the big city can wear you out. And if it's true about a bad breakup being the primary reason for her so-called sabbatical, that explains a great deal. I'm glad she's taking time away to heal."

"Doing the wintery Christmas here in Harmony, but then back to the Florida coast for January sounds wonderful," I said. "Did I tell you we'll be heading down to see Scott's sister in Florida for our honeymoon?"

"We're happy to spend time with you guys next week." Sophia joined our conversation. "We plan on going down to our boat on the Gulf shoreline. The marina we're in is close to Seaside. I know Scott wants to visit Paddy while he's there. He might be able to give him guidance on the construction he's doing with the old building he bought. And I'd like to talk more with

Katie about her experiences with the LA party scene. I do more corporate, large-scale events, but there is always a cross over."

Rocco asked Beverly if she was happy with her book signing at the Book Nook.

"It was delightful. So many kind words from readers, and that cozy, warm atmosphere was great. I'll be honest, it's harder to get the chill out of one's bones as we age."

Ruth and Rocco chuckled.

"Tell us about it," Ruth said. "You'd think we Midwesterners would be used to it, but the cold is still a hard hit every winter."

"That surprise you sprung on Jacqueline was quite a feat! Funny how we both knew Sonja while she lived in California," Rocco said.

"So true," Beverly said. "Jackie, do you think Lynette brought the trouble here with her?"

"I don't know. Jeff has not completed his investigation, but she's a person of interest. Rocco, did you have a chance to talk with Kim about Gerard Singleton yet? Jeff's wondering if he's the same man as the stalker at Shady Pines. That would be a little too much of a coincidence."

"Stalker? I'm out of the loop. Do you have a stalker, Ruth?" Mandy asked. "That's creepy!"

Ruth batted the suggestion away. "That's just the tag Eunice gave him. Harry, our watchman, saw him a couple of times. It might have looked like something strange or suspicious to Harry, but he does react very protectively regarding our little community. I'm not sure why Jeff thinks he'd have anything to do with Sonja, though."

"It's more that he wants to eliminate the stalker as having any connection to her. The excuse he gave Harry for being around Shady Pines was that he was interested in property in Harmony," I said. "So he could be the same man Kim has been showing properties to."

"As Beverly and I both know, Sonja's husband died under suspicious circumstances, and she'd been keeping out of sight for years," Rocco said.

"He's right," Beverly added. "She just dropped off the face of the earth. I was so happy to hear that our paths crossed here in Harmony. She was going to come to the signing so we could catch up, but sadly that meeting didn't happen."

Mandy looked puzzled. "So, you think the creep hanging around Shady Pines might have been looking for Sonja Bernardi? I remember seeing Kim's client in the studio. He did have an air of mystery about him. Well-dressed... all proper like. But just a bit of flash. Was her husband in the mob or something? Maybe she'd been in witness protection and this guy found her. His cover for being here was that he was searching for properties. After all, he wore sunglasses and diamond rings if I remember right. Classic mob attire."

"Mandy!" Ruth scolded. "You have a vivid imagination."

Mandy grinned. "It might be the champagne!"

"The young lady is not far off," Rocco said. "Sonja led a different life than 95% of the residents of Shady Pines. She very well could have been right to drop off the face of the earth, as Beverly said, to protect herself all these years."

"Has Kim gotten you a photograph of Gerard Singleton yet?" I asked Rocco.

"Did someone call me?" Kim and her husband Stuart Walters approached our table, arm in arm.

"Sorry for my wife interrupting your celebration," Stu said, "but congratulations. Jackie and Scott. We can't wait to see you get hitched tomorrow. Come along now, dear, they have our table ready."

"Hold on, sweetie. Jackie was asking if Rocco had heard from me. I'm here to tell him in person that I did finally find a photo of Mr. Singleton. But it took my unique detecting ability to do it. Did Jeff let you know he ditched me?"

"Jeff ditched you?" Rocco asked.

"No silly, Gerard did. He just up and left town after all the properties I showed him. Even Stu with all his skills couldn't find the guy's photograph on the web. Not on LinkedIn or Facebook or Pinterest. I love Pinterest, don't you Ruth? I see how all the quilters can pick up patterns and ideas. And I follow pins for..."

"Kim, honey, can you get to the point? These people are having a party and the hostess is waiting to seat us."

"You go run along to our table, I'll be right over," Kim said. "Now where was I? Oh yeah, finding Gerard. Do you know that hotel by the expressway? The one with the free breakfast? Turns out that is where he was staying. I explained what he looked like to the manager, who was a happy client of mine. Sold him a house in that little subdivision where the mill workers lived in the Flatlands. Anywho, he helped me out by letting me peek at the security camera film and there he was. Got a grainy photo of him and his license plates on the rental car!"

She paused to reach into her oversized leather purse. "Here you go, Rocco. I made a few copies and gave one to Jeff to show Harry out at Shady Pines, and he said you'd be looking for these because you're a man with connections with characters on the seedy side of life."

Rocco looked at the images on the papers Kim handed him. Something in his demeanor changed, but he looked up with a calm smile and said, "I have connections on both sides of the law, Kim. Thank you for these. You did a good job."

Kim walked away with a proud sashay.

CHAPTER TWENTY-THREE

"Again with the nudging, Libby." I stretched and reached for my little buddy. "Last night on this couch for us."

As I folded up my bedding, that wonderful smell of coffee brewing floated out from the kitchen again. Last day as a single woman. Life as I knew it would only get better. Bundling up, I grabbed a cup for our walk. The winter dawn added a soft, deep blue tinge to the sky, but it would be half an hour until the sun rose, and even longer before we saw it above all these tall pines.

I felt surprisingly relaxed. Today's things were scheduled, prepared, and laid out as best as they could be, and what would be would be. The weather looked like it would cooperate. That was a plus. Sure, I didn't have a new manicure, but a quick fresh nail polish application would fix that. I had closed-toe shoes, so the lack of a cute color on my little piggies wouldn't even be noticed. I was an old hand at pinning my hair up in a French twist. The caterer and florist were all set, and Mr. Kramer and his sleigh would pick Scott up first, then come in here to Shady Pines to get me.

Returning to the cabin, I heard Aunt Ruth's voice say, "Here she is now."

Who would be here at this hour? Oh please, no more murders or mayhem… I've had quite enough!

"Jackie, look who's here. You remember Martha and Jean?"

"Yes, of course. Good morning, ladies." Ruth caught my questioning expression and cast her eyes up in frustration.

"We're very sorry to disturb you on this special day." Martha winced, signaling that this visit wasn't her idea. "But Jean was adamant that we talk to you this morning. In fact, she explained her concerns to me last evening and wanted to come over to talk with you, but Ruth had mentioned that your family would be having dinner at the Wildwood. She agreed to wait until now."

Aunt Ruth began making busy movements to show them this wasn't a good time either, but I thought I might as well listen. After all, in this age group one doesn't show up at someone's house at this hour of the morning without it being pretty darn important, and poor Jean had been nervously wringing and twisting her hands in knots the entire time.

"It's okay Martha, we have time to hear Jean's concerns. Ruth, did you offer them a cup of coffee?" I said.

"Ah, no. Sorry, where are my manners? Would you like a cup? And I have s'mores cookies I made yesterday."

"No, no, none for me," Martha said. "But thank you."

"Jean?"

"No thank you, Ruth," Jean said. "And I appreciate you listening to us, Jackie. I've heard that you are practically part of the police force by helping them solve crimes, and I think you'd understand this from a woman's point of view better than Chief Jeff would."

"I'm not part of our police force, but if this has anything to do with the tragedy that befell Sonja Bernardi, you should probably go directly to Jeff. He really is a good listener and a sympathetic person."

Jean's hands clenched into tight wrinkled fists. "Oh no, I just couldn't. He'll think I'm a crazy old lady. But you all understand a woman's intuition. Those feelings we can't explain. Men just don't get it."

With an uncomfortable chuckle, Martha said, "Jean, that's not always true. But why not just tell Jackie what you and I have been talking about so we can get out of her hair and let her get ready for her wedding?"

Jean looked miserable, like she hadn't slept in days. I leaned forward toward her, trying to encourage her and let her know I was listening carefully to what she had to say.

Jean took a deep, cleansing breath. "As you can tell, I'm anxious to speak to you, but also very uncomfortable. I don't like gossip. I assure you this isn't gossip. I want you to know that. It's things I've observed that wouldn't matter one iota if Sonja hadn't been murdered. But with that horrible truth, they took on a different meaning. That poor woman didn't recognize what was happening."

"Go on, Jean. What was she missing?" I had no idea what to expect we all would hear, but Martha knew what troubled Jean, and it must have made enough sense for her to come here this morning.

Jean looked toward Martha, who nodded her encouragement. "It seemed like he was always there. You saw it too, Martha. You're her neighbor."

"She's right. Don did seem to be at Sonja's often," Martha said. "But I didn't… oh never mind. You go on, Jean. Finish your thoughts."

"I take strolls in our neighborhood. My dog needs walking and I like to make sure I get the exercise. Plus, I often visit with Martha or other lady friends in my quilting circle.

"I saw things going on at Sonja's place. Don shoveled her snow and scraped off her steps. He would run errands for her. I know because the grocery store clerk asked if Don was drinking white wine instead of beer. I knew he wasn't buying white wine for himself. The remodeling job never seemed like it would end. It just was too much. I felt it was like he wanted a relationship with her, and not just as a friend."

Jean looked around at all of us, trying to assess what we thought. "I'd never seen Don behave that way before. He's always been helpful to all of us women who live alone, so I know he's a kind man, but this went further than that."

"Did you notice this too, Martha?" I asked.

Shifting in her seat, Martha hesitantly said, "Yes, I guess so."

"But I don't understand your concern," I replied. "She was an attractive woman. Maybe Don and Sonja were just enjoying each other's company."

I tried to gauge where Jean was going with this and with her next words, my thoughts about what she was driving at were spot on.

"I think it went too far. She wasn't the nicest person. She seemed to push away our efforts to include her, like our quilting group. It wasn't her cup of tea, I get that, but she could be cold. Stand-offish. I think poor Don was drawn to her like a moth to a flame."

Ruth gasped. "Jean, are you saying what I think you're saying? My god, how can you even think that?"

Jean trembled and covered her face with her hands.

Martha said, "There, there now. You're right to express your thoughts to us, but it is a shocking accusation."

Not as shocking as they might think. I knew Jeff already considered Don a suspect, and this might provide him with more proof. Had he been rejected outright by Sonja and in a fit of passion stabbed her? It was not out of the realm of possibility.

"Jean, calm down," I said. "I know this was hard and that you don't want to accuse your friend of murder, but you're right to bring up things you saw."

Jean's eyes peered over the tops of her fingers. She slowly lowered her hands, and they fell loosely to her lap.

"Then you'll take this to Chief Mathis? It might mean nothing, but I've gotten it off my mind now, and that's all I wanted."

"I still think you should talk to him directly. You are obviously upset, and I understand you're wanting to avoid talking to the police about a friend, but you must do it yourself."

"You are so good at solving murders and talking about evidence and all that. Please, can't you help Jean by telling Jeff what she just told us?" Martha pleaded.

"I'm not really involved, and he'll have questions that I can't answer."

Ruth's voice was barely above a whisper. "And she's getting married today."

"Jackie's right. Jeff might want to know more. We can't put her in a tough spot." Martha stood, pulling her coat's hood up and her gloves on. "We've taken up enough time. How about I take you into town for breakfast, and maybe we can go by the police station then?"

When Ruth closed the door behind Jean and Martha, she turned and leaned back against it. "Now that was one weird scene."

CHAPTER TWENTY-FOUR

Rocco arrived to escort Aunt Ruth to my wedding.

"You look very handsome. My aunt is a lucky woman."

"Thank you, Jacqueline, but I am the lucky one," Rocco countered as he took off his black wool overcoat and hung it on the coat tree inside the door. "Am I too early?"

"Not at all." I understood why he was asking because I was still in my robe. "Just finished my hair and makeup. I couldn't risk getting anything on my dress. Ruth is ready. I'm going to have her help me with the back zipper. I'm not quite as flexible as I used to be. You two can leave then and I'll meet you at the Harmony House."

"Nonsense," Ruth exclaimed as she walked out of her bedroom. "We are waiting until it arrives. Remember, I'm one of your unofficial wedding photographers! I must get a photograph of you in your crimson coat, stepping into the sleigh."

"Oh, you're right. Thank you for thinking of that. Are you okay with waiting a few more minutes, Rocco?"

"Rocco, is that alright with you?" Ruth asked. "We'll still get there ahead of the bride and groom's arrival."

A tender smile rose on Rocco's lips and his eyes softened as he took Ruth's hands. "Certainly, it is alright. Ruth Parker, you take my breath away with your beauty. You not only look gorgeous but radiate pure inner joy."

"Oh my, Mr. Montalvo, please. You're too kind." Ruth ducked her head, but not before she shared a flirtatious smile with Rocco.

I was happy to see her extra efforts were appreciated. The dusty blue of the dress she'd chosen highlighted her eyes. The shade of lipstick we'd shopped for brightened her complexion. And she bought a new pair of heels, which flattered her legs. But not before protesting that she'd agree to no heel higher than an inch, claiming she'd twist her ankle. I finally convinced her that the wide, chunky, two-inch heels were stable, and she should at least give them a try.

"Now wait until you see how Jackie looks! Come on

my dear niece, let's get you dressed and get this party started."

Aunt Ruth and I had a teary moment as she fastened my mother's pearl necklace for me. I'd always planned on wearing the necklace, and it fit perfectly with the dress I'd chosen. Thankfully the dress was designed for Pauline Dubois' last wedding. Beverly had explained that where it fit in the soap opera's timeline, she was playing a mature Pauline, so that called for less flash and more class than her earlier weddings. And it was perfect for me. The color was very close to the porcelain I'd chosen before, and I loved the way the dress fit.

When I received Scott's text that he'd been picked up by Mr. Kramer, I was completely ready to go. As Rocco helped me put on my coat, it all seemed like it had been designed this way… the full-length coat was a perfect complement to the gown.

When the sleigh arrived, Libby promptly ran to check out the draft horses pulling it. But with a couple stomps of their large hooves and a few snorts directed her way, she wanted nothing more to do with them.

Scott stepped out of the sleigh and came to me. What a handsome man! And with the simple words whispered in my ear, "You and me now babe… together forever," I about melted down into the cold snow. He kissed my cheek before stepping back to compliment me on how stunning I looked, before greeting Rocco and Ruth.

Mr. Kramer climbed down from the raised driver's seat. He took off his cap and swept it across his chest with a small bow. "Good day. It's a pleasure to take you to your nuptial's, ma'am. Would you like to meet Beauty and the Beast?" He chuckled at my puzzled expression and added, "The horses that will be taking you for a ride today."

I'd never been close to horses of this size. They were enormous, majestic animals. As Mr. Kramer led me toward them, I sensed the rich, leathery smells of the harness and the musky, almost sweet, horsey odor. Brass bells on the back strap jingled with each slight movement of their bodies. He introduced me to Beauty and Beast, who nickered softly as he rubbed their noses.

"Now if you're ready, we should be on our way. Your wedding awaits."

Scott and I settled in, and Mr. Kramer offered us lap robes to drape over our legs. In the crisp air, steam rose from Beauty and Beast's nostrils as they snorted and neighed.

With a wave goodbye, we were off. The solid, rhythmic clopping sounds from the horses' hooves accompanied by the tinkling harness bells serenaded us.

I was cozy and warm under the plaid lap robe and

snuggled against Scott. We rode along toward Harmony House on a route Scott and I had mapped out weeks ago. It took us on the river road past the Harris and Sons Marine Maintenance where Scott's pontoon boat, *Playing My Toon*, was stored. Next, we glided along by the Stone Mill Brewery, which got its name from the old stone building that had at one time housed the paper mill operations that built this town.

Slowing as we entered the retail district of Harmony, I was lost in all the memories created there. Shorty's Tavern, where Val, Wanda, and I had tried to sneak a little underage drinking in but failed. Past Sutton Antiques, which had once been my mother's dress shop, Vogue on Main. And of course, my own Parker Photography Studio and Gallery with its second-floor balcony. Libby and I had spent many a morning there while I drank my coffee and watched the world wake up, and many an evening sipping my wine watching the village streets quiet and the lights go out.

Next door, Val's salon, the Cut-N-Curl was closed, but next to it, Dolly's Diner was open. Crossing past the village green, I thought of all the celebrations that had been held there, from the Winter Wonderland going on now, to the Taste of Harmony held earlier this year. The horse and carriage drew attention from the people enjoying the winter festival. Little children with red noses pointed, jumping up and down. Adults waved, their big smiles cheering us on.

The village offices, library, and police station were closed for the day. Ahead was Murphy's Coffee Shop and Bakery, Ginger's Book Nook, and the offices of our own newspaper, *Harmony Happenings*, where I'd had many a discussion with Stu over a maple-frosted donut.

Light wispy flakes began to fall as we continued along the river, then took the turn to head up past The Hills Resort and the Driftless Golf Course, and on toward the Harmony Museum and Nature Center where our friends and family waited.

Mr. Kramer reined the horses in, guiding them to a stop at a small pull off at the side of the road. "Thought you might like a look out across the village," he said as he loosened the reins and turned to look out himself. "This is one of my favorite places to pause and take it all in."

Below us, the snow-covered roofs of the houses in Harmony proper blended in with the snowy branches of the trees that surrounded them. Christmas lights peeking out between tree branches twinkled. It was like a miniature vintage Christmas village.

"Shall we continue on now?" he said after a few minutes. "You have a party waiting for you."

"We do?" Scott kidded. "Well then, let's get on up the road so I can marry this lady and celebrate."

CHAPTER TWENTY-FIVE

Just as we turned on the entrance road to the mansion, Mr. Kramer spun to look back at us. "Hang on, we're going to give them a dramatic entrance."

He called out a *giddy-up* and snapped the reins. The horses broke into a trot. He must have texted ahead at the turnout, because I couldn't believe the cheers that rose as the house came into view. There, on the pine bough and red ribbon decorated veranda, stood our guests, waving and smiling as Mr. Kramer reined in the horses to a stop at the front walkway.

Scott squeezed my gloved hand. "How blessed we are."

I nodded in agreement. "I love you. Now let's get married."

* * *

Our simple ceremony was performed by Pastor John. We exchanged modest gold bands for our wedding rings, then, with permission from Pastor, we sealed it all with a kiss.

Next up was the bouquet toss. Kate, The Flower Girl florist, had convinced me to do a separate bridal toss bouquet. She said it would be so fun and was a long-standing tradition at Wisconsin weddings. I stood at the second-floor railing in the huge entrance hall, looking down at the group of single ladies gathered below.

There was Kay, who'd been dating Jeff, our Chief of Police, for over a year now. Ginger, who I knew was in a serious relationship with Patrick Murphy, better known as Murph. I watched Eunice push her way into position… hope springs eternal! Aunt Ruth stood at the back edge of the small crowd of mostly twenty-somethings.

Hands were held high, hoping to catch the bouquet. With my back to the group, I tossed it over my shoulder. I turned and saw it was a clean catch by Ginger, who stood wildly waving it for all to see. Tradition meant the person who caught the bouquet would be married soon. Murph was one of the good guys, and seeing Ginger with the bouquet made me happy.

Scott had adamantly refused to do a garter toss,

calling it a tradition for the young kids. I'm not sure who convinced him he had to do it, but he surprised me by walking up the stairs with a silky beribboned garter twirling on his finger. His slow ascent was accompanied by hoots and hollers from the group of bachelors who had replaced the single ladies below.

"Where'd you get that?" I asked.

"From my son. He told me too many of his buddies are still bachelors, and he wants to see them jumping for the garter." Scott shrugged. "I figured why not."

I laughed when the garter was caught by Lon Harper, Kate's father. He lived on Oak Street, just down the block from the house I grew up in. I remember encouraging Kate to ask him to join us tonight. She assured me he would be here because he was helping her set up the flowers.

Scott and I congratulated the winners, teasing them about the importance of maintaining traditions.

We directed our guests to the buffet set up in the dining room. I'd chosen Darlene to cater my wedding. I'd first met her at a fundraiser here at the Harmony House. When I called her about the job she was surprised because one of her wait-staff that evening had turned out to be a murderer. I assured her that her professional and polished image remained intact, and I looked forward to working with her. When we finalized the menu, it included Patti Hunt's renowned cranberry orange relish and her yummy corn soufflé, and wedding cupcakes from Murphy's.

Ginger had a side gig as a vocalist in a local band. That's how she'd come across the band who was now playing in the atrium. They had a good reputation for reading the crowd and could cover decades and styles of music with ease. After dinner, tables would be moved to clear the way for a small dance floor.

Scott and I walked around the scattered tables, hoping to chat with everyone here tonight. I received oodles of compliments on my dress, including one from Eleanor Harmony. She also remarked on the evening coat I'd arrived in. "What a lovely coat," she said. "It seems familiar."

Her fourth husband, Tom Lemke, who was formerly a groundskeeper here at the Harmony estate, helped her dab away a small bit of butter from the corner of her mouth.

"I think there is one similar to that in the collection of your ancestors' garments," he remarked.

"Really? Is that so, Jackie?"

"It is, Eleanor, and good memory, Tom. I always loved that velvet evening coat and used it as the inspiration for mine. Now to figure out where to wear it again."

"Even if it is a one and done, it was worth it. You looked like an arriving queen!" Eleanor said.

"Thank you so much. Your family had good taste," I said with a wink.

Scott and I moved on to the table where Orin from the Stone Mill Brewery sat with Kim and Stu Walters.

"Are you enjoying yourselves?" Scott asked.

Kim was the first to answer. "I sure am. And I can't wait to get Stu up there to dance. We've completed more lessons. Stu's been practicing, and he's doing great, aren't you sweetie? You guys make the best-looking couple. I'm so glad Ginger caught the bouquet. Her and Murph make such a cute couple too. Oh, Jackie, I think Jeff got to talk with Gerard. I finally helped connect a face to the name. Or did I tell you that already?"

Stu interrupted her, "Honey, you told them last night. No police business talk now. We're all here to celebrate Jackie and Scott's marriage."

"Agreed," Orin said. "I'm grateful that Kim is still working hard to find a tenant for the rest of the building."

"Believe me, I'll find you a good neighbor, Orin. I will never give up working to fill that space by a business that the entire community will be excited about," Kim added.

"That's good news," Scott said. "Don't forget Drake

Construction. We'd love to work on a project like that. My son Matt is showing great promise as a designer for commercial interiors. He'll be doing much more with the business in the future."

Patti and Charlie Hunt were seated at a table with Mandy's parents. Both couples were playing with their grandson Ty sitting in a highchair between them. Patti was Scott's ex-wife, and yet again, the gratitude that they had managed to remain friends washed over me. It certainly smoothed the way for everyone in this small town.

"Who's taking over the babysitting for the night?" Scott asked. "Or has this little one-year-old convinced you he can stay awake and party all night long?"

"Yeah right! He can try, but our bedtime might be earlier than his nowadays," Patti said with a laugh. "He's headed home with us so Matt and Mandy can relax and enjoy their evening. And a great big congratulations, you two! I'm so happy for both of you."

Patti's farm-to-table foods passion grew into a business that was our studio's go-to caterer for events. For some odd reason, the time we hid out in the loft of her family's old barn to catch a killer came to mind. I reached to give Patti a hug. She'd become a big part of my life here in Harmony.

Next table over I stopped to thank Grace and

Dermot for the wedding cupcakes they'd created. "The cupcakes look scrumptious! I hope there are a few leftovers for us to take home."

"Dermot will drop some off at your place. He froze them in a special box for you to open on your first anniversary," Grace said. "We had the best time decorating them."

"I love all the beautiful colors of frosting. And the varieties! There is something for everyone," I said.

"I'm claiming the dark chocolate with raspberry drizzle," Scott said.

"Excellent choice, but you should try the salted caramel too," Dermot said. "They have the copper-colored metallic sprinkles. I never knew edible sprinkles came in so many shapes and colors. We're planning on offering more dolled-up cupcakes in our shop in the future."

Grace laughed. "We have to use up all those bags of sprinkles!"

"I was hoping your niece Katie would be here," I said.

"She's around here somewhere. I think she went with Ginger and Murph to put in some song requests with the band. I'm so glad the cousins are getting to spend this time together. I really feel it's cheering her up being here. And I know she's looking forward to an old-timey family Christmas."

CHAPTER TWENTY-SIX

The guests, finished with their meals, began to mingle. The buffet had been taken down and replaced with a dessert and coffee bar.

I found Celeste and Felicia, my Chicago friends, at the portable bar talking with Todd and Alli. They'd driven in this morning, and we greeted each other with girlish squeals.

"You look maar-velous, my dear!" Celeste said. She licked her fingertip and touched Scott, while making a sizzling sound. "And this hunk is hot, hot, hot. I always had a thing for construction guys."

Scott grinned. "Tell you what. I have a bunch of construction workers right here that might want to take you for a spin on the dance floor. Course they could be younger than you…"

"Ohh. I can be a cougar for the night," Celeste said with a provocative grin. "How about introducing your buddies?"

"Sure, if my wife will excuse me."

"Go ahead. Just give the guys fair warning these are big city girls," I said.

Scott took a deep bow from his waist. "Will do. This way, ladies." Scott hooked elbows with each of them, and off they went.

I decided to take a moment to head to Aunt Ruth's group, who'd commandeered one of the tables. Ruth patted the seat next to her, and I collapsed into it.

"Ahh, nice to get off my feet for a few minutes. How's your evening going?"

"Other than relearning to walk in heels, just fine. You've pulled together an awesome bunch of people to celebrate with you. Great party!"

"I saw you hovering at the edge of the bouquet catcher group."

"Eunice dragged me out there with her," Ruth said with a dismissive laugh.

"Well, you do have a beau, and maybe he would have felt compelled to ask you to marry him if you'd caught the bouquet."

Ruth leaned in and whispered in my ear. "This is between you and me, and please keep it that way for now. He has asked me. I've accepted. We didn't want to overshadow your wedding day."

My jaw dropped and my heart swelled. I squeezed Ruth's hands in mine. "We've both found love late in life. That's awesome."

"What's awesome?" Betty asked as she brought a plate of cupcakes to the table.

"Just feeling the love," Ruth said.

"Yes, love is in the air. Do-do-do-do. Love is in the air," Betty said in a sing-song voice. "Did you know that more than one of our Shady Pines friends have crushes on Rocco? You'd better hang on tight!"

"Oh, I will!"

"Geez!" Eunice blurted out from her seat across the table. "It's getting to be like junior high. The winter is long enough as it is. People stuck inside acting crazy." Eunice knew how to cut to the chase.

"Is it really that bad? I mean, so what if there is a little flirting and courting going on?" Betty responded.

Eunice groaned. "Dear sweet, naïve, out-of-touch Betty. Did you know there is a love triangle right under Ruth's nose?"

Betty looked perplexed. "Love triangle? Who?"

Ruth shook her head. "Stop all this. If you're talking about Harry and Annie liking each other and Elmer being jealous, that doesn't make it a love triangle for goodness' sake. Elmer might resent Harry spending so much time with her, but it's not a love triangle."

"That involves three people, right?" Betty pinched her eyes in confusion. "And a triangle has three sides. So wouldn't it fit?"

I cracked up at Eunice's facepalm as she said, "Yes Betty, it would fit. But that's not what I was talking about. There were shenanigans going on…"

"If you all will excuse me, I think I'll find my husband and get him to dance with me," I said, wanting to escape the Shady Pines gossip.

Scott stood with Jeff and Kay, watching the dancers.

I walked up behind Scott and hugged him around his waist. "Want a dance with your wife, Mr. Drake?"

"Jackie, you know I'm not a big dancer."

"Oh, come on buddy. You can sway back and forth," Jeff said, grabbing Kay's hand and leading her out to the dance floor. "We'll go with you."

Reluctantly, Scott agreed to step out to the dance floor. He had a nice smooth rhythm to his movement. And being out there with others of all different levels of ability, he managed to loosen up. Celeste and one of Scott's employees twirled past us. A thumbs up from her prompted a low chuckle from Scott.

"Hope he knows what he's getting into," I said, before being jostled from behind.

"Keep it moving you two. You can't just rock back and forth in the same spot all night," Wanda said as she side-stepped to get around us.

"Who's that she's with?" Scott asked. "He's the guy who caught the garter, right?"

"Lon Harper," I said in astonishment. "I didn't know they even knew each other. I'll have to ask her what's going on."

"Just because she's dancing with someone doesn't mean something is going on, does it?"

"You're right. But remember the garter catch? That counts for something! Maybe you empowered him to make a move."

Scott squeezed my waist. "I hope so. Wanda has been alone too long."

"It would be so nice if she could find a partner again," I said. "After John died, she threw herself into refurbishing the motel. But now that it's up and running and seeing success, I wish she had someone special to share things with."

Like me, I thought, leaning securely against Scott's chest. And like Jeff and Kay, who were slow-dancing nearby. Like Ruth and Rocco, and maybe Annie and Harry. I wondered if it was true that they were courting.

Through the abundant glass windows in the atrium,

I saw the clear winter sky revealing thousands of twinkling stars.

After a couple of songs, Scott begged off, explaining that he wanted to say goodnight to some of his employees who had to take off early. I joined Hannah and Mark Sutton, who were mulling over which cupcake to choose, consulting with Shorty Schuster and Dolly Watson. There were so many memories between this gathering of Main Street neighbors.

"Congratulations, Jackie!" Hannah said. "You look amazing. We couldn't be happier for you. When will the gallery reopen? Everyone is excited to see what it will look like."

"Fingers crossed it'll be ready to go by early May. I want to be open for the tourist season. Did you see Val?"

"She's coming this way," Dolly said. "And I have to get going. Diner opens early. Hope you don't stay holed up in that big house on the bluff, now that your cozy little apartment is closed up."

"No way, Dolly. I'll be in town tomorrow in fact. I could never stay away from your home cooking for any length of time."

"I'll hold you to that. Night all," Dolly said with a wave goodbye.

Val had a wide, expectant smile.

"Okay, I'll bite. What's the big grin for?" I asked.

Val's eyes lit up as she spoke. "I think I may have found a buyer for my salon!"

"Val, that's terrific! Who is it?"

"She's the wife of one of Scott's carpenters. She's coming over tomorrow to take a look. If it works, we'd partner up first, and then eventually she would find financing so she could buy me out. I can't even believe what I'm saying. I'd almost given up and thought I'd end up selling the building and just letting it all go."

"I'm so happy for you, and have a feeling it will work out," I said. "Say, did you see Wanda dancing with Lon Harper? Is there something going on there?"

"During the winter months she's been having flowers delivered to the Riverview Motel, and Ron is the delivery man. Kate told me her dad seems to spend a long time delivering to the west side of town. So yeah, I think there's something going on. Pretty cool if they got together."

The rest of the evening flew by. Scott and I stayed until the last guest left. We were beat, but the party had been a success. The food was delectable, the flowers were gorgeous, the band was terrific, and we were man and wife.

CHAPTER TWENTY-SEVEN

s we pulled into Scott's driveway, I felt an overwhelming sense of peace and calm. Sure, I was tired, and my feet hurt, but none of it mattered a bit. This would be our home together. We were starting a new chapter in both of our lives.

Scott pulled into the garage. When he opened the door to the house, he had me cover my eyes, saying he had a surprise for me. He guided me through the back hall and kitchen, then stopped at the edge of the living room.

"Now stay right here and don't peek. I have to do one more thing."

He moved away, and then in just a few seconds he said, "Okay, you can look now."

Scott stood next to a tall, completely decorated Christmas tree with an expectant smile on his lips.

"Wow, Scott! It's stunning!"

"Merry Christmas, Mrs. Drake."

"How on earth did you manage to get this done without me seeing it?"

With a sheepish grin he said, "Christmas elves are real."

"I'm overwhelmed. It's perfect." I went closer to look at the ornaments hanging on the fragrant branches. "These are some of mine. From my little fake tree. Oh, and here's the one your sister picked out for us. But what… this ornament… it was one I made in grade school." I turned to Scott. "How on earth did you do all this? Was one of the elves Aunt Ruth?"

"Yes. She kept your family's ornaments and knew that now was the time to give them to you. She had stories about each one. And Jackie, I want us to start adding to these. Build the collection with our own new memories. Let's start with hanging this one together."

Scott reached for a red gift box, pulled off the ribbon, and opened the lid. Inside was a hand-painted ornament lying in white tissue. I reached in and pulled it out. The scene that ran around the circumference of the delicate globe was our village of Harmony nestled in the hills surrounding it with the river flowing by.

Together we hung it prominently at the front of the tree.

"Scott, can we do a Christmas Eve dinner here? For our family and any friends who don't have somewhere to go?"

"I was hoping you'd want to do that. I've already invited Sophia and Jack. I know Matt and Mandy are taking Ty to Patti's on Christmas Day, but we've usually done Christmas Eve together these past years. I'd love to start that tradition with my… with our grandson."

"Aunt Ruth and Rocco. Beverly and Alli. And Todd. I don't think he has plans. I'll have to get some food together, but I can do that Monday or Tuesday. This will be our first Christmas Eve with our loved ones gathered together under one roof. I love you, Scott Drake."

"And I love you, Jacqueline Drake. Hold on, I almost forgot. Matt said I should flip the switch turning on the deck lights. Guess he and his elves put decorations outside too." As soon as Scott flicked the switch up, a twinkling magical landscape appeared. The railings were wrapped with thousands of small white lights. Just beyond that, a large evergreen was lit by colored lights that climbed up its full height.

Scott gasped. "How on earth did they get that done? The tree is so tall."

"So, you didn't know about this? I love that kid of

yours! We're ready to celebrate the holidays in style. I can just picture Ty when he sees all the lights."

Scott took me in his arms. "Having a little one around sure does add to the Christmas experience. My house has never felt this lived in, Jackie! Now let's turn in. Tomorrow will come soon."

CHAPTER TWENTY-EIGHT

The next morning Scott and I hit the ground running. We had a Christmas Eve dinner to shop for, invitations to extend, suitcases to fill for our Florida trip, and final business details to set up with both of us being gone for two weeks.

By the time I arrived at Parker Photography to check out the progress, Scott had been there and gone. Matt said his dad ran into Madison to get a particular adhesive they needed. "We're working with some unique materials and want to be sure to use the best products to adhere them. It was a blast last night. Mom and Charlie kept Ty overnight, so Mandy and I got to sleep in past five for once. She's in the back moving out the last of her supplies. Did you need to talk with her?"

"No, I'll catch her later. Did your dad tell you about our Christmas dinner?"

"He sure did, and we are looking forward to it. How'd you like our decorating?"

"Matt, it was perfect. And all a surprise for me. Thank you so much. The way I've been welcomed into your family means the world to me. See you tomorrow night."

Val was inside her salon, so I popped in to hear more about the potential partner. It sounded like it would work out for her. The young woman, Missy, was fully licensed and had been renting chair space in a salon in Greensville. When her husband got a job with Drake Construction, they moved to Harmony. Val explained that Missy had planned on applying at Cut-N-Curl after the holidays.

"I told her I didn't want to rent out space, but I was looking for a hairdresser who would seriously consider taking over the business in a year or two. Well dang, if she didn't offer to buy in right now. But I said, let's see how you do here first before getting all legally tangled up. I talked to Scott this morning when he was at your place and he vouched for her husband being secure in his job with Drake Construction, which spoke well of them both. Can you tell I'm pretty positive this Missy is the one? Retirement here I come!"

"That's terrific news, Val. I'm so happy for you! But you know I'll miss seeing you when I walk by the salon's windows."

"Hey, you won't be here downtown much yourself, Mrs. Drake," Val said. "I bet I'll hallucinate about seeing you and Libby up on your balcony. Things are changing, that's for sure. But now Chris and I can spend more time together. Especially fishing with the grandkids. And Travis wants to expand the marina, so he might be putting Chris and I in charge during the summer months."

"Then maybe you can get away for the winter?"

"The extra income might make that possible."

"Tell me more about Wanda and Ron. I totally missed that. Are they dating?" I asked.

"How about the three of us have one last girls' get together this year? Then we can get the whole scoop on Ron Harper. The Wildwood is closed tonight, but I think the Stone Mill is open. Say appetizers and a drink? I'll give Wanda a call and see if it works for her."

"It's a date! I'm meeting my Chicago friends for coffee now. They're taking off this afternoon. I'll see you at the Stone Mill later."

Celeste and Felicia were at Murphy's when I got there. We had time for a quick coffee before they had to start their drive back to Chicago.

We said our goodbyes on the sidewalk. Through the windows of the Book Nook, I noticed Katie was browsing the shelves. I decided to pop in to say good-bye, as I might not see her before she left. The book section she was perusing was the mystery section.

"Mystery lover?"

"Hi Jackie!" Katie held up two books she had tucked under her arm. "I've already bought a couple of beach reads here. But in case we get bad weather, I'll have a good mystery to cuddle in with. Congratulations on your wedding and the terrific party you threw. That's one thing I miss living in a big city. The sense of community coming together."

"Thank you, Katie. I do value my small-town roots and am glad I returned here. But there are advantages in big cities, too. Hope you get more Florida time. Is Seaside Cove a small town?"

"About the size of Harmony, I'd say. I'll be there at least as long as it takes to read these books," Katie said with a chuckle. "I'm missing the holiday party season, business-wise, but sure am enjoying the slower pace of life. Just don't know when or if I will get bored without the excitement and energy of the West Coast."

"At least you still have beaches and warm weather there in Florida," I said.

"Right. That's a good thing. I'm loving having a white

Christmas this year though. By the way, thanks for the introduction to Sophia and Jack. I'm glad they are looking into docking their boat in Seaside's marina."

"They're sounding positive about that. Jack said the rate is good, and there they might be able to afford a little getaway house too, instead of sleeping on the boat. How's the Irish pub dream going for Paddy?"

"It seems like things are stalling on that. Small towns have their own issues. Paddy says he hates dealing with a gombeen man."

"Who and what, is this gombeen man?" I asked.

"Are you impressed with my Irish? I had to look that Irish expression up myself. It means like a conman, someone who's a wheeler-dealer, looking for a profit at someone else's expense. In this case the gombeen man Paddy's complaining about is the mayor of Seaside Cove. He's giving my uncle a hard time with the remodeling permits and inspections. And even forcing him to postpone the opening of the pub."

"Sorry to hear that," I said. "We recently had an issue with a small-town mayor who thought he was a big man. Fred Foster was supposed to golf in our recent tournament. He ran Foster Town his way, and many of the residents butted heads with him. What some people will do with a bit of power, huh? I'm going to grab a sandwich at our local diner, want to join me?"

"I'd love to, but I'm helping Grace clean house for our Christmas party. My cousin Murph is bringing Ginger over, and Aunt Grace is holding her breath that he'll have bought her an engagement ring for Christmas. She couldn't stop beaming after Ginger caught your bouquet last night."

"I'll keep my fingers crossed! Those two are so good for each other. Now I'll say goodbye and safe travels if I don't see you before you leave."

"Thanks, and same to you! I'll most likely still be in Florida reading books when you and Scott get there."

"I hope so!" I said.

CHAPTER TWENTY-NINE

From behind the front register, Dolly waved me off to find my own seat. Back toward the far corner of the diner I noticed Jeff sitting with his back to the wall. A typical seat choice as he could keep an eye on his surroundings.

"Mind if I join you, Chief Mathis?"

"Not at all, Mrs. Drake, it would be a pleasure. And how did you sleep last night?"

I had to think of a quick comeback to Jeff's suggestive tone of voice, but words failed me, and I just gave him a saucy grin before saying, "Why Jeffrey, that's rather forward of you to ask such a personal question."

We were interrupted by Dolly arriving with a coffee for me. With a bawdy body wiggle, she too asked me, "How did you sleep last night?"

Jeff answered for me, "She's not divulging any details from the wedding bed. I've already tried."

"Oh lord, I don't want details. I know how it all works. Just give me a thumbs up or down."

With uncharacteristic boldness I gave her two thumbs up.

"Alrighty then, just as I suspected. Scott has it going on," Dolly said with a wink and a nod. "What can I get you for lunch?"

I ordered a club sandwich with a side salad, and Jeff asked for the same. A big part of me wanted to ask how the murder and break-in investigations were going, but I'd made a promise to Scott and to myself to stay out of the drama of any more murder cases. But these crimes had felt so personal, being that Sonja was creating my once in a lifetime garment. I refrained from asking but felt a pleasing satisfaction when he said how much he would appreciate my input.

"Sure, Jeff. Don't know how much feedback I can give but go ahead."

"Kim was instrumental in finding Gerard Singleton for me."

"I heard she did that. Bet she was tickled that she could help."

"She was, and I gladly listened to her entire explanation of how she did it. But the point being that with her help I got a photograph of Gerard from the hotel security camera. The hotel manager refused to divulge personal customer contact information without a warrant. But they did give me a copy of the grainy photograph. Kim also gave one to Rocco.

"He contacted me this morning, identifying Gerard as a former FBI agent turned private investigator. Rocco said he was currently working on the West Coast and put me in contact with him. Gerard explained that Lynette hired him to find Sonja Bernardi, so that explained why he was here in Harmony when Harry saw him."

"Ah, so you already took the photograph to Harry?"

"I did. But he couldn't identify him as easily as Rocco because the guy was wearing sunglasses and sitting in his car when Harry saw him. I asked Gerard if that was him hovering around the old folks' home. He said it was and got a good laugh when I told him he'd acquired the stalker misnomer."

"Will you be letting Harry know he'd been fending off a former FBI agent?"

"I should do that. He'd wear it as a badge of honor. Anyway, Gerard was very forthcoming in the way he felt about Lynette. He agreed to take the job of finding out where Sonja Bernardi now lived, but also felt Lynette herself needed to be watched. He sensed a deep and hostile anger in her. Since he knew Sonja Bernardi's story and that she was widowed, he wanted to make sure she wasn't the target of Lynette's anger and that what she told him about getting a family ring and journal back was truly all she wanted to do."

"That's the first I heard of that. What journal?"

"Gerard was told it belonged to Lynette's brother and should have stayed with the family. He suspected it contained incriminating information that the Bernardi family or the LA Mafia wouldn't want exposed."

"Jeff, I might have seen that journal. It was on the nightstand when I was at the house on Thursday for my final fitting."

"Hmm… so it wasn't hidden. Makes sense with what I've found out. But first let me explain why Lynette is no longer on my murder suspects list."

"Glad to hear you're making progress. What cleared her?"

"Gerard stayed here in Harmony, unbeknownst to Lynette. On Thursday night, when Lynette checked in at the Riverview, he put a bug on her car, then tailed her to Shady Pines. He saw her go into the cottage and leave a short time later. He observed Sonja close the door when Lynette left, and then stayed to watch her move about the house, closing the blinds, stuff like that. So he knew she was alive at that point. When he heard about the murder the next day, he knew Lynette wasn't the murderer. Her car never left the motel until the next morning when she drove back out to Shady Pines."

"Do you think she might have realized Gerard was tracking her movements and tried evading him? Could there have been another car she used to return to Sonja's to commit murder?"

"Very good questions. I had the same ones for Gerard. He explained that he was certain she didn't. And Rocco agreed, telling me that Gerard was one of the best and wouldn't have gotten caught surveilling Lynette."

"So that takes Lynette and Gerard out of the murder suspects category."

"Right. Lynette returned to me with the email chain evidence that validates what she said about the ring. She proved she and Sonja communicated about it and that the ring was to be given to her when she arrived in town."

"She's legit then. My feelings about her were wrong."

"Hold on, there's more. Besides Kim being instrumental in my identifying the so-called stalker, she also confirmed that the unique style of boots Lynette wore matched the few new footprints we observed around the cottage on Friday night. Thanks for that tip, Jackie."

"You're talking about after you were notified of the break-in, right?"

"Yep. When confronted with that footprint evidence, Lynette was trapped into confessing. She'd gone back to the house for the ring, since Sonja was murdered before she got to get it from her. I've charged her with breaking and entering. I still have the ring in police custody, but I'm waiting on Sonja's attorney to find the next of kin before I turn it over to Lynette."

"What about the journal? Do you think she stole it?"

"She haltingly offered it up to me when I asked her about it. I was glad she didn't think to ask me how I knew she was looking for it. It was like a diary her brother had kept. In going through it I didn't notice any nefarious information or lists of gangsters' phone numbers, so I guess she really was just here for personal family items and not for some more nefarious reasons."

"Now let me see. That leaves you with only one suspect for the murder, Don Stone. Sonja would have allowed him in that night, because she knew him. He lost his bloody glove when he fled. I'm assuming there was blood on the glove."

"There was, but we haven't confirmed it was Sonja's."

"One thing that would confirm who did it would be if you found clothing with blood spatter evidence on it. Since you suspected Don, did you check his garbage?"

"Yep, checked his trash. No evidence of bloody cloth-ing. But you are definitely right about finding blood spatter evidence on the murderer's clothing. That would break the case wide open. I'm going to be interviewing him again and hope I will get a confession."

"Passion as a motive?"

"That's all I can come up with. Some sort of twisted evil rose up inside that nice guy. Jean and Martha came to me this morning and said that very same thing."

"I was hoping they'd talked to you. They came to me and Ruth on Sunday morning and told us about their concerns. But I, in my determination to back away from murder investigations, gave it right back to them. They needed to tell you themselves. What a sad story to hear. I hope that the additional information they gave you can get him to confess. Remember how we forced a confession in that Fourth of July boating issue?"

Jeff's knowing grin told me he remembered. "How we hid in the bushes at the Langdon's cottage to set up Sylvia Nash? I remember. Are you saying we should set Don up? Get him to confess? Not a bad thought, Jackie."

CHAPTER THIRTY

After picking up fixings for Christmas dinner the following night, my final stop before heading home, which was now the house on the river bluff, was to pick up Libby at Aunt Ruth's.

"I'm going to miss her," Ruth said as we watched Libby bounce and leap in the soft snow next to the cottage. "Have time for a cup of coffee?"

In my hurry and scurry, my first inclination was to say I had to run home because I had groceries in the car. But since it was winter, and the temperatures were below freezing, the groceries would be fine. What was my big hurry? Aunt Ruth was like a mother to me, and I'd be leaving on my honeymoon soon, so I decided to stay and chat for a bit.

After holding yet another cup of coffee in my hands

today, I told Ruth about our plans for Christmas Eve dinner. "Since we have a huge tree decorated with priceless Parker family ornaments hung on it, I want to have everyone over to enjoy it with us. Will you and Rocco be able to make it?"

"I'm sure we will. Our plans were up in the air, so I'm glad you decided to do this. It will be lovely to check out that completed Christmas tree. Scott worked hard to pull that all together."

"Ruth, there was something I wanted to ask you about. Last night Eunice said there was a love triangle going on right under your noses. What did she mean?"

"Oh, I don't know." Ruth tapped her nose. "I try to keep this out of other people's business."

"But you must have some idea. Who are your neighbors here?"

"This place isn't all that big, but I have lots of neighbors. Annie is a close neighbor, and I think she enjoys Harry's company a little more than others. They are actually quite a lot alike. Poor Betty, she's still trying to figure out the Annie, Harry, and Elmer thing. Why are you asking?"

"I left before Eunice finished explaining what she meant. Did she have more specifics?"

Ruth indicated her disapproval with a quick tsk-tsk.

"Just gossip?" I asked. "Or does she know something you didn't?"

"What she said, I took with a grain of salt, as she'd had a couple of glasses of champagne. It's not worth repeating."

"Ruth, there's more, isn't there? Does it have anything to do with Martha and Jean and that uncomfortable exchange with them yesterday?"

"I agree that conversation was peculiar." Ruth seemed to stop herself from saying more.

"Care to elaborate?"

Ruth pinched her lips. "You know how I dislike talking behind people's backs. Not giving them a chance to explain, clarify, or defend themselves."

"Yes, I know." I let that hang in the air a moment. But then pressed once more. "Ruth?"

And I was glad I made that decision to push her to talk, because what I heard put things in a new light.

* * *

That night, while catching up with Wanda and Val at the Stone Mill Brewery, I was distracted by what I'd learned from Ruth. It appeared to add a surprise suspect to Jeff's now list of one. Don. I needed to think it through. And this wasn't a good time to do that. My lifelong friends deserved my complete attention. I could share my thoughts with Jeff in the morning.

We had cheese curds and flatbreads to nibble on. Orin treated us to his newest appetizer, a garlic shrimp dip with pita chips. I ordered my favorite Pulp Man Red Ale, named in honor of the men who'd worked within these walls. Wanda and Val decided to split a bottle of wine.

We toasted to Missy's success in being able to buy Val out of her beauty salon business.

"I'm already working with my accountant to put a value on the business. This week when Missy starts working, I'll be able to judge if she's up to it. The Greensville salon she's been with for over five years has high praise for her. But enough about me. We both want to hear if the wedding garter catcher has any prospects."

Wanda's smile said it all.

"So, it's true? Oh Wanda, I couldn't be happier for you. How long has this been going on?" I asked.

And Wanda proceeded to tell us about the attraction that had been growing over the fall and into the winter. "His neighbors throw open houses on Christmas Eve, and it's his turn to host. He's asked me to join him. Then we're going to catch a Christmas movie at the Greensville theater on Wednesday and go to that new

Asian restaurant for dinner. I imagine you and Scott have plans, but if not, it would be fun to have you join us."

"I remember how that neighborhood had the best house decorations when we were kids," Val said. "And your family's home was always one of the most beautiful ones. Remember, Jackie?"

"I do. I loved growing up there. But enough about all that. Let's dig into this yummy looking food."

CHAPTER THIRTY-ONE

Christmas Eve day arrived with clear skies and sunshine. Scott took Libby out for her morning walk as I watched through the window with a mug of coffee. I could get used to sharing doggie duties with him. Getting ready for tonight's gathering was on my mind, and I looked forward to it, but first I needed to get what I'd learned yesterday off my mind and into Jeff's hands.

I'd barely waited for Jeff to get seated at his desk before I began jumping into what I wanted to get out. "Do you remember meeting Martha, Jean, and Annie at Sonja's cottage? They were there both

Friday morning when the murder was discovered, and late Friday night when you were alerted to the break-in."

"Sure, I remember them. Couldn't have told you their names then, but now that Jean and Martha came in to talk to me, I can put a face to those two."

"Did Jean suggest you should look into Don Stone as a suspect?"

"She did. She laid out her concerns that he seemed to be overdoing it with helping Sonja. Shoveling her snow, running errands, and dragging his feet on the remodeling he was working on at her house. All valid points."

"Hmm… did Martha agree with Jean's story when they talked to you?"

"I asked her about that. Since she lived right next door, surely, she too would have observed things like that too. Her response was a weak, watery one. She seemed to want Jean to take center stage. Any agreement with what was being said came with some reluctance."

"I got the same vibe from her when they came to Ruth's on Sunday morning. She couldn't understand why Jean would think Don's attraction to Sonja would lead to murder. But Jean pushed on, saying Don was like a moth to a flame."

"Okay, but so what?" Jeff asked.

"That wasn't the only odd conversation I heard on Sunday. It was at the wedding when there was teasing and silly talk about love triangles at Shady Pines."

"Spare me the details." Jeff crossed his hands in front of his face.

"Ah, but the devil is in the details, which I didn't wait to hear on Sunday night. I left before Eunice shared them."

"And in her usual colorful, direct way, that probably was a good idea," Jeff said. "Okay, so have you found out what she was going to say?"

"I did. This afternoon when I went to pick Libby up from Ruth, she told me that the love triangle Eunice was remarking about was between Don, Jean, and Sonja. Ruth doubted Sonja was even aware of what was going on with the residents of Shady Pines."

That got Jeff's attention. "Do you give any credence to what Eunice said? She is known to exaggerate."

"In this case I do. That's why I'm here."

"I didn't go into everything I've been doing in the case since you've been clear you want to stay at arm's length. I had Don come in for a second interview like I said I would. He just doesn't seem capable of murder. I brought out the glove Libby found in the snowbank. When I asked if this belonged to him, his first reaction was confusion, then he dropped his head into his hands and began rocking back and forth. I pushed on by asking him if he killed Sonja Bernardi."

"Way to get to the meat of the matter. What did he say?"

"He kept his head down and grudgingly acknowledged that it could be his glove, explaining he's bought the same style of winter work gloves for years. Then the guy looks up and there is such a genuine pain and sadness in his face. So, there I sit thinking he's going to confess, but what he says next left me completely flummoxed."

"Go on." I leaned in, he had my complete attention.

"Don claimed he didn't want to have to say this, but he also couldn't let me think he killed Sonja. He talked on as though in a daze, saying he hadn't put this together until he saw Jean Friday night at the scene of the robbery. Jackie, Don told me he thinks Jean could be the murderer. I instinctively thought he was trying to mislead me."

"He could have been." Biting my lower lip, I said, "But it fits with what Ruth said. Ruth offered a possible explanation for the glove too. She said many of her friends at Shady Pines knew about Jean's crush on Don. Is crush even the right word? Anyway, it was known. And one of the things that happens when someone has those feelings is that they want to keep a little personal piece for a souvenir of time together.

"Good man that he was, Don helped many of the residents at the Pines, but Jean took it on herself to keep a pair of his gloves for when she shoveled her own snow. Other people could attest to this. They saw her. If Jean wore Don's gloves during the murder, it could have been some sort of symbolism for her."

"Hmm, very interesting thought," Jeff said. "Don gave me several other things in Jean's behavior that led him to even speak of this. He told me about the late-night calls from Jean to help her open a stuck window, the little gifts like a potted plant to brighten his place, and the dropping by with fresh baked brownies. He knew she was building up his kindness into something more."

"Are you left believing him or her?"

"It's the classic his word against hers. I listened to Jean but didn't press her. She was obviously upset with what she felt she had to tell me. But I've made notes on the information you just brought me and will keep all possibilities open. There is something else involved."

That got my attention. "The tire tracks?"

"No."

"A new eyewitness?"

"Not new, but a trusted one. Gerard. As a good investigator would do, he noted things around him.

Thursday night, when he left Shady Pines, he noted someone walking near Sonja's just as he left the area. Could that have been our murderer?"

"Did he identify anything about the person?"

"Let me think. It was a woman. Average height. Wearing a big, puffy sort of coat. She shielded her eyes from his headlights."

"Jean has a coat like that. If I'm remembering right, she had it on Friday morning."

"But think about it, Jackie, Jean has a dog she walks. Gerard didn't mention seeing a dog. So, it's circumstantial evidence only. Lynette was there the night of the murder, and if not for Gerard seeing Sonja alive after she left, Lynette might still be a suspect."

That truth sucked the air out of my sails. How could I have jumped to that conclusion so quickly?

"You're right, Jean could have been there the night of the murder and not be the murderer. But why didn't you tell her that she's under suspicion? You let Don know he is."

Jeff puffed out his chest. "It's a delicate balancing act, Ms. Parker. Oops, excuse me, Mrs. Drake. We police detectives must keep all our balls in the air, juggling them carefully." He collapsed back to a slump. "Wait, that's a bad analogy. Maybe I should say we police detectives have to sift meticulously through dirt, mud, and stones to find the buried treasure. Hmm… still doesn't sound right. Let me see…"

"I got it Jeff, I got it. Now you need blood evidence or a confession. Next step, Chief Mathis?"

"A pre-Christmas Eve visit to Shady Pines is in order."

CHAPTER THIRTY-TWO

*O*ur Christmas Eve dinner was a success, and we all agreed it would be the beginning of a new tradition for our friends and family. Beverly and I raised a toast to our first sisters Christmas together. Ruth and Rocco announced that they planned on marrying in the spring, and that news prompted a second toast.

Dinner flew by with conversation and laughter. My heart was happy.

Alli helped clear the table after everyone was finished while I set up a Christmas cookie spread on the large coffee table near the fireplace. Scott showed Todd around the place explaining what he needed to know, as he would be staying here running the business and taking care of Libby while we were gone.

Ty, who was being allowed to stay up late, stole everyone's hearts with his bright smile and shining eyes. Having a baby around at Christmas was the best. He was beginning to walk by balancing himself on the furniture, impressing us all. But then, much to everyone's delight, he let go of his grasp on a chair to waddle over to Sophia, who was holding Libby.

"Oh, Ty, good boy. You love the puppy. Look at you go, big boy!" Mandy applauded Ty's effort as he reached Sophia. Libby was fine with Ty as they'd been together often over this past year. Mandy and Matt exchanged proud parent looks.

"First steps! So cute. A boy and his dog," Sophia said. "Too bad about your allergies, Matt. I hear there are dogs that don't shed so there's less dander."

"We're looking into getting one of those for a family dog, but not before..." Matt took Mandy's hand, and she gave him a small nod. "Ty's little sister arrives in May!"

"What!" I practically screamed before running to give Mandy a big hug. "This is the best news!"

Everyone's cheering startled Ty, who dropped to the floor and began crying. But his cries soon turned to giggles when Grandpa Scott scooped him up and began playing airplane by holding him high up in the air singing, "You're going to be a big brother. Hooray!"

This may be just about the best Christmas I've ever had, I thought.

Absorbing all that happened the past few days made me realize what a wonderful year lies ahead of us.

* * *

Since everyone else had plans for Christmas Day, Scott and I decided to join Wanda and Ron for the movie and dinner. Beverly and Alli had early flights back to LA, hoping to avoid the packed airports. Mandy and Matt were having Patti and Charlie over for Christmas morning brunch, so Ty could be home to open presents from Santa. Then they'd go to Mandy's parents for the afternoon. Shady Pines had a planned day of food and games, which Ruth and Rocco looked forward to attending. Sure, we had some packing to do for our trip tomorrow, but we could complete that in no time later.

The day went by at a wonderfully easy pace. The specialness of the holiday was felt all around us as the four of us enjoyed each other's company.

We packed our suitcases and updated our travel plans as a winter storm front threatened to drop four inches of snow. We upped our departure time, hoping to get south of it before it barreled into Wisconsin.

. . .

Thursday morning, in the pre-dawn, we left Harmony for our drive to Florida. Murphys wasn't open for to-go coffees, but luckily one of Scott's employees had gifted us insulated travel mugs, so we were all set.

I realized I hadn't thought about Jeff's investigation until I saw his name come up on my caller ID. The call went to the truck's Bluetooth speaker.

After exchanging Christmas greetings and words about what we did for the holidays, Jeff asked how far we were. I explained our leaving early decision meant we were already in Kentucky.

"Good to hear. The snow has started, and this is going to be a big one," he said. "Safe travels and I know you'll enjoy Florida. Say hello to Paddy for me when you see him."

"Thanks Jeff. We'll be in Tallahassee a few days before we head down to the Gulf shore area."

Though I was curious, it was Scott who asked how the investigation was going.

"I didn't call sooner as I didn't want to disrupt your holiday. But since you asked, I can tell you that the murderer has been charged and I'm confident the charge will stick. So, both cases have been solved before the new year."

"Jeff, that's great news. Since we're driving along on clear roads and it'll be another hour before we stop for the night, I'd be grateful if you could give us a rundown on what transpired."

Jeff went on to explain that he'd gone to Shady Pines to talk with both Jean and Don.

"Part of my interview with Jean was asking if she knew who had a puffy coat like you and Gerard described. She feigned ignorance of what such a coat looked like. When I described it, she said she couldn't think of anyone who wore such a coat. I told her a witness saw her in one."

"Did that get her to admit it?" I asked.

"Not at first, but then she gets her coat out, trying to say she didn't know that's what it was called. When I said I need to take it for testing, she got real defensive, all puffed up just like the coat, with words flying out of her mouth. 'Why? What for? Are you serious? There's no blood on this coat. You're crazy.' Things escalated from there. She threw the Don thing at me again and I told her he'd handed over his coat without hesitation."

"Wow, you figured out a way to let them incriminate themselves," I said. "So, then she gave you her coat? And now you'll have them both to test."

"Nope. She still didn't want to give her coat to me for testing. I said if there is no blood on it you don't have a problem. I paused, and she still clutched her coat. So, I added the words that I could get a search warrant."

"And that was the moment she confessed?"

"No, but she gave me the coat. I thanked her and left to do the preliminary tests, knowing the coats could be sent to the state lab if nothing showed up. But it did. Enough blood had spattered on her coat to charge her. And not a trace on Don's."

I congratulated Jeff on solving both the robbery and the murder. He in turn said he appreciated my help before disconnecting.

I looked over at my husband and patted his leg, letting my hand rest there. Scott kept his eyes on the road, but he was obviously confused about all of this. I told him I'd explain later.

To our right, the sun was setting. Ahead of us, our hotel for the night was booked. And further down the road Florida waited.

All the homicide havoc and murder mystery had been left behind.

CHAPTER THIRTY-THREE

Katie Murphy...

I ended up staying longer in Harmony than I'd planned because of the snowstorm that arrived and took over everything. It was crazy. The howling winds blew snow into big drifts, and we couldn't even leave Uncle Dermot's house until the plows came through. But that was okay, because my cousin Murph and his fiancé Ginger took me to a toboggan run and riding down that shoot was super fun!

When things cleared up enough for me to travel, I was itching to hit the road. Between the snow and the temperatures outside, I didn't think I'd ever warm up until I got to Florida. Once I cleared the snow zone, there was no big rush. As a kid, I dreamed of attending Space Camp, so I made a stop at the U.S. Space and Rocket Center in Huntsville, Alabama.

The next morning, I drove straight through to Seaside Cove, still not sure when I'd drive back home to Los Angeles. I know that I've been putting it off. Was I just avoiding the inevitable? I took this sabbatical, calling it that because running away sounded like I was a little kid, to give myself time to clear my head. I'd built a lucrative party planning business in California and then put it on hold. How'd I let myself get that wimpy over a guy?

And what grown man breaks up by text? Even though the odds were slim, I didn't want to run into Joel anywhere, ever again. But I can't stay away forever. Or can I?

I'll think about that later.

What was the *Gone with the Wind* line? Oh yeah, I remember. *After all, tomorrow is another day.* Wish I was as pretty as Vivien Leigh. Watching her play the southern belle, Scarlet O'Hara, was mesmerizing with her dark hair and sultry eyes. I'm okay in the looks department, or so I'm told, but with my auburn hair I'm more of a Maureen O'Hara than a Scarlett O'Hara. At least I have Vivien's blue eye color instead of Maureen's green eyes, so I'll take being a mix of both looks. Can you tell I'm a little infatuated with the old-time movie stars?

Aunt Maeve called yesterday asking how things were going with me. She's such a sweetie. It sounds like she's worried about Paddy, saying his pub opening is being postponed again! And Paddy told her the bleeping mayor, I knew he didn't say bleeping, but Maeve simply couldn't swear, is still not happy with something or other in the building. She said he grumbled that Mayor Trimble had his inspector tell us, but he knows it's just him making all the brouhaha and fuss. Even small towns have power players.

A power player, that's what Joel wants to be. He had his eyes set on moving up through California politics, and that meant having the right person on his arm. And I guess me being a self-employed Irish chick didn't fit with that plan. But the blonde bimbo whose daddy practically owned Orange County is a better bet? He thinks so.

I'm left with an ugly distaste for crooked politicians and political wannabes.

When the smoke clears for the Irish pub build-out to continue, they will need marketing advice, and I already have some ideas. That is if I'm still there of course. I can just imagine a St. Patrick's Day party in the pub. Oh, and there's that annual pirate festival I heard about.

Halloween would be crazy in that old building. The building is spooky in its own right because it used to be a mortuary. And who doesn't love a costume party?

The ideas kept rolling through my head as I crossed into Florida. That was me. Get an idea and it could get stuck in my head for hours.

*K*atie Murphy Cozy Mystery series coming in 2024!

ABOUT THE AUTHOR

Here are a few ways to reach me…I'd love to stay in connected!

Please sign up for my monthly newsletter. I'll share things about my life…both personal as Brenda Felber and professionally as my pen name Suzanne Bolden.

Email me at suzanne@suzannebolden.com

Like/follow Suzanne on her Facebook page.

Suzanne Bolden's Amazon Author Central Page. If you follow me, you'll be updated when new releases are available.

Check out my website www.suzannebolden.com

Thank you for reading my books. If you enjoyed them, a review is much appreciated!

ALSO BY SUZANNE BOLDEN

Katie Murphy Cozy Mystery Series

#1 Pour Decisions

#2 Pick Yar Poison

#3 Raising Spirits

#4 Auld Lang Stein

#5 A Wee Lepre-Con

#6 Paws for a Pint

7 The Elf Did It

#8 Matrimony and Malice

#9 Read Between the Lines

day in and out to protect folks like you from chaos. There's a war going on out East. You want it coming over here, finding that little girl in there?"

"It's already found her, sir. Where do you think her parents are?"

"Well, if they're fighting, good for them. They're fellow patriots. Shit. If you were doing your part, you wouldn't be standing here holding me up for a few bucks, keeping me from my duty, from my job."

"Without my gas, you couldn't do your job."

"Your gas? This here is Union's gas. We're standing on Union's soil. I got Union's next soldier in the back of this jeep here. I'm a man for Union." I pulled my weapon from its slumber in the holster on my hip. "I'm starting to think you aren't a man for Union. And this is Union's gun. So, I'm going to take what belongs to it. Or are you going to try to stop me?" I pulled back the hammer of my magnum. "Are you spitting on the grave of those who've died for Union?"

"No, sir."

"My girls—good soldiers—would be rolling over in their graves right now. Are you for my girls?"

From the corner of my eye, I saw the young cashier peek her head through one of the larger breaks between the wooden slats of the shack. She fought off tears. Good girl.

"You for Union?" I asked again. Carl stared down the barrel of the gun pointed at him. He nodded calmly. "Good."

I put my magnum back to its leather bed at my side, brushing past Carl on my way to the driver's seat. The engine fired up and I began to roll ahead, but I put my baby back in park suddenly, sending my payload against the floor of the back cabin with a thud. I stepped out, approached Carl, and reached into his breast pocket. From the coveralls, I pulled a few folded, dirty bills. I raised the money to his sights.

"For Union," I said, got back in the jeep, and sped off into the goddamn dust.

Hundreds of kilometres passed before I noted the stinging in my forearm. Perceiving blood was difficult through the deep red of my shirt. There was no need to pull over. Seeing the oval shape of the dried, brown liquid from within, I knew my catch had broken the skin when she bit me before I got the cuffs 'round her wrists. Her teeth marks made my stomach grumble, so I tore into the recently acquired jerky. No doubt, she made wreaths of torn flesh on herself as she struggled like a maniac against her restraints in the back of the jeep. Dodgers confused the hell out of me. Their commitment to combat the draft, which paid them to fight for the great West Caribbean Union, was baffling. Youth provides strength and frustration that combine so well in a soldier. Too many jobless peasants went hungry. So many died resisting Catchers like me. Why not fight for the Union instead? Never do what you're good at for free. I lived by the same principle. Holding up gas station attendants wasn't my best work, but I reminded myself it was necessary to fulfill my deeper purpose. Carl's cash would tide me over on my journey to the coast to collect on my catch. That feeling of nervous excitement churned in my belly with thoughts of a new case file, a new warrior awaiting me in Los Muelles. The constant ups and downs of the rough and broken road furthered the roiling in my stomach.

The ships of the Union port town became visible as the winding highway descended the mountains gave way to the sea. Fissures cracked the asphalt road in twisting veins. Although the highway of heroes was fractured and unruly, the magnificent wall that stretched along the coast below remained perfectly whole. Union's top engineers came together in a brilliant display of human ingenuity and collaboration to create the barrier between us and them. Never again would a tragedy like the coastal raids occur. Where the blood of our natives was spilled, rose an impenetrable shield. No one in; warriors out.

My catch would be leaving the island for the first time. She was unaware that she was about to see the world on Union's dime. She was on the precipice of unearthing her true potential. Her aptitude for greatness remained an undiscovered mystery. The battlefield would extract the glory dormant beneath the surface of her peasant life. By no fault of her own was she born into mediocrity. I myself was once a simple farmer, long before my years of soldiering. The girl was not unlike many other cases I'd encountered. She continued to fight the call to grandeur in the back of the jeep as I pulled off the crumbling road to savour my favourite part of my vocation.

With Los Muelles in view and the vast West Caribbean Union spread out in every direction, my purpose always came clearly into focus. The highway of heroes was the route my father took to deliver me to the armed forces. It was the very same course I used to bring my girls to the port to enlist and depart. I inhaled the salty air blowing off the ocean. The breeze climbed the mountain where I stood. Love of country welled up within me. Tears came to my eyes as I thought of my girls in their fatigues boarding the ship to leave the Union. Their bravery was unrivaled. Their valour not forgotten. There was nothing I could do to protect them once transported abroad, but no daughter lives forever under the protection of her father. All there was left to do was deliver them reinforcements. The catch to be dispatched would make for a feisty ally in the war against Eastern invaders.

The town of Los Muelles did not live up to its initial, honourable purpose. Brothels lined the narrow streets. Whores walked the shattered asphalt, which locals tried to pass off as cobblestones. Drunks and lechers hung over the ornate, wrought-iron balconies reaching out over the long line of Catcher cars in the lane. I waited in the queue. Break lights bathed the graffitied walls in a sultry, red hue. My pants got a little tight at the seam in anticipation of delivering my cargo and succumbing to a woman's warm embrace. Eight months was the longest it ever took me to close a case. In all fairness, the girl rattling around behind me like a ricocheted bullet had a lot of spirit. Military sentiment had fallen off considerably. I used to be greeted with open arms when I arrived at the doorway of future soldiers. Mothers prepared me food for the road. Fathers shook my hand in earnest as they handed their children to me. The draftees used to ride shotgun, sharing stories from their young lives, divulging dreams for their futures. Eight months was bad for business. Eight months saw my allowance dwindle, my confidence fade, my stomach empty, my legs weaken, my pursuit wane. But, for all my eighteen years of Catching, my sense of duty never dulled my faith in cause or country.

Shallow rivers of mud ran through the streets as the skies opened. Rains streamed down the dusty mountains and filled the cracks between the crumbling concrete beneath the jeep. The fetish seekers seemed to pay the warm showers no mind. It seemed as though the sweat and moisture only heightened their sense of desire. I hated to have something in common with the lazy, paper-pushing dock workers living in Los Muelles full-time. They enjoyed government salaries and a fixed place to live, but extorted the whores in Union's name. Desire is desire all the same, and I would share a thin wall with one of them later that evening, no doubt. A prostitute came to the window. All the stopping and starting sank the jeep deep into the softening road. I stepped gently on the gas pedal; the jeep went nowhere. The tires spun but failed to grip. Pressing too hard would have sent me into the chrome bumper of the chicken bus ahead of me. Mascara flowed down the street woman's cheeks. Her voice could not compete with the raging showers and engine roars between the narrow, concrete lanes. She pressed her hand against the window. Her sad eyes made me long to console her anguish, but I wasn't in the market yet. I hoped to find her later. Mud sprayed backward under the jeep, and the car lurched forward. The pro bowed her head and stepped back. My catch groaned after being slammed against the interior.

"Not much farther," I reassured her.

Black wires sagged in their tangled complexity between timber poles that softened in the downpour. I tried to follow their routes as I sat in the steady traffic. The cables were a stark reminder. Too many people wanted too much. Hoards descended on places like Los Muelles in search of increased luxury and decreased workloads. Without the coastal wall, foreigners would return. The appetite for our resources would arrive with them. I refused to come to town without delivering an offering to the cause at home and abroad.

The great gates finally came into view as the jeep inched out from the alleys. Bright, fluorescent lights beat down from thirty feet above. Gunmen patrolled the top of the wall, looking below to the screening area where the soldiers congregated on one side, a view to the ocean beyond on the other. I breathed a sigh of relief to be amongst my own once again. There was order to the unloading process. Barbed wire partitions zigged and zagged on the way to the guard booths. Each drop of rain caught the overhead rays and shimmered against the dark sky. The portal was a thing to behold. Its scale not only served to keep intruders at bay, but the gargantuan feat of human engineering also reminded all who basked in the glow of its spotlights that we were all part of something far bigger than ourselves: The West Caribbean Union.

"Documents," yelled the young man from the guard box. Despite his age, he managed to speak over the torrential rain in a deep, booming tone.

"Yes, sir," I replied, passing the case files and my Catcher identification through the open window. "How about this weather?" The soldier either didn't hear me, or chose not to respond. He seemed focused on the task at hand.

"Says here you've been on this case for eight months?" Just then a great *BANG* came from the back of the jeep.

"She's been a handful."

"Everything seems to be in order." The young man returned my IDs and held on to the case file. "Park your vehicle in bay nine. Our men will extract the Dodger."

"I usually unload my case file."

"That won't be necessary. One of our men will park your vehicle on lot six."

"I can park my own damn car, son."

"Those are my orders. Please report to the Section Supervisor's office for debriefing as well." We both sat there a moment, staring at each other.

"You going to pay me, kid?" I asked.

"I don't have authorization to provide your allowance at this time, sir. The Section Supervisor will have more information."

"Whatever you say, soldier." I pulled the jeep into the unloading bay, submitted my keys, and stepped down into a knee-high puddle. My only pair of boots and pants were soaked through.

The section office was between the line of guard booths and the great gates. Behind it was row upon row of the few hundred jeeps and other all-terrain vehicles reserved for us Catchers. I felt at home for the first time in months. A bath and clean clothes were at the forefront of my mind, second only to getting paid. As I jogged through the rain, I looked back at my vehicle being pulled into the caged receiving area. A soaking wet soldier went to the rear of the jeep. Moments before he opened the double doors to collect the Dodger I brought in, the soldier took a long cattle prod from his utility belt. The tip began to glow neon blue as he activated its charge. When he finally swung the jeep doors open, the girl I captured leapt out toward him like a bat out of hell. The soldier was not phased and rammed all two million volts into the girl's chest. She went limp before she even hit the ground, falling face down in the mud. I looked away. Things had changed since I enlisted.

A bell rang as I opened the glass door into the section office. My boots and pants were no longer my only attire drenched in rain. I could feel the moisture sinking into my skin. A young woman sat at a chest-high desk in the middle of a room full of Catchers. Each of us donned the same red shirt, black pants, gold badge, and government-issued weapon. It was a dangerous yet familiar group. We were united in our work, commiserating in silence about the toils shared on our solitary hunts. It reminded me of my eight years in the East. Knowing I belonged to a scattered battalion linked in common purpose did my old, tired bones some good. I stood a little taller as I approached the desk.

"Name," said the woman in uniform.

"Strickland River," I replied. "You the one who's got my allowance?"

"The Section Supervisor will have more information about your pay," she didn't meet my eyes as she spoke, keeping her focus on the computer illuminating her hard, attractive face. "He'd like to speak with you personally."

"So I've been told."

"You can take a seat if you can find one. We have a long line. Please make your report as succinct as possible when your name is called."

"When will that be?"

"Sometime between now and when you hear me say it." The woman locked eyes with me. I knew all too well not to trifle with administrative staff. Gunshots frightened me far less than the typing on a keyboard.

As I turned around to seek out a seat, a dozen rows of weary Catchers greeted me from their seats. Despite all the time on the road, I wedged my way between two large, odorous men near the rear of the room to get off my feet. They grunted as I squeezed my shoulders between them. My aroma was as foul as any other man's, but I braved the stench to be among my associates. Being surrounded by so many others who fought for my side brought a smile to my face. And there, I waited patiently for my name to be called.

GENERAL LAMENT
AUGUST 2174

A frustrating six months passed before I could firmly stand on my own two legs again. Sergeant Antoine Porto was at my side through the whole ordeal, teaching me to shoot. Rehabilitating my body proved a far easier task than my mind. I was moved from triage along the beach to an inland hospital where I lay bedridden for months, paralyzed in sorrow with nothing to do but replay the undoing of all that kept my life and sanity sewn together. My seemingly endless wounds were dressed and treated, yet my anger and hatred were left to fester, rotting deep within until I was able to convince the Sergeant to accept me into his service as a part of the West Caribbean Union military.

I had little gratitude for the modern instruments used to keep me alive when I was injured. The only contemporary machines I had much interest in were weaponry I could use to unleash revenge upon my enemies. Many lonely nights were spent cursing the doctors and nurses who had attached me to the tubes and wires that kept me breathing against my will. If given the choice, I would have died in the sand with my husband and child. Instead, I returned to the shoreline to hone my aim and cultivate the art of soldiering. A barracks was erected a few hundred metres from the white sand where my family, my people were buried. From their graves rose the foundation of what I was told would become the prodigious protector of the Union going forward. Promises of a barricade gave me no solace. While the concrete barrier was constructed along the coast, Sergeant Porto was building a warrior from the simple fisherman I was before combat chose me to join its faithful.

Charges exploded all around as my new family and I crawled facedown in the sand beneath a low canopy of taut barbed wire. The very same sand could have been my tomb if not for Sergeant Porto. Antoine was a generous, compassionate man, but I had little place in my heart for such things in those days. I had assembled an internal barricade of my own. It corralled my rage and blocked out the kindness of others, which I soon learned were great qualities in a soldier.

Sergeant Porto screamed over the deafening blasts, distant waves, and gunfire surrounding me. He was an entirely different man in training than he was during my time in hospital. The same person who gently massaged my legs to reduce the swelling when my casts came off was one and the same to the Sergeant encouraging me to dig the bayonet at the tip of my AK-47 deeper into the sandbags hanging along the training area. For every pull of my trigger, for every thrust of my knife, I imagined having such skill with my assault rifle in the face of the invaders responsible for the coastal raids.

Spit from the Sergeant's mouth sprayed my cheek as I lay flat in the sand spewing bullets into a distant target made from palm fronds and driftwood. He spun his hat backward so that the brim wouldn't bump against my hand or weapon as he screamed obscenities over the sound of my firing weapon. My eyes remained on the mark, but I could see the furrowed brow of his dark, bushy eyebrows in my periphery. Antoine could not go an hour after shaving without a shadow reappearing along his square jaw. His olive skin was quick to absorb the island sun. Tan lines were bold along his biceps when he removed his uniform before entering the barrack's showers at the end of a long day of simulating combat and chaos. I would watch the water fall on his head of thick black hair, attempting not to stare as the stream ran through the dark hair covering his chest. The sorrow from losing the love of my life was still all too fresh to find any carnal pleasure in the attractive display of masculinity. Somewhere deep within me, desire survived, but even the slightest spark of lust was snuffed out by sadness foremost, and anything that lingered, guilt stamped out. Sex had little to do with the enjoyment I found in the Sergeant's cleansing demonstration. It merely took me back to the quiet hours we spent together as he read to me in my time of healing.

A whole new world was brought to my ear by the Sergeant's lips. I was not ready for new beginnings from the outset. Restraints were required in my first days. I tore at the careful dressing of my wounds. The Sergeant was one such bandage who I clawed in reward for his gracious treatment. For all his attempts to soothe my sores with promises of a better tomorrow, I cursed the Sergeant for his aid. Hearing the words of the nation's great authors for the first time felt like a betrayal to my man and daughter. Why was I alive to enjoy the beautiful tales? It wasn't fair that I could be inspired to fantasize when my little girl never knew the joy of dreaming about her future. Each hope for my remaining years opened the thin scabs growing over my injuries. The burden of survival seemed insurmountable. Joining the armed forces seemed the only path forward without forgetting. Revenge was the only road left to walk with my family by my side.

Stepping into the fresh water falling from the steel spout above, I made certain to keep retribution at the forefront of my mind as I averted my eyes from the Sergeant's glistening contours. Our common showers were our daily ablutions. Each evening I washed away any doubts about my vocation. Soldiering was my last link to the forsaken love I once knew. No future beyond the death of my enemies warranted consideration. Every time I cleansed my mending skin, stretched my nagging legs, loaded my weapon, fired at a target, opened a book on the topic of war, I was stacking moments one on top of the other, and I managed to build some semblance of a life on the ashes left behind.

Dining in the mess hall wasn't so different from the way I once ate with my people. Boots replaced bare feet in the sand beneath the wooden harvest tables. There were far more shaved heads in the crowd than I was used to. The food left much to be desired. Every meal I'd enjoyed before the force-feeding I endured in the hospital was plucked from the nearby sea or sourced from the hills rolling down to the coast. It took a rare breed of imagination to taint the fresh ingredients native to the area. The grouper slapped on the steel tray I slid along the mess counter was robbed of all colour and flavour. Avocados were injected with hormones that doubled their size and halved their taste. I ground chilis and mixed them in with the lifeless corn and beans served at every meal. Seconds after I put my tray down on the only uninhabited table in the entire tent, Sergeant Antoine Porto took a seat next to me. His knee grazed my thigh as he came to my side. I feigned ignorance to the contact.

"Mind if I join you?" He asked. It would be an egregious error to deny an officer. He was already cutting into his grouper anyhow.

"Of course, Sergeant." We chewed in silence for a moment. The tension in my stomach made me thirsty for honey wine.

"I'm going to tell you something I'd like to stay between us," the Sergeant spoke softly, leaning his mouth closer to my ear, keeping his eyes on the blank tarp rustling in the wind. "Can you keep a secret?"

"Of course, Sergeant."

"You're far and away the best soldier I've got." He turned his eyes to me. I nodded in agreement, which he found amusing. I'm not sure why. "Your age is a huge asset."

"You calling me old, Sergeant?"

"Look around you, Private. I've got nothing more than boys and girls in my squadron. The other thirteen are here for a cot, running water, three square meals a day, and something to do. You have a purpose."

"God damn right."

"That's why I'm counting on you." The Sergeant took a mouthful of fish, corn, and beans off his spoon, spending time to chew and swallow. "You're the first to know. We're being deployed."

"I'm ready, Sergeant." A lump suddenly bunched up in my throat. I gulped it down with a chili paste chaser. The fire in my belly burned away the fear and gave way to the slightest sense of relief I'd felt in months. Finally, a chance to alleviate my rage was coming to pass.

"Yes, you are."

It was later that evening that I tossed and turned on my bottom bunk in the dormitory. Crews worked late into the night constructing the nearby wall, but it wasn't the power tools and beastly machines that kept me from my slumber. The racket of steel saws and excavators actually grew on me. They silenced the ever-present screams echoing in my memory. Noise didn't keep me from sleep. Thoughts of taking my first life prevented me from closing my eyes to the night. I stared up at the bed overhead. My comrade above certainly wasn't still either.

The dawn of a new me was breaking. I would be a red sky in the morning: a warning to all who looked to cross me. From the depths of my meticulously packed rucksack, I withdrew the military scissors issued to me. The teenagers in my squad raised their heads from their pillows as I strutted across the earthy floor toward our shared washrooms. A bare bulb hung from a thin wire at the tent's centre. No light filled the thin glass orb. Our eyes were trained to adjust to the darkness. I could feel the thirteen stares upon my silhouette, the pointed shears like a dagger in the shadows. They feared me. They revered me.

By the light spilling through the seams of the barracks, I looked upon the face in the small mirror hanging over the sink. My thick black hair fell down to my feet with every snip of the scissors. I gripped the strands at the roots in handfuls. Multiple hacks at the clumps were needed to free me from the weight on my head. The long, dead cells piled up in the dirt. I took good care to cut down to the skin. Never again would my hair be burned away. That very smell came to me as I continued to reveal my virgin scalp. I ran my fingers over the short stubble left behind. A born warrior was framed in the mirror opposite me. I was conceived in the ashes of combat and emerged with nothing left to lose. I floated back to my bunk like the angel of death. Others in my squadron hid under their covers as I passed. They were fortunate not to be in my wake. I put my smooth head on my pillow. The whispered prayers from the other bunks lulled me into a deep, peaceful sleep.

EZRA ATUN
FEBRUARY 2185

We felt all grown-up. And for all our crimes, I guess we were.

Eleven years had passed since the coastal raids; we were eighteen years old and I was in love with an intimidating, intoxicating girl. It seemed most nights Vallah loved me too. Plus, there was always rum. The ocean was my backyard, the waves my playground until the Union began building its divider from the sea. With no more waves left to surf, we were always lacking. With no water left to fish, we were always hungry. Don't underestimate the influence an empty stomach can have on the conscience. Being one in a pack of strays didn't help much either. We were prepared to do just about anything to eat. And eat we did.

Our horde of waifs did not go unnoticed upon entering the town limits. We were accustomed to making our presence known when we drifted from village to village, plundering as we pleased. Los Muelles was different. No one was frightened by Mick's size, Carmen's ferocity, Vallah's beauty, Cash's gall, or my cunning. Shopkeepers didn't close their doors as we passed. Residents didn't bring in the clothes hanging from their lines. What few lawmakers there were did not cower in their forts. Reputation did not precede us. We only added to the streets that were already teeming with vagrants. The only looks we got were from the admirers of Carmen and Vallah.

The narrows were littered with men: mostly soldiers and construction workers. Cooks, whores, and hustlers rounded out the field. Our little mob didn't intimidate anyone.

We heard the Union broke ground on the wall in Los Muelles. It spread like wildfire across the coastline, but that was the first portion I saw fully complete. Laying eyes on the fully-grown, concrete giant for the first time was a moment that burned into my memory. Rumors about an immense, terrible fortress promised jobs and security, which brought the poor and fearful flocking in. None of us had seen so many buildings built so close or so high. Setting foot on the main strip of asphalt that lead toward the great gates was another sensation I never forgot. My bare soles had never touched a paved road before. The blacktop was hot as the sun descended just below the daunting barrier at the street's end. Laying eyes on the concrete giant was yet another unforgettable moment. Vallah stopped in the lane, below the dangling, painted sign of the Grandview Hotel. Music, laughter, and glassware spilled into the street from its open door. It was six storeys high, towering over the other ground floor shops, restaurants, offices, and garrisons. It sprawled out in a grey, concrete maze across the land tilted toward the barricade. The top floor and its wrought-iron terrace bathed in the rusty orange sunset. I gazed up at the lace curtains blowing in the breeze. The penthouse was the only view above the wall. Stepping into the sun, a woman in military uniform leaned against the railing painted in gold. I couldn't make out her face from below. I saw a man's shape emerge onto the balcony behind her, wrapping his arms around the officer, kissing her neck.

"I'm going to live there someday," Vallah daydreamed, setting eyes on the same scene.

"I'll make sure of it," I looked at her. She kept staring at the penthouse.

"Yeah, right," she laughed.

While roaming the main funnel into the city, it was nearly impossible to keep watch in all the dark alleys breaking off from the street in seemingly endless tangents. Whistles, catcalls, and kisses surrounded us. My heart beat faster in my chest. I could hear it pumping just as loud as the devils lurking in the fading light. Instinct put my hand in Vallah's. She tossed it away, knowing she needed both fists at the ready. I took her lead and concealed my knife in the sleeve of my tattered khaki shirt. We were the fresh meat. Our tender flesh wafted through the narrows and called out to the villains. Suddenly, the echoes materialized. A grimy hand reached out from a small break in the concrete blockhouses, snatching Carmen's wrist, pulling her into the glooms off the road. She did not scream. Mick rushed into the blackness before I had time to think. By the time the rest of us followed, Carmen had already put the bastard who grabbed her on his back. When the offender tried to rise from the alley floor, Mick brought one of his massive fists down on the bum's face. The sound of bone hitting bone filled the small space between buildings. They didn't kill him. Our knives stayed at the ready, but Carmen and Mick gave the man the beating of his life. It was important to have the attacker back on the streets to spread word about the consequences doled out by our band. No one said a word. We were all too familiar with the scene.

When Mick and Carmen grew tired of their mugging, Vallah went to the mangled body to check the assailant's pockets. Without even looking up from the man's soiled clothes, she reached back toward her brother with an open palm, holding a bunched-up piece of foil. None of us had any want for the crystal, except for Cash, who, in an instant, darted around a corner to lose himself in the company of the reed, the spoon, the smoke, the high. He was stealing away to get a beat on the crystal, running like a subterranean sewer throughout the Union's affluent and impoverished alike. It was weeks before he turned up again and Vallah almost seemed relieved to have her brother gone. Carmen never thought much of him for introducing Mick to crank. Cash's desire for Mick didn't endear her to Cash either. Vallah continued rummaging, investigating the holey, worn-out boots on the bum's gnarled feet. There was a small roll of filthy bills tucked under the right's insole. I considered taking them for my own bare feet, but Mick did the work, and it was harder to find anything to fit his uncommonly large bottoms. He put them on. His toes poked through the front as he wiggled them to get Carmen to break a smile. Mick looked as frightening as I knew he could be in the changing colour of the alley. Daylight drained from the tight space. Break lights from the road only deepened the red blood that stained Mick's t-shirt. Sweat caused the cotton to cling to his skin, displaying the broad shoulders and taut muscles beneath. Carmen burrowed under his arm. They kissed.

Countless victims were left in our slipstream on the journey to Los Muelles. We were in search of the promised land. A dangerous reputation was necessary and couldn't be had without foes. Myths told about our band served us better than any weapons we fashioned. Rumors of our violent deeds were only effective when united with the transient lives we led. Constantly moving meant we never had to live up to all the tall tales. There wasn't actually a killer among us. I, myself, had been credited with taking at least two lives. I stabbed a man once. I cut a woman too. Neither died; I was sure of that. But neither of them ever pursued Vallah again. She used to find my theatrics attractive. My temper entertained her in the mundane times we spent living hand to mouth. Mick was a brute. That never appealed to her. I was always calm and calculated, so when something riled me up enough to spill blood, Vallah relished her hold on me. We both knew such a flame waned. My affections never faded, but chivalry drained from my spirit in spurts. Exhaustion poked holes all over me. I was tired. It was having a terrible effect on my libido, and sex was one of the few pleasures we could enjoy for free. It got harder to want to touch her after seeing her bite into another girl's ear after a card hustle went wrong. I didn't feel sexy in her eyes after she'd seen me hold a torch to a man's foot to extract the location of his buried savings. It was impossible to reconcile love and survival. We sought a new backdrop to play out our star-crossed affair, a fresh canvas to smear our future.

At eighteen years, we decided to sink our teeth into Los Muelles, make it home like it was to so many other grifters. We thought ourselves so much smarter than the rest, but with the shield of perpetual movement no longer protecting us, we badly needed a new defence against the many who would gladly wipe us out to turn our band's reputation into a feather in the cap. A stronghold was my idea. I think I missed our home on the coast more than the others. The life of a rolling stone wasn't a concept I knew of until I lived exactly that.

Night came quickly, so we set out from the alley to search for the city's cheapest rooms. The beggars, the soldiers, and the barkeeps suggested Miss Holly's. Rates were, in fact, the lowest around — so long as paid company wasn't required. A robust, fast-talking woman put the money Vallah handed over into the front of her sauce-covered apron. It was tied tightly around her thick hips. A host of kitchen knives hung in holsters from the same line across her body.

"You'll have no trouble from me unless you give me cause," Miss Holly barked, turning up the heat on a gas stovetop between fixing two drinks for the patrons swarming the bar. "How long you plan on staying?"

"A while," Vallah answered with determination.

"I hear that a lot, honey. Money goes fast in Los Muelles and don't always come as quick as jumping a junky for his."

A silence fell over the four of us while the boisterous main room continued to buzz.

"Mhmm. Word travels fast in the narrows. You can count on it reaching Miss Holly first."

"What's your first name?" I tried to turn the topic to the multi-talented cook, bartender, and madame .

"Don't get ahead of yourself, handsome. Now, I can see you don't have any bags. Take them seats by the bar. I'll fix you something to put some meat on those bones before you head up to your room."

"Whatever's cheap," Vallah spoke up.

"Mhmm. Hear that a lot too, honey. First meal is on the house, which is to say: it's on me. Can't help my soft heart for you young bucks."

Vallah and I pulled up stools to the sopping-wet bar top.

"We'll just take the key for now," Carmen called over the crowd. Mick's arm was draped over her shoulder. He surveyed the room, already anticipating his next bout. Blood dried on the puffy skin around his knuckles.

"Sure thing, sweetheart." Miss Holly held out the key close to her chest, forcing Carmen to lean in close to Miss Holly's lips. "You could make a good living doing what you're about to do for free," she said, under her breath.

Carmen tugged the key away from Miss Holly's meaty grasp.

"We'll be up in a minute," Vallah assured our friends.

Steering Mick toward the stairs leading up to the rooms, Carmen kept her glare fixed on Miss Holly until she disappeared down the hall above.

"There goes the muscle, so now I know I'm talking to the brains." Two steaming, heaping plates of coleslaw, rice and peas, and chicken thighs in jerk seasoning were set down as if from thin air. "You kids are new in town. I could keep that roof over your head, your bellies full if y'all are looking for work."

"What kind of work?" I pointed to the rum on the bottom shelf behind Miss Holly, and raised two fingers. A pair of short glasses were placed in front of me and Vallah.

"It would just be a short while." Miss Holly poured as she spoke, constantly tending to the stovetop. "Just until you get on your feet." The air was hot and thick. The rum felt good going down. It slowed my heart after watching the beating in the alley. "I'm guessing y'all don't have papers on your names."

"Who needs 'em?" I chirped, motioning for my glass to be refilled, knowing full-well we were being propositioned, taking full advantage of all that was offered on the house.

"Anyone who doesn't want to be deported. You all come up on the coast?"

Vallah and I looked at each other from out the corner of our eyes.

"Thought you were about that age. Damn shame about the raids. That way of life is long over now. Business has been good in Los Muelles since though. Why shouldn't y'all take advantage? After all, it was you who lost the most."

My mouth was busy enjoying the tender, dark meat with the perfectly kicking sauce.

"You think this is the first time I've been approached about tricking?" Vallah didn't touch her food or her drink.

"Not just you, honey. Your boyfriend too. All sorts of appetites in Los Muelles. More soldiers and workers arrive everyday. Union is all for it. Keeps morale up. Hell, I pay taxes. Only work I know you can get without papers. A lot of lonely souls here need company."

"We ain't that desperate." Vallah slid off her stool.

"Not yet, honey, but you've hit the end of the road. The wall's going up and you don't got any papers. No birthdate, no residency, no proof you were born in the Union. You don't want to be on a ship looking back on the wall from the outside."

"We'll get 'em," shouted Vallah.

"Only two ways for coast kids like you."

"How's that?" I spoke through teeth full of rice and peas.

"Once they arrest you—and it's only a matter of time before they arrest at least one of you little hustlers—you got two choices: labour camps or military. That's the only way they'll recognize your name, your country. Can't get work without papers. Can't live without work."

"We've done just fine so far." Vallah shoved a man who stumbled drunkenly into her shoulder as she stood with fists clenched. I sucked back another rum.

"World's getting smaller, honey. Union's closing in on your kind. I'm just trying to offer a helping hand."

"We don't need it." Vallah stormed off. I scraped what was left from my plate onto Vallah's untouched portions, drank her rum, and before I could turn to follow her with the plate in hand, Miss Holly called after me.

"That girl wants something you can't give her, handsome." I gave my back to Miss Holly, but she kept on yelling. "A job or papers. Let me know what you decide."

My stomach roiled: not used to all the starch, the space being taken up with food, the greasy goodness dished up by Miss Holly. That feeling in my gut and that twisting concrete hallway—where I walked behind Vallah— have remained regular features in my nightmares. Aluminum sconces cradled small candles on the walls. No outside light penetrated the hall upon hall of shabby rooms harbouring moans, raised voices, silence, and infinite mystery. Only the dark hair falling halfway down her back, her thin waist, womanly hips, and determined gait could be seen in the moment I was forced to replay over and over in my dreams. Countless nights I watched Vallah strolling down that corridor away from me.

Our room resembled what I imagined a prison cell to look like. There were two cots on either side of the rusting metal sink and toilet that were dead ahead as I entered after Vallah. The door sat loosely on its hinges, and the feet of the beds kept it from fully opening into the cool, damp space. Showers were communal, but I hadn't seen a sign despite all the doors we passed along the way. Mick stood ass-naked, relieving his bladder. Carmen sat up on the bed. The single, discoloured sheet covered her breasts. Her hair was askew. Sweat glistened on her skin in the dim flame flickering in the sconce over the toilet and sink.

"Not exactly the stronghold I had in mind." I closed and locked the door behind me. A gentle push could have broken it down.

"Think Cash will know how to find us?" Carmen asked. Her eyes bulged when I presented the jerk chicken and sides.

"He always does." Mick shook his leg and flopped down next to Carmen and shared the food.

"It's a lot bigger here." Vallah paced the bottom edges of the beds.

"Too big." I sat opposite Carmen and Mick, leaning toward them. "We'd need an army to run this place like you planned, Vallah."

"It took us too long to get here. No one said there'd be so many people. Where the fuck were all these soldiers when the East Caribbean Republic attacked?" Vallah continued walking back and forth, not looking at us.

"Why don't we just roll on to the next spot?" Mick scratched himself. "No harm done."

"There's nowhere else. Union's deporting everyone we steal from and Union's got too big for us to steal from them."

"I ain't scared," said Carmen, eating off the plate with her fingers.

"We'd get pinched in a second," Vallah dismissed her.

A long pause gripped the room.

"So, why don't we get pinched?" I said, hands together, resting my arms on my knees. My stomach churned from the meal and the ramifications of my suggestion as I leaned over.

"Fuck that." Mick chewed with his mouth open.

"We've spent the last eleven-years running from the law of some kind," Carmen added, after swallowing.

Vallah fell quiet. I could see her wheels turning inside her head.

"Think about it." I sat on the cot's edge. "We keep pulling jobs the same as we've always done. Nothing too big. Nothing too violent." I looked at Mick. He flipped me off. "If we don't get pinched, great. We hole up here for a while and sit on our riches. But if we do get snatched up, Union has to book us, has to give us papers. We do a short bit at some farm or factory somewhere on the interior, and we'll walk out without looking over our shoulder for fear of being shipped off the island to some other godforsaken place."

"Woah. Hold on, man. They'll give us jobs if we get pinched?" Carmen sat up.

"That's what that lady downstairs says. We get scooped for something small, Union just puts us to work for a stretch."

"Or we can sign up. Fight for Union. Still get our papers." Vallah stopped in her tracks, biting her nails.

"To hell with that. I won't die for those bastards. They left us for dead when ECR came. Now they're trying to kick out survivors because we don't got proof of citizenship." I snapped. Vallah was still cross with me for not doing more when Miss Holly propositioned her, questioned her honour. We were knee-deep in a muted row. They happened enough after spending every waking hour together for over a decade.

"I don't like that lady downstairs." Carmen said.

"I don't trust her either." Vallah kept biting her fingernails.

"We'll look into it for ourselves. There has to be someone around this town that got booked that way, or knows someone who did. If it's true, how can we pass up not being hunted, not being hungry, not existing anymore? Hell, Vallah, maybe we'll find jobs here after we get papers. We can live in that top room at the Grandview Hotel."

She didn't answer me. She went back to pacing.

"I kind of like it here." Mick licked the plate. Grains of rice fell to his cot.

"This can't last. It won't." Vallah broke her silence.

"She's right," I chimed in, ignorant to her true meaning. I should have seen it then, but I was blinded by my hopes, my foolish belief that peace and comfort was really within reach for someone like me.

* * *

It wasn't six weeks before the four of us were in handcuffs. Cash was in the wind.

Holding up a liquor store with knives in a town populated by heavily armed soldiers proved difficult. Vallah and I were usually able to cook up better scams. Neither of us had our hearts in the job. Fatigue was setting in. I felt it in my bones as a tall, stalky man in uniform gripped my arm and ushered me down the dank hallway in a long line of delinquents who were awaiting sentencing. My body embraced his sturdy grip while I let my legs go limp, forcing him to nearly carry me to where the other felons stood waiting. The support didn't last long. I collapsed to the ground. Warm blood trickled down my neck and along my back from the inflated wound left by the nightstick blow to my skull after the failed heist. Pain rushed in and receded like the tide. If only the arresting officers had listened. There was no resistance from me. A court date was exactly what I was after. Silly me.

The concrete floor was cool to the touch when I propped myself up onto my hands and knees. That sharp ammonia smell from urine filled my nostrils. I was brought to my feet again by the swine in military attire. He leaned me against the wall. My swollen cheek came courtesy of the series of blows I received before being tossed in back the transport to the holding cells. All was going according to plan — my plan at least.

The cold stone refreshed the puffiness around my eye. Shackles were wrapped around my ankles, linking me to the chained queue shuffling forward slowly. Faces in the narrow row, lit by the fluorescent lighting above, turned to see all the commotion made by Carmen and Mick being hauled in behind me. Their curses and spitting only made my head throb more. I was relieved to be on our way to getting booked, to finally being acknowledged by a higher power, officially recognized by the Union. My friends' rage surprised me for all the years we spent without the guiding hand of a government to aid us. I was so naïve.

I gained enough of my balance to inch ahead in the line when the door at the far end of the hall filled with light and silhouetted whoever found themselves at the front entrance. Vallah's hair swayed across the small of her back as I discerned her shape from the rest. She did not turn. If only she twisted a little, I might have better remembered her face. There wasn't anything to shout to her over the sound of chains clinking together, the steel dragging across the hard floor. I believed there was plenty of time to speak ahead, conversations without perpetual hunger inside to distract from our many musings. The gods must have been chuckling heartily at my folly.

When I finally stepped into the white light, my eyes ached, and shooting pains jabbed at my temples. There was little worry in my heart, though. I'd taken many far worse beatings in my time. The shackles were removed from my ankles. I was about to become a Union man. My back straightened, my chest rose, my shoulders lifted. A woman in uniform sat at a high desk, towering over me. Medals in various shapes, sizes, and colours were pinned to the shoulders and chest of her pressed olive-green uniform. The Union flag hung behind her, bathing in the electric light shining down from the ceiling. Each fixture hummed in all its brightness. There was a door to my left, another to my right.

"What is your name?" The woman asked from her seat at the desk. Her black hair was pulled back tightly from her face. She was beautiful, with jet-black eyebrows, and large, alluring, ink-coloured eyes. In my daze, she was a stunning vision in the all white room.

"Ezra," I mumbled in a mixture of fright and anticipation.

"Speak up when you address the General," ordered the armed man standing at my rear.

I cleared my throat.

"And your family name, Ezra?" The General inquired, her entrancing gaze fixed on me as her pen moved frantically across the paper below her.

"Atun." My voice filled the small room. "My family fished mostly tuna."

"Ever been arrested before, Ezra Atun?"

"Not officially."

"I can see that from your lacking of paperwork. You've slipped through the cracks too long. So, consider this your birthday. The Private behind you is going to take your picture and the file of Ezra Atun will be added to Union records."

I nearly leapt for joy. My brain damage is the only excuse I can conjure for such stupidity in the face of such disaster.

"First, we must determine your sentencing. You have been found guilty of assault with a deadly weapon, robbery, mischief, and conduct detrimental to Union interests. I'm sure there's a lot missing from this list." The General winked at me. "For your crimes, you have been sentenced to eight years in service to the Union. Lucky for you it's your first recorded offence, or the term would be far more severe. You have two choices: begin an illustrious career under my command in the armed forces in protection of the Union at home and abroad, or contribute to the Union's efforts to remain a shining light in a world sinking into shadow by making yourself useful at one of the Union's various labour interests at the interior." The General was writing throughout the entirety of her speech, staring into my soul with every stroke of her pen. "Simply say: 'option one' or 'option two'. How do you plea?"

"Option two," I said, almost giddy. I never forgave the sinful errors made in my youth to put myself in such a position, to be so excited about relinquishing my freedom.

"Tell me, were you a victim of our enemy's attacks on the coast? You look to be about eighteen or nineteen."

"Yes, General. They killed my mother and father."

"The fishmongers?"

I nodded.

"And you don't wish to avenge them?"

"Not much of a fighter, General."

"That can't be true if you've survived eleven years on your own. But, so be it. I don't want any man in my military who lacks the courage to honour the memory of his people. Private, take this worker's picture and bring him to the holding cell."

The soldier pressed me against the wall and pulled a wet rag from a filthy bucket at my feet. He wiped the blood roughly from my face. The scent of alcohol was strong. My cuts stung. He then raised the small camera to his eye.

"Be still," the soldier demanded.

I'd never had my picture taken before. I couldn't help but smile, so I did, and a great flash filled my eyes. My head hurt. Blurry, white spots speckled my vision. Instinct told me to rub my eyes. I couldn't reach them with my hands cuffed behind me. A small rectangular piece of paper poured from the camera. The soldier handed my picture to the General and then shoved me toward the door to my left. Warm, thick air greeted me in the cell stuffed with other people. Odours from the unwashed horde hung in the air like a cloud. Vallah was nowhere to be found as I rubbed shoulders with my fellow convicts. I expected to see more happy faces, more delighted, newborn citizens. Then I came across Cash. He was sitting curled up on the floor against the far wall. Sweat beaded across his nose and forehead.

"Cash, it's good to see you. How'd you know to get locked up today? We thought we lost you for good this time."

"I got booked a few days ago." His voice was weak, his skin pale, which wasn't uncommon. "Gave some junky soldier a good stash to keep me in until you guys came through here. When I heard in the street Union was giving two meals a day, beds, and papers to new arrests, I knew you and Vallah would be all over it." Cash was hunched over his stomach. He was shaking.

"You've kicked before. You'll be alright. A few days and you'll leave that stuff behind for good."

"No need. Word is there's a dealer at the interior. They call him The Kid. They say he's got the best stuff on the island. We're heading to paradise, brother." Cash made his true motives known. "Where's everyone else?" He coughed and spat on the floor.

Just then, Mick came bursting through the door with two guards corralling him into the cell. They threw him against the throng. A soldier hit Mick square between the eyes with the butt-end of his rifle. Mick didn't go down. He kept wailing like a banshee, spit collecting around his mouth. Carmen wasn't long behind him, doing her best to gnaw off the faces belonging to the men who forced her in. I whistled to them and a path cleared for them to pass through to me and Cash. No one wanted a head-butt from Mick or a bite from Carmen.

"Hey, Cash ol'boy," Mick said, his chest rising and falling quickly from his fervent breathing. He began to calm a little, but still looked menacing from the gash in his forehead that spilled red across his face.

"Vallah's not with you?" Cash suddenly looked panicked.

"She was ahead of me in line. I thought she'd be in here already," I said.

"This cell is for the camps, the other is for the military." Vallah's brother struggled to his feet to tell us.

It wasn't until we stepped out into the rain, and I saw Vallah's long hair dripping in the sunny showers, that I believed it. My herd of outlaws was loading onto one bus with barred windows. Cash, Mick, and Carmen trailed in the same pack. Looking over a waist-high, concrete partition, I saw Vallah's crowd headed for the door of a different bus enclosed in cages. Soldiers steered us toward our transport with their nightsticks.

"Where's that other bus going?" I yelled over the downpour to an armed woman.

"Those are Union's future heroes." She pushed me onward.

"There's a mistake." My voice hardly carried over the torrential rain beating down in the strange, yellow sun.

Without a word in reply, the soldier sparked the blue tip of her wand. I called out to Vallah. Her long brown hair fell over her face as she entered the barracks-bound Union bus. With hands cuffed behind my back, I tried to force my way to her. I couldn't see her face. Then I felt the volts travel through my body. All went black.

STRICKLAND RIVER
MARCH 2192

If your life has been anything like mine, the looming truth that every story begins with an undoing becomes welcome. I don't recall the exact moment I learned that no matter how hard I squirmed, my fate as a mortal man was shut by the red wax seal called death. My life really started when my inevitable end was brought to my attention. It gave me a reason to get out of bed in the morning, knowing that I had an undefeated foe to contend with. That respect quickly turned to servitude. I sat in the waiting room with all those other filthy men. We were a fleet hired to shovel coal on the raging flames. The world wasn't big enough anymore. Soldier, father, Catcher, I fed the fire. I knew it as a child: a day would come when I could no longer feed the blaze with anything other than myself.

"You can come back now, Mr. River," said the girl through wisps of smoke. I stopped staring at the cracked, concrete floor long enough to notice her open hand leading back to the Supervisor's office.

When a man comes to town from far away, his superiors do not enjoy the dark they've been lingering in while the agent was in the field, so it behooves the Catcher to tell a tale to secure his pay, but for all my time alone, my failures amassed in far greater number than the adventures of my hunt. Tracking is all in the subtle, treacherously tedious details. The assumption was that all us Catchers did was follow trails of breadcrumbs left behind by the drafted. In a country defined by mountains and jungle, I was a hound under constant assault from new scents, watching my step and my back one square metre at a time. There was no room for excuses in my reports. The deadline was queen, and the Catchers her loyal subjects. We existed at her mercy, trying to deliver more fighters to the cause before the sands of time were scorched once again on Union shores.

I snapped to my feet when I was summoned. Fatigue wasn't allowed even the briefest audience with the Supervisor. I evoked thoughts that brought my precious baby girls to mind, feeling a tinge of the excitement I first knew when I heard there was a job to do that would serve their memories and honour the debt I owed them. It helped for me to think of myself as a prospector sent to seek out gold flakes at the riverbank. Each new soldier was an extremely valuable thing.

"Strickland River, you ol' sonuvabtich," the Supervisor said, as he came around his desk to give me a handshake. His skin was smooth and soft. "Have a seat, please. You must be exhausted. Did Sharon offer you a glass of water on your way in?"

"No. Thank you, sir. Rather looking forward to a real drink." I took him up on his offer to sit.

"Sure. Sure. Of course."

"I'd like to apologize, sir —"

"I'll stop you right there, River. I should be the one apologizing. Eight months ago, you sat in this office. I noticed your limp, despite your best efforts to hide it."

"Sir —"

"Please. My list of reservations was long before handing over your most recent case file. That was before this..." the Supervisor flipped open a folder on his desk. My name was written vertically along a tab going down the side, "…eighteen-month catastrophe. How did you eat? Your allowance couldn't have lasted any more than six months."

"I'm clever."

"That you are, River. But, unfortunately, your wits are no longer enough to warrant a salary, gun, or badge."

"Please, sir. I beg you: give me one more case to prove myself."

"You've had eighteen years in the field, over fifty cases to your name. You've done more than enough to prove yourself a true friend to the Union."

"Let me continue that friendship."

"River, it can't be news to you that the situation across the border has deteriorated."

"So why not have another Catcher to gather reinforcements?"

"We don't have the resources to carry dead weight. You and I both know a chain is only as strong as its weakest link."

The pit of my stomach rose to my throat. I could feel my eyes dampening despite my best efforts.

"Listen, River. I know why you first got into this business. Your girls were decorated soldiers at their end, and I'm aware your wife followed soon after the news. There are few who can say they've given more to the West Caribbean Union than you."

My heart pounded in my chest. Air went in and out of my lungs as fast as a hummingbird flaps its wings. I could hardly see the Supervisor's bullshit sympathy as my sight thinned.

"Your delivery didn't fetch you much after this length of time, and the discharge package isn't what it used to be, but there will be a ceremony—"

"Just one more case, sir."

"There's just no room in the budget for you. I wish there was another way to slice it."

My face fell into my hands, then my head dropped between my knees.

"The name Strickland River means something in this town."

"I'm on my bottom dollar, sir. Just one more case."

"There's some work here in Los Muelles. I'm sure your reputation will serve you well."

"You're killing me, sir. Catching is all I have left."

"Look here, River," the Supervisor changed his tone impatiently. "You have the Union's gratitude, but I don't have to tell you there's a war going on beyond that wall outside and I don't have the time to hold your hand through this. I don't have a job for you anymore."

I ground my teeth and rose to my feet. I wiped snot from my nose along my sleeve.

"River—"

"You're right, sir. Thank you for the opportunity. I'll take my pay and be going."

The Supervisor unlocked the top drawer of his desk and withdrew a small stack of cash. He put it on the desk between us. I slid the wad of paper bills off the edge into my pocket. The Supervisor stood and extended his hand. My arm felt heavy as lead. It took all my strength to lift my mitt and squeeze the empty palm offered by my superior. I gave him my back as I went to leave.

"River."

"Sir?"

"I'm going to need your badge, weapon, and keys."

Without a word, I hauled my magnum from its holster and dropped it on the desk. I placed my badge beside it. The keys to my baby jangled in my shaking hand before I released them to fall in a silent moment below the fluorescent, sleepless judge shining down from the ceiling. Papers were pushed across the desk towards me. My dismissal numbed me for the ensuing signatures bringing an official end to my service. I couldn't bring my legs to bend. Getting to my feet again after returning to the chair seemed impossible: a thought that kept my legs straight as I scrawled my name in messy chaos across discharge forms. Father taught me better than to disrespect his name in such a fashion.

Anything the Supervisor might have said was lost like screams in the depths of a tumultuous sea. All my focus stayed with my tools for the job. Wide eyes fixed on my weapon, my instrument of transportation. Black ink was spread beneath Union letterhead, and I was likewise spread thin, reduced to a few stamps in records to be disregarded from that moment forward.

I stood there stripped, going for the door in a spinning daze. A room full of Catchers served as a stark reminder that I was a newly helpless, naked man without a tribe. Torrential rains continued as I burst through the exit. A waterfall engulfed me while I staggered through the mud. All that came to mind was: drink. The Catcher bar of Los Muelles was the lone port in the storm, the single connection my sputtering mind could find. A sudden desire to rub elbows with the kind who look you in the eye while tightening the grip on your balls overcame me in the rain-drenched streets. Even the deep, red warmth coming off the taillights in the lanes relieved the tension in my shoulders. The alleys embraced me and hid me from the exhausting gaze of official reports and legal documents. A patriot with no nation, I stepped through the ornate passageway leading into my refuge, into Miss Holly's hotel.

There was a middle-aged veteran and one of the men who turned tricks at the guesthouse singing, clapping their hands, and stomping their feet in the far corner opposite the bar, below the staircase leading to the second floor, to the privacy of the rooms for rent. Catchers gathered around them at their plastic tables, leaning in their plastic chairs, sheltered from the rain. They sang with power together. Their thunderous rhythm filled my chest as I approached. Hoots and hollers punctuated the duet as they sang:

You better run from the sun
You better flee from the sea
For here comes the Union men
Who show all brav'ry,
Strength, utility

I nearly collapsed to the floor before my ass fell on a stool. I braced myself against the bar. The bills in my pocket were damp as I rummaged through my wad of crumpled paper. Miss Holly immediately appeared before me when I slapped two depictions of a former Prime Minister down on the bar. The moisture made the bills stick to the surface.

"Looking mighty troubled there, River," she said, putting a glass under my chin, filling it with my favourite rum. Miss Holly collected the bills and reached into her front apron pocket for change. I waved her off.

"Leave the bottle," I muttered.

"Can I fix you some fine food? I'm damn sure you ain't eaten as well as you do here out on the road."

I tipped back the drink and shook my head as I gulped.

"You going to be needing a room?" Miss Holly inquired.

"An hour." I drank again. "Let me know when she's free." Four more wet papers stuck to the bar after I tossed them out.

"Sure thing, River. Enjoy your rum." Miss Holly deposited my funds in her apron and whispered something to a small boy at the end of the bar. The thin boy in a tight pink shirt proceeded to run up the stairs, into the dim glow illuminating the twisting tunnels of rooms.

To have a place once remembered with reverence usurped by a new trauma was painful beyond expectation, and likely because it was indeed not anticipated. Surprises were not among my pleasures. It was my belief that I'd die on the job long before my efforts were deemed to do more harm to the Union than good. My ship had run aground in a familiar port. Miss Holly's had always been a place of celebration, a pitstop between cases when confidence and funds were at all-time highs, a haven for those who faced troubles each and every day without retreat. Maybe that was the lesson lingering in my glass as I sucked back another rum and replaced it as easily as my Supervisor replaced me.

No one grants permission to serve the country, just as no one grants permission to be a father. Responsibility grows from within. My loyalty, my drive, and my responsibility were in question. I hadn't been discharged. I was being challenged, tested, and pushed. The Supervisor knew me too well to think I'd ever quit. He called me to read between the lines. I knew it to be true. And suddenly, my mood drastically improved. What kind of patriot requires compensation for his trade? Duty is not virtuous if returns are expected. I thought I'd been canned, fired, kicked to the curb, but after a few short rums, the pounding music, the smell of familiar pros, I realized I'd been given a promotion. The Supervisor granted me a special task because he knew the true value I offered. After a few short breaths, I almost pitied the

Catchers all around me. When I first walked into the room, I felt less than, like dirt beneath the feet of those who still got to do the job I loved, but I soon recognized I'd been anointed, pulled up beyond the ranks to a nobler class unto its own. My strength was renewed, my course presented, my faith restored. Just as a smile came to my face, the boy put a hand on my shoulder. I turned to face him, but my eyes were quickly drawn to the magnificent figure atop the stairs.

"Listo, señor?" he asked.

"Si, mi amiguito. Yes I am."

I snatched the bottle from the bar and grabbed another glass to go with my own before making my way to the foot of the stairs, eyes fixed on Lola. Of course, that wasn't her real name. She wore it like a uniform, a gorgeous Union servant like me.

Crushed lavender, hibiscus, and bougainvillea petals floated at the surface of her washbasin in the room. She stood nearly six-foot-two, a few inches above me. Lola's strong arms embraced me. Born a man, she evolved into a stunning creature by rituals and procedures I couldn't begin to understand. Her breasts were hard and strong. There wasn't an ounce of weakness to be found within her. It was impossible to define the attraction. There was no need for explanations in the humid candlelight, in the unequaled release. No words were spoken. We took our time, but Lola knew how to maximize the earning potential of an evening, how to provide solace to as great a number as she was able, how to contribute to the Union cause with the greatest efficiency, which only made me pine for her all the more.

My skin stuck to the thin sheets as I lay on my back with the rum bottle on my chest. Lola was gone without a single kiss, knowing to leave me to the newfound task at hand. I could not linger long. The crowd would be most full in those hours between midnight and dawn. I needed the chaos, the noise, and the confusion to cut my target from the herd. There was a bounty of Catchers undeserving of their recently procured case files, just waiting to be relieved of the charge greater than them, more deserving of someone like me.

The wind kicked up as I descended the stairs. Rain and a stout wind shook the tin roof attached to the wooden beams above. No one seemed to notice. They certainly didn't notice me: another contented man primed to fulfill his purpose. My bottle was lighter, the rum sloshing about with each step down. I returned to my seat at the bar. Miss Holly slid a plate of rice, beans, fried plantains, cucumber, and breaded snapper between the bottle and my arm. She took my attention from the herd.

"Everybody's gotta eat," she said, void of any tenderness.

"Thanks," I picked up the fork buried in the pile of rice. A full stomach would aid in the night ahead.

"Everybody's gotta pay too," Miss Holly added with a fist dug into where her apron was tied around her hip.

Another dead Prime Minister was handed over.

"Enjoy."

I licked my plate clean. Miss Holly always appreciated compliments to her culinary prowess. The room became drunker with every passing minute; not everyone could hold their liquor as well as me. All the dancers seemed too confident on their feet. They sweat out the alcohol in small, consistent portions. It was those sitting down that I watched closely. Without standing to track fluctuations in balance, a drunk could rise and be caught off guard by an abruptly spinning room. Off guard was exactly what I needed. Los Muelles was populated by beggars, thieves, bounty hunters, street workers, cooks, and soldiers. Not one from this crowd was likely to drop their guard with any haste.

A subtle sign was all I needed. The signal appeared when a young man of slim build proceeded to spit on the concrete floor in repetition. Excess saliva is a telltale caution for the onset of vomit. The young Catcher leaned forward in the cheap chair, dropping his forehead on the back of his hands interlocked on his solitary table. Empty beer bottles and short glasses littered the surface, but he was alone. Head down, he continued to spit between his knees onto the floor. I summoned Holly's errand boy over with a wave. It was the same boy who called for me when Lola was washed and ready. The urge to have her again was hard to stymie. Time didn't permit another hour upstairs. Time was quickly rising up my list of enemies. Short of breath, the boy stood next to me while I asked him if the man I stalked had a room for the night. He shook his head. Perfect. Dry heaves came on strong for the young Catcher as I watched his back rise and fall in small, intoxicated convulsions.

"Go tell that man there's no puking here," I told the little boy. He put out an open palm and I placed a few coins in his waiting grasp. "That Catcher has to leave, understand?" The boy nodded.

Off he went, swift as the wind. The last drops of rum fell to my tongue while I watched the boy deliver the message. He pestered the young Catcher until the drunk rose to his feet, leaning on the boy for balance. When the boy brushed the Catcher's hand from his shoulder, the inebriated serviceman nearly toppled over, staggering for the doorway. I patiently waited for him to exit.

Rain washed the young man's vomit down the gutter, joining the mud, urine, and god only knows what else. He continued to expel Miss Holly's food and drink. The young Catcher turned a gaping mouth up toward the downpour to chase the bile. Puddles sprayed as his service boots shuffled through the sludge. I gave him a good lead to stay off his radar. Balance seemed to be his primary concern. There were few shadows to be found among the bright bulbs hanging over food carts and doorways, blaring from cars and motors. Finding the dark corners came naturally to me after eighteen years of hunting others. My target scraped his shoulder on the corner of a small shop as he turned into a lightless alley. All the falling water avoided my face thanks to the brim hanging low at my brow. The sound of keys jangling against each other echoed in the narrow where I followed the first figure in my plot for redemption. Much of the bustling noise from the main strip was at our backs. Each step had to be taken carefully. A profound, rose-coloured radiance from the young Catcher's taillights illuminated me as he turned the key in the rear doors attached to his jeep. I crept along the alley wall, camouflaged in heaping trash piled high between me and the crucial player in this unfolding divine drama.

The young Catcher checked his backside, not noticing me. He spread a blanket in the barred back cabin of his all-terrain ride. For all the showers trickling down the concrete walls in the scarlet hue behind the car, it seemed as though the blood, the writing, was already on the wall. When the young Catcher rolled an empty duffle bag to make a pillow before crawling in back, I snuck up so close he could've felt my breath on his collar. I gripped the rum's bottleneck. Not a sound until I brought the hollow glass down on his skull, shattering the bottle, slashing the young Catcher's head, sending him to his knees in the river of mud collecting in the narrow. But he did not fall unconscious. My strength was not as it once had been.

Spinning quickly, he wrapped his arms around my waist and dragged me to the soggy ground. I lay on my back, looking up at him in the crimson glow. Before he could bring his bony fist down on my face, I drove the jagged end of my bottle into his throat. His life drained down on me, filling my gaze along with the mud and rain;

my hat flung off, unable to protect me from the spray. The young Catcher stayed perched there for a moment until I felt his body go limp. It took all my power to toss him aside, sending a splash from the alley floor. His boots seemed too big for his feet as I dragged him behind the pile of garbage I hid behind the moment before. I had to act quickly. A badge and magnum were returned to my hip. Relief pulsed through my veins as I buckled his belt around my waist. His keys hung in the right rear door. I claimed them before shutting the back. The engine fired up, roaring magnificently in the narrow. Before I put the jeep in gear, I turned to the case file sitting on the passenger seat, flipped it open, and ran my fingers along the name: Ezra Atun.

GENERAL LAMENT
JULY 2190

Defecting was no easy task. My life was in greater peril as a deserter than it ever was as a soldier.

I don't omit the details of my twelve years in service to the armed forces lightly. It is not an error, a lapse in memory, or a desire to protect any reputation I might have once claimed. My twelve years as a soldier made a monster of me. There is no debating the issue. Any deplorable act your mind can conjure, I committed it twice, three times over, offending the gods in ways your mind can not imagine without having spent time in the field, in hell on earth, in a state of mind that is subhuman, which is what I became. The conscious exclusion of my role in the Union's atrocious eradication of our neighbours to the East can best be attributed to the fact that those who suffered by my hand need no record of the sins perpetrated against them. I will not depict them in words or any other means for the simple reality that the matter of this world I transformed into evil still lingers in the souls of so many, like a virus lurking in the ether for a host. It was, and remains, my greatest fear that some poor, disillusioned individual would find inspiration in the retelling of my wartime deeds. No. Those twelve years will not be recounted. Please do not let a lack of vivid detail persuade you into thinking I am a good person. Not knowing the treachery unleashed on my account and command does not change what I was, what I have cursed myself to be until the end of time, in memory or myth: an ogre, a demon, a leviathan of hatred, a plague on the island where I lived.

Were my husband and daughter avenged? Of course not. All I accomplished was a thorough stamping out of the woman they once loved. The wife and mother they knew died in the ash and sand along with them. It was not a phoenix that arose from the cinders left behind. I emerged a hideous pariah, a troll consumed by death's will: an eager, sharpened scythe ready to eviscerate anyone described as an enemy of the Union, an enemy of my husband, my daughter, my people. If only I had allowed for a moment's reflection like my battered body attempted to force upon me at the time. Twelve years were spent foolishly attempting to satiate my ravenous thirst for retaliation. I will give no more credence to that era. Too much time was lost killing in the name of something I didn't even slightly understand. That is why I began to write the *Exile Manifesto*. Once I'd wiped the blood from my face and opened my eyes to the truth staring at me head-on, it became my solemn duty to recount the Union motivations behind the war — not the war itself — which I only derived from over a decade in its service. I had to tell an entire generation of people scorned by the coastal raids why joining the Union armed forces was the antitheses to a solution for their troubles. If only I'd been handed the *Exile Manifesto* in my hospital bed as I mourned the loss of my loved ones, perhaps I could have walked an alternative path to fury. But I didn't dwell on that fantasy. I didn't blame ignorance for my atrocities. I wanted no forgiveness. My dream to spare others the horrors I committed was my lone, selfish realization. I did not come to it on my own. A vision for the future was provided to me by the kindness of a stranger. She first put the worm in my ear that I could begin my penance on Earth, that I could do good without ever being fully redeemed. It was the only thought that kept me from taking my own life, something I considered daily, and in many ways, attempted in empty gestures. She was the true leader of the Exodus. The manifesto wouldn't have spread across the Union without her guiding light. It took four years from the time I defected for our paths to cross, four years of despair. I don't know if she found me or if I simply stumbled across her, but I remember in great detail the beginning of our work together.

* * *

It was a small town somewhere deep in the interior — civilians were few, soldiers fewer — a pitstop really: a place between places. The odd transport truck passed along the packed-earth road. All was black besides the moon, the stars, and the dim bulb hanging over a single food stall lining the unpaved highway. I was nocturnal then. My fame had mostly faded from the general public. The military was not so quick to forget my betrayal, which was why I roamed while most others lay sleeping. I felt comfortable in the anonymity the night provided. Darkness was my great protector. Even the dull light over the yucca and plantains for sale hurt my eyes as I stepped into the faint glimmer's edge. A young farm boy was startled when he noticed me from behind the stall's wooden counter. It was my scent that first alerted him to my presence. He pulled a handkerchief from his back pocket and covered his mouth and nose. His eyes became watery.

"Closing up for the night, miss," he spoke through the thin cloth. He looked to be about twenty years old. His clothes were filthy. A patchy, scraggly beard covered his gaunt face. A few teeth were missing from his head — not enough to make him completely ugly.

"Drink," I blurted. My stomach was empty. My priorities in those days were obvious.

"Don't got anything to drink out here." He looked out from under the open hatch making a little awning over the stall. "Let's have a look at you. Step into the light some, so I can see you." The farm boy's priorities were becoming obvious as well.

I noticed a saddled horse with a small cart behind it standing in the dark beside the booth. Squinting, I moved forward slightly. The shakes were already creeping up on me. Quivering limbs were usually what awoke me from my drunken slumbers, reminding me to feed, to drink. Deep, heavy bags hung under the boy's eyes as he looked me up and down. My black mane with streaks of grey was bunched in dreaded, stinking clumps atop my head. My clothes were holey and rotting, revealing my discoloured skin to the bugs. I had no shoes on my feet. As sweat ran down my arms it made tiny rivers of clear liquid between the layers of dirt and dust caked on me like paint. My tattered pants were stained all over.

"You from around here? Don't get a lot of women on the supply routes."

My lips stayed sealed. I rubbed my arms as I shivered.

"You poor thing. Looks like you haven't had a bath in a dog's age. You hungry? Need a drink to warm you up?" His handkerchief covered his mouth, but I could have sworn he licked his lips.

I nodded at the prospect of a drink.

"I'm just packing up here." He went out the back of the vegetable stand and came around to my side. Lowering his handkerchief for a moment, my stench made him regret letting his nose guard down. He tied the bandana over the lower half of his face. "Please, hop in the cart. I'll take you back to my father's farm. We'll get you cleaned up, put a little food in your belly. How's that sound?"

"Soldiers?"

"You speak English?" He paused, looking me up and down again, sizing me up, wondering if I was worth the hassle. I was harsh on the nose. The eyes were a different story. "No. Don't worry, beautiful. No soldiers. My father runs a Union farm. He's a powerful man. There's more food and drink than you can imagine. But my father doesn't allow visitors. He can't know you're there."

The thought of a drink was the real motivation behind my decision to accept the invitation. Even the horse seemed to turn its nose up at my disgusting odour as I approached.

"Can't make a sound when we get there," said the boy as he stacked wooden crates of produce around me. "Promise?"

With one hand on my heart and the other in the air, I made my vow. The only light for kilometres went dead when he unscrewed the bulb and locked the stall. He mounted the steed, and we set off into the seemingly endless night. Only by the light of the pale moon could I make out the silhouette of a lone, stubby mountain a few kilometres toward the horizon. Eyes to the distance, I reached into a crate holding what felt like avocados. I tossed the rinds along the flat land and helped myself to a few. The boy looked back in my direction, and he smiled at my cheeks full of avocado.

"See that little light up ahead?" he asked, pointing to an orange speck in the short mountain's heart. "The farmhands say a mystic lives up there. My Pop lets her come down and preach to the workers every now and then. They think she's got powers. I don't buy it. Only power around here is the Union, so far as I'm concerned."

We ambled along slowly for a little over an hour. Stars passed overhead as the boy spoke aimlessly, and I devoured anything within reach. I would have tossed him off his horse and taken the cart if the crates had booze instead of fruits and vegetables. There wasn't a sound in the air besides the horseshoes stepping on the odd stone. The cart's rubber tires were silent on the mostly smooth terrain. My feet were grateful for the break.

"Shhh," the boy put a finger to his bandana when he turned to make the noise. He leapt swiftly from his mount, coming back to the cart, a folded blanket in his hand. "Coming up on the farm now. Get down. Silent. Like you promised."

Nothing aside from the occasional burp escaped my lips along the way. Only once the boy warned me did I notice the great, wide shadow at the foot of the stout mountain ahead. The fields seemed a consistent height, stretching out as far as I could see in either direction. Razor wire glinted in the soft, silver moonshine. The menacing blades were taut above a twenty-foot fence bordering the farmland. Alarm bells started ringing in my head, but I was in the middle of nowhere, hadn't eaten in days, and might not make it back across the flatlands before sunup. The boy was right, Union farmers were powerful people, but their power lay in their trade, not their weaponry.

My impulse to flee abated when the boy said:

"We'll get you a drink in a minute."

I ducked my head below the cart's lip. All went black when the blanket was tossed over me and the produce. The horse's footsteps began again, and the cart rolled forward. For years in the service, I lived off the supplies shipped to the front lines from places like that farm. Never before had I set eyes on one, let alone set foot on the fertile soil.

We came to an abrupt halt.

"Evening, sir." The boy said aloud. I couldn't see who the greeting was directed toward. Then I heard the unmistakable sound of military-issued boots stomping in the dirt.

"How'd you do today, Samuel?" Asked the voice connected to the boots.

"You know how it is. Most truckers only stop at the stall for cigarettes and a piss. They can get all the grub they want in Los Muelles when they get there," said the farm boy, Samuel.

"You ever tempted to catch a ride with one of 'em?" The guard baited him.

"No. I like it out here. Nice and quiet. It'd be nice to a see a lady once in a while though."

"What's that smell?"

"I guess ol' Lightning here needs a bath." The horse neighed when Samuel pat the beast. I knew full well the guard was referring to me.

"Get that thing out of here."

"Yes, sir."

The crackling of a radio was audible over the crickets.

"Samuel's coming in."

"Thank you, sir. Have a good evening."

The guard didn't respond. I heard his boots again as he stepped away, a few high-pitched beeps, a loud latch, and hinges screeching. My body lurched forward against the crates when the horse pulled forward. The hinges screeched again, a loud latch immediately after. Another crackling on the radio: "Samuel's clear. Gate secured."

The cart was still for a long while. Unfamiliar sounds and smells drifted in and out as I tried to orient myself. Soft candlelight surrounded me when the blanket was finally pulled back slowly from over my head.

"Sorry about that," Samuel whispered. "Here you go."

He handed me a mason jar full of clear liquid. I unscrewed the top and guzzled what smelled like paint thinner, which I admittedly huffed from time to time when other means to kill brain cells weren't close at hand.

"Easy." He snatched the glass from my hand. "That's strong stuff."

Not strong enough, junior.

Waiting for the booze to do its work, steady my hand, quiet the screams, I looked around to where I'd been taken. The cart was parked in the middle of a small barn. Wax candles were placed sparingly around the space. Samuel unsaddled the horse and wrapped its lead around a post. A small fire burned just outside the doorway, barely wide enough for the cart to pass through. The auburn light spilled onto the crops beyond. Fires were a luxury I couldn't afford in exile. Steam rose off a large bucket hanging from a spit over the flames. A tin trough sat on a patch of hay by the horse's stall. Samuel motioned for me to join him by the tub. He placed the jar next to it like a lure.

"Were those soldiers at the gate?" My voice was grave.

"Shh," he spat softly. "She speaks again," he added, under his breath. "Don't worry, we're safe so long as no one hears us. I'll take you back to the stand in the morning."

It was foolish for me to venture into a Union snare so carelessly. Four years spent mostly in solitude had softened me for the promise of food, drink, and a wash. I got out of the cart, brushing past Samuel on my way to the barn door, peering out to discover endless field in one direction and a guarded gate when I turned my head.

"What the hell are you doing?" Samuel whispered furiously, tugging my arm to rip me from the doorway.

"You said no soldiers."

"You don't have to worry about them. They're not soldiers. They're security guards. They work for my father."

"They work for the Union."

"Keep your voice down." The grip he had on my arm softened. He ran his fingers along my filthy skin. "You're here for the night, like it or not. Only way through those gates is in my cart come morning." The farm boy's expression softened. He wasn't bad looking. It'd been a while since I'd satisfied any carnal desires. I didn't deserve satisfaction. I hated myself too much for it, but it seemed the only way out the gate was to let him in mine, so why deny myself a little pleasure amidst all the pain?

"Pour that warm water in the tub," I breathed the words. "First you're going to wash my clothes. Then you're going to give me a bath. And when are you going to take me back to the stand?"

"At first light, ma'am."

"That's right." I pulled him by the collar to bring his ear to my mouth. "Or else I'll cut your goddamn throat." I hissed.

The farm boy stayed true to his word. Before daybreak, he packed crates around me in the wooden cart. I took care to be better hidden this time around. He looked down on me before tossing the blanket across my body. There was no more need for the bandana over his mouth and nose. He used the horse's brush to untangle my hair the night before. It felt good to be beautiful in his eyes. He wasn't bad looking. Then all went dark beneath the fabric.

"Going to have a good day today, Samuel?" Asked the guard.

"It's already a good day, sir."

"Got any smokes back there?"

Samuel paused.

"Of course, you do." The soldier's boots were heavy on the dirt. I could hear him breathing just above me. Suddenly a burst of light filled the cart. A corner of the blanket was tossed aside. Greasy, tobacco-stained fingers reached into a crate full of hand-rolled cigarettes. The blanket blocked out the light yet again. "Thanks," said the soldier. I heard him strike a match. The smell of burnt paper wafted through the air. The radio, the latch, the screeching hinges. "Samuel's out. Gate secured." And the gentle ride over flat land began again.

It grew hot as the sun rose over the cart and dark blanket. The warmth and swaying cart lulled me to sleep after a night spent satisfying my hunger and my lust. Samuel fucked like so many of the young soldiers I enjoyed throughout my reign as General, mistaking pace for rhythm. A small smile came to my face for the first time in years, thanks mostly to being clean, well-fed, and still drunk. I dozed in back the cart. My nocturnal schedule knocked me out cold.

Comfort betrayed me. When I awoke, the cart was still moving. It couldn't have been a short nap for all the stiffness in my joints when I opened my eyes. There was no way we were still on our way to the food stall. I maneuvered my head just above the cart's lip and folded back the blanket slightly to discover there was no light in the sky, nothing but the white orb, the speckling of stars. Horseshoes clinked against stone yet again. Night had returned. I tossed the blanket off me completely, sitting up in the cart to see Samuel back in the saddle. He had us riding toward the farm and the stout mountain again. The faint, golden-brown light in the centre of its portly silhouette confirmed as much.

"What the fuck is going on?" I yelled at the farm boy.

"I didn't wake you. It's alright, you'll be my secret. I'll keep you," he spoke from his saddle, over his shoulder.

We weren't moving fast enough to keep me from getting to my feet. I stood up and tossed my legs over the side of the cart. The small stones scattered about the ground were no match for my callused feet.

"Woah," Samuel called to stop Lightning in her tracks. "Where do you think you're going?"

I didn't reply, sending long strides back into the night to catch up to my escaping exile. The farm boy dismounted and ran up behind me.

"Stop." He grabbed my arm, I shoved it away. "I shouldn't have brought you out this morning. My father has his girls. He'll let me keep one." Samuel wrapped his arms around my waist and lifted me off my feet, carrying me back toward the cart.

Guilt and excitement swirled into one as I was given the excuse to unleash violence upon a Union man. I squirmed up high enough to free myself enough to throw my elbow square into the farm boy's jaw. He dropped me, quickly approached, and was greeted by a blow to his diaphragm, which folded him over in want for oxygen. His head lowered to my waistline. I interlocked my hands behind his head and pulled down as I drove my knee square into his nose.

Lightning stirred from all the commotion. I stepped over Samuel's body on my way to the horse. The farm boy wasn't quite unconscious, and he was trying unsuccessfully to get to his feet. All his strength was gone. I detached the cart from Lightning's saddle, knowing I'd be faster without dragging the food, and I'd just eaten more than I consumed in an average week.

I afforded myself yet another pleasure I vowed to deny myself after deserting when I mounted Lightning. We went dashing into the night. Whether surfing or riding: wielding nature's power makes titans of mortals. But for all the dominion I assumed to be mine, Lightning immediately took command. She ignored my tugging on the reins and my heels dug into her sides. A route was in her veins, and there was nothing I was going to do to stop her. Her course was set. She sped toward the tubby mountain, toward the farm. Just as I considered leaping from off her back, I heard a rifle ring out behind me. Where did that farm boy bastard get a rifle? It must have been stashed somewhere on that goddamn cart. I was a moving target in the dark, there was no chance he'd get me, and I could still beat him to the hills on foot. The winds were with me until my curse caught up with me. Samuel's second bullet caught me square in the right butt-cheek, the same cheek he'd had his hands all over the night before. There was no choice but to stay with Lightning and hope to the gods I could keep her from returning to the farm. Dying didn't scare me, but I'd be damned if I was going to swing from a Union noose. No farm guard was going to claim the price on my head. No fucking way. Another gunshot bellowed across the open plain. This time the farm boy's luck ran out. He fired a fourth time, hitting nothing but the cool evening air.

Lightning surprised me as she began to veer from the ample fields. She wasn't headed back to her Union captors. She was headed for the mountain, so I let her lead the way. Each gallop sent agony shooting up my back and down my leg. My body was littered with scars from bullet wounds, cigarette burns, and countless gashes. Years weakened my threshold for the throbbing damage brought on by the gun. I struggled to keep conscious, to keep my grip on the reins tight. My chest lowered to the firm saddle and robust shoulders supporting Lightning's neck. She barreled into the night, keeping her nose pointed toward the amber blot on the horizon. All my resistance to passing out was futile. I was losing blood at a troubling rate. Most of my internal reserves were rotted in alcohol. Each blink lasted longer than the next until my gaze could no longer stay fixed on the tawny glimmer beckoning Lightning.

The sun burned my eyes when they finally split open. Lightning was still, drinking calmly from a clay bowl between her front hooves. Every muscle in my body ached. I could hardly move, straining my neck with all my strength to look out over the vast fields spread out on the flatlands below. The green crops were separated from the otherwise dry earth in sharp, precise edges. My breathing was off pace with Lightning's hefty inhales. When I tried to see what lay on the other side of the horse's well-built frame, gravity yanked me from the saddle onto the rocks scattered in the dirt. It didn't seem as if I'd been followed or tracked, but I still kept myself from moaning as I twisted amidst the dust in case I was within earshot of any unfriendly company.

Raising my cheek from the pebbles, I heard growling coming from the gaping hole in the mountainside. As if a dragon's yawning jaws extended out to take me in its fiery throat, a blood-orange cave encircled my body from above. A low rumble stirred deep inside the earthen hall, growing louder as my fear awoke my adrenaline to ensure I wouldn't blackout again. The thunderous growl warned that this place harboured some ghastly creature deep within. Was I fleeing the Union noose for the waiting jaws of some mythic living thing? All I could do was tilt my head and stare until a figure materialized in the luminous doorway to the belly of the beast. She emerged from the radiant depths, strolling gracefully along the smouldering tongue rolling out from the squat mountain, which didn't seem so short from my new perspective.

The woman stared deep into my eyes when I looked up from her immaculate feet. She came into focus, as if nothing at all materialized into a radiant being. The stranger held a bottle of pale brown rum. A drowning bee writhed in the bottom. Pouring the last bit of liquid and the little buzzing insect into her mouth, she chewed and swallowed. I could have sworn I heard it pop as loud as Samuel's rifle when he blew a chunk from my ass. She put the empty glass in the dirt and ran her hand gently along the horse's neck before reaching into Lightning's saddlebag to withdraw a mason jar of white rum. Her silky smooth, brunette hair fell over her face as she bent down to put the open lid to my lips. A sun-kissed, dainty finger tucked the loose strands falling down over her eyes behind her ear, revealing playful, green eyes and a gentle smile. White lightning spilled from the side of my mouth when I wolfed down the liquid. Hoarse, burning coughs rose from my chest and escaped my throat. The stranger seemed unconcerned while the spirit leaked onto the ground. She took my hand in hers, somehow lifting me from the dirt without the slightest hint of effort. I put all my weight on her. I could not stand by my own strength.

"Come with me," her voice echoed in my head. I could have sworn her lips hadn't moved.

Hand-in-hand, she carried my burdensome load through the threshold. The growls coming out from the tunnel reverberated off the walls surrounding me. For all the warning signs, I was no longer afraid. An elemental trust told me this person meant me no harm, told me that even if I were about to meet my end, it would be in a manner most agreeable. It was when we passed a small, petrol-run generator that I laughed at myself for all the images of dragons my imagination conjured up in my dread. The engine ran loudly just beyond the main chamber of my saviour's hollow. It wasn't the primitive dwelling I'd expected from a shelter carved out of the swollen earth. My personal condition put me in no position to judge any standard of living, but I was amazed at the beauty that greeted me. Silver layers of foil lined the curved walls, which filled the dome with shimmering light while trapping the warmth of the burning coals heaped in a small pile at the centre of the cave. She welcomed me to lay on a mat made of hay beside the fire. To this day, I don't know why I so docilely accepted her invitation. That was until she ripped open the backside of my pants.

"Squirm some more and I'll stick this hot knife in all three holes staring up at me," she uttered, somehow tender and calm despite the threat. The stranger placed a firm hand on my lower back, her strength amazed me as she kept me in place without changing her reassuring expression.

"I can't stay here. I'm in trouble."

"Yes, yes. You're in exile, honey. The Union wants your head on a pike, but you'll only be doing them a favour going back out there with a slug in your ass to slow you. You'd be dead as a doornail if Lightning hadn't brought you here."

I said nothing more. Did she know who I was?

"The farm guards won't risk leaving their posts. The field hands grow restless and already outnumber them. *If* they send scouts, they'll have to come from Los Muelles. We have time. I visit the field hands on Sundays. They don't miss a beat on the farm; one of the few benefits of being invisible to their masters." The witch held a blade to the small mound of glowing embers. "We'll know in a few days if Samuel has raised the alarm. No doubt there will be questions about the gunshots. That farm boy fears his father, though. I'm sure the truth rests with you alone now. A curse you're familiar with, eh?"

Turning in an attempt to read her expression, her meaning, she winked at me, extending a small stick toward my mouth.

"Bite. We need you quiet for the time being."

Just as I clenched my teeth onto the wood, I smelled, heard, and felt the searing pain on my ass as the stranger dug the red-hot blade into my flank to remove the bullet. No sounds escaped my lips. I relished the pain. It was well-deserved.

What once seemed a grotesque and terrifying growl became a comforting, welcoming purr. The small generator sat far enough outside the cave's main chamber to lull me in its humming. I soon learned the lone machine in the humble dwelling powered a radio scanner, picking up signals between soldiers, superiors, and Catchers operating in and around Los Muelles. No wonder the farmhands shrouded the stranger's knowledge in myth and lore. She could predict whatever came over the wire. The scattered reports and discussions were turned down to the volume of low whispers when my host and nurse returned from the small tunnel.

"Samuel couldn't have known who you are," her smile was reassuring as she sat cross-legged beside me.

"Who are you?"

"My followers call me Lou. We're safe for tonight. Rest dear."

There was a lot of "we" talk from the woman, but with my bare ass stitched, warm coals, fruits, vegetables, and a half-full mason jar close by, my fears about the stranger and my identity were quelled. Bullet removed, horse at the ready outside, I knew I could take her down if need be. I'd faced much worse odds and came out unscathed. Besides, she was a stunning creature, surrounded by an aura that assured me that my best interests motivated her. Fellow outcasts were always the best at keeping secrets.

By the time night returned, and I was at my most alert and sociable, we began to interact with an ease I'd not felt since splaying my toes in the sand on the beaches I once called home. Drunkenness certainly didn't hurt in greasing the gears of conversation either. We both seemed loose, in a hurry, in a muted relief to be alone together as exiles.

"So, who do you seem so sure I am?" I didn't pose the question with aggression or suspicion. It simply came time to clear the air when I was offered a steaming bowl of meticulously prepared snake meat soup to go with the poured spirits.

"That's a question for the mirror, General," Lou said, smiling from the corner of her mouth, at once presenting a riddle and tipping her hand.

"And where do you stand on my decision to desert if that is in fact who I am? Is the General in the presence of a rebel, or can I expect to be throttled in my sleep?"

"I'm in exile just like you. I'm someone who believes everyone's life is their own, but you know better than to let vague answers fly. I've been waiting for you to usher in the new era. The Union's time is up. To put it plainly, General: I'm on your side."

"There's no General here."

"Your rank is the same. Those who follow you and your direction have simply changed. You are as god made you, General. I have spent most my life waiting for such a conductor to channel the plight of my people into action. They have looked to me far too long to do something as I've watched helpless from this cave. You've changed all that."

"Why do they look to you?"

"I was one of them, an orphan who came to them in a hurricane long before the war. I don't remember any of it aside from the visions that return to me in my sleep. They were so sure the weather foretold their doom. They were preparing for their end, their final judgement, but then I arrived, and all were spared. I was just a girl with no memory of my life before. There was no explanation I could give, so they spoke for me. All I wanted was a place to stay, to call my home. Those prisoners in the farm below clothed me, fed me, raised me. When Union came — gathering them up in trucks to fight or farm — lives were sacrificed in hiding me. They all seemed so certain that if only I could survive, they would one day be free again. I had nowhere else to go, so I followed them here. Samuel's father is a believer now too. Even he knows I will deliver our people from the Union's grasp. I've dedicated my life to repaying their kindness, their faith. They will live to see their trust in me rewarded. Now I am not alone. I have the powerful General to aid me."

"What makes you think I'm that terrible monster?"

"You arrived in the midst of a great storm, just like me. It was not made of clouds and rain, it was made by the Union. I've been following any account of you through the radio that I could find. The airwaves are full of stories about your exile. There's still a pretty price on your head. You don't know your own power, the sway you still hold on this nation. Now I've found you to join your rightful side. I am your chance, General. And you, mine. Together we can live up to the power that's been granted us."

My role in the Exodus was a decision made beyond my will. Deserting was certainly my choice, one made with haste when I learned the foundation of my military service was built on a lie. It was reinforced with deceit and betrayal, which pushed me to erect a monument to the warlords, built on the bodies slain in the twelve years I spent killing in the Union's name. As soon as I learned the truth, I fled. That much credit in the Exodus is mine, but if Lou had not cast her net into the sea of anguish in which I drowned, the hordes of men, women, and everyone in between, who I showed the way, would have never made the journey to the East Caribbean Republic to the truth about the Union. The *Exile Manifesto* came gradually. Lou eased me into the role she conjured up in her cave over the years, using the desperate ears from the farm below already turned to her lips to hear what we discussed that very first night together.

"There must be a way to get East, to penetrate the wall. I've seen it in my dreams: where I first saw you. You were once the leader of the entire armed forces. Even the most enlightening dream can't replace what you must know." The coals reflected off the foil walls and shimmered across her soft skin as she spoke. It made my soul glad to sit in the stubby mountain's heart, the auburn jewel that so intrigued me the night before.

If I were being entirely honest with myself at the time, Lou's proposal would have been quickly recognized as my innermost shameful fantasy. The possibility that I might still harbour the influence to make changes for the better was under constant assault from alcohol. The crystal taking the country by storm never appealed to me in the same way as my beloved booze. To think that there was some mechanism I had the power to set in motion to even slightly correct the fallout of my past was more hope than I allowed myself to enjoy. The military already had me believe in false idols. Being the master of disaster and the example of peace in one lifetime was like pulling double duty as an arsonist and firefighter. Whatever judgement awaited me in the afterlife would do little justice to those living in the wreckage of my wake.

Again, if totally truthful, I was petrified at the thought of getting it all wrong for the thousandth time. I tried to tell myself that mistakes were only lessons I refused to acknowledge. Saying as much to my victims, their families, their friends, and their lovers could never be enough. Apologizing for all the Eastern lives I had claimed condemned me to live out the rest of my days in the West. Mercy from my former enemy was more than I could bear. Even the possibility that I might be welcome in my repentance brought suicidal thoughts rushing in. No. The Union made a destroyer from a fishmonger. My gift from the gods was determined. Lou provided a new purpose for such flairs. The Union would be undone brick by brick, soul by soul. I knew to demolish the West by extracting the parts of its sum. A mosaic of treachery was about to be unmade, dispersed by my hand under two conditions: "No killing," I almost screamed the words at Lou as I lay perched on my elbows, my ass still bare and raised.

"You will not be asked to claim another life."

"And I will never set foot across the Eastern border again. Not until the Union is bled dry, sinks into the Caribbean, or is crushed in the vice of the continents will I allow myself to partake in whatever new world comes next.

"That means you'll die here, General."

"So be it."

My military acumen immediately served me well when Lou and I plotted the first in what would become a rich jailbreak tradition. How better to grind a large-scale invasion to a halt? Starve out the invaders. The farm below the mountain set the stage for the hush-hush networks I would beat out from West to East with Lou and countless other brave exiles. We planned and executed the escape for those few dozen farmhands. Word that there was a pilgrimage to a new world in the East began to spread. The news traveled at a pace much too slow for Lou. She had waited years in a cave for the revolution to begin. She observed and underwent the anguish, dread, and hopelessness of her people on some mystifying wavelength. Lou urged me to write every day amidst our schemes and perilous undertakings. My companion insisted the Exodus needed to become an idea, one that had no want for the General, which killed the dependence on my life with every stroke of the pen, reducing my significance to wind-blown pages. It was imperative that others learn to free themselves despite my craving to be their liberator. All they needed was a map and a clear night sky to read the stars in their darkest hours.

<u>EZRA ATUN</u>
MARCH 2192

Calluses protected my hands and fingers from the ceaseless rigors of production. Every three minutes on the factory floor, an eighty-pound bar of lead was loaded into a hydraulic press where the metal was compressed in a die. The lead was hardened and churned out in spools of dense wire. High-caliber bullets were made using the thickest lines on the reel. Copper alloy jackets were cut by the second, lubricated with soap, and filled with lead. No room for error or air pockets were tolerated. Performance and accuracy in the field were paramount. The war would never be won without straight-shooting rounds. I averaged three-thousand bullets per day on the factory line.

* * *

Multicoloured fireworks burst across the sky as if waging war upon the moon. I was envious of the flatlands beneath, seemingly undisturbed and never-ending beyond the fences.

There was my friend — dancing in the cage — drunk to ease the apparent end to his youth's liberty. Old, country songs about god and nation fanned the flaming bonfire surrounded by blonde, brunette, redhead, and black-haired youths partying under a big, dark, starry sky. The draft thinned the crowds at each celebration shared by those of us in the ghetto.

"Drink?"

I lifted my palm to the constellations above, and Cash Desear put a mason jar in my hand as he took a seat in the plaid lawn chair on the dusty earth next to me. We clinked our jars, tipped back our heads, closed our eyes, and savoured the burn, feeling no fuller, no drunker. A loud bark from the mutt chained up outside our casita spooked Cash. He spilt some rum down his chin when he sprang forward in his chair.

"What's that about?" Cash asked, referring to the mongrel.

"Finally cornered him in the coup this morning. He must have dug under the fence," I said. "He's cost us four chickens in as many weeks."

Cash kept a wary eye on the dog. Into the jar once more and another melancholy cheer. In the distance was the main event: Private Mick Tatum of the West Caribbean Union prepared for deployment the following day. He was filled with as much chemical vice as the gods allow before pulling the chord.

"He'll be dead before the week's out," I said, watching.

"Guys like Mick thrive in chaos," Cash came back at me in a hurry, his stare forward and steady. "He's been at war with himself so long, no one else with a gun's gonna get him." Putting his jar in the dirt, Cash moved on to rolling a joint.

"I'm not counting on anyone coming back anymore."

"Keep that shit to yourself for now, man. It's a going away party." My friend's eyes went from rolling leaf to roaring fire, never meeting my eyes. "And I'm trying to tell you: people like Mick weren't meant for life in the ghetto. Some people are just survivors.

They don't move unless death's chasing." Cash's affections for Mick were obvious, but years spent hiding his fondness dulled the signs.

"So we're not living unless we're dodging bullets?" I was being facetious, but why not ask a wise, young drunk about love and war in the midst of a good binge?

"How long you known me?" He wet his lips and dragged his tongue along the thin leaf cradling the coarsely ground herb. "You know that's not what I'm saying. I just mean that not everyone wants peace. Hell, boredom might claim more lives than the enemy."

"I wish they'd all just devour each other and leave the rest of us out of it." I put my jar in the dirt at my side.

"Amen, man, but that's not the way things are. It's fight or flight times we live in. We stay here much longer and the decision is going to be made for us."

"How about deciding to smoke that?" I pointed to the crafted joint.

"There's the Ezra I know and love."

We rose and strolled toward the flames to spark our high, crackling along the dusty earth like a trail of gunpowder igniting its way to the powder keg. Dirt was kicked up in the air by all the dancing feet. It rose up with the smoke, swirling faster than the thoughts churning round in my mind. Any of their names could have been called, mine too, just the same.

Throwing his arms around his pregnant wife, Mick kissed Carmen with more tongue than love as she tried to steady his imbalance. The civil ceremony was a point of pride for them, considering all the years we spent without papers. From his open-mouth kiss, Mick turned his gaping mouth to the stars and poured our handcrafted rum down his throat. Pale blue dots were scattered above him in their organized chaos.

"They'll name stars after me by the time I'm done over there," Mick raged at the sky.

"Where they sending you?" Cash asked before a swig from the same jar. He relished putting his lips to where Mick's had just been. Mick shrugged his powerful shoulders.

"Ask the Dog Catcher over there."

Cash and I turned toward our lawn chairs in the dirt a dozen metres away. Neither of us noticed the man who'd been just over our shoulders. He leaned against a large, white jeep that managed to camouflage in the night just beyond the fence. It reflected the dancing shadows and lively flames of the party across its bulky body and snout-like hood.

He wore a blood-red shirt tucked into ink-black pants where a golden badge — turned amber in the firelight — sat on his belt, which also held his spare ammunition and holstered magnum. His eyes seemed to glow as the blazing bonfire portrayed itself in each frame of his sunglasses. Cash gave him the finger and wet the dry earth with his spit. The Dog Catcher tipped the brim of his Stetson hat like a devil in the dust.

For all the stars and gods filling the night sky, none seemed to pay us any mind. We raised our fires high. We were the only sound or light as far as the eye could see across the flat, parched earth. The rippling mountains on the horizon were merely silhouettes against the wispy Milky Way beyond. We didn't have our backs to the wall. We remained a herd of sheep with coyotes ever-circling. I observed the scarlet, button-up shirt on the evil spirit beyond the fence. The black ridge of his lid looked like horns in the night. All the revelry at my back sent marigold specks swirling around his figure. It seemed he could have appeared with the blustering soil as if he had no need for his government-issued, egg-white ride. His large, oval shades gave him a menacing, sandstone stare. I couldn't take my eyes away. Evil finds a way to be witnessed.

Another shade of wickedness caught my attention when the all-too-rare sound of the fence screeching open filled my ears. Every head across the ghetto turned in reverence to the uncommon noise. It was hard not to notice The Kid's arrival. He too seemed to appear from the churning, dirty wind. The rusty wheelbarrow he pushed looked like a reclaimed chariot awaiting horses. He stopped at the gate to glad-hand the guards, offering each of them their pick from the contents heaped in the deep tray of his wheelbarrow. None of them paid for their packages. They offered a strong-handed frisk in return. He saluted them as they completed their thorough search of his person. A book was removed from his breast pocket and returned without concern. The narcotics The Kid gifted the men and women in uniform were enough to gain entry to sell his goods, but he would be shot dead on the spot if they discovered weapons.

An oversized West Caribbean Union uniform hung off The Kid's slender shoulders. The shirt was rolled up at the sleeves and open down the middle to display his stick and poke tattoos. His pants were baggy around his thighs and hemmed at the bottoms to keep from dragging across the ground. A few of his thick, black dreadlocks fell over one side of his face. The rest were pulled back and tied behind his head. Cash caught The Kid in his gaze and immediately gravitated toward his presence. He drifted from our group without a word.

"Like a moth to the flame," Carmen said, watching Cash wander off. "He still owe you money from the last time?"

"There's only so much you can buy at commissary." My eyes followed him as he approached The Kid and his wheelbarrow. A small group began to gather round.

"I think they call that enabling."

"You're one to talk," I motioned to Mick who was stumbling into small crowds, spilling rich, amber rum from the mason jar in his hand.

"We can't help who we love."

"Nope."

"You loved Cash's *sister*. You don't owe *him* anything."

"Family is family."

"Guess we don't got much more than that out here, huh?" Carmen fought off tears.

I wrapped an arm around her shoulder. Carmen laid her head on my collar. We looked upon the blazing fire to save her an audience as she cried. Cash stood well beyond the flames. His shape became distorted in the heat waves emanating above the pyre. The neckline of my shirt became damp and warm with Carmen's tears. I noticed The Kid fix his attention on me as Cash flapped his lips quickly. Keeping his eyes on me, The Kid handed Cash a small parcel wrapped in foil. Cash stuffed the crystal in his pocket — the burden of addiction lightened slightly for the moment —and he waved me over. Carmen took notice too.

"Go on," she said. "It's a party. There'll be plenty of time for tears tomorrow." She wiped her eyes and feigned a smile.

I squeezed her close, attempted a reassuring grin, and sauntered toward my friend and his pusher. My stomach tightened as I approached them. If I was an enabler, The Kid was the architect of Cash's illness. It was difficult to veil my distaste for him as a result.

"Good to see you, Ezra." The Kid had to speak up to me as he stood about shoulder high. Even he didn't know his age, but I guessed him to be about seventeen.

"Wish I could say the same, Kid." I took a slug from my mason jar.

"Why you always gotta be so mean?" The Kid asked. Cash awkwardly backed away into the darkness with his hands in his pockets. A small line of desperate ghetto citizens clamored at the contents in the wheelbarrow's bed. The Kid collected coins for the letters, trinkets, and drugs he dispersed. He didn't look me in the eye as he tended to his business.

"You and your cooks have made a small fortune killing my friend with that shit."

"We're on the same side, Ezra."

"How's that?"

"We're rebels."

"I'm no rebel. I live in a cage."

"But your words escape the fence." The Kid leaned in close as he spoke. "I've read your journals. Cash shared a few. He's a good man. Better than you think." The Kid pushed aside some of the hands emptying the wheelbarrow. "Enough! That's everything. I'll be back soon," he yelled over the commotion. Respect for the boy was apparent. The crowd dispersed quickly, leaving a lone, small package in the rusted metal. "Moving crystal is how I feed my people. A small package here and there for the guards, and I can do some good in the ghettos too. I hate the Union just the same as you."

"Is that why you wear a Union uniform?"

"Got it off a meth-head soldier. My product is my weapon. You fight with your words."

"I don't do anything with my words." I was taken off guard. It was news to me that anyone other than my closest friend had read my scribbling. I feared the trouble that might find me if those pages got into the wrong hands.

"We'll never have peace as long as the Union stands." The Kid handed me the small package remaining in the corroded tray. "I hear commissary is light on paper and pencils." I peeked inside the parcel. Firelight fell on the hosta leaf wrapped around the stack of papers bound by a string that The Kid gifted me. "The General says every rebellion starts with the words of a slave. It's already begun, but we could still use you."

"Screw the General. I don't want anything to do with soldiers." I tried to force the writing utensils back into the pusher's hands. Just as The Kid was about to continue his appeal, the guards called out his name, informing him his short welcome had expired.

"I have to go." He gripped the handles of the wheelbarrow and lifted the legs from the dirt. "Remember what I say: keep writing. We're on the same side. I'm sorry about Cash, but I don't have the heart to deny the desperate the few pleasures left in the West. Be well, Ezra." The Kid nodded, pivoted on the deflated wheel of his chariot, and walked out the gates.

* * *

The dog's crazed barking shook me from my slumber. It tugged at its chain, merely choking it all the more. Damn mutt was like Sisyphus, fighting gravity for lack of anything else to do. Of course, the chain could have, one day, broken.

My cheek and head felt like a grid as I ran my hand over the short stubble along my jawline. The grid on my face came from sleeping face down in the hammock on the porch during the few hours between the party's climax and the blue hue of the morning. The rambling land around my shared, tin-roof casita had the look of a battlefield. Bodies were spread throughout the dirt, incapacitated from over-consumption, run into the ground by the weight of mortality looming so heavily over the evening's festivities. Survivors stood around small fires as ash from the dying bonfire blew past.

Through a diamond space in the woven hammock, I saw the Catcher and his jeep upside down with the tires pressed to the red earth sky. I groaned and rolled over in the mesh bed to turn the world right-side-up once again. The hangover made the horizon rock back and forth until I could focus on the Catcher's mirrored glasses staring back at me.

It was when I walked into the casita and saw Carmen and Mick sitting naked on my bed, looking at the drawing on my ammunition-crate nightstand, that I realized why the Catcher loomed over my home like death's shadow. Without delivering Mick to the ships, there would be no pay.

The bunk that Cash and I managed to sever in two was only a little nicer than the bunks in the casita a few doors down. I was too deep in my slumber to hear Mick and Carmen's farewell thumps from the hammock outside. Giving them my bed was the least I could do.

"This is a great sketch of her," Carmen said. I passed the foot of my rotting bedframe. Looking at Vallah's picture was reserved for nights of self-loathing.

I said nothing. My bare feet dragged along our dirty, concrete floor as I went to the drape dividing Cash's side from mine. Just as I raised a bent finger to knock on the wall where the old bedsheet hung, a small, dark-haired, caramel-skinned guy slithered past me without clothes, without eye contact, on the way to the compost toilet. He wore nothing, exposing the myriad of red dots in his thighs that he seemed unconcerned with hiding.

"Cash. Mick's leaving soon." I peeked around the curtain. It seemed a distant place from the rest of my home. Stacked cardboard boxes from the commissary were the best attempts at furniture. Plastic wrappers, candles, and other paraphernalia covered the floor and parts of the foam pad that Cash slept on in the corner.

"You awake?" I called at full volume. The naked gentleman returned from his audible piss through the wood seat over the hole in the floor and again eked past me without a word or glance before closing the discoloured curtain behind him.

Carmen's eyes were without tears as Mick enveloped her and their due baby just outside the casita. A crowd was gathered around. Many had just come from the party. Some remained in their drunken slumbers elsewhere, but the friends Mick had known better than his departed siblings or deceased parents surrounded him with our love. Cash couldn't bear the heartbreak of the farewell.

"You're coming back to me and this baby. I don't care if this war lasts a thousand years. You better come back. I'll be here, waiting." Carmen kissed the father of her unborn child one last time before he climbed up into the open, steel-barred double doors of the white, four-wheeled beast driven by the Catcher. The gun-toting man closed the doors and secured the lock.

"You're a motherless piece of shit," Carmen said.

The Catcher tipped the brim of his Stetson hat yet again.

* * *

My shift ended; it was marked by the clanging bell. The sun set over the end of the assembly line at the far end of the factory. I had watched it rise in the frame of the enormous sliding steel doors at the opposite end of the line that morning. We worked as if the sun went up and down by the will of our toils. I wasn't sure how to feel about that. Twelve hours of darkness before I would continue the loop from bed to my place in line yet again. That wasn't so bad. I was on my way to a simple meal at the dining hall, then I was free to drink myself silly under the stars if I cared to. It occurred to me to do just that. The Kid's paper and pencils wouldn't go to waste. Cash and I crossed paths in the narrow spaces between the casitas. Purple light striped Cash's otherwise colourless face through the slats of the neighbouring cabin.

"Lucky, bastard," I said to Cash in hopes of lifting his eyes from his dragging feet. "Thermometer in the factory said thirty-two degrees. Should be a cool one for the overnights once the rain breaks this heat. Clouds are rolling in." A commissary cigarette hung from Cash's pale lips while I talked at him.

"Guess so," Cash spoke with his eyes turned to the pastel fluff above. He stood, staring up. The ghetto wasn't entirely bankrupt of beauty and Cash was the perfect example. If I could paint, he would have made for an excellent subject. Smoke spilled from the open half of his mouth and rose above the shacks, drifting toward the pale moon, revealing its face in the darkening sky. I couldn't help but catch glimpses of Vallah in that living portrait of her brother. I tried not to think of her that much. It proved impossible within the fences, where new, good memories were hard to come by. Cash took another drag from his cigarette. He grinned while he let free a slight chuckle. "I wonder if she's looking at this same sunset somewhere." He gazed over the flatland.

"Can't beat a beachside sunset," I tried to change the subject for fear of wailing in a place far beyond its quota of tears.

"Vallah always liked a desert sunset. She said the ocean was too loud for her. I wonder if she's gone deaf from the sound of her gun."

"Better get to work. We don't want her running out of bullets."

"My sister would have a laugh knowing I was stuck here, working in a factory to fill her magazines. Thinking of *you* doing it might not make her so pickled," Cash said as he stepped from the light of the falling sun. He approached and put a hand on my shoulder. Red dust flew up from my shirt, filling the space between us. "She loves us, man. Wherever Vallah is — alive or dead — she'd never forget us. We might not see her again, but I hope you know she didn't leave for any lack of love for you and me." Cash pat me on the back. Moisture came to my eyes. I couldn't speak. "Don't worry, man. We won't be here forever." He walked off toward the factory wreathed in rays of orange and pink.

I looked down at my shoes. I grit my teeth, took a deep breath, and walked to my casita in the dust. Shift change brought out all the ghetto faces. On the clock. Off the clock. We all had grease under our fingernails. Pleasantries were often interrupted by patrolling guards. For as much as I would have hated to see Vallah subjected to enforcing curfews and labour schedules, the prospect of her duties as a glorified babysitter in some other godforsaken ghetto was far more comforting than envisioning her on the front lines of a hopeless battle.

I nodded to a few familiar neighbours before picking out Carmen in the crowd of dozens drifting between each other. She was the only stationary soul in the shuffling horde. Her pregnant belly pressed against the chain-link fence as she looked forlorn at the abyss. A guard just beyond the perforated wall quickly inserted himself in her view. His moving lips were all I could see in the noisy commotion between myself and the scene unfolding in the distance. Carmen lifted her hands to the fence and grasped the metal wire, staring over the head of the short, young guard. The man in uniform stepped back and raised his weapon. His lips moved faster. My friend didn't release her hold on the cage. She began to shake the barrier. The workers continued to weave around one another on their way to and from the factory. No notice was paid to Carmen as she tightened her grip. Another guard joined the scene at Carmen's back. She refused to turn and see him. The second guard raised the butt-end of his rifle above his shoulders and brought it down on Carmen's skull. She fell to her knees, but her fingers remained clenched around the fence while I watched, leaving her arms extended over her head as if reaching out for the heavens after the rest of her body went limp. The guard outside our enclosure slung the strap of his weapon over his shoulder and carefully loosened Carmen's fingers one at a time. Damaging a worker's hands would have landed the guard in hot water. I stood helpless as a statue.

The sight was nothing new. Violence and labour were the twin pillars of my existence after the coastal raids. Stupefied, numbed, shocked, paralyzed, asleep — call it what you will — I did nothing as I watched Carmen's life-sustaining body crumble to the dirt. The thief of her consciousness put his hands under her arms and dragged her away just as the final factory bell tolled. Hustling, shuffling feet of the remaining stragglers kicked up the dust in a terse instant. An immediate hush claimed the space once more. I was left to amble back to my home alone. The freedom to drink myself to sleep seemed to lose its lustre in a hurry. Night closed in. Sadness took hold of my weary bones.

A piercing screech from the rusted hinges holding the casita door shook me from my daze as I arrived home. Silence greeted me in the empty room once filled with bunks, conversation, and occasional laughter. Many of the wooden bedframes were burned in the courtyard when the number of residents went into steep decline. I didn't always have my own space. I used to share it with seven others — another reminder of my dumb luck. Papers were stacked next to my bed. Pencils were scattered on the floor. Vallah would have appreciated the privacy. Most nights we slept together in our adolescence, we were surrounded by the snores, whispers, dreams, nightmares, and breathing of others. My bed would've been more enticing were she still around. I took a seat on the floor, sliding my legs beneath the rickety legs of the bed. The foam pad where I slept was firm enough to write on without piercing the paper with my lead tip as I began to write. What good did my words do Carmen's head? No prose or poem would protect Vallah. I was not a vessel to channel and scrawl any details about her condition, her whereabouts, her feelings, her kill count, or death. Words couldn't remedy Cash's unrequited love, forlorn heart, or habit. My pencil was no wand to conjure Mick for the sake of his impending child. But still, I wrote. What else could I do?

I continued to record my story and scribbled my origins beyond the ghetto. I refused to let Carmen's pain, her bloody skull, go unwritten. Her toughness deserved to be immortalized. There were few memories before the five of us were cast out on our own. Did the invaders not account for us children growing into men and women with deep seated terrors that would one day bloom in revenge? Did they not think us worth the bullets? Were they so doubtful we'd survive? Perhaps the raiders were right. If not for Vallah, Mick, Cash, and Carmen, there would be no lead spread across the pages piling up beneath my bed. The schoolhouse was our saving grace. If it had been any of my other classmates, I would have been buried in ash and sand like our teacher, like our parents, like our hopes for a future beyond the ghetto or the gun.

Rays from the ochre-coloured sunset broke through the vertical slats serving as walls for the rickety casita. The floor was covered in the red dust I drove through to make my way to the ghetto. Despite the dry heat, a mouldy smell filled the space. Empty, rotting bedframes and bunks lined the walls. My rubber-soled footsteps were silent on the concrete ground. I hadn't checked and cleared the entire room to be able to make noises carelessly. No ghetto punk was getting the drop on me. Not again. A sheet hung in the middle of the room. I drew my weapon and pulled back the hammer, using my barrel to catch the edge of the makeshift curtain. Dirt went flying into the bright beams streaking the space when I tossed it aside to reveal a body curled on a foam pad. The figure lay motionless, hardly breathing at my feet. I held up the picture from Ezra Atun's file against the face on the floor and immediately knew it wasn't a match. Bits of foil were littered about the scattered, decaying wood. A charred spoon lay next to the heap of skin and bones. The smell left by burnt crystal filled the air. It made me miss the salty breeze in Los Muelles.

Suddenly, the echoes from the striking of a great bell rang out, shaking the decaying sides of the enclosure. I quickly snuck back behind the sheet as the junky stirred. There was a small door with a crescent moon carved in its timber door along the wall. Flies, moths, and mosquitos swarmed me when I ducked inside the tiny space built around the shithole carved out from the earth. I held my breath from the stench. The sound of feet shuffling across the dusty concrete was audible as the figure broke the rays of light spilling through the cracks in the decomposing lumber. The door squeaked on its rusty hinges, the setting sun filled the cabin as the young man took his exit. I breathed a sigh of relief in the brief moment I stepped out from the crap stall. Not a minute later, I was forced back in as the bell tolled once again, and the casita door swung open. The element of surprise was turned against me. I refused to inhale the pungent odour in the fear I'd alert my casefile and end up with winged bugs in my lungs.

Ezra Atun walked about the room for a moment. From the space between the boards, I set eyes on my catch for the first time. He shuffled some papers beneath his bed, unscrewed the lid of a mason jar that sat on the floor, and gulped in earnest. Then he turned towards me. I moved my eye from the open space. It was too late.

"You want a drink?" The voice came from just beyond the shithouse door. I noticed the daylight coming through the crescent moon cut-out was blocked.

"Sure." I sheepishly stepped into the casita's main room. "Long drive. Needed to use the can."

"There always used to be a fight for it at shift change. Not so much anymore." The young man extended the jar that was filled halfway with clear, varnish-smelling liquid toward me. He stood eye-level with me, just over six feet, with hair cut almost to the skin. A scruffy beard grew across his jaw about the same length as on his head. I imagined him filling out a uniform well.

"Thanks." I stepped forward and accepted the drink. It burned my throat on the way down. I refused to grimace. My authority was already compromised by being discovered before I intended. "How'd you know I was here?"

"Been stuck in this box over seven years now. I've gotten to know the shadows pretty well."

"Observant. That's a fine quality in a soldier." He immediately noticed the Catcher's badge on my hip. There was no use introducing myself. He'd seen plenty of my kind before. I relaxed a little, aided by the strong drink. I took another slug from the glass.

"You can holster that." Ezra motioned to the cocked magnum in my other hand. "I'm no rabbit."

"Heard that before. But I'm going to trust you. Can I trust you Ezra?"

"Can't trust anyone in your line of work, I suppose," he replied. The young man had a quiet, confident way about him. His presence in the rundown casita somehow made the space a hair more refined. "Want a seat?" He folded the holey blanket on the bed overtop the stacked papers.

"Sure." I returned my weapon returned to its holster as I put the moonshine to his hand, making sure to stare long and hard into his eyes before crossing his face so close he could smell the liquor on my breath. The rickety bedframe shifted under my weight. Ezra sat on the bottom bunk closest to me.

"So, I got twelve hours?" He asked, taking a swig, placing the jar between his feet on the floor, putting his hands together, and resting them on his knees.

"Plenty of time to organize a hell of a send-off. I threw my girls parties fit for queens before they shipped out. Drove 'em to the coast myself too. Wasn't much need for Catchers in those days. Weren't so many Dodgers then. But, I'm happy for the work."

"I'm happy too." Ezra leaned back nonchalantly on the bunk.

"How's that?" I hadn't seen a case so respectable in a dog's age.

"I've been stuck in this cage going on eight years now. About time I got out to see the world, fire some of those bullets I've been making since I was eighteen. Plus, there's someone I've been hoping to catch up with. Someone in the service."

"Your girlfriend, right? Vallah Desear."

"You know her?" The young man perked up. I could practically hear his heart beat faster.

"No. It was in your file. She mentioned you at her sentencing. That her brother you're shacked up with?" I took the jar from the floor and wet my lips.

"Yeah. I'll be glad to be rid of him. All he cares about is crystal."

"It's everywhere, kid. Nothing like a tour of duty to keep a young man such as yourself on the straight and narrow." My throat was warming from another drink.

"Where are they sending me?" Ezra accepted the jar. We passed the drink freely like I had done so many times on the farm with my girls. They were only a few years younger than him when they enlisted. He might have made a fine match for my youngest.

"That's above my pay grade, son."

"I'll ship out from Los Muelles?"

"Sure. I understand you lived there for a time."

"I used to sell palm frond roses in the square with my girl."

"Got yourself into some trouble too. Armed robbery, I understand."

"Those days are behind me." The young man looked ashamed.

"Cheer up, kid. A bright future awaits." I stood up and put my hand on his cheek. My balance was a little off on account of the white lightning. "I spoke to the guards. They're going to let the night shift off a little early to celebrate with you." I found myself hoping for an invitation but quickly sloughed off the ridiculous notion. "Enjoy yourself. Not too much. We take off at 0600. I'll be parked right outside them gates. Don't make me come toss you out this bed."

"I won't." Ezra stood, a look of melancholy in his eyes. "What's your name, sir?"

"Strickland. Strickland River." His manners were a pleasing surprise.

"Pleasure to make your acquaintance, Mr. River, sir."

"The pleasure's mine, Mr. Atun." We shook hands. I felt a lump in my throat for the respect shown to me after all the scorn I endured over the years and those recent weeks in particular. "See you in the morning." I walked to the splintering door and turned back to stand in the frame a moment. "Remember: I'll be right outside that gate."

All the commotion at shift change caused quite the dust-up. It began to settle, turning the air into a bronze fog. A sudden ease came over me. The young draftee reassured my faith in the crusade I was charged. Loyal patriots were not extinct in the ghettos despite so much evidence to the contrary. As the sun fell over the small hills on the horizon, I envisioned Ezra sitting shotgun on the journey back to Los Muelles. Delivering an eager soldier in such short order would surely appease the Supervisor's concerns about my talents as a Catcher. After all, men exchanged cases over card games, cockfights, horse races, and betting of all sorts on a regular basis. Only a few days passed since the divine intervened in the narrows around Miss Holly's. There were too many bodies strewn in the Los Muelles alleys for that underserving young Catcher to be discovered with any haste. Even if he was found, his death wouldn't be reported by the louts in the streets. His pockets would be picked clean, and he'd be left for the rats. Soldiers wouldn't touch him. Catchers were beyond military jurisdiction. They had enough to worry about without an investigation. Other Catchers were the least of my problems. One less badge meant less competition for the dwindling casefiles bringing any worthwhile reward.

The bell was struck for the final time, and the vibrations pulsed throughout my body. By bringing Ezra in before the week was out, all would be forgotten. I could reclaim my life in service to the country, to Union. I saluted the guards on either side of the gates as they let me pass through to my jeep, waiting patiently beyond the fences. Union law demanded twelve hours for draftees to put their affairs in order. I had drawn a fine case for the first time in what felt like forever. Ezra Atun deserved his final hoorah as a civilian. I envied him. Sunrise would bring about his baptism into the holy fraternity that defended all Union glory.

GENERAL LAMENT
MARCH 2192

I knew I was growing old when I awoke in the bed of a boy whose name I didn't care to remember.

In earlier years, I could have snuck out from beneath his sweating body, exiting into the night a satisfied woman, leaving him still thrusting and unsuspecting. But the old gal was slipping.

Light spilled in through the wood planks and aluminum sheets. Yellow streaks lined his strong and muscular back as he lay sleeping on the woven straw mat he shared with me. The rum removed his name from memory. The day-old alcohol stripped the taste of his lips from mine. It must have been a good night because all the lust was gone from my bones. I just wanted to get the hell out of that hut to return to my perch on the misty mountain above the village.

His pale, white rear shifted slightly in his slumber, and as it did, I rolled off the worn bed onto the cool, ashen floor. Soft breaths were the only sound in the room. Snoring hadn't begun to plague his sleeping yet, which was another benefit of the younger ones. I held my lungs full of air and decided not to let it out until I was beyond his door.

My uniform lay in a pile right next to my face. I could see my medals pinned to the material, catching the light of the rising sun.

They always impressed the boys, the aspiring soldiers, guerrillas, freedom fighters, rebels, or whatever they were calling themselves in those days. Each little badge was only worth its weight in how much it could get an aging woman laid. As they dragged against the packed earth when I stood and grabbed my clothes — making all too much noise in an all too quiet room — I didn't even think they were worth that. The young man stirred at the sound. I could hear his breath shorten as he woke. Still keeping my mouth sealed, I threw my shirt over my bare breasts, which stood the test of time pretty well for their size, and I made my way for the exit at the other end of the small room. While making my escape, I snatched the bottle I'd brought the night prior. The wooden door swung shut behind me as I entered the street. All was silent. I exhaled and buttoned my top. A mischievous smile formed itself on my mouth. I turned to the door and saluted.

"General?" I heard a sleepy voice say from the other side of the thin wood, and I was out of there like a laugh in the wind.

✳ ✳ ✳

Only by the magma's dim light at the belly of the abyss could I see my feet at the crater's edge. It was a moonless night. No ash spewed from the opening in the earth. I looked into the lake of fire a few hundred metres down and considered going for a swim. Tears filled my eyes. I blamed the toxic gasses found so close to the peak but knew my memories were the root of such evil. It was quite a way back down to my cabin on the mountainside. The fall would only take a moment. Arriving in such a state of despair took years. I took my last sip of wine before the plunge. Nearly half the bottle remained as I tossed it over my shoulder. Sins like wasting good wine no longer worried me. Death would provide me all the drink I could ever imagine.

Taking in the noxious fumes, I looked over the small, makeshift village of my last remaining followers. Air left my lungs in a sigh of relief. My eyes closed. I stepped over the edge, weightless.

Then, suddenly, I felt a shooting pain across the surface of my skull. Trying to turn my gaze as best I could, I jerked my neck and set eyes on Lou. She had my thick, black hair caught in her talons, leaving me dangling over the precipice. The wine was titled up to flow into her waiting mouth. Her spread lips wreathed the redness of her tongue like the basin of the volcano. I could hear her gulp the fruit of the vine, and she exhaled, thirst quenched. Only then did she pull me from my place over the void. She moved me effortlessly, like the towering cranes I'd not seen since leaving Los Muelles behind in twenty-one-eighty-six.

Back on my feet, I realized how tipsy I'd become in the darkness atop the lofty fault line in the earth. I was entrenched in the winter of my seasons with my right hand. Lou was accustomed to my antics for all our time together. As much as she possessed other-worldly patience, I could see her waning desire to put up with such suicidal stunts, which only made me want to leap off the edge all the more.

It was time to work. Lou arrived to tell me as much. A group of five had travelled twelve days just to meet me. My ability to inspire courage never ceased to amaze me. The desire to swim in a river of fire began to fade. Little did they know it was only a two-day ride to the ECR border. Their arrival at my home, down the mountain, marked the end to the most treacherous part of their journey, and somehow, they felt as though they had to find me in order to make the final stretch. Did I not make the path clear enough in the *Exile*

Manifesto? It did wonders for my ego to be needed, but it reinforced my distaste for the never-ending evidence of each person's need for a leader. I followed Lou down the steep volcanic face. The ash shifted beneath my feet on my way to the cabin where the small crew was gathered. I agreed to help them, yet again joining forces with strangers to win the battle for freedom being waged against the Union. Hold the applause. Don't forget the guilt and shame that motivated me.

The son scowled. He had his parents' pleasant physical features. But while they oozed with fear, I saw in the boy the rage of a lifelong victim of Union circumstance. His hatred for the unseen forces steering his family to slaughter was palpable, intense, attractive. He was at that age just entering manhood when a gun would've been welcomed if offered to him. I considered recommending the firepower between my thighs to appease him before crossing into the ECR, where there was no more use for his fury. There were carnal uses for it. I was getting distracted. The daughter peeked out from behind her mother's thigh and saluted me. I asked that she not do that. And then there was an outlier, a young woman in a frayed Union uniform that defined her curves. The name stitched over her breast had been torn away. She obviously shared no relation to the family of four.

"You a deserter?" I asked of the stunning young lady. Her chestnut-coloured hair was pulled tightly back from her face in a large bun.

The former soldier simply nodded. She looked exhausted — a feeling I knew all too well.

"Where did you serve?"

"Hispaniola mostly, before it joined Jamaica, before I got my hands on your book, on the truth." She had an unwavering voice.

"She saved us." The trembling father chimed in. My eyes stayed with the stunning deserter. "We were discovered along the way. She fought off the soldiers."

"Did you kill them?" I stepped toward the girl in uniform.

"I've killed many people, General."

"You still got a gun?"

She reached into the waistline at her back and held a pistol in her palm.

"Come with me," I told her.

The family began to follow me and the deserter up the volcano's face.

"We're going to get you across the line," I vowed, my speech slurred. "We just have to get rid of this weapon first. Can't go into a foreign land bearing arms. We'll be right back." I gave the little girl a thumb up. The little girl returned the gesture. "Lou, can you fix them something to eat?" My right hand obliged, ushering the family into my quarters. I ascended the powdery slope. The deserter followed closely. "Don't worry. She'll take care of them."

"Thank you," replied the former soldier, still holding the pistol in her hand like a waiter carrying drinks on a tray.

"Don't thank me," I said over my shoulder.

"That's what I keep telling that family down there."

"I hear it's hard for people like you across the line." I walked with my sights on the faint red glow hovering over the volcano's lip.

"It's always hard. I'll manage. I just wish I'd stayed in Los Muelles, bided my time until I was deported. Anywhere must be better than the West Caribbean Union."

"I see you missed that in my writing," I chuckled, thinking of all the other details I must have left out or were passed over by my readers. "No one was deported. People are a nation's greatest resource. The Union only gave two options to those of you on the coasts without papers: labour or military. Those who refused faced the firing squads I commanded."

"My limited options don't excuse what I've done. I should've chosen labour or faced death."

"The world knows what we've done in Union's name. They have every right and reason to hold a grudge, but the greatest onslaught of hatred comes from within. That's the Union's great trick: we blame ourselves."

"Does the world know we were trapped? That the Union set fire to their own coasts to start the war?"

"For the most part. The ECR denied any military action against the Union. Once the Union started invading other islands and bays of Central America, it was impossible to hide the fact they waged war on the nations set to collide with our island. The world knows the coastal raids were a Union ploy. I wish more of our own people knew. Doesn't mean we've been forgiven, though. There's still a lot of distaste for us in the ECR even though they take in so many refugees."

"I did terrible things before I read the *Exile Manifesto*. I wouldn't forgive me either," the deserter's voice trailed off. I could see her holding the gun away from her like it was week-old fish.

"You have to forgive yourself first, soldier. That's the mission you're on now. You have to get past what you've done to get past the line."

"Have you?"

"Can't ever forgive myself. But I'm never crossing the line, so I don't have to." I winked at the deserter as we came to the volcano's sweltering crest. "Do as I say, not as I do, and definitely not as I've done. Now, throw that gun away. You don't need it anymore."

The deserter looked at me, then back at the silver pistol iridescent in the red light rising up from below. She let the firearm slip off the skin of her palm, and it disappeared into the bright crater.

"What's your name?" I asked the girl.

"I've told you before." Her eyes stayed transfixed on the bubbling depths just over the edge of where we stood.

"I sentenced you?" Sweat started to bead on my skin.

"Seven years ago."

"Tell me your name again. It belongs to you now. Not me. Not the Union."

"My name is Vallah Desear. And I defect from your service."

"Congratulations. Now let's have a drink and get you East of here. I've learned that's the best I can offer in apology."

"It'll do," Vallah said, smiling out the corner of her soft lips. "Better be a strong drink."

The parents, their two children, and I stood in awkward silence as Lou readied the horses. I was piss-drunk. The deserter could handle her fair share, but her eyes were quite glossy too after we made amends with raised glasses. Our three steeds stood shoulder to shoulder before us. The family of four and I were in line with Vallah opposite the beasts. Lou was in the middle of us travellers. She reached into the pouch hanging from her hip, took up a fist full of red, powdery sand, and lifted the blood-coloured ball to Lightning's snout, blowing a scarlet specter up her gaping nostrils. The ash-coated mare inhaled the merlot cloud deep within.

Trueno's stomach rumbled as she awaited the ritual of courage and good fortune. Each muscle in her massive body showcased its perfect form when she stepped back on hind legs and neighed so loud I could see silhouettes of the villagers in their candlelit shacks coming to their windows to catch a glimpse of the mighty horse that would be used in tall tales around their fires. I knew all too well they couldn't see her deep black hide from down below.

Lou snickered when it came time for Diva to receive the rite. The horse's tan jacket and blonde hair made him stick out in the night, but he'd carried me to safety through too many getaways to judge him by his undeniable beauty. When the rose-tinted mist made its way into his lungs, Diva dropped a steaming pile of dung out his backside.

Then Lou turned to us to provide the same strength she'd gifted to the beasts. She held the small mound of deep red dust in her hand and raised it to our faces. The father sneezed. The mother cried. The son coughed. The daughter giggled. Vallah closed her eyes. I smiled. And together, we mounted with crimson faces. It was obvious the son was a little embarrassed to be riding behind his mother. He was about the age my daughter would've been if not for the coastal raids. My attraction to the young man waned as thoughts of my only child came to mind. With thoughts of my departed daughter, it was impossible not to conjure images of her father. Comparing any man to my long-deceased husband also cooled the flames of my drunken desire. Anyone standing next to my great love in mind's eye would be a distant runner-up in a contest of beauty, brawn, or wisdom. The decision to resist seducing the young man was made as quickly as we were about to take off across the mountain slope. With Vallah wrapped around me on Diva's back, my lewd thoughts turned to her ample shape pressed up against me. Lou slapped the steed's behind, and we were off.

Diva leaned uphill as the ash shifted beneath his hooves. The soft surface under me and my countrymen muted the sound of our travel as much as the clouds overhead subdued the starlight waiting behind. We soared across the steep face of the volcano as if taking flight from the giant's nose. I felt like a titan. Delivering five souls to the East Caribbean Republic was yet another act of defiance against the powers of the Union. When combating the forces of those who think themselves gods, it did my followers good to be led by someone with similar, drunken delusions of personal grandeur. I became the product of war my superiors wished me to be in my years of service to the Union army. A period of my life was spent in a warlord's frame of mind. With every kill collected, with every battle won, with every rise in rank, I experienced the power accumulated from a fallen adversary. Such bloodlust was branded on my DNA, but when I deserted, I lost my outlet for destruction. It nearly ended me, until I met Lou. Without her guiding light, I would have never ferried all those souls beyond the Union's reach. In exile in my own country, fanning the flames of the Exodus, I found the only shred of happiness left for me in life. The slight joy was never completely devoid of disgrace. I rode hard until my eyes burned.

The whispered lore of Lou's ability to wield magic was crucial to our message. When a feat seems impossible, feed the faithless with tales of miracles. Returning to the city in daylight always caused a big commotion. The mission was a success: five more souls were freed from Union's coffers. I didn't always come back to the village with good news to share. Ash padded the steps beneath my boots as I strolled the narrow, shanty lanes. Tents were pitched on the rickety rooftops of the single-storey expanse of dwellings. Plastic umbrellas and clothes drying on lines caught the smoke rising from skillets sizzling over open fires along the main drag. Each vendor thrust one tantalizing aroma after another beneath my nose. Reverence was paid to Lightning, Diva, and Trueno as they trailed behind me. The horses bowed to acknowledge the praise they received. They graciously accepted the food presented to them in great quantity. Diva was never shy about eating more than his belly could hold. Villagers simply buried his droppings with the ash piled outside their doors.

My stomach rumbled after the four days spent navigating the subterranean avenues leading to the ECR. Every time I thought my decision on a dish was made, I lost Lou in the crowd. Packs of her doting devoted teemed when we stopped at any cart or stall. The faith we cultivated for the Exodus bloomed in Lou's presence. She had usurped the volcano for the people's focus of admiration. They marked her as their protector from the Union. A sea of hands reached out to get closer to the source of their salvation. It was said that Lou was the force that caused the eruptions that lay waste to the easternmost reaches of the Union wall.

In truth, it was the landmasses of Cuba, Jamaica, and Hispaniola converging on the island that forced Montagne de Feu's eighteen-year-old peak to burst into a scorching wave across the Union's concrete barricade, which failed to keep the world from penetrating its borders. The West Caribbean Union was no longer an island in the year twenty-one seventy-four, when the coastal raids began, when tragedy befell my departed family. It collided with its neighbour, the East Caribbean Republic, which opened the earth to the vast oceans of molten rock flowing beneath the thin surface of our planet. There was no use telling Lou's loyal subjects about the natural powers at play that forever changed the West Caribbean Union's future. I wrote all about Pangea's reformation in the *Exile Manifesto*. The Union secrets I uncovered in my ascent to military and political power were laid bare on the page for all to read and disseminate. When I worked diligently to detail all I knew in my book, my concerns always centered on the lacking resources I had to spread the word. Never in my wildest notions did I think people of the Union would simply not believe what I told them in writing.

When the Union became one with the ECR, the fault lines in the earth redefined the lines on the map. Rich in resources, financial and social supremacy was firmly consolidated within a small, elite class. A deplorable, disturbing scheme was invented by Union leadership to make enemies with the Republic to protect existing claims to sovereignty. A singular tragedy had to be inflicted upon the people to justify the Union's dominion over the land once bordered entirely by the sea, so the Union raised East Caribbean Republic flags from its ships and set fire to its own citizens in the coastal raids of twenty-one seventy-four.

I decided on battered, fried chicken that was handed to me in a basket woven from palm fronds. The drumsticks were easy to eat with one hand during the walk back to my post above the village. Smoke from the cookfires rose up to a blue sky. All the dark ash absorbed the ample sunlight. Only the noises of chatting villagers, busy pots and pans, and wash buckets being tossed in the lane filled my ears. The unpredictable fault line we straddled was quiet for the moment. I always felt unsettled when rubbing shoulders with the people making camp on the low ground. If Montagne de Feu erupted, I hoped its lava would take me first, to give fair warning to all others to flee if the worst should happen. It was a precarious thing living in the shadow of the very active volcano that was simultaneously our protector and greatest threat. The massive formation represented the Union's greatest fears. Montagne de Feu dissolved the boundaries between the West and East islands. An untameable force undid all the Union's work to construct a divider between nations, which blew a gaping hole in the promise that leadership could keep the world from penetrating the utopic vision Union sold the desperate, gullible population. The military sent me all over the Caribbean to wage war and lay claim to the islands that would one day arrive on our shores and take what was promised to Union citizens. At first, I stormed beaches with the blinding hatred the coastal raids instilled in me. Union counted on such emotions to barricade its soldiers from remorse and consideration for our fellow man simply divided by the sea. The more I went abroad, it was impossible to ignore that I became the raider. Years were spent plotting how best to lay waste to the Republic to the East, how best to destabilise our neighbour so that when Pangea pulled us together, created a bridge between us, we would be the conquerors, they the vanquished. The ECR accepted refugees in great number when the Union's draft became uncovered by the *Exile Manifesto*. It was a humanitarian disaster.

Montagne de Feu kicked open the doors for the Exodus. The propensity to praise Lou in a holy, sacred way didn't surprise me. Who was I to impose my godless attitudes upon the faithful? My right hand was their patron saint for escape from Union's clutches. I gave up trying to keep an eye on her in the crowds.

The salty, greasy chicken grabbed my focus while I walked toward the camp's outer limits, slowly climbing the mountain. Lou could catch up. I grew thirsty for rum after the journey through the tunnels. But as I looked at the makeshift huts erected on the ashes of the town that was buried repeatedly by almost twenty years of Montagne de Feu's impulsive, volatile eruptions, I both admired the courage the villagers maintained in the face of their destroyer, but also scoffed at their folly to forgo the passages East in order to live in squalor close to Lou, their deity. I just wanted so badly to save them, but they believed their faith had already done so. My duty was to ferry those who wished to reach the Republic to their desired destination. That was my charge, my penance, and my reward. I hoped to be long dead before the volcano displayed its power once again. It didn't surprise me that Earth's welcome expired. All there was left to do was dance upon the drifting lands like melting icebergs. Fight for flight. I first chose combat, but mother nature was and forever remained undefeated. To flee seemed to be the only reasonable response to the chasing rivers of rancorous heat. It was this realization that brought me into Lou's fold. An armed rebellion against the Union would have been ludicrous, but I was not prepared to accept extinction. In exile within the country, I fused fight and flight, understanding that to escape is to battle with the instinct that screams: us or them. The Exodus was my best solution for all the killing I'd seen. I was no longer a soldier. I was a conductor calling "all aboard" to all who would listen. Everyone was free to stay on the platform or get on the train.

I wasn't sure if my Catcher believed my little act. Playing nice at least bought me a little leash. The hammock swayed gently while the stars began to appear above. I wished Cash's shift would end. I wished Carmen wasn't in solitary for her incident with the guards at the fence. Twelve hours was too tight a window to plot an escape. I'd never heard of anyone who made it to beyond the gates. I racked my brain to remember if anyone ever tried it in my time. All things considered, it wasn't that bad of a life in the ghetto. But seeing the running sun escape over the horizon while I sat drinking in a cage made me feel ashamed, gave me a hint as to why Vallah chose a different path all those years ago in Los Muelles. I watched a grand, cosmic display of the universe's awesome scale, and there within the confines of a rusty fence, I moped as a compliant, well-behaved prisoner. The delusion that the Union would let me walk free with my papers once my eight years were up was a fantasy I clung to far too long. My only excuse for buying what the Union sold us as a better life was the alluring opportunity to turn inward for the first time in my life. Only someone given the gift to spend so many nights drinking and staring at the stars could travel as deep into the darkened passages of the soul as I had.

The ghetto was my cocoon. I felt my will bursting against my enclosure. No living thing to ever take flight is a stranger to the fear of falling. It's not as though an escape never crossed my mind before my Catcher came calling, bearing news that I was drafted. Every bullet I constructed on the factory floor brought with it the urge to run and never stop again. For all my inner searching, writing, thoughts, and feelings, I'd been running on the spot so long that I forgot my soles needed to touch the ground to get anywhere of any true importance. Years on the line made me sturdy but stationary. Between fugitive, prisoner, or soldier, the choice seemed clear. Even the very thought of a jailbreak brought a smile to my face, a steep hike in my pulse. Thrills were hard to come by since turning eighteen when I walked willingly into my snare and forfeited the life of adventure I took for granted. Chasing liberty was the only way I knew to tap the source again. The first thing was to puncture the surface and let the outside world come rushing in. Just then, I saw a moth dancing circles around the rising moon. I hoped Cash would come with me. I feared the logistics of busting Carmen out. All I knew was the reign of compliance was over. Not another day would I spend enslaved to another's cause. At least as a thief and beggar, I fought for myself, for the ones I loved. Signing up for the ghetto was my best effort to keep them safe, but the Union betrayed me over and again. The armed forces wouldn't take me captive to do the same. I bid good luck to the Catcher who arrived to claim me. I spent eleven years on the run after the raids. The ghetto was just a rest stop. If Strickland River was going to catch me, I'd make him earn it.

The Kid arrived much earlier than he usually did on the lucrative nights when the draft took another soul from the ghetto. He pushed his wheelbarrow across the dirt. It was piled particularly high with bribes for the guards, letters for the workers, fireworks for the celebration, and crystal for the bored and desperate. The factory bell echoed early, just as the Catcher promised. Seas of greasy workers drained from the workshop, few stopping by to bid me farewell and share a drink. I was obviously distracted from the well-wishers, watching The Kid roll by Strickland River's parked, olive green jeep. Business proceeded. Guards plucked from the wheelbarrows as they pleased, stuffing their uniforms with whatever chemical, lewd photograph, or other valuable The Kid could scrounge from the outside world for his caged brothers and sisters. He passed through the gates as I'd seen him do so many times. I definitely wasn't getting anywhere as a stowaway in the shallow bed of his wheelbarrow.

Cash intercepted The Kid on his way to the ghetto's belly. Stopping only for a second to place a foil-wrapped care package in Cash's hand, The Kid was swarmed, and Cash strolled toward me as if I were none the wiser that he just copped for the thousandth time before my eyes.

"Word got through the line that Catcher out there paid you a visit." Cash leaned against the casita, gazing out over the commotion to the jeep.

"We've known a long time we'd never see parole." I went back and forth in the hammock, dangling over the dirt.

"I'm sure they'll be coming for my ass any day now too." My friend lit a cigarette. "Guess they'll wait for Carmen to have the baby before they snatch her up."

"Not if we fly the coop." As the crowds dispersed around The Kid, I caught his attention and waved him over.

"What are you talking about?" A smile came to Cash's mouth around the cigarette.

"You ready to run again?"

"Lead, and I'll follow, brother." Cash clapped his hands and rubbed them together in delight.

"You trust The Kid?"

"No one hates Union more than him. The enemy of my enemy is my friend. Ain't that right?" Cash knew The Kid best for all the wrong reasons.

Just then, the wheelbarrow and its teenage pusher pulled up just shy of bumping into the rocking hammock.

"Shame to hear you'll be leaving, Ezra. I had big plans for you." The Kid rested down the rear legs of his cart on the ground.

"Don't be cancelling those plans just yet. I got a proposition for you. All I can offer is my credit at the commissary." I put my foot to the ground to stop swinging.

"All The Kid wants is damage done to Union. That's payment enough. Isn't that right, Kid?" Cash bit his smoke, grinning.

"Don't tease me, fellas. The Exodus is real." He replied anxiously.

"Then sign us up." I stood and offered a hand to The Kid. He paused a moment and then shook it with a surprisingly strong grip.

"You guys want to escape?" The teen blurted.

"Yeah, but we won't get far if you don't keep your voice down. We have to get Carmen out of solitary too. Is that possible?"

"Hell yeah, it's possible. I've been waiting years for some of you pricks to work up the balls to get the fuck outta here and stop slaving for the enemy."

"Can you actually pull this off?" I asked. The Kid certainly wasn't lacking enthusiasm. "That Catcher hasn't taken his eyes off me." I looked to the shape sitting, staring from behind the jeep windshield.

"I've got distributors all over the country. More trade routes than you got hairs on your head. I can get you to the General."

"Why haven't you gone yet?" I inquired, lacking the time to diligently vet my accomplice.

"I fight the Union from the inside. You'll see. I got a camp in the valley. That's our first stop. There's a revolution going on. You just been in the dark, my friend."

"How long does it take to get to your camp? Your crew won't make it back here before morning if it's a safe distance from here." I played the devil's advocate as I did so often when plotting with Vallah.

"I just play the simple peddler for the guards, Ezra. You think I'm stupid enough to make the trip alone? I've got scouts hidden all across the flatland waiting on me. They're ready for anything."

"You sure about this, Ezra?" Cash turned to me.

"What the fuck we got to lose?"

"Great night for a jailbreak, fellas. Just a few orders of business: you both know how to ride bikes?" The Kid was visibly excited. The guards at the gate gave him a whistle, warning our short time was running out.

"Sure. We've stolen anything on wheels at least once, but we really going to try to outrun that Catcher's jeep on fucking bicycles?" My doubts were being realized much too quickly.

"Relax. That jeep ain't going nowhere. I'll be back in a few hours with bolt cutters, a crew, and a few other things. Just be ready to haul ass when I say so." The Kid looked over his shoulder and waved to acknowledge the whistles coming from the guards. "One last thing." He reached into a pocket sewn on the inside of his baggy Union uniform and revealed a booklet bound by string. "Read what you can of this." *Exile Manifesto* was scrawled in black ink across the cover. "It'll explain everything. I bet you'll pedal a hundred times faster once you know the truth."

"Not that conspiracy shit, man. You gotta focus, Kid." Cash exhaled after a long drag from his cigarette.

"What's this?" I took the thick, worn pages.

"That's the map to freedom, brother," said The Kid, and he took up his wheelbarrow to push toward the gate. "I'll see you soon. Don't forget to bring the book. Don't bother coming without it." His expression was grave. "There aren't many copies left. We need it." I nodded, and he walked off across the dirt as a gust of wind sent dust swirling around him. I looked down at the booklet and quickly tucked it behind my back when I noticed my Catcher glaring.

* * *

It was difficult to believe such strong words written by the person who sentenced me to the ghetto in the first place. My fingers ran over the final period after reading the document aloud.

"Why'd The Kid wait so long to show us?" I looked up from the booklet that sat open on my bed in the casita's dim candlelight.

"He's been spouting that shit to me for years." Cash was sprawled out on a bunk, staring up at the wood planks hanging over him. "He's tried to tell you too, but he knows you've always hated him."

"I hate that he sells you crystal. I never knew much more about The Kid." The worn, stained pages were in my hand when I stood and started pacing. "You think any of it could be true? I mean, the islands all coming together? Sounds pretty farfetched."

"Who cares? What does it change?" Cash lit a cigarette.

"How can you say that? Union killed our parents, burned our homes, turned us into beggars and criminals."

"We were always going to be poor thieves. I think the raids just hurried us along. You were the only one who ever had any trouble with it." Cash kept his eyes upward on the smoke rising around him.

"Why do you even want to leave if that's what you think?" I leafed through the General's pages, scanning accusations, remembering the day she sentenced me to the life I found myself in.

"Because I'm tired of being looked at like nothing more than a faggot junky."

"You know I couldn't care less who you fuck, but you *are* a junky, Cash."

"Who the fuck isn't? You're a user too, man."

"I've never even tried crystal. I guess I got a weakness for rum, though." I didn't pay the debate much attention. Me and Cash fought about his habit limitless times. My focus was on the General's claims.

"You just asked The Kid to bust you out of here, knowing full well he'd do it because you're afraid." Cash spoke calmly and slowly. He was high, honest, reflective.

"Didn't you hear what I just read? The East Caribbean Republic had nothing to do with the raids. I'm not fighting for Union, for those fucking murderers."

"We weren't much better in our time. You ready to go back to ripping and running?"

"That's different. We never killed anybody."

"It's a fine line you might have to cross this time."

"If they're on Union's side, they have it coming."

"What about Vallah?" Cash sat up on his bunk, and we locked eyes. "She's a Union soldier."

"Vallah's gone. I've spent too long chasing her ghost. I'm going East. I won't let the Union ruin the rest of my life." The moment the words escaped my lips, the factory bells rang louder and faster than I'd ever heard them clang before.

We hurried into the bright red, blue, and yellow bursts raining down from the fireworks in the clear night sky. The explosions overhead illuminated what caused the commotion below. A mass of Union guards writhed in the dirt at their posts. All the workers stepped back from the fences to show the armed and uniformed young men and women twitching uncontrollably amidst the popping flares filling the air with smoke and vivid colour. I went to rush forward to get a better look at the fallen, convulsing guards. Cash quickly grabbed me by the collar to keep me still. When I turned to question him, he motioned subtly to my Catcher stepping out of his jeep. Strickland River paused to meet my gaze in the incessant ringing from the rocking bells and the increasing flashes from the fireworks display that could not be stopped once it began. My Catcher looked torn between pursuing me or aiding the incapacitated guards. He ran for his fellow Union officials. I was still locked in a cage after all. A few guards seemed untouched by the strange affliction that had befallen our other captors. There were too few on their feet to resuscitate their comrades. Even the Catcher seemed dumbfounded as to what action he should take. And then the startling scene came into focus when a small posse of three teenagers, led by The Kid, huddled behind Strickland River's jeep, hiding on the shadowy side away from the pandemonium going on at the gate and surrounding guard posts.

The Kid's team made quick work of slashing open the jeep's two tires on their side. They sliced the rubber carefully, causing the vehicle to lean toward them, and the tread went flat. I watched all of this in awe, unsure what to do, confounded as to what would happen next, ignorant to the plan playing out on my behalf. The Kid pulled the backpack from off his shoulders and spoke to the two figures with him in the dark. He handed the others items I couldn't quite make out from this distance. Only by the rapid illuminations made by the fireworks could I see The Kid wave me away from his position. He seemed to be signalling for me to go toward the opposite end of the yard, to the fence behind the casita rows. Two teens rounded the fence corner at The Kid's direction, and their leader disappeared into the darkness beyond the jeep. It dawned on me like a kick in the ass that the escape was on, and it was high time to act accordingly. I gave one last look to the distracted Catcher tending to the shaking soldiers on the ground around him. Pushing Cash into the wood alleys between shacks, we ran along the fence to where the two teens were headed from the adjacent side.

"Shit, the book," I hissed at Cash.

"Forget it, man," he said.

Helpless, I threw up my arms. The Kid told me not to bother showing up without it, so I doubled back without even thinking to scan for the Catcher. Pops and sizzles continued outside the wood panels. Flashes of yellow, green, red, and blue broke through and fell on the *Exile Manifesto* on my cot. I took it under my arm, turned to leave, and decided to grab the loose-leaf pages covered in my writing from under the bed.

Back with Cash in the alley behind the houses, along the fence, I gripped the stack of papers. There were multiple fallen guards along the way. As we passed the regular guard posts, we witnessed bodies with limbs gnarled gruesomely, with foam about their mouths, littering the dry earth on our way to where we eventually saw the two teens kneeling in the dirt against the fence. We arrived before them short of breath, separated by the rusting, metal enclosure. I noticed the tools The Kid must have given them when they used small, handheld wire-cutters to snip the steel threads one by one. The blasting fireworks began to slow their pace in the distance, leaving the bell to toll wildly in the night. Cash and I stood helpless while the boy and girl about ten years younger than us performed the daring rescue.

"You got the book?" One of them asked hurriedly, neither of them taking their eyes from the task at hand.

"Right here," I replied. My mouth was dry.

A short line was eventually cut about knee-high from the ground, and the girl with braided, blonde hair folded back the severed barrier so that Cash could crawl through the opening to be pulled through to the other side by the ginger-headed, freckle-faced boy. I was next, but I was much too excited and didn't crouch low enough. When Cash and the boy yanked me toward them, my shirt and skin caught on the razor-sharp wires, opening deep cuts in my flesh.

"You alright, man?" The blonde girl released the fence, noticing the blood left behind.

"Haven't felt this good in a long time." Adrenaline numbed my pain.

"The book?" The freckled kid had a satchel slung over his shoulder. I handed over the pages along with my own. He put the writing in the leather bag at his side.

"What about Carmen?" I demanded.

"Don't sweat it. The Kid's on it." The ginger boy looked up at me from shoulder height. His pale, round cheeks seemed to glow in the darkness. "We gotta go."

I noticed the faint reflection coming off the blonde girl's braid, almost twenty yards ahead already.

"Where we going?" I asked the pale-faced boy.

"No time." He sprinted off after the girl with impressive speed.

Me and Cash looked at each other. I didn't realize his cigarette was clutched between his teeth the whole time. He took one last haul and flicked it into the dirt, a small spark flying when it hit the ground, and we chased after the teenagers, struggling to keep up.

It felt like hours that our four sets of feet pounded the small rocks and dust underneath us. Only by the stars, being blocked by the rising, black hills on the horizon, could I tell we were approaching the beginning of higher ground. Cash wheezed, coughed, and spat every half kilometre or so. We finally entered the hills. The pace set by the teens was remarkable, reminding me how long it had been since I had run with the thrilling knowledge that someone was chasing. Surely my Catcher would call in a ride from somewhere else, but it would be hours before he could get repairs or a replacement vehicle, which would only get him so far before the terrain got too difficult for four wheels. I wondered if he knew the land well enough to track our course. The only dread I felt was for the all too likely scenario that The Kid couldn't spring Carmen from solitary. Those bolts were made thick. Then there was the fact that Carmen had the added weight of life inside her belly for the seemingly endless kilometres we ran.

When it felt as though my heart was about to give out, I noticed the ground begin to slope down. It was a gradual descent at first, which quickly turned into a steep, winding grade where shrubs and patches of grass came underfoot with more regularity. Valley walls eventually came to rise as we entered the twisting halls that became visible in the faint, purple light creeping over the hills. Humid air began to fill my lungs, slightly moistening my dry, gaping mouth that sucked for oxygen. The trickling of running water became audible in the rising light, and I found myself praying that a cool drink from a small stream or humble puddle was awaiting me shortly. In the soft pink morning, we wound a dell wall to find The Kid, his companion, and Carmen all sitting on bicycles atop a long, steep, grassy decline into a waiting river valley. Cash vomited when we finally came to a halt. I wrapped my arms around Carmen and her wide mid-section, immediately embarrassed that I ever doubted her ability to do anything she put her mind to.

"The book?" The Kid asked in a heavy tone. The Ginger boy handed him the satchel. The Kid looked inside to confirm, and he looked happy to be reunited with the words before putting the leather bag over his shoulder. "We're about half way now." He looked as though he hardly broke a sweat. Carmen was practically holding me up. She noticed the blood on her hands after embracing me.

"Half?" I moaned.

"Don't worry." The Kid winked, motioning to the four other bicycles leaning on kickstands next to him. "It's all downhill from here."

"Wait. What did you do to those guards back there?" My genuine concern was also a convenient stall before continuing on.

"The necessary, my friend." And with that, The Kid pushed forward, confirming my fears that the sudden seizures were inflicted on my account. I found myself half hoping the results were fatal. After reading the General's allegations against Union soldiers only a few short hours before, I couldn't help but wish suffering upon my enemies.

The skills necessary to ride a bike really are as unforgettable as the saying goes, especially when doing more braking than pedaling. As soon as I gripped the handlebars and felt the hard seat under me, the motions came rushing back to me. We carved jagged lines in the quenched soil below our thick tires, zig-zagging down the steep slope toward the stream glistening in the new dawn. Wind blew over my head and across my scruffy cheeks. I would have howled with delight if I wasn't afraid it would alert anyone around to our jailbird gang. My feet dug into the pedals, and I stood hunched, bending over handlebars to grip the brakes. The blood across my back felt cool in the fast-moving breeze. Only while standing on a breaking wave did I feel so in touch with the slipstreams left by the gods for us like playthings. A life in combat — or death at the hands of my Catcher — was hot on my heels. All I could do was enjoy my flight for as long as it lasted.

The Kid led the way, weaving through shrubs, rocks, and trees as he fought playfully for a position at the front. Carmen came next, with Cash doing his best to keep up. She crouched low to reduce her drag and barrel toward the water as fast as possible. I watched my partners in crime and innocence during my wide, meandering curves. The ginger teen and his blonde partner nipped at my rear wheel to keep me on course like dogs herding witless sheep toward the pen. Only once my legs began to tire from steadying myself on the prolonged descent did I see where we were being steered.

Tall, thin palm trees formed the outer limits surrounding an even more dense interior forest. The canopy's varying shades of green looked impenetrable from my view above. Soaring birds seemed to be the only things able to penetrate the natural roof sheltering the mysterious woods. The river formed the lone break in the foliage, and even it became engulfed by the boughs and leaves as the ground beneath my tread began to level toward the valley floor. Even after the spirit-testing run and perilous descent, our guides called for our burning legs to pedal hard when we entered the hall of pillars supporting the palms providing shade. I felt like a wild horse galloping through the trunks and falling coconuts to flee cowboys just waiting to break me. Loud thuds from the falling debris were heard on one side and the other, But I couldn't lift my eyes above for fear that I might ride smack into the narrow, innumerable towers. Bugs began to fly at my face to add to the rough, exhilarating trek. I spat out those that made their way into my mouth when I gasped for air. Midday came, and I thanked the gods for the shadows cast by the palms that gave way to cocoa, lime, avocado, and mango trees growing in irregular sizes and patterns. Thankfully our teenage leaders slowed their speed shortly after we started dodging the low-hanging fruit hovering along our course.

"We dismount here," The Kid shouted. Those of us behind struggled to stop so abruptly in the fallen leaves. He swung his leg over his seat and stood proudly.

There seemed to be nothing but vines, spider webs, flowers, and foliage in every direction. Roosters crowed from unknown locales. Mosquitos buzzed around my ears. My clothes were drenched with blood and sweat from the humidity percolating in the lush forest. The Kid cupped his hands about his mouth and produced a call that sounded somewhere between a barking dog and a meowing cat. The reply came rustling from the bushes just metres from where we stood. I half expected a four-legged little animal to emerge. Instead, a short, stalky guerrilla came forth from the thicket with a rifle slung over his shoulder. A purple bandana was tied around his wavy, black hair.

"Stay close." An impish smile was written on The Kid's face. "Easy to get lost in the maze."

The deep green brush became thicker and taller with every few steps. Each of us pushed our bicycles through what I recognized to be the croton plant known for its unruly growth. It was a hearty, wild-growing bush that had been trained into a winding hedge. Tight corners and jagged edges marked our way deeper into The Kid's lair. More guerrillas emerged from alcoves cut from the croton, which was red in some patches, purple in others, and green everywhere in between. There were surprisingly many armed teens stationed along the twisting gauntlet. They harboured far more menacing motivations in their eyes than the ghetto guards ever could.

"I'm going to smack one of these little shits if they keep gawking at me like I'm some Catcher or Union soldier." Carmen raised the back of her hand in warning to one of the guerrilla's prowling close by.

"They mean well," The Kid replied. "They're orphans of the storm just like you and me."

Carmen lowered her hand guiltily. Her expression softened, understanding their rage all too well.

"We almost there, man?" The journey obviously took more out of Cash than the rest of us. "Could use a little something to keep me going, you know?"

"What happened to the stuff I gave you last night?" The Kid seemed unconcerned with the volume of our voices as he called back in the single-file line.

"Never got the chance to light up. Left it behind. Things went down pretty quick."

"Thanks, by the way," I added.

"Don't thank me yet." The Kid looked to me. "You got a long way still. Wish I could see you through." To Cash: "we'll get you your medicine soon. Where do you think we make the stuff?"

Turning the final bend in the croton hedge, The Kid revealed his woodland sanctuary. The maze opened into a massive courtyard encircled by great, emerald walls composed of intricately woven vegetation that climbed nearly four metres tall, almost meeting the drooping bows from the canopy above. Light broke through the fort in crisscrossing beams, speckling the roughly two-dozen trailers and mobile homes scattered about the jungle stronghold. A chrome-covered school bus sat parked in the centre, shimmering as it reflected the rays poking in. The flamboyantly long vehicle was further decorated in spray paint that depicted curvy women, marijuana leaves, dragons, and machine guns. A clay chimney rose from the bus roof at the middle and stretched up toward the palm trees until it disappeared in the concentrated fronds. Heavily armed children ranging from seven to seventeen ran and played about, seemingly undisturbed by our presence.

"Welcome to my humble abode." The Kid looked about his homestead with pride. "The morning's hunting party should be back with dinner soon. There's water from the river in the drums behind the bus there. I'm sure you're all thirsty."

"What is this place?" My curiosity got the better of my thirst.

"This is where we make the crystal that pays to keep these kids fed." The Kid's hands were on his hips, obviously satisfied. "The war, the draft, the labour camps, all leave a lot of kids without people to look out for 'em. I do my best for some of 'em for a little while." The Kid walked us around the bus to where fifty-litre barrels with spouts out the bottom sat in crates attached to the rear bumper. We cupped our hands and drank the cool, clean water with a slight metallic aftertaste.

The full tour of the grounds, measuring about two acres, was complete with tales of the daring adventures The Kid carried out to acquire each little house on four wheels. If he'd told me the astonishing, inconceivable stories while pushing his rusted wheelbarrow in the ghetto, I almost definitely wouldn't have believed him. Yet, after he sprung me from prison with such relative ease, I found it hard to put limits on what The Kid was capable of. Each mobile home gave lodging to about five kids. All of the dwellings seemed well-equipped and stocked with fruits and vegetables from the abundant forest. It was impressive to see how many children and adolescents were given a place to stay, food to eat. I knew my friends, and I would have killed to stumble upon such a haven when we were left without guardians. Then I paid attention to how many kids toted weapons. Many of them likely had to kill, in some form or fashion, to keep their place in The Kid's guerrilla ranks.

"And this baby here," The Kid paused as he patted the chrome hood of the bus, "…is the generator that sustains us."

He called it the village of Nevermind, a place for the disregarded, forgotten generation he shepherded for better or worse. The Kid pounded a fist against the folding glass doors cut from the long, reflective surface covering the outer shell of the bus. Bullet holes punctured the small, grimy panes, and similar damages were peppered across the murals painted over the chrome siding. The door squawked on its track. The Kid forced it aside, revealing an armed boy in the driver's seat wearing a gas mask. One hand was on his weapon and another on the lever that allowed us to climb the three steps to the vehicle's belly. There were no seats other than the guard post at the steering wheel. Two older boys stood in goggles, ventilators, thick rubber gloves, and aprons. Their gear looked like it was military-issued. The olive-green attire protected them from the chemicals bubbling in glass jars and beakers feeding into the chimney at the roof's low centre. A workbench ran along the walls where seats used to be. The Kid took the bandana from around his dreads and held it over his mouth and nose. We followed suit, lifting our shirts over our lips and nostrils, watching the two teens in fatigues toiling to make the crystal in the hot, tin bus.

They were approaching the drafting age. The Kid told us he saved them. Pushing a wheelbarrow and crystal across the ghetto plains, I condemned the opportunist he was for meeting a feral desire in an otherwise captive community. Setting eyes on the village he called Nevermind stirred a great pride in me for The Kid's mission. I was surprised to find myself impressed by the measures he went through to give the young boys and girls a home worth protecting. They had food and refuge by his hand. As I began revering The Kid, the question I pushed from my mind in my determination to avoid capture came sharply to my attention. I interrupted The Kid's speech about the sprawling routes of his enterprise.

"What happened to the guards?" I asked The Kid. He stared into my eyes. The two crystal cooks stopped their busying around. The Kid seemed angry that I had the audacity to ask the question with such an ugly answer. Tension wisped about the crystal kitchen in clouds thicker than the steam and smoke catching the light. I could see him deciding how he was going to scold me for acknowledging his deeds, the deeds done to spring me. His expression softened quickly, and The Kid shrugged his shoulders.

"We gave 'em hot shots." The Kid looked to his cooks. They appeared to take his subtle glance as approval. They went calmly back to work without a word. "We're at war, Ezra. Don't be confused about it."

"You poisoned them," I said loud enough for the cooks to hear me from my place closest to the driver's seat.

"I made a choice to get you out before we lost another ally to the Union killing machine." The scales of justice were level in his opinion. My scale was teetering. It was going to be a shame to tell him I wasn't worth the trouble despite my gratitude.

"They're dead?"

"Most of them. Likely. Yes." He was a stone in his countenance, losing himself in the cooks' measured, calculated process. "You're going to tell the General about what you've seen here in Nevermind. Let her know we have a solid network to support the Exodus. This war is going to end one day. Tell her I've got the people who will rebuild this country when that day comes. She'll know what to do." The Kid sighed. "More arrive every day."

"Why don't you tell her yourself?"

"My people need me here." The Kid waved us down the steps, nodding to the cooks before he joined me on the soft ground outside the bus. "I could find other ways to get a message to the General. Your repayment starts now. I need you to look around, make observations, write, spread the word about the revolution once you get East. We need all the fighters we can get. Others will come."

"I didn't just bust out and run from one war to get caught up fighting in yours."

"The only path East goes through the General. I scratched your back, asshole. Can't pass along a message?" He hunched toward Carmen, Cash, and I as if to tell a secret. "Listen, my cooks are getting older. I am too. We can scare off a Catcher or two when we need to, but an army of them is different. We need reinforcements. My name's going to be called soon too, Ezra."

"You risked having a Catcher around when you busted me out." I was truly grateful, but I couldn't stop trying to tally the lives my freedom cost.

"Leaders have to take chances sometimes. Can you lead, Ezra?" It sounded strange to have The Kid — almost ten years my junior — toss around orders like I was a subordinate. The fact of the matter was that our causes happened to align for the moment. We shared the weight of a grisly deed done to take us farther on our respective courses. He was my only ally in my bid to escape across the line. I shook his hand, knowing full well I had plenty more shady deals ahead if I was going to get where I wanted to go.

"I'll tell the General you've asked for reinforcements. I'll tell people in the East about your revolution," I lied well with years of experience in the field. "You just have to make sure I get there."

"I'll have my two best take you to the river that leads to one of my distributors. She'll have instructions from there." The Kid waved over the freckle-faced teen and his blonde partner, who cut the wire to set me free.

"Wait. I need to light up before we hit the road." Cash was shivering despite the humidity. The years spent on opposite shifts in the ghetto veiled the cancerous takeover his addiction performed on him. He could go days without crystal before Los Muelles, before the ghetto. I quickly realized that the duration of our escape was the longest he'd been without since being introduced to The Kid.

"We'll take care of you, friend." Our host whistled to the kids playing outside the closest mobile home. "Get a pipe for our countrymen," he said and turned to Cash. "There will be plenty more waiting for you downriver. Colonel Couture is one of my most trusted distributors." Then The Kid turned to me. "She'll be able to put you on the right path. You should get your back patched up before you go too." Cash walked off toward the small shelter, following the children.

"And the Colonel will take us to the General?" Carmen asked. Her face was pale. She held her hands around her stomach, looking as though she were about to burst.

"It's two days on the river before Colonel Couture's temple. It's a hell of a sight. Worth the trip itself. From there, it will be another week or so to the General, another few days to the line if you make it to Montagne de Feu."

"That could be two weeks." Carmen looked at me. Exhaustion, worry, and frustration welled up in her moist eyes. "I'll never make it, Ezra." This baby is coming any minute." I didn't know what to say. She focused on The Kid. "Do you have room for me? I could lend a hand. It would just be until the baby was old enough for us to head out on our own."

"We can't leave you, Carmen." But I didn't see any other way. "We've made it this far because we've stuck together."

"Vallah's gone. Mick is god knows where. We haven't stuck together at all. I have someone else to protect now, Ezra." Carmen fought off her tears, furrowed her brow like I'd seen her do so many times, and addressed The Kid. "I'm a good fighter. All I need is a few weeks."

"We'd be happy to have you." The Kid put his hand over his heart. "You and your baby. There's plenty you can teach the rest of them here. Union fears guerrillas and mothers the most. You're both."

"Then I'll stay too," I said quickly. "I have to meet your baby."

"You've got a Catcher on your tail, Ezra. Lead him away from here." Carmen couldn't hide her relief to have a safe space to bring her pending child into the world.

"You're sure about this?"

"You can make it, Ezra. You don't need me. And Cash will only slow you down," Carmen advised.

When Cash eventually emerged from the trailer, he looked lighter on his feet, as if he were floating over the grass towards us. Carmen delivered the news that she wouldn't be coming with us. He simply gave her a sad smile, embraced her, and backed away without saying anything.

"The river will keep them moving," The Kid rubbed his hands together. His ulterior motives for our successful mission were not well hidden.

The blonde and redhead teens who cut the hole in the fence arrived at his side with inner tubes from tires over their shoulders. They handed one to Cash and one to me. Patches had been melted over the puncture wounds in the rubber. I immediately realized that we were not the first people The Kid had run down shit's creek with nothing more than a floating ring and a Colonel's name. I wondered how many lives were lost failing to deliver his message to the General. Our escorts led Cash and me back through the maze. Carmen disappeared behind the croton hedges, holding her stomach with one hand, blowing a kiss with the other. Rustling in the bushes could be heard all around us as we passed the guerrillas in their hiding places. My life was no easier at their age. The blonde and redhead kids strolled ahead of us, apathetically carrying out their orders.

I heard the river long before I saw it. We walked for hours while being accosted by mosquitoes and the thick jungle heat. The bandaged cuts on my back became a gathering place for all the flying insects seeking a drink or the cool, wet relief provided by the drying blood. Sweat collected under where the inner tube rested on my shoulder. Cash appeared unperturbed in his state of chemically induced bliss. Then we came to it: a turquoise lagoon carving its way through limestone, gushing under the branches and vines growing out from the valley walls. It looked refreshing and dangerous in the same instant. The Kid's emissaries took us to the riverbank and gawked at us expectantly. Our route was in no way charted. The entryway to the raging waters was only slightly calmer than the peril we were sure to encounter along the ride. Boulders peaked up through the white water ahead. Debris from upriver barreled by us as the logs and branches collided with rock before submerging and reappearing on the waters Cash and I were supposed to travel.

"Is there another way?" I inquired.

"Colonel Couture doesn't want to be found. She keeps herself well hidden. This is the only way to find her." The ginger-headed boy turned to walk away.

"Any advice?" I called after him.

"Keep your ass up."

Cash licked his lips as his glossy eyes feasted on the running river. I glanced at him, but he did not acknowledge me. He hovered down to the water's edge like a spectre. Pale yellow sunlight from the orb lowering through the trees covered Cash. A calm, confident glow surrounded him as he stepped into the shimmering water. Somehow, he made the frightening rapids appear to be nothing more than a gurgling pool when he encouraged me to follow him into the water as if to be baptized. We needed to be on our way before we lost daylight. No amount of time would pacify the violent river, and I had no plans to navigate such a wild stream in the dark. Cash bowed his head to the water and took a drink. He smiled back to me, calling to mind the features he and Vallah shared as brother and sister. Then, with a serenity that quieted my doubts, he settled himself in the rubber ring, pushed off from the limestone bank, and drifted off into the yellow gateway between jungles on either side.

My experience was not as serene as Cash made his appear to be. I learned fast why the ginger-headed boy warned me to keep my ass up. Hard, jagged rocks assaulted my hips, thighs, and boney butt through the hole in the rubber ring. I shifted and adjusted my weight, trying to perch my entire body on the inflated inner tube without toppling into the surging river. The scratches along my back were at least cooled by the foaming, perilous waters. Drowning seemed like a constant possibility until I eventually embraced the turbulent path and resigned myself to the tributary's will. Only once sunset engulfed the jungle did the water level out and give way to a flat, reassuring lagoon.

Music I'd not heard since I was a child filled my ears. Tranquil, tired voices sang in harmony inside my head and deep within the hollows of my chest. Gentle drums and clapping hands welcomed me back to the water as I broke the still surface with my fingers and toes. The river moved beneath me. My ancestors, at once long gone and ever-present, carried me, doing their best to return me to the sea. The only true friend I still knew in life was drifting farther from me with every metre travelled. Cash found his freedom, but as Carmen revealed to me, he would do something entirely different with it than I planned to. That's what I told myself in my solitary pursuit for liberty. Survival would no longer cut it. From the time Cash, Vallah, and I were forced inland from the sea, our simple pursuits were water, food, and shelter. In the ghettos, I was given as much in exchange for my labour, but freedom was mine to lose. I scarcely thought that I was born with something worth stealing. I gave it away so flippantly in light of my hunger and thirst, but as I floated downstream, concerned about my next meal, I rediscovered that freedom I'd traded away so long ago. The right to Ezra Atun, which was once handed to the Union, became rotten fruit. My new life took seed. The void in my stomach was my own. Even if starvation, infection, or virus claimed me, it would be a satisfying end to know that I drifted downriver on my own accord in hopes of finding something I could not explicitly name. If I died being eaten by animals or drowned in torrential rain, it would be a death all my own. The body was mine, my life belonged to me, and so, I wanted to die for my own foolish beliefs and desires. I would not die for a stranger's vision.

STRICKLAND RIVER
MARCH 2192

I wiped the foaming spit from around her mouth with the sleeve of my shirt. Her ribs cracked under the weight pushing down on her chest from my interlocked hands. No matter how fast, how hard I pressed, nothing would revive her. The rattling sounds she made just before her last breath escaped her lips were deafening. Her eyes went dead. She lay lifeless in the dust when I ran towards the next Union guard writhing in pain, driven insane by fear. One after the other, I tried in vain to save a single guard.

Much of the night was rife with such horror. Only once the sun began to rise, when a new day came, did my mind turn to my case: Ezra Atun. He would bear the full brunt of my ire, but that moment would have to wait until after I helped the few remaining breathing guards bury their young comrades. Few had the displeasure of getting the hits that weren't spiked by The Kid and his merry band of murderers. The survivors grabbed shovels and drove their spades into the dirt while the crystal deepened the damage done to their minds. No amount of training or procedure could have prepared the Union guards. The Kid and his faithful counted on the chaos. Their time would come. I had graves to dig first.

My girls were a world away when they met their ends. They were not afforded a final resting place for their father to visit. A foreign battlefield cradled their bones. Time and distance scattered their memories like sand in the wind. I wept for my girls while I poured red dirt over the strangers piled on top of each other in the hole I made with other Union sons and daughters. It broke my heart to leave them in their despair, but I couldn't wait around for Union officials to arrive and begin their investigation. I was not prepared to answer any questions from my superiors. My mission, my calling, was a solitary one.

The gates were locked. I posted three heavily armed soldiers at the break in the fence where Ezra and Cash escaped. I found footprints in the red earth around where the chain-link fence was cut. Four sets of tracks trailed off toward the horizon. The keys to the jeep jangled in my shaking hand when I started the car. I was so intent on chasing the outlaws down that I failed to notice the flattened tires. The fugitives bought themselves another hour in the time it took me to get the remaining guards to jack up the jeep, patch the slashed rubber, and inflate the tires enough to resume my pursuit.

A determination unlike any I'd ever known overcame me as I followed the imprints left by those guilty of treason. I kept my distance from the markings while I drove slowly beside Ezra's trace, careful not to disturb the ground leading me to my target. Footprints eventually gave way to the thin tread marks left by bicycle tires. Each narrow trail showed the dodgers for the snakes they truly were. Ezra was a serpent with a mouth full of venom. He was a poison to the Union. I was the antidote.

I took my foot off the gas when the tracks came to a steep valley with the jungle in the distance. The jeep handled well on the rough terrain. My teeth were clenched while I pressed down on the brake pedal with all my weight. I hadn't slept much and descended into a bad dream. All the hatred and rage welled up from the events of the night were channeled into that steering wheel. Each finger of my hand was frozen solid in the shape of a claw when I went to open the car door and step into the world governed by the dodgers. Flexibility was necessary. It was time to wake up, stretch out, and be alert enough to watch my back from that moment forward. I unfastened the strap over the magnum in its holster at my side. The sudden interaction with my mortality rushed up my nostrils. My chest puffed forward with extra air in my lungs. Maybe I wasn't as fast as I once was, but I was confident to draw quicker than any dodger, deserter, or guerrilla. Union trained me. It was time to hunt.

The trees were too tight for the jeep, so I went into the dark green world on foot, following the footprints left in the mud. It felt like the better part of the day that I scanned the jungle floor for any trace Ezra left behind. Snapped branches, splashes of water, even the smell humans left behind; they all led me to him. Night fell and awoke the nocturnal beings always lurking in the wildest places on the island. Moonlight betrayed my targets. Their trail was too fresh and overpopulated. I followed deeper into the forest until I discovered a dense living wall stretching up from the forest floor. Fallen leaves were ruffled nearby. The hammer of my magnum was cocked. My hand rested on the handle. No amount of humidity could quench my thirst. Amidst all the chirping, mating calls, and rustling, I made out a human sound.

A demon from the darkness assailed me from above. Thin limbs wrapped around my neck and head. The weight brought me to my knees. It felt like a rabid monkey was doing its humble best to strangle me to death. I was able to slide the creature's arms from my throat. All went black when the hairless forearms covered my eyes for a moment. My attacker clawed at my face, tugged my hair, bit me all over. Not a grunt or wail escaped my lips for fear that my presence would attract more devils on The Kid's perimeter. Many horror stories about the fledgling insurgents in the jungle reached my ears from other Catchers brave enough to chase their prey into the guerrilla's domain. The little monster assaulting me made no such attempts at silence. He shrieked and hollered with terrifying, primate-like ferocity. I had to quiet him quickly. Other lost, evil menaces lurked close by, and I didn't need them alerted. Little ones strike in packs. Shame already welled up inside me for letting a sprat get the drop on me. From my knees, I ripped the childish rebel off my back. His feet were thrown over his head as I pulled him over my shoulder. A teenage boy landed flat on his back in front of me. His ginger hair looked fire red in the moonlight spilling through the canopy to the muddy forest floor. Before he could roll over to pounce from all-fours, I found myself on top of him, knees pressing into his arms, hands squeezing his windpipe. The young guerrilla's face was smeared with dark dirt. His eyes bulged. His teeth shone white as he chomped at the air in desperate attempts to wound me in any way possible. I could feel his legs flailing behind me. The noises he made were muffled for lack of oxygen. His snarling was still audible and disturbing in the woeful, sleepless jungle.

"Where is Ezra Atun? What did The Kid do with him?" My lips were inches from the boy's ear while I restrained him with hands harbouring the strength earned by many years in combat. "Tell me now." My warning was issued in a hissing whisper. "Don't make me kill you." I loosened my grip slightly to let air pass into his lungs. He coughed wildly.

"Fuck you," the ginger-headed teen managed to say between frantic gasps. I pressed my magnum to his forehead. The calluses on my other hand tightened around the ginger's throat once again.

Then I felt it: a bullet ripped through my bicep. The muscle used to lift my gun. The pain seemed to strike long before the shot rang out and further stirred the teeming jungle. My eyes rose to the shooter. Shock and darkness made me see my baby girl holding the smoking rifle, taking aim at me. Blonde streaks — unlike any I'd seen since my daughter left for the front — were what tricked my eyes in the delirium infiltrating my senses. I reached out toward her beautiful face. Only by the sound from the second blast whizzing past my ear did I snap out of my daze. The hand I used to squeeze the life from the red-headed boy felt around on the black ground for my magnum as the blonde guerrilla charged me. She was not my baby girl. I had to remind myself before I took up my weapon and blew a hole in her leg. My cover was broken. Going on undetected was impossible. A choking boy and a wounded girl were my best bet to ascertain Ezra's whereabouts. The girl's blonde hair felt soft in my grasp. She was small. I dragged her beside her comrade, away from her rifle. Her screams brought tears to my eyes, but nothing would deter me from my mission, not even harrowing thoughts about the way my girls left the world. All my efforts were in their honour.

"Where is Ezra Atun?" My dominant hand hung lifeless at my side. The magnum's weight was awkward for my left's lack of practice taking aim. Little marksmanship was required. My gun was pressed to the ginger hair of the boy, who was slowly regaining his breath.

"I'll never tell," said the blonde. She managed to stifle her wailing and wrapped her arms around her injured leg on the ground.

"Maybe *you* won't." I stood over the diminutive rebels and pressed the sole of my boot onto the boy's neck. "Where is Ezra, son?" The fear of being heard was long gone. Time was short. My spirit was trembling in startled recognition of my deeds. I wished for escape from the hell I entered. The fastest route required answers. Kicking the girl's open wound was a shame that never left me. "Don't make me hurt her more, son." Shrieks from the girl fostered even greater gloom in the haunted jungle overwhelming me. I took my boot from the boy's throat and pointed the gun at the girl. "Tell me, or she dies."

"The Colonel," the boy coughed wildly. A spectre carrying the truth came forth from him against his will. "Colonel Couture. The temple."

Hope at last. I knew the Colonel well.

"You're a bastard," cried the girl in agony.

"The side with the most bastards always wins," I replied.

With my left hand, I shot both the children dead. My journey to the temple, to Colonel Couture, to Ezra Atun, would take me deeper into the blackened heart of the nation, into the rebel stronghold, into the most sinister depths of my soul. I shifted my holster on my belt to sit where my one good arm could reach it, departing the jungle to climb aboard my jeep and end the war I was fighting within since being a husband, a father no more.

Descending into hell wasn't the jarring fall many true believers claim.

Every visit was a slow, beleaguered crawl to the place reserved for mankind's ugliest, most powerful traits. I never thought my next encounter with the damned would sneak up on me so unexpectedly. Especially considering how well acquainted I was with humanity's uncanny talent to discover the apple in Eden and bite through the skin.

The sun was high in the sky when I returned from getting a middle-aged couple across the line. Their children had been lost to the conflict. Why is there no name for parents who lose a child? I was carrying a heavy load of despair for all the sorrow that rubbed off on me during the latest delivery from the West Caribbean Union to the East Caribbean Republic. Drinking water never flowed with any regularity on the two-day journey to the crossing point. Every trip made me grateful to be riding Trueno through the streets of Valle Oculto upon returning. I was considered a rich woman for having horses. Usually, the townsfolk would gather around my steed when I entered the village in the valley. But that day was different. Crowds brushed past Trueno's monstrous legs without the slightest bit of interest. They packed the narrows and trampled the ash in the streets until it was pounded into the hard, black ground. Men, women, and children rushed toward the faint screams echoing in the short alleys.

I sat forward in my saddle and made my way toward the old town square. Palm trees sprung from the black mounds of ash filling the Spanish plaza. The colonial buildings bordering the square were bathed in bright sunlight. Heat waves hovered just above the ground. From my place on Trueno's back, I could see Lou at the centre of the surging mob gathered in raging suspense. My right hand hung before a man tied by the wrists to palm tree trunks. The fronds and coconuts were hacked away. No shade fell on the assembly or the captive. There was not a lick of clothing on his naked body. His blue eyes were piercing from behind the grey mud caked all over his otherwise pink skin. His lips were cracked and bleeding. He was splayed out like a Christ of the tropics. Lou had an arm wrapped around the soldier's helmet, using it as a bowl to mix water and ash to form the sludge she smeared across the delirious, wounded man.

I dismounted and entered the horde. Trueno turned tail and forced her escape from the unpleasantness unfolding. Her space-black hide zigged and zagged on the volcano's face as she climbed out of the valley to the stables, to the home I longed to return to after another harrowing journey. But Lou's display of magic and madness could not be ignored. Designs drawn using the same grey muck pooled in the prisoner's helmet ran across the surface of her skin. Quetzal feathers in all their rich green, vibrant yellow, pastel blue, and radiant red adorned her braided hair. Her show was premeditated. It was only a matter of time before some Union official wandered into Lou's snare. I had seen a power brewing in her since our earliest days together in her cave.

Lou fought the war on a different plane, in an alternate dimension. What did the Union care about one of its scouts being abducted without a report from the barren edge of the country? Soldiers were bred to die. No one knew as well as I how inconsequential one infantryman's life was to the nation. Lou was not confined to the battle in those terms. Gods joined the human conversation most ardently in wartime, and Lou knew their language. She plotted to sway favour with the spirits. For all of her exploration into the dark arts, it seemed Lou was preparing to conjure something great to further the Exodus' cause. Perhaps she had a malevolent tidal wave in mind. Maybe the instantaneous presentation of an oasis to inhabit was her plan. I didn't know. All I knew was: the pain my witch inflicted upon the scout was but a slight fraction of the damage she was dishing out to the evil force at the Union's very core.

When you watch people long enough, they can't simply hide their nature. Boil down any person to their genetic code, and the words "us or them" will be scrawled there. We all inevitably pick sides. Most days, it's usually as simple as, "I want the ripest tomato on the pile in the market for my family that I feed". But on days when a Union scout is captured by an entire population – nearly a thousand souls – who've had their lives ruined in some form or fashion by the Union, and who live in constant fear of servitude, it was no wonder they reacted the way they did. I knew what it was like to entreaty the gods to spill the blood of my enemies, but no solace was found in the puddles spattered by the dead. I had witnessed rivers turned red from the lives draining downstream.

Lou had her devoted followers at a fever pitch. She served them a potent cocktail of anger, desperation, and faith. It was as if they had finally awoken from their years spent in terror. Too long had they lived helplessly. The wisdom they once had to govern their collective force was lost and forgotten in all their years as victims. Only when that Union scout was captured did their terror deform into wrath. People screamed at the man, they kicked him, they punched him, they flailed themselves at him like deranged anarchists. Their frenzied indignation was precisely the emotion I preyed upon when recruiting for Union ranks.

A child rode her father's shoulders and approached the sufferer. The soldier's groans were scarcely heard over Lou's surging flock. When the father lingered in front of the Union man, he drew back his fist and unleashed it on the defenceless skull dangling before him. His daughter used her seat on high to empty her mouth of all the spit she could collect around her baby teeth. I heard the bubbling saliva sizzle on the grey muck preserving the soldier's anguish in roasting, crispy flesh.

"What in the name of all the gods is happening here?" I grabbed Lou by the arm and shook her with all my strength.

"Judgement day has come." Lou wore an eerie grin. "Montagne de Feu has stood dormant too long." Just then, I felt the earth rumble beneath my feet. "The gods sent us the Union man as a sign. The time has come for Valle Oculto to empty." Sweat dripped out from under Lou's Quetzal headdress. The feathers pulled my eyes from the tormented Union scout. I looked beyond the dazzling colours to notice the small plumes beginning to rise from the crest of Montagne de Feu. "The river of fire will flow soon enough," Lou yelled out over the swarming, ravenous assembly. They cheered at the very sound of her voice. "This soldier is our sacrifice," she cried. Uproarious applause exploded throughout the square. The garish praises bursting from my people echoed from the walls bordering the pit full of palms and ash.

"What did we vow just two short years ago?" I wailed into Lou's ear, still gripping her by her arm.

"This is not killing. This is recompense to the powers that be. This soldier is being purified. He would've died a soldier. Now he dies a saint. But first, he will bear our people's hatred. They must pour their malice into him, into Montagne de Feu. Our people will be clean when the volcano wipes the Union from the world. We will remain, exorcize the evil inside us, and rebuild this nation with pure hearts."

Watching the rapid rate that my people adapted to the ugly horrors of our time was disheartening. The world went to shit, and it wasn't long before the population followed suit. I thought I could turn the tides for them. Under my wings, they were supposed to be alright.

Coded messages between neighbours became unnecessary. Our environment grew too ugly not to speak freely. Small talk was as extinct as humanity looked to be in a few decades. Lou and I spoke in biblical terms. We used rhetoric indicative of Armageddon. It was a scene from those novels Sergeant Porto used to read to me in the medical tent before the book bans.

The soldier just hung there. His flesh cooked. I almost expected the crowds to feast on him. Terror set in. I'm sure the scout's sense of fear died long before I arrived. The panic was all mine. All hatred to be found in the human heart was on display. Every second full of the sights, smells, and sounds recalling wartime memories was too overwhelming to bear. My nerves were shot for far too long to keep my sanity while standing in hell incarnate. More bludgeoning ensued. Each citizen was introduced to the devil inside us all. By no means did I want to interrupt such a rite of passage. I lived with the devil for years on the battlefield. We had some great talks. The bastard is a good time. No words quite describe looking at the most detestable of fallen angels straight in the eyes and realizing you're no better than the beast. Maybe that's what drew me to Lou upon our meeting those few years prior. She had seen the other side. She had gone over the edge, and she was back with unwavering lunacy. Torture performed for a participating audience was somehow not as shocking as what she experienced living in solitude in the barren hills bordering a Union farm all her life. She used me for my power. I used her just to have someone as mad as me around to talk with. That's how things got so far down the road to public execution. We were always broken people trying to lead broken people. I shed a tear for my dear friend, Lou. It rolled down my dirty cheek, and I pushed my way through the ravenous mob packed into the square.

My palm was sweating around the leather handle of my knife. People stepped aside once they recognized me. Some bowed their heads when I made my way to the prisoner. What a sad thing it was to be an honoured member in such a scene. I never understood why military heroes wanted their conquests painted and hung on walls with distinction. Such depictions of that hot summer day beneath an erupting volcano would not reflect favourably on my legacy for what I was about to do. Lou tried to stop me, but I threw her aside, pulled out my blade, and stuck it in the ear of the Union scout to save the entire town of Valle Oculto from plummeting further into such miserable depths with no return. The lights went out behind the soldier's eyes in a hurry. I relieved him of his life, of his duty. A collective outward breath actually echoed up against the colonial bricks enclosed around us.

Silence overtook the people. A profound sobriety gripped them in the loss of a single stranger's life. More blood was smeared on my hands as it sprayed from the victim's head when I withdrew the steel from his skull. Men fainted. Women collapsed to wallow in tears. Lou had her sacrifice. She healed them of their bloodlust in a single blow. I didn't disagree with it, but I vowed to never play games with the gods again. Never killing a man again was a promise I had to live with failing to keep. My season with the mystic was over. She conjured a terrible storm over Montagne de Feu to cast me out of the valley.

I tried in vain to beg many to leave before they were consumed by fire. Their faith in Lou was steadfast. Slander was spread against me. Source material was not difficult to find. The *Exile Manifesto* was at once my greatest recruitment tool and a confession of my most heinous deeds. It was impossible to convince the people I was any less evil than my holy counterpart.

On Trueno's back, I rode out of the valley in an endless pursuit of redemption. It became clear at that moment that two things were invariably true: I would never leave the country, and I would live the rest of my days in exile. It was naïve to ever think a home would embrace me again. Being alone suited me better anyhow. Another thing I knew without a doubt was my enemy. Whenever my path crossed with the Union, it would be a bad day for their side. There was no flag to fly but the colours of my own salvation.

A purple and orange sky lit the brightly painted concrete that made up Valle Oculto as I ascended the ridge leading West to the interior. Light rain coated the glossy buildings. Under the precipitation and falling grey flecks, the town shone with the brightness of a dying star. At least they were free to perish how they wished.

<u>**EZRA ATUN**</u>
MARCH 2192

It was then, surrounded by the haunting monkey moans, that our tires leaked and whimpered, giving out as if too afraid to go on any further. The rubber tubes beneath us took a beating on the river rocks along the way. Sunlight likewise leaked away from the day. It was time to make camp beyond the gaze of any other passengers on the water. Many eerie times had been shared between Cash and me on hunting trips in the cacophony of the jungle night, in the back alleys across Los Muelles, but there was something about the primate warning calls that made me, a dodger, feel most unwelcome and afraid. Yet, onward we went as all with a purpose must do in fear's sweaty grip.

After tossing our deflated inner tubes into the thick brush to hide our tracks, we walked onto the sacred ground worshipped by our ancestors. The discordant sounds bellowing from the howler monkeys encircled us as we crossed the clearing bordered by abundant jungle. Cash gave me a nervous grin reserved for times portending adventure. A stiff breeze blew through the blades of grass. Walking across the manicured lawn, I recalled the legends overheard in my village, in school, in the late barroom hours when men look desperately to myths of the distant past to provide refuge from the uncertain future. It was said that the gods fallen from heaven built Templos Desiertos to hide from the others residing amongst the stars.

I never thought I would live long enough to knock on god's door to see who answered.

The gusts parted the foliage to create tiny windows and revealed canvas tents flapping in the wind below the trees. People emerged from beneath the makeshift shelters scattered throughout the ruins. Many used the larger of the fallen rocks as foundations for their simple homes. Our presence brought some out to offer shy waves and faint smiles. The deeper into the old blessed site we sauntered, the denser the community grew. They looked like us; hardened, afraid, suspicious. Only by promises from The Kid did we believe the public around us wouldn't capture us and turn us over to the Union to claim the hefty price on each dodger's head. Our trepidations were complicated when loud whistles were offered to us. Brief applause, hoots and hollers all sounded as we entered under the stone arch, giving way to hundreds of tarps of wood and canvas, and other constructed shelters sprawled across the lawn leading to the monument aligned with the twilight. A hollow space was formed from boulders at the temple's apex. Moss-covered rocks framed the fiery orange orb falling over the horizon. A silhouette stepped into the space and began to sparkle. I wondered if it could be General Lament. My heart leapt into my throat. Cheers rang out, reverberating in low echoes off the white and black stone slabs overtaken by vines. The shadow backlit by the sun raised up its hands. We were quickly surrounded by congratulatory embraces and encouraging pats upon the back. I could not have been more confused, but only an idiot rebuffs a warm welcome. Especially with the law chasing. With as much humility and gratitude as I could muster in my bewilderment, I tried to hush the frenzied temple dwellers. Cash reveled in the greeting.

"What's going on here?" I was embarrassed to ask, which was surely apparent on my red face.

"Welcome to Templos Desiertos," a voice bellowed out from the crowd. The sound of her words seemed to quiet the rowdy bunch. "It's a rather confusing place for new arrivals, I must say. People like us aren't accustomed to a warm welcome." The speaker revealed herself in the form of a large woman who owned her mass as a consequence of her heavy presence. She wore deep fuchsia and teal makeup around her eyes. Purple lip paint covered her mouth. Her hair was short, messy, and pink like a pixie. "My name is Colonel Couture," she declared, striking a diva's pose that swayed her floor-length dress and jiggled the array of hand-beaded jewellery hanging around her thick neck. All those around exploded into merriment at the sound of her name. I thought I saw a glimpse of stubble on Colonel Couture's chin, which she held proudly to the sky. "Come now, boys. If you get swept up in this now, you'll wake up sore and even more befuddled. Follow me to my quarters," she said as if in invitation, though she placed her gorilla-sized hands over our shoulders and ushered us through the sea of people. Cash looked back, seeking the source of the burning crystal in the air.

Onward we were pushed. After nearly a hundred metres, weaving through dancing bodies, we came to an old testament tomb. Three boulders, each only slightly larger than the giant Colonel, formed an archway that was magnificently painted in pastel hues of turquoise, pink, yellow, green, and orange. On the stone beam above the doorway was a face, painted in the old tradition, surely not meant to depict the Colonel, but rather the persona that encased her like a triumphant aura.

Our doubts about entering the Colonel's modest cave were soon shoved aside by curiosity. We went inside the candlelit womb.

The inside was just as extravagantly decorated. Intricately sewn cloths were draped over wooden furnishings. The smooth, stone walls displayed in majestic colour a story of battle and migration. I could only get a glance of the tale.

Dirt and years filled the grooves found in the weathered faces of the countless stones stacked in primeval order. The temple walls were painted in colours cast from the setting sun. Torches sat in sconces along the corridors. Colonel Couture performed a greeting surely perfected through years spent welcoming the lost souls exiled to the jungle. She threw her voice round the winding halls traversing the temple interior. Her radiant pink wig entered the shadows ahead while her gentle, alluring voice persuaded from behind. Templos Desiertos — the buildings erected for religious rites — were converted to a theatre for Colonel Couture's dramatic talents.

"Look around you, sweethearts," the Colonel's speech enveloped us like a warm blanket as her words filled the hollows between the rocks. "This temple is a symbol for our times." We came upon a dead-end suddenly, as if the wall materialized at Couture's will. An intricate portrayal of the temple construction and its labourers was painted there. I thought the Colonel was leading us, but we stood at a barrier, and I felt her strong hand land on my shoulder from the darkness as she spoke.

"A disposable workforce is the link connecting the rise of any empire. Thousands of years ago, the foundation of this kingdom was laid by the hands of the enslaved natives. Those competing for the power owned by the gods aspire to greatness through the collective sweat, blood, and tears of marginalized people. It is impossible to resist admiring these great structures. King Solomon and his descendants ruled this region for centuries, relying on the fear brought about by the magnitude and reputation of this sacred space.

Those who resided within its walls were said to access the divine gifts of healing, wisdom, and soldiering. The West Caribbean Union is no different. I once belonged to the inner circle of the empire, entitled to the gifts bestowed by the government. To kill in the Union's name is rewarded with statues and riches. To question the plans set out by the masters is punishable by further servitude. When my battalion came upon this place after reading the *Exile Manifesto*, the parallels were too apparent to ignore. We were a band of trained assassins. Instead of laying bricks, we tallied corpses, forming the foundation for the empire that exists today." The small flames in sconces across the walls erupted in raging dances. Firelight burned so brightly it nearly blinded me. Colonel Couture continued preaching.

"When we learned this structure was built on a bedrock of magnetic ore that sheltered us from the Union's gaze, we accepted the gift of our ancestors. It was as if the slaves — our blood relatives — enacted a long game escape plan." The torches dimmed. "Compasses and satellites go dormant in the vicinity of the temple. You are free now." Couture materialized from the shadows before us. She walked to Cash. She stared deep into his eyes while I watched with fright. A golden bowl sat smoking in her hands. I knew the smell of burning crystal all too well. The Colonel blew the wisps into Cash's face. "Free to breathe whichever air you wish, free to fuck whoever you wish, free to strike the Union back when it raises its hand to your loved ones." The Colonel turned to me when she mentioned love contaminated by authority. "How does it feel to be out from under the Union's thumb?" She tried to bring the fragrant concoction under my nose. I turned away.

"I feel reborn," Cash spoke in a breathy whisper. A trance overtook him. His eyes glazed over. The Union may have caged us, but Colonel Couture plied my companion with her high ideals, using the crystal Cash inhaled.

"Yes, handsome," she said. "The moment you entered the veil hanging over our kingdom, you shed the chains shackled to you the moment you were born into poverty. We were the bricklayers. We were the labour, the disposable workforce, the killers, the killed. Now we are protected by the temple constructed by our ancestors. Welcome home."

* * *

Cash never stopped loving Mick. He told me so, time and again over the years. "Home" was always a tricky word for us. The first place we gave the name was burned to the ground. Any other station we lingered in our youth never came with any true sense of safety or security. Home was wherever we found ourselves in the company of loved ones. I was home so long as Cash was still at my side, but romantic love is another shelter altogether. Cash was my brother. I loved his sister. With her gone, I would never be truly home. The same could have been said for Cash. He had to watch the man he loved go to bed with another person every night. Cash had to stomach being spurned by Mick for the simple fact that they were born with different preferences in lust and tenderness. I considered myself lucky to fall in love even once in my woeful existence. Cash would have said the same, but on the temple grounds, he found an affection he never knew.

There were dozens of men who wished to share Cash's bed. Some even said they loved him. I knew Cash developed feelings for at least one of Colonel Couture's retired assassins. Validation and heavy narcotics are a potent mix, which is why we delayed so long. My intentions were to cross the line. My only friend in all the world was drowning in cock and crystal. Cash had a hard time picturing much better in the East, especially remembering the ghetto we so recently escaped.

I must admit: it was an enticing place to want to make camp as a dodger in his twenties looking to heal a broken heart. The temple grounds housed a wild group of liberated radicals who were all too familiar with how fleeting the future can be in wartime. It felt good to thumb my nose at the gods and follow the impulses stamped out by the Union. But I had gone too far. There had to be something over the line to make all the suffering worth carrying on. Hope pumped through my veins. Cash mainlined crystal. His affliction was having its day.

Vallah left all those years ago. Mick was taken to serve. Carmen stayed with The Kid to bring a child into the world. I couldn't bear to lose Cash too. The temple grounds were just too alluring to his weaknesses. He was in a junky daze. Cash didn't share my delusions about what world awaited in the East. Colonel Couture embraced him in a way he had never felt before. In some ways, I was happy for him, but he was at the mercy of his illness. If we didn't leave soon, Cash would be dead before Mick, and the latter was on a battlefield.

Cash stood before me, completely naked. His skin was glistening from his time with the man who left our tent when I arrived. There was hardly room for the two of us to stand in the lean-to held up by sticks, rope, and rubble. I asked him to cover up. He wrapped a woven, military-issued blanket around his shoulders. It wasn't the sight of his genitals that disturbed me. Years together numbed me to that. Cash's grey flesh clung to his ribs. All colour left his face. His shoulders slouched under the thick cape. A concave chest barely supported his collarbones. I asked him about making preparations for the next leg of our journey. He changed the subject to the throes of passion he so recently enjoyed. The smell of sex and melted crystal hung in the trapped, dank air. I took my exit.

Appointments with the Colonel were difficult to make after our introduction. Questions amassed over the weeks. She would not receive me to answer them. The temple was a maze. Returning to her chambers without a guide was impossible. No one seemed eager to help a dodger either. When I offered the information that Cash and I had never seen active duty, the eager welcome we first received faded like the soft edges of the eroded temple boulders. My inquiries about our overseer, our temporary residence, and a safe route East had to be run through Cash. His intimate relationship with the men who still donned their Union uniforms afforded Cash enough social capital to gain answers to the questions I fed him. Trying to steer someone as persistently inebriated as Cash to extract sensitive information from a community of former soldiers was no small feat. Information came in bits and pieces. Eventually, my friend discovered that a supply train delivered the goods we enjoyed to a makeshift depot hidden somewhere in the surrounding wilderness. Our meals that included dairy, fruits, vegetables, poultry, and other assorted meats were no longer such a mystery. Knowledge of the train wasn't enough. Where did the supplies come from? Where were they going? Could I hitch a ride?

Cash used his influence on those lusting after him to get me on a crew that unloaded the train cars during the monthly deliveries. The deserters on the temple grounds were a well-oiled machine. Colonel Couture was the unseen conductor operating the controls from her stone sanctuary in the sky. I recognized a proletariat apparatus from my years in the ghetto. There was little context Cash could provide before my first shift on the jungle train crew. All I knew was that the provisions convoy ran from Los Muelles through Templos Desiertos on its way to a place called Valle Oculto. The directions Cash acquired led me to a set of tracks embedded in the tropical forest only a few kilometres from Templos Desiertos. I stared at the steel coursing through the jungle-like silver streams. Turning my gaze to the left, I looked upon the way back to Los Muelles, to the life I left behind so many years ago, to a past that would never stop chasing me so long as I remained within the West Caribbean Union borders. To my right, a path to the East was laid out before me. The Kid said the General awaited in Valle Oculto. The Kid said General Lament held the key to my exodus. I was presented with a path leading directly to her, so I followed the tracks to the East, toward Valle Oculto. The grass was soft and damp beneath my feet. My shoes had finally dried from my journey on the river. Sunshine broke through the trees in thin beams. Birds sang. I was totally alone, lost in the timberlands with nothing but a narrow path to guide me. As the trail curved along a densely forested hill, I was taken back to the day of the coastal raids. The jungle transported me back to that nightmare, to when I hurried through the crops and smoke to find my parents, my home, overcome with fire. Each step required a reminder that such a scene was not waiting for me around the bend. I felt like I could walk all the way to Valle Oculto with nothing more than train tracks and bush songs to keep me company.

Keeping Los Muelles and the ghetto in mind was crucial as I marched toward my first shift in service of Colonel Couture. Once reunited with liberty, I was every bit a slave to it as Cash to the crystal. Never again would I take my place on an assembly line. My work on the Colonel's crew was not another passive resignation of my sovereignty. The Kid sprung me from my prison. He told me to seek refuge in the General. His word was the only counsel I could trust in a country that used freedom like currency. Discovering the supply route vehicle was my mission. I went undercover to chart my course across the line. Tracing the curve in the tracks, I almost walked directly into the headlights of the train's lead car and the dozens of staff there to collect and protect the cargo.

Wooden crates were stacked in my arms by other volunteers standing above in the supply car. A red, waxen seal marked the slit between the lid and thick slats. Straw peaked through the thin breaks between pieces. The dry hay scratched my skin as I carried the boxes to the wheeled dollies. An armed guard stood at each car's open door. Colonel Couture's deserters left their duty behind. Their automatic weapons were another story. Looking down at the seal beneath my chin while I hauled more crates, the Colonel's initials stared back up at me. The outline of the Western half of the island and the letters C.C. reminded me of the Union labelled crates I filled with bullets in the ghetto. When I next filled my arms and strained my back, I walked in stride with another labourer on our way to the dollies.

"How long has the Colonel been ripping off the Union like this?" I asked the bald, sweaty man next to me.

"We're just taking back what's owed," he grunted as he dropped the sealed cases and went back for more.

"Owed?"

"Everyone in Templos Desiertos fought for Union. These supplies are our retirement. We just pushed up our pension payout a little."

"Union discharged you?"

"Not exactly. We started as the Colonel's battalion. One of the fiercest the Union has ever seen. And that's saying something." The bald man tilted his head toward the armed guard on the stationary train. "It was a few years until we realized we were getting screwed, not fairly compensated for our work, so we started taking what was owed. From soldiers to thieves."

"Why all the guns then?"

"We might not want to hurt our former brothers-in-arms, but I've never known a Union man to give up supplies without a gun pointed in his face. The colonel didn't want no civil war. That doesn't mean we don't fight when we have to." He threw down another large crate. Lugging, walking, and talking seemed to be too much for him to do all at once. His body shape made it difficult to imagine him as a hardened killer, but his eyes told a different story. "You excited to go on your first run?"

"My first run?"

"Don't worry. You won't be stuck doing this unloading shit forever. You'll go out to collect soon enough. Quitting the fight cold turkey would've been tough. At least we still get to see some work in the field. Just consider yourself lucky you arrived after we laid these tracks. That was some real backbreaking work. We lost some good people. We eat a lot better now, though."

"Sacrifice a few for the many," I suggested, trying not to disagree with the part-time killer.

"Exactly. We invite everyone to join us before they die. They're welcome so long as they pitch in. We just can't have our little secret getting out. Know what I mean?" Sweat beaded on the man's head. He stared at me the rest of the walk back to the supply car. His threat was heard loud and clear.

"Loose lips sink ships," I said.

"Right on, brother. So does dead weight. You aren't dead weight, are you?"

"Hell no, sir."

Dodgers had no place in the West. There was always a side recruiting with some divisive logic and slogan. Too much of my youth had already been wasted waiting in a cage patrolled by true believers. The bald man predicted how my time on the temple grounds would inevitably end. Killers were rewarded. Pacifists were buried in unmarked graves. It was time to hitch a ride. I couldn't risk staying still to have misfortune discover me yet again.

STRICKLAND RIVER
APRIL 2192

Riding a horse evoked a memory taking me back to a long-gone childhood on my father's farm. Each stride sent pain shooting up my arm from the wound I dressed just below my shoulder. Blood seeped through the sleeve, and I ripped off my shirt to tie around the hole in my bicep. I could feel the metal slug moving around in my muscle, tissue, and nerves. It hurt every bit as much as the beating I took when my father locked me in a pen to break a wild horse he corralled for me to ride. He was waiting for me outside the wooden enclosure with a rope when I climbed away from the bucking bronco, determined to kick my head free from my weak body. I never liked horses after that, which made it all the harder to ditch my jeep along the river leading to Templos Desiertos. The natives on the bank would have no use for the vehicle. One bullet was enough to introduce them to the power I wielded in my magnum. They would have given me all their horses if I had any use for them. Following the water on four wheels was impossible. Four legs were the only way, despite my distaste for the smelly beast I rode.

Colonel Couture stuck her needle through my skin while I looked about her lair. The slug taken from my flesh sat in a tin bowl on the sealed crate at my side. She fed me. She kept my cup full with amber rum from the supplies stacked high in the ornate room nested in temple stones. Her care was not enough. Nothing she did could ever redeem her in my mind's eye. Colonel Couture led my girls into battle. The cross-dressing war machine gave the orders that got my daughters killed. No amount of thread could repair the damage done.

"Tell me where he is." I took a sip and avoided eye contact.

"You know I can't do that, Strickland," Colonel Couture muttered while she tied off the knot she sewed into my arm.

Knowing their commander saw them alive more recently than their father burned worse than the alcohol Colonel Couture poured over my stitches. Her only sin was being with them in the badlands where they fell. Union didn't tolerate remorse in such matters. Guilt and officers go together like water and oil. How many prayers were said each night with the hope that suffering finds me? When news telling about the ambush that took my girls returned to me from abroad, fury consumed me so ravenously that I rode to Los Muelles with the men who carried the unconscionably vexing message. Shame usurped rage when Union officials no older than my departed daughters turned me away from enlisting because of my age. They told me there was a way to channel my frustration, to put my woe to work.

"I suppose I owe these last few years to you. My job, I mean." The rum went straight to my head for all the blood I lost along the way.

"You don't owe me anything," she replied.

Her regret for saying as much was clear when she quickly turned from me to pour another drink. We both knew I didn't owe Colonel Couture a damn thing for the debt still due to me. Questions are all that linger in a mourning father's heart. The Colonel didn't have the answers the day I tracked her down when she was in Los Muelles on leave after her failed campaign in Guatemala. Anguish and embarrassment carried me from the departure docks, where I was turned away.

Couture was still recognized as a man back then. Union never recognized that women were trapped in men's bodies and vice versa. I approached the Colonel at Miss Holly's place. It was my first time setting foot in what would become a regular haunt. A handsome man was on the Colonel's arm. They shared a bottle of rum and a few laughs while I watched them from the bar. I reached over and grabbed myself a short glass before shuffling over to their table. There was thunder and lightning in the air, but it had yet to rain. Couture's shirt hung open to his naval. Gold chains hung from his neck. The yellow metal reflected the lit candles and electric light flashing in the street. His face turned pale blue when lightning struck, and I stood over them to pour each of us a drink from the bottle between them.

"To my girls." I stretched my arm out over the table, over their heads, and drank with the man who gave the orders that got my girls killed.

"Cheers, patriot," the Colonel offered distractedly. He didn't acknowledge me directly. There was no way for him to know who I was. His gold rings clanked against my glass before he tilted his own, and rum went dripping out the side of his mouth.

"My girls died for you." More thunder rumbled the concrete inn filling up with those looking to escape the storm. More lightning spattered the interior walls like a rattling gun illuminating a dark place.

"Sir—" The Colonel rose to his feet. Eyes full of remorse looked back at me. "They didn't die for nothing, I need to finish what they started, but they won't let me fight." I blubbered like a scolded child.

"No one tells us if and when we fight, sir," the Colonel said. "If it's Union work you want, come with me."

Colonel Couture rose and immediately led me away from Miss Holly's inn. Through the driving rain, the flickering luminosity in the sky, and rolling booms, he walked me through the narrows of Los Muelles to the wall being erected there. Couture took me to see the Supervisor right away. Before the day was out, I was enrolled in the Catcher training program. The ranks of outcast, aged, casualties unfit for active duty embraced me thanks to Couture. I was a Union man again.

The Colonel and I met in and around Los Muelles numerous times after that fateful day. She was a grand drinking partner, which I could only admit to myself after a few years reluctantly talking over spirits and accepting visits in my room from Miss Holly's staff at Colonel Couture's expense. Time didn't spare us any complication in our loose affiliation with one another. We shared a history that bound together the sorrowful souls left alive in wartime. In many ways, she was the closest thing I had to a friend.

The air was moist in her den. Humidity weighed down upon my shoulders. Everything I wore felt heavy. It was about to rain. My head began to dip toward my chest. I fought hard to keep my eyes open, to question Colonel Couture. The moment had been long ordained. I was on the path to that night in Templos Desiertos well before I could change course. Providence led me to my seat in the jungle, next to the woman responsible for the three medals dragging down the chest pocket of my crimson shirt. Destiny demanded such a confrontation. Ezra Atun was my last chance to contribute, to help my girls. I knew it. Colonel Couture did too.

"Why not stay here, Strickland. You deserve to retire in peace." She refilled my cup. Her deep voice was soft, reassuring, tempting.

The sky cracked open. The Colonel's tower looked out into the clouds. We were the source of the storm, brewing on a divine plane, ready to be unleashed in real-time. I slammed the medals down on the table between us. She fixed her wig, and her stare swam in my eyes. Neither of us could hear a thing in the suddenly lashing rain. Water leaked through the temple stones. The clouds screamed and roared.

"Tell me where he is, and these are yours," I yelled. She couldn't hear me, but I saw her read my lips. I looked at hers.

"You can forgive me?" She pointed to me, then back to herself.

I nodded.

She looked down at the Union medals shimmering in the sparkling moisture swirling through the tower and all around us. Couture had tears in her eyes. Her mascara ran down her stubbled cheek. Her lipstick ran. She did not wipe her eyes. The rain was cool on my face when it dripped from the temple's peak. My tears were hot when they fell down my face. Colonel Couture took my hand and pulled me so close I could feel her warm breath on my ear.

"Come with me," her voice somehow distinct from the ongoing tempest outside.

"Where?" I asked for her to read.

"The train." I saw her say.

"Wake up. Wake your ass up!" Cash smacked my face while I groaned in the damp heat trapped in our pitched tent.

"What the fuck is it?" I didn't smoke crystal, but the temple grounds were the first opportunity to drink in quite some time. Daybreak had yet come, and I was deep in a drunken slumber when Cash delivered my rude awakening.

"The Catcher," Cash breathed frantically. "He's here."

"What?"

"I was fooling around with one of the guards by the Colonel's chambers. Strickland. Yeah, that's his name. He's here for you."

"Are you high?"

"That's irrelevant. I know what I heard. We gotta get you out of here."

"How?"

"The train for Valle Oculto leaves tonight. Apparently, they like traveling during heavy rain. It helps cover the sound to keep Union scouts off the scent."

"Your boyfriend can get us on a supply car?"

"I have a lot of boyfriends here, but we have to do this alone," Cash said.

"Lead the way."

The night brought heavy rains indeed. Every former soldier and junky around sought shelter from the torrent falling from above. Tents glowed from within as Cash and I weaved through the rows in the downpour. My clothes were soaked through in a matter of seconds. Cash didn't wear a shirt. The soldier's belt he must have claimed from one of his companions had extra holes punched in the leather to keep his pants up around his fading waist. Each crack of lightning made his wet skin sparkle in the clearing just before the jungle. There was not a single bone hidden beneath layers of fat, muscle, or flesh. His insides were on full display. My friend looked like death as he led me through the trees and vines. I couldn't help but worry that he had imagined the impending doom in some drugged-up stupor. There was no time to doubt him despite years worth of evidence stacked against my lifelong friend. A wild look possessed him when he turned back toward me to yell instructions. He was drowned out by the heavens pounding down on the canopy that served as drumskins for the frantic rhythm falling from above. I was immediately transported to that chillingly secret place Cash and I ventured into at times of crisis. There were no words to describe the lengths we were prepared to go in our maniacal drive to survive. Instinct kicked in, and I did not question the beast within that took control. It appeared as though Cash relinquished the reins to the devil inside too long ago to reclaim his life's direction. I knew I could tolerate a little more before surrendering. Cash tried to kill himself too many times before. He was cracking. I only knew because I, too, was on the brink of breaking from within. Even my thoughts struggled to keep up over the sound of the ear-splitting rain. My eyes were the only thing I could trust.

Then I saw the flashlights struggling to penetrate the downpour. Orange bulbs failed to find any moving forms in the dark.

There was no way to hear our approach. Cash pulled me by my shirt collar toward the slowly accelerating train, toward the open car door inviting us inside. The moment the flashlights turned away, we crawled about the moving vessel. With every burst of lightning, we searched the car for a crate that could fit us. One near the top of the pile met our specs. It would be a long ride packed like sardines served in the ghetto. Time in transit was undetermined. The destination was unclear. But there were air holes in the wooden boxes. I knew it wasn't the first time the crate carried something breathing. I prayed there wasn't something alive inside waiting.

We gnawed at the wax seal over the seam between pieces of wood. We clawed with our fingernails at the lid until we got the nails to give up their grip. The top came flying off. The train increased its pace. There were no clues to let us know if the guards were on to us. Speed was all I could think. We quickly emptied the box filled to the brim with machine guns, tossing the weapons through the dark portal into the night. I leapt inside. Cash put two hands on the lid and pushed down. I heard him pile crates above to keep the top tamped down.

"There's room for both of us in here," I wailed from within the confines of the crate. The rain wasn't so loud in the train car, but the storm raged on as it passed by the doorway. I put my eye up to one of the holes in the box. I kicked and fought at my cage like a rat turned rabid by a country determined to exterminate my kind.

Cash appeared in the dim glow above the lighter he struck to create a flame. He held a stick of rose-coloured wax in one hand. In his other hand were a military-issued lighter and a stamp with the Colonel's initials.

"What the fuck are you doing, man?" My screams fell on the deaf ears of my friend made crazy by crystal and a life defined by slow torture. We both knew what he was really doing. "You're leaving me all alone out here? Just like Vallah?" He could hear me somewhere deep down.

"Let me do this one good thing." Tears streamed down his face and joined the golden sweat and rain catching the light of the flame. "I love you, brother," he said.

Suddenly the light went out. Cash pressed the Colonel's seal to the wax. White light flashed beyond the train car door, and I watched from the hole as his silhouette flew toward the thick forest. He was gone. The train sped on into the darkness.

GENERAL LAMENT
APRIL 2192

Supplies were necessary before I left altogether. A train was due. Heavy rains rolled in from the West, and my conscience didn't allow me to depart the valley without first informing the Colonel's foot soldiers that Lou and her faithful still required resources and they were to take over delivery duties. Pride made me camp out at the tunnel opening with Trueno, Diva, and Lightning before the train arrived. The thought of remaining in Valle Oculto while Lou's new regime dawned a fresh age following their first kill turned my stomach.

I usually brought two dozen volunteers and four sleds to ease deliveries into the valley. Not that day. All I wanted was some water, medical supplies, and dried food for any dodgers I encountered along my way to yet another era in exile. To imagine seeing Lou at the train pained me too much to arrive second. Being first required patience. Trueno rested on the ground behind me, and I leaned back to relax against her comforting bulk. Lightning stood in the sun, casting her shadow over me to protect me from the heat. I made sure to position myself where the tracks came to an end, which was thankfully upwind of Diva. I stared into the deep, dark tunnel weaving through the mountains all the way to the jungles surrounding Templos Desiertos. The bleak, hollow cavern foretold the future awaiting me after yet another failed attempt at redemption. Were the people better off without me? Or, did I let down more frail human beings looking to someone, anyone, to make any sense of the nation's horrors? Was there any clean route through the weaknesses of mankind? Belonging to anything larger than myself only ever ended in turmoil. Solitude seemed to be the only possible way to peace in my time. I let my head back against Trueno's ribs as her chest rose up and down in powerful breaths. My eyes felt heavy, and I slept soundly for the first time in weeks.

When my eyes opened, I noticed the faint glow rushing toward me from the depths burrowed in the mountainside. In the distance, Montagne de Feu towered above the small mountain range where the tunnels ran. Plumes veiled the peak. I turned my focus to the convoy of supply cars pulling in. The people in Valle Oculto had their chance to leave with me. Ensuring a steady flow of provisions was the last good deed I mustered for those that once called me their leader.

Two of Couture's soldiers jumped down from the train and pointed their guns, as militants are wont to do. When they realized it was me, they blushed, lowered their weapons, and took me into the tunnel to survey the transported goods. I informed them Lou was in charge from that moment on. I didn't field any further questions.

The air was rank and moist in the packed-earth underpass. A robust stench grew all the stronger when I climbed up into the open supply car with my saddlebag slung over my shoulder. More of Couture's warriors gathered around the gaping vessel with their arms at the ready. They were not truly deserters, as Colonel Couture liked to claim. Union no longer commanded them — that much was accurate — but they were every bit the killers they once were. The enemy of my enemy was indeed my friend yet again. I knew where the Colonel's raiders procured the antibiotics, vitamin supplements, medicines, vaccines, water, dried food, and crystal I rummaged through to fill my bottomless leather purse. They were a menacing group unfazed by taking lives. All that changed was where they took their orders. I admired their desire to murder for their own benefit at least, but the Colonel became rapidly responsible for a great deal of mercenaries that weren't so much taking orders as they were operating as a dangerous unit for as long as the rewards were plenty. Colonel Couture and her legionnaires stole from the oligarchy, enjoyed the exploits, and distributed the rest to the destitute lot not willing to kill for themselves. Those in the Colonel's company had no desire to lead. A coup was not in their plans. Responsibility gets in the way of revelry.

For all their sins, the group that made the four-day, arduous journey in the dark to bring goods to the doleful souls in the valley was actually very helpful as I packed my saddlebag for the unknown hazards ahead. Colonel Couture's seal was split using their combat knives. Crowbars propped open the various crates that held the valuable stores I pilfered. The war dogs assisted me in loading up the horses. And just as I was about to step out of the train for the last time, I noticed a crate stacked high that seemed to be leaking. An acrid smell of urine filled my nose when I took a whiff from the fingers I dipped in the liquid.

"You got some live cargo on board?" I asked one of Couture's mercenaries.

"No prisoners." He immediately raised his rifle to the box above us. His comrades followed suit, and the train car filled with the sound of loading guns.

"I'd like to have a look in that box, soldier," I said.

The man with his finger on the trigger motioned to another jumpy trooper. A nimble woman quickly ascended the pile of wood and hay with her weapon over her shoulder and a crowbar in one hand. She moved crates aside. Another young man followed her up. I brought up the rear and stood with them, gazing down at the sealed package seeping bodily fluids. The boy had his gun at the ready, the barrel pointed directly at the small box. The girl cut the seal and pried off the lid to release an awful waft of rancid air. Sitting in the crate, in his own piss and shit, was a stoic dodger.

"Don't shoot," he cried, his hands raised.

"It's alright, son. We've all spent time rolling around in our own filth." The soldiers covered their noses and kept their barrels locked on the stowaway.

"General?" asked the vagrant.

"Not anymore."

"You sentenced me to a ghetto back in eighty-six."

"I'll do everything I can to make it up to you." A lump rose to my throat. "Why don't we start with some water."

Meeting that dodger felt as though my ships had come in. I sat next to him on the black ash mountainside beside the horses, knowing full well that I didn't have enough years to begin again with a lone disciple.

"I read your book." He wiped his lips after a swig from the canteen. Flies circled him, but he seemed unfazed by his odour and soiled pants. Maybe he was aware that the only person between us with any reason for shame was me.

"What do you think?" I rummaged through my saddlebag for a jar of rum.

"There were some good parts here and there." Only because I had sentenced the man to the ghettos did I let him speak ill of my life's work. Quiet courage rose to his surface. He had the look so many had by the time they found me. No doubt he started the journey with company. Blank stares have an odd way of resembling each other. Rum couldn't wipe their faces from my memory entirely. The parched dodger was like all the rest who followed my words to the collision between East and West. Anyone who trailed my words, my deeds, my commands all went unquenched. He didn't have to say that I caused him great suffering, that my manifesto did nothing to amend my failures. I already knew getting him across the line would do no justice as an apology. He looked at me and saw me naked in all my disgrace.

"What were some of the not-so-good parts?" I asked. He gazed at me out the side of his eye and somehow recognized my desire to kiss his feet and beg forgiveness. If I could do one thing to repay the dodger, it was to spare him having to console his woeful tormentor. Such great things awaited him. My only wish was that he wasn't broken too far beyond repair.

"You just skim over the fact that you were lied to as if it were all your fault. There's no fucking time for what you've done. Everyone already knows. We were there." The words burst out of him like champagne from a shaken bottle. That was the foulest thing he allowed himself to say to me.

"How would you have gone about it?"

"With a little more hope."

"For what?"

"Whatever comes next," he said, allowing himself for a mere instant to glance toward the horizon, between the break in the mountains, where the line called out to him. "There's no use mourning the past when there are still so many futures depending on you. We all have sob stories. It's high time we shared some good ones." The man was on the road to becoming a prophet and had yet to realize.

"So, you write some yourself?" I didn't know what else to say. My rope's end was fast approaching. History would have no choice but to paint me a monster without the last chapter of my life told. The daring to recount it myself evaded me as well as I eluded the Union. How do you ask someone you've so damnably wronged to do you a favour? I wanted the filthy man before me to get to the ECR. I wanted him to relay my message, which existing in wartime prepared him to deliver. For all the hatred in his heart, he knew freedom would be his great revenge.

"I've written a bit, but there's nothing to show for it now," he turned his pockets inside out. Ash fell from the holey fabric.

"Your story is plenty," I replied. Then Lou arrived. People began emerging from the valley. Many who had been there in the piazza for her sacrifice.

"What's your name?" I turned away from Lou and looked at the dodger. No one would have blamed him for shaking in fear. His hand was steady around the canteen.

"Ezra."

"You want to get out of here?"

He nodded, gazing off past the drove coming to pilfer through the Colonel's stolen treasures.

"I see the irony here, but you're going to have to trust me."

"All the trust I had, I left with Vallah. You have my will to survive. Nothing more." A far away daze came over him.

"Vallah Desear?" My breath was suddenly short.

"You remember sentencing her?"

"I won't mourn that past," I said. "But I recall getting her to a refugee camp over the line a few months back. Pretty soldier."

"Don't play with me." He stood over me to speak. Flies circled his face. He did not swat them away.

"Let me take you to her. Please." The urge to grovel welled up inside. I could not have been more desperate for the chance to be what a soldier dies waiting to become: redeemed. Ezra took pause. Only the sound of the soft breeze and crates being unloaded onto sleds was heard in the valley.

"Fine," he said, likely unaware that there were other options available to him.

Chills of gratitude became goosebumps on my flesh. Lou made her way over with unsettling grace. Her lips were so close to mine that I thought she might kiss me, just as Judas did Jesus before the end. Maybe things would have been better if that new testament soothsayer lived long enough to write his own story. Maybe things would have been worse. Even in my unfulfilled attempts at salvation did I insist on comparing myself to a long-forgotten god.

Lou stared into my eyes, but I glanced past her to see her followers unloading all kinds of life-taking instruments from the train. The Union military codes stamped on the Colonel's sealed crates were the same combinations of numbers, letters, and dashes I wrote on classified request forms when I was in charge of arming the masses. Lou and I stood toe-to-toe while her devoted faithful unloaded what I read to be firearms, explosives, ammunition, and anarchy. Lou's rescue from the doldrums after I defected from Union service abruptly came into focus. From the depths of that shallow cave in the stout mountain where I met her, she plotted everything until the moment I defied her. An armed rebellion was always in her visions for the future. Even as we stood on the mountainside forever severed in our battle against the Union, her lips moved, whispering spells to sway me back into her grasp as leader of the assault against peace in our time.

"The volcanos will bury the West before you have time to wage war." I was weeping. I yelled for her people to hear. "Can't you see that in your visions?" Lou's whispers screeched in my skull.

"Our victory will come in the afterlife. The gods see that we fight for good. We have heaven to look forward to," Lou replied. "Is that not what you seek, General: salvation?"

"I'm on my way there," I sniffled, and Lou's voice immediately went silent in my head as I turned to Ezra. "Care to join me?"

A life in the ghetto didn't prepare Ezra for riding a horse. Our grand departure was undermined when I put Ezra's feet in the stirrups one by one. Lou chuckled mildly and betrayed my confidence in her I once believed to be so enlightened. I was not too proud to request Union's uniform from Lou's haul. She obliged. No doubt she promised Colonel Couture the power of the gods for their revolt, their coup, their place in the circle of rule and egress.

Water washed away the bugs and anguish swirling around the dodger. I watched him bathe in a small stream trickling down the narrow mountain pass we traversed on our way to the line. There was no fat on his bones. Wrinkles from an entire youth spent in the blazing sun settled into his skin. His back and bare ass were to me until he sauntered over to the horses and put on the clean military threads I took from Lou as a parting gift. Ezra was unperturbed to dress in full view. He was a homeless, restless defector with an uncertain future, and my carnal propensity to find such uncertainty attractive was unrelenting.

"So, who is this Vallah Desear to you?" I did my best not to stare. The dodger exercised his right not to speak. "I assume she's the reason you came with me."

"I don't know what you're playing at, but I don't believe much of anything you say." Ezra clumsily struggled his way back into the saddle on Lightning's back. The horses pushed forward. "Can't you just tell me where to go? I don't want to ride with you."

"Trust goes both ways. How can I be sure you're not a Union spy?" To this, he had no answer, leaving us in a state of mutual skepticism as Trueno, Diva, and I led the way.

For all the souls I ferried across the thinning runway between East and West, none granted me the communion I laboured so severely to discover. Only in the company of husband and daughter on the sun-soaked beach of my past did I belong. Not in Union ranks, not in Lou's care, not in exile did I feel what I promised others awaited them across the line.

"Did you love her?" I sheepishly broke the quiet.

"Yes," replied the dodger.

"She's alive."

"I can't believe you."

"If only everyone else learned the same from my book, maybe we'd all be a little better off. Will you write when you make it?"

"I don't know."

"You can't forget about the West. It will be burned away soon enough." My heartache shook my vocal cords.

"The West can burn." Ezra tightened his grip around the reins drooped over Lightning's mane. "But I won't let the memory of my friends drown with it. That's what Vallah knew that I never understood. She left because she couldn't watch. Mick got dragged away right in front of my eyes. I let Carmen go because she doesn't need a ghost hanging around her child. I pretended to resist when Cash closed that crate down on me. The Kid only had to hand me a silly book before I ran away. I didn't know it then, but I wanted Vallah to get gone more than anything. The only thing worse than living in a cage is realizing you're the cell your loved ones are trapped inside. When the West is in ashes, at least my friends will have a chance to get out without me weighing them down. I won't forget them, General. My freedom is theirs. History will remember their names. Yours will go unwritten."

"Your friends sound like true patriots," I said. The dodger's words were like a stake through the heart. "Tell me more about them."

"I'd never give them up."

"It probably hasn't hit you yet, but you're about to start over in a new country. I'll still be here. Your friends too. Who says they don't want to get across too?"

STRICKLAND RIVER
APRIL 2192

Horseshoes clacked against the tracks and filled my head with consistent, maddening noise amidst the absence of light in the never-ending tunnel, calling to mind the ancient tortures I saw Union use to interrogate the enemy when I was in the service. After five days, even the tiny glimmer I saw in the distance made my eyes ache. And I realized I was the last of a dying cowboy breed. To venture so far from the belly of my country drained what remained of my energy reserves. Colonel Couture managed to close the hole burrowed in my bicep by that rat bastard little guerrilla. Too much blood was lost anyway. Five days riding in the black made me believe the bright tunnel archway was the exit from my body.

When I emerged from the void cut through the mountains, a gentle rain awaited me. Turning back crossed my mind too many times to count until I felt the droplets and found myself back in the light. I was still getting used to being without my daughters' medals resting heart-to-heart on my chest. All divine purposes come to a place of such doubt. No worthy cause undertaken for a nation is done without a few litres of blood given in offering.

Soft ash pushed about by the wind was slowly tamped down by the rain. Evidence of a great sum of people and sleds to carry the Colonel's supplies were written in the patterns on the ground. If only there were more than one train, I might have been able to preserve some strength. As it was, even stepping down from my horse was too great a chore, so I observed the breadcrumbs from on high despite my weakening eyes. Where the train disappeared, I never knew. Legends of the East were littered with tales of magic. The mist descending on the black, sooty valley supported the claim that such ominous powers lurked at the Union's fringes. Home was a long way behind me. But I was not entirely beyond the reach of the gods. They turned my attention to a small tributary weaving its way through the pass. Flies circled a pile of discarded clothes I knew to be Ezra's at the edge of a pool steaming in a volcano's shadow. The moisture in the air made it nearly impossible to cover the horseshoe footprints pressed into the dirt nearby. I counted three horses, twelve feet. Who was helping my case flee further from his duty? It wasn't that junky buddy of Ezra's. The drughead queer had a life in service to the Colonel to look forward to for his crimes against the Union. I wanted Cash's sacrifice to be for naught. It was only a matter of time before Colonel Couture returned to Union command. She played the mercenary, but I knew she was as much for Union as my daughters and I. I was certain she would rejoin the fight against foreign invasion and internal insurgents. With my daughters' medals in hand, she could return to the favourable grace of the gods and Union. Cash Desear forfeited his chance when he helped Ezra steal away on the supply chain. The Colonel put him to work with my blessing. Cash was sentenced to a life in the temple or a death building a new one in honour of the nation.

Tracking Ezra and his unknown companions mercifully kept me from returning to the mysterious passages burrowed in the valley like red herrings. I was on their scent like a bloodhound bred to seek and find for its master. Their company would slow them down.

Bounty hunters travel alone for speed and simplicity. I was a lone Catcher unburdened by the weakness of others. My duty propelled me forward. My calling provided the vigour to stick it out a little longer, to bring in my case and have my gun and badge returned to me with praise.

The ash beneath my horse's feet slowly turned from smooth, moist soot to coarse, wet coral. Waves crashed against the exterior of the subterranean passageway General Lament led me into. Each collision of water against rock made me flinch in my saddle, unlike the fearless steeds I always heard were so skittish. They calmly walked through the submerged thoroughfare resembling some ancient freeway built by the sunken citizens of Atlantis. Scarlet lava oozed from the walls and ceiling around us. A thin luminescent river ran like honey mere metres from the hooves that carried me forward. We were in the very heart of our country, navigating the depths of a volcano to flow forth from the unblocked artery only the General knew how to find. Only by the light of the leaking magma and torches we held could I see General Lament's face. The fierce heat and spontaneous flames bursting from cracks in the underpass did nothing for my optimism regarding the new world I was about to enter. If biblical imaginings of hell were to be believed, I was sure I'd found the place.

My guide made me think she was a descendant of the devil. Glory and prestige did nothing to quell my pity for the General, and she was all too aware for me to bask in the hatred I felt for the woman who sentenced me. Not a minute passed without a glance from over her shoulder as she led me to the line and watched for any hint of gratitude, warmth, or forgiveness. Desperation spilled from her mouth when she asked about the story I shared with Vallah. It was another reason I had to rub the sweat falling from my face between my fingers just to be sure that I hadn't fallen into a dream and was talking with the devil on the banks of the river Styx.

The General poked and prodded about my feelings toward the beautiful soldier she smuggled into the ECR not more than two months before. I saw General Lament hating herself for seeking thanks. The devil existed only for lack of love, I guess. The General begged for me to see her as the repentant hero. She drew my ire and my mercy. For better or worse, General Lament was my ferryman through the glowing, corroding coral tube, the single thread still linking Union and Republic. I knew better than to trust her word completely, but I found myself following the General through that infernal underworld just as I lived in perdition with Mick, Carmen, Cash, and Vallah. Every step closer to the line brought me to the realization that General Lament was my compatriot in the abyss between nations. Something resembling sympathy for my fellow exile forced its way to my mind while our horses trotted over the sharp, black, coral road. She swore on the gods, her departed daughter, her dead husband, and everything else in the world the General valued that was no longer in her grasp. Vallah was only a day's ride away if Lament was to be believed. What was so different about accepting her word in person? Why was I so quick to have faith in the stories told in the General's book? The Kid almost thought her a deity. Maybe I was the one too eager for a doctrine, or at least some claim for hope in the disintegrating country I was born into. Escape was my only motivation when The Kid's guerrillas ripped me through the ghetto fence. I was a dodger. It was better than being a slave but it left me pining for connection, a history, a people to belong to. In chasing Vallah and the line, I left my only other family in the wake of my disappearance.

The sad truths I faced in solitude began pouring from my mouth like a river coming to a steep fall. Of all people to become a confidant, why General Lament? We knew regret and shame, but she long ago stamped out any allusions for a brighter future for herself. Reluctantly accepting her aid was all I could muster as absolution. No lava, seawater, or deed could wipe her slate clean. Even as I smelt the salty liquid sizzle and evaporate after seeping into the hollow channel with the molten rock to humidify my hell, I tried to articulate to the General what else she could do in atonement. Mick was lost to the war. Carmen and The Kid were left to shepherd guerrilla orphans in a thinly veiled jungle escape. Cash's fate was a mystery. For all I knew, he was knee-deep in handsome men and fine narcotics, fading gracefully into an early grave with a sly smile on his gaunt face. That was my wish on the path across the line. But General Lament rode alongside me like a satanic genie yearning to do my bidding in the West I was about to leave behind. I told the General their names. I recounted the virtues of those responsible for the freedom within my reach.

Our final exchange was fraught with conflicting ebbs and flows of love and hate. We did not dismount. The General told me the horse I rode was named Lightning, and she was mine until I made my way to the refugee camp just beyond the border. A solemn vow prevented Lament from seeing me all the way across. She said she was to remain in the West until the Union was saved. We both knew that meant she would go down with the ship, fighting fate until the very end. General Lament wanted me to know she was sorry, and that she needed me to find Vallah for the sake of her soul. She demanded I find peace in exile. And, with a blown kiss, the General took up her reins, guiding her two horses toward the Union. I watched her figure fade in the auburn haze filling the underworld I was left alone to navigate.

* * *

Torch in hand, I leaned forward in my saddle to push Lightning closer to the new country awaiting me. The water level began to rise slowly with every passing metre. Firelight did little to combat the thickening darkness, merely turning the mist rising from the puddles beneath into a blurry, golden fog. Lightning's hooves splashed into the growing pools and echoed all around me. I allowed myself to dream about a swim in the ocean once I made it through the volcano range dividing East and West. And then I came to the very manifestation of that divide. Grey concrete reflected the flickering flame I carried. The treacherous wall surrounding the Union confronted me. Its foundations pierced the coral, stretching from floor to ceiling like the mineral pillars strewn throughout the void in the earth. Lightning sauntered up alongside the colossal partition, and I ran my hand against the grain. My fingers traced the archway cut from the otherwise impenetrable stone. Endless blows from a pick-axe were written in the channel excavated by the will of a woman bearing the weight of unimaginable contrition. The passageway was no wider than my steed, no taller than my head when sitting in Lightning's saddle. Before entering the General's hole burrowed through the Union wall, I went to the place where coral and concrete met. The ocean outside eroded the slightest crack for me to press my eye, and for the first time since I was a child, the sky and sea met on the distant horizon before me. Joy released butterflies in my gut until I heard a soft splash from behind. I couldn't see a thing in the darkness from whence I came.

"General?" I called out into the black.

Rapid slaps against the shallow water began charging toward me. Lightning was right on cue. She turned swiftly and plunged us through the door in the wall. I ducked my head and held the torch out before us. The air was suddenly cold as we stormed furiously through the wall. No matter how fast she ran, the concrete kept stretching out ahead of Lightning's nose. I gripped the reins with all my might.

The bullet went through my back, and I fell from Lightning's saddle onto the coral floor as the gunshot still reverberated throughout the underpass. All the air in my lungs left me. I gasped for breath to no avail. My body froze in terror on the jagged ground until Strickland River stepped into the light of the torch that was illuminating the tight hollow. Instinct couldn't overpower my pain. I was glued to the rocks, forced to watch while the Catcher unbuttoned his holster and drew his magnum. The flame danced on the silver barrel pointed at my skull. A grave smile came to his floodlit face. I tried to suck in one last breath and managed to close my fist enough to lift my middle finger to the Catcher.

Another shot rang out, but I heard it rebound against the Union wall when Lightning bucked her hind legs to kick Strickland just below the heart, shoving him against the markings chipped away at the concrete. His back slid down the rock, leaving him slouched next to me with eyes jammed wide-open in panic. The Catcher coughed, and blood spurted from his mouth onto his deep-red uniform. His silver pistol rattled against the coral within reach of my hand, still giving him the finger. I struggled onto my side to take up the weapon. The steel felt icy against my skin. Pulling back the hammer took every bit of strength still surging in my body. My finger rested on the trigger. We looked deep into each other's eyes without a word.

"Not today," I muttered. Lightning huffed. The metallic taste of blood was still on my tongue, and the magnum shook in my weakened grip.

GENERAL LAMENT
JUNE 2192

An armed guerrilla emerged from the croton. I found myself staring down the barrel of yet another child's gun. She couldn't have been more than twelve-years-old. Her tattered Union uniform was all too familiar. The fear and anger spewing from her mouth were quickly silenced when she laid eyes on Trueno and Diva. Such four-legged beasts weren't found running wild in the valley forest surrounding The Kid's little compound. Horses must have only existed in stories told to the adolescent rebel. The girl wasn't hasty to believe me when I told her who I was, but she had read my book, so we exchanged a few memorized passages in substitute of whatever password was required to enter the hedge maze. She couldn't stop staring at the horses as she led me through the twisting, turning labyrinth.

We entered the manicured courtyard together. Beams of yellow light broke through the foliage overhead, and I thought of where Ezra might be after breaking through himself. The tiny village was lively with playing children, construction, and gardening. I was reminded of my seaside camp before the coastal raids when I heard the high-pitched cackles of young laughter. Trailers and rows of vegetables were arranged meticulously around a chromed-out bus releasing smoke up toward the canopy. The air shimmered as the cloudy wisps caught the buttery sunlight falling down. I dismounted. Children gathered to touch the horses. A woman emerged from one of the trailers, holding a baby to her breast for feeding. She came right towards me.

"Is it really you?" Asked the mother.

"I think so," was all I could manage to say.

"I'm Carmen." She held the baby in one arm and extended her other hand to shake mine.

"Ezra's friend," I replied, taking her palm in mine.

"He found you."

"Maybe Vallah too." The look we shared once I spoke their names was worth every sorrowful kilometre I travelled throughout the Union. Just then, a trailer door exploded open to reveal a handsome young man with dreaded hair and tattoos across his chest. His smile stretched from ear to ear as he ran in my direction.

"General?" Asked The Kid.

"Please. Call me Sloan," I said through the lump in my throat.

"It's a pleasure," he laughed. "I loved your book."

Ezra Atun was a bastard for sparing my life. At least my corpse could have done something to plug the hole between East and West. Instead, I found myself back in Los Muelles with my tail between my legs. A kind receptionist draped a blanket over my shoulders while I sat in the waiting room outside the Supervisor's office. The fluorescent light burned my eyes. A few days in the back of a Union jeep adjusted my sight to the dark. I didn't remember where they picked me up. My internal injuries didn't allow me to get too far from the line, but I was certain I would only heal if returned to my nation's heart. The bounty out on my capture couldn't have been worth much. Failed Catchers were strewn all over the country and often left to rot. They had me on two charges: failure to deliver a case and murder of a fellow officer. I thought I might be able to trade the General's last known whereabouts and the location of the hole in the wall for a reduced sentence. The very thought of withholding intel from the Union for personal gain turned my stomach. All the churning in my belly could have also been the blood pooling throughout my organs. Either way, it felt better being back in Los Muelles, amongst Catchers and patriots.

"Mr. River," called the secretary. "The Supervisor will see you now."

Getting to my feet took a moment. I heard the others snicker. Exhaustion stamped out my shame, and I shuffled my way down the hall to the Supervisor's office. He did not offer me a seat, so I stood trembling as I recounted my divine purpose. I told the full story about the Catcher I killed, the guards poisoned in the ghetto, The Kid's guerrilla orphanage, Colonel Couture's mercenaries, the General's latest movements, Ezra's escape, and the route cut through the Union's great defense against foreign invaders. The Supervisor took meticulous notes while I preached the gospel delivered to me by the gods throughout my odyssey. When I finally came up for air after laying all my sins bare, my knees failed me, and I collapsed on the floor before the Supervisor's desk. He whistled, and his office door swung open. Two large soldiers each put an arm under mine and picked me up. I looked at my superior for any hint of clemency. He did not meet my gaze. Rather, he nodded to the soldiers on either side of me.

"Thank you for the opportunity," I struggled to say. The door closed behind me without a reply from inside. They whisked me away through the station exit. A hard rain fell on us when we stepped outside.

"Can you stand?" Asked the soldier on my right.

I nodded.

"Face the wall," he yelled over the driving downpour. I followed the orders, turning my sights on the immense feat of human engineering keeping our enemies at bay. "Last words?" He shouted.

"For country," I whispered, with a hand over my heart.

I saw my blood splatter against the concrete wall before all went dark.

EZRA ATUN
APRIL 2192

The gun still hung from my fingers when Lightning stepped out from the tunnel into the East Caribbean Republic. Water bordered either side of the narrow stretch of land. Sunset turned the sky shades of lavender, sandstone, and magenta to be reflected off the waves rushing toward shore. A pair of symmetrical bays transformed the thin runway into a vast terrestrial landscape after the first hundred metres. The coral strip soon gave way to sand, grass, and dirt covered in row upon row of mirrors tilted toward the setting sun.

I was hunched over in the saddle. Blood seeped through my clothes, staining Lightning's ashy hide. She walked along the water's edge as the tide lapped up against her holy legs. The sea air filled my lungs, and I conjured enough spirit to lift the gun and heave it into the surf. I knew the bullet entered my back, and I was grateful to see the exit wound in my belly when I tied the Union uniform around my gut to slow the life draining from me. To see the ocean once more before I died was my only wish. Gratitude pulsed through me. My vision blurred. Lightning kept on walking.

Only once night fell could I see the vague shapes of people casting shadows against a large, square structure bathed in warm orange light. After the long road, those last few hundred metres seemed like the longest. I pulled into the refugee camp in disrepair under a blanket of stars. People uttered prayers and led Lightning by the reins toward what I could only compare to a hulking barn. I finally slid from the saddle and fell from Lightning's back, expecting to meet the ground, but I landed in the many arms congregated in the grand entrance hall. Strangers carried me through the crowd in silence. The weight of my head was too great to bear, and I felt it rest in a pair of linked hands, letting me look up at the balconies towering above in countless number. I watched people gather at their railings and shed tears for me. I searched their faces until Vallah's stared back at me. She covered her gaping mouth from fifty-metres high. The gatherings parted for her as she sprinted down the steel gratings zigging and zagging from one floor to the next. I was already in triage before Vallah took my hand and wept.

"Oh, Ezra. I'm so sorry." She kissed my bloody knuckles.

I shook my head, saddened to think Vallah believed she owed the apology. There was so much I wished to say but couldn't muster the breath to speak the words. They placed me down on a stretcher, and people in white coats began examining me with flashing lights and strange instruments. Vallah was pulled away, but before she left my side, she crouched down to the dry earth in the enormous gallery, took up a pinch of dirt, and rubbed it in my hand, leaning toward my ear to say:

"We made it."

ABOUT THE AUTHOR

Born and raised in Toronto, Andrew Calderone wrote *Borders in the Sand* while roaming Central America and the Dominican Republic. His first novel, *Thirsty Scholars*, was crafted at the Humber School for Writers before writing and co-directing the award-winning films *Cold Is My Brother* and *Exit Interview* (CBC). He has studied literature at University College Cork in Ireland, the University of the West Indies in Barbados, York University in Toronto, and is writing his third novel at the University of British Columbia's School of Creative Writing.

www.ingramcontent.com/pod-product-compliance
Lightning Source LLC
Chambersburg PA
CBHW030938210726
48290CB00007B/2240